Rips

Peter Owens

AmErica House
Baltimore

First Printing

ISBN: 1-893162-55-9
PUBLISHED BY AMERICA HOUSE BOOK PUBLISHERS
www.publishamerica.com
Baltimore

Printed in the United States of America

For Mary, Syb, and Jay

Acknowledgements:

Special thanks to Consulting Translator Robert Watson of Quebec, Consulting Editor Catherine Houser at UMass Dartmouth, and History Consultant Robert Smith of Massena, NY.

For further reference:

For a concise history of the St. Lawrence River and the border region, please visit **www.powens.com.** The site also includes a bibliography relevant to the Rips era, scores of useful Web links, a photo history of several river islands dating back to 1943, and information about boats and shipping from past to present.

Chapter 1

1759, St. Lawrence River, Quebec and New York Border Region

A light west breeze whispered over the immense reach of the St. Lawrence River as far as the eye could see, nudging up gentle waves. The breeze flowed softly up the easy slope of Everett's island and shimmered the long, thin leaves of the seven willow trunks leaned out over the point in a lightly swaying canopy. Île du Cèdre was one of a dozen islands visible from this broad swath of river known as St-Francois du Lac. It was not a lake, really, but an immense patch of flooded valley that simply never drained and was so large it could whip up furious waves and turn ordinary inland storms into furious river killers.

In the distance on this hot July day, a French Army patrol bateau lurched slowly toward the island, four sets of oars plopped unskillfully and in odd, unsyncopated arrhythmia, chopping clumsily at the water as if manned by bored and distracted children. Holding firmly to the stern gunnel and affecting a determined pose of military dignity stood a French officer barking out orders and profanities at his inept crew, most of whom had seldom rowed a boat and cared little about learning or developing a smooth and productive stroke.

With one very good shot from his buried canon, Everett could have taken out the French patrol boat in the middle of the channel. Anyone surviving the blast would drown in the powerful current. No one would ever know. Except the widow Ella, who stood hanging clothes and gazing inscrutably at the French officer directing his crew to row a bit goddamned more stiffly or they'd miss the fucking island altogether. Or something to that effect, Everett's French being poorly.

Ella's friendly, bemused look pained him to no end. She'd been under Everett's protection for six months, and he'd developed such an attraction to her, his belly quivered just to look at her blond curls trembling in the west wind. He wasn't so sure that the little flirt she'd developed for the French officers might just be real and that some day she and Jamie, her 13-year-old son, might climb in one of the patrol boats and leave the isolation of Everett's island and join the French side until the war's end.

On the other hand, if he missed his shot from the buried canon, the French landing party would know he was there hiding and would surely kill him and take Ella and Jamie prisoner for harboring the enemy. So Everett just lay still in his hot, dusty underground hole, the shape of a shallow grave, peeping through a thicket of raspberries and feeling the spiders and ants crawling along his sweaty neck and up his ankles, mosquitoes singing at his ears and his whole being itching beyond toleration.

The French officer directed his oarsmen to the edge of the mossy bank, tossed an anchor onto the island, and pulled the stern in close with series of loud clunks from the boat bouncing on shallow rocks. Everett chuckled in derisive silence at the boatmen's ineptitude and trained the bead of his flintlock pistol on the forehead of the officer as he stumbled clumsily up the slippery bank.

"Ah, bonjour, Madame, bonjour. Comment allez-vous cet jour qui est brutalement chaud?" the officer asked with cheerful irony, adjusting his blue tunic.

"Je suis très bien, merci, et vous?" Ella smiled.

"So, so. Ees too many hot for me," he shrugged looking over the island. "Ze husband, ees here, ici, aujourd'hui?"

"My husband is dead," she said evenly.

"I am sor-ry. Je suis désolé, excusez-moi," he said clumsily, sweat beading on his forehead, forming rivulets that darted in starts and stops down his temples and cheeks. "Keeled in thees war?"

"Yes. It's been one year now."

The officer squirmed awkwardly. "Thees war ees very bad," he said mournfully.

"Pointless," she said, "but that's not your fault, is it?"

"Oui, exactly," he said. "My name ees Henri. Je m'appelle Henri," he said with a courtly bow. "Pleece don't ask me why I am here. I have no idea, real-ly. Crazy, no?" he said with an effeminate flick of his wrist.

Ella tossed her thick tangle of blond curls to the downwind side of her face and gripped a knot of locks in her fist. She smiled. *An unlikely soldier*, she thought, but quite likeable, really.

Mosquitoes whined and hummed at Everett's neck and ears, injecting him every few moments in the sweltering snarl of prickly shrubs. It was all he could do to keep himself from shooting the gabby Frenchman just to hurry him off the island. *Get yer ass gone,* he muttered silently to himself, feeling each bite stab his flesh with a fiery itch.

The Frenchman asked, "You take many visitor to zis island?"

She puzzled a moment, then shrugged as she replied, "Non, vieux indiens in leur canoe, cherchant leur tribu et pas en condition pour le fighting."

"Madame, faire non laissa la Indians sur la ile. C'est très dangereux. Madame, do no let ze Indian on zis island. They very dangereux," the officer cautioned, looking at her musket tilted against the enormous trunk of the grand willow hanging out over the point.

"Oh non, non, monsieur. Je suis très prudent. Très, très prudent. Don't worry. I'm very careful. Very, very careful," Ella smiled.

Is she flirting with this guy, Everett wondered with a mix of depressed jealousy and squirming impatience, lines of stinging ants weaving up his sleeves and pantlegs, his hands trembling from his unrequited urgency to swat and thrash murderously at the emerging army of insects devouring his flesh. But he could not move for risk of death or capture.

The officer gazed suspiciously at Jamie who sat on the sod mound of their roof, his grim face streaked with dirt, his musket draped over his knees.

"Tu viens avec nous dans notre bateau. Pour safety? You come in ze boat, yes?" he offered.

"Non, ici c'est my home, merci," she said firmly.

"Oui. Yes, yes. Pardon." Then he shrugged and nodded to his bowman to push off. "Bonjour, madame. Be with care," he said with an elegant bow. "Je te plait soient prudent, madam. Je sort de cette paradise. I leave madam to zis paradise until next we meet, no?" he added with an odd, resigned irony, before smiling and tipping his hat, the boat clunking on the rocks as the officer stepped in and pushed off. The current quickly seized the boat and pulled it away from the moss bank into the swirling eddies of the silent, powerful current.

Everett watched her release her hair, smile warmly, and wave to the officer, her hand pausing a moment as if to say, maybe someday, maybe yes I'll go with you. A half dozen oars plopped in odd, undisciplined chaos into the dark water, and the French officer rolled his eyes in annoyance at his crew, then shrugged again helplessly while saluting Ella as if to say how unfortunate they both were to be stuck in this overheated wilderness trapped by a very stupid, befuddling war.

In a few moments, perhaps thinking he was out of earshot, he shouted, "Plus vite, mes maudit bâtard," and other assorted insults as his bored and dreary crew splashed their oars into the current and lurched limply away from the island. They would continue their largely pointless patrol far from any active front, the officer stuck in a lonely outpost with demoralized soldiers wishing to be half a world away in France rather than in the hot, bug-infested North American wilderness on a large and dangerous river looking for an enemy that was sometimes Indian, sometimes scruffy American, sometimes foul-mouthed British, sometimes wild-eyed Scots clad in skirts, but an enemy mostly elsewhere or nowhere.

Everett squirmed in his hot hole and waited until they were out of sight as Ella hung more wash. *Jesus what an odd arrangement this was*, he thought. He hid from the enemy, yet was her protector for some sudden moment when her smile and good looks and firm resolve might provoke an attack rather than hang-jawed admiration. And then Everett would burst forth and in moments they might all die. The island was their sanctuary, its isolation keeping them out of harm's way, away from roads, away from strategic forts and crucial villages, away from troop routes and random, idiotic massacres.

Both the British and the French claimed they could not control their own Indian allies, so massacres were depressingly common. So it was far better to be away from the action, more than 100 miles from Quebec to the north and 60 miles west of Fort Henry on Lake Champlain where 400 French prisoners were not long ago murdered by their Indian captives despite half-hearted attempts by British officers to stop the carnage.

* * *

Upriver 60 miles west, the British had captured Fort Frontenac but so far Everett's patch of the river was safe from combat. It seemed to Everett that here they must be as safe as anywhere could be. Yet, from time to time, their isolation made them extraordinarily vulnerable to the slightest whim and murderous mood from their few passing visitors.

Everett couldn't quite figure it except to believe that Ella and Jamie possessed a certain power over the nasty, rotten dispositions of men. She surely had a power over him, and each day it grew stronger and more urgent. She had a way with the Indians, and the Frenchmen loved her. But the American and British trappers who roamed the river were tough, brutal men and less enamored with natural beauty of any kind. And the irascible Brits and Scots-if they ever found him-would surely force him into battle or kill him as a deserter or lock him up to die in some putrid, disease-ridden prison.

When the French patrol boat was but a speck down river, Everett squirmed out of his hot hole and brushed the dirt and stinging red ants from his neck. The fresh breeze offered a glorious cooling bath of air into which Everett twisted and danced and shook himself like an old, water-soaked dog, gradually moving closer to Ella who sat pensively on a log staring out at the river.

"That Frenchy there's got an eye for you, ain't he," Everett teased.

"Would he now?" she said, "Is that what you think?"

"I'd cut his bloomin' throat," Everett snorted, scratching feverishly at his itchy neck, swatting at the stinging ants.

"Aye, you would," she said with a skeptical frown.

"Oh, what a gentleman, though," Everett grinned, with a mock bow.

"He's got good manners," she said quietly. "I like a gentleman with manners."

"Then I need to work on mine," Everett laughed, in a mock twirl, bowing to his knee close enough to catch her scent.

She pulled back a bit and grinned at Everett, her eyes twinkling with bemused tolerance at his boyish, dopey charade. "A jug of cologne after a good bath would suit me," she smiled.

Everett leapt to his feet and ran down the slope and thundered into the river, diving into the cool current, twisting and coming up squirting water from his mouth, and then losing his nerve with his little flirtation and rolled back over and dove beneath the surface and swam deep and long into the channel where great, 15-foot strands of weed grass undulated and waved with the roiling current, glowing a brilliant golden-green from the scorching sun above.

His stomach churned and ached with longing, not knowing what to say or what to do, but knowing he liked her nearly as much as she scared him, which was a lot. He first felt this strange and conflicted churning the first day he saw her standing with her son before the smoldering ruins of her burnt-out cabin on the shores of Lake Champlain.

He was paddling his empty canoe north from Albany after unloading several hundred pounds of beaver furs at a trading post where he'd been told the prices were double what he could get in Lachine or Montreal. By the time he got there, the prices had dropped in half, and he cursed himself for his greed and left fuming at the wasted trip.

On his way home he saw Ella and her son standing like statues gazing at the crumpled ruins of the fireplace chimney that set the cabin ablaze from an early morning pine pitch fire. It was cold, misty March day, the lake still marbled with floating patches of ice. Everett pulled up to the bank to offer his help and stretch his aching legs. She was covered with soot, her face smudged with wood char and her cheeks stained with white streaks where tears washed through soot and char. They stood amid a clutter of metal pots, salvaged metal tools, and the skeleton of a flintlock rifle burned clean of its wooden stock and tilted against an enormous cast iron pot.

"Anyone hurt, ma'am?" he called from some distance so as not to startle her witless at his approach from behind.

She turned and shook her head no. He half expected she might faint away in a swoon when to his surprise she turned back and kicked a copper pot in looping arc back into the smoldering mass of ash. This was his first inkling of her capacity for anger, and he stepped back a bit lest she launch something in his direction.

"You got kin or a husband can help you out?" he asked cautiously after a respectful silence.

"He's dead six months. I have no kin save Jamie, here."

"I'm sorry, ma'am," Everett said, noting to himself that beneath the soot and char was a pretty face and smooth-curved jaw twitching hard and fast.

"I be glad to give yas a ride up to the settlement by the fort," Everett offered.

"It's overrun by diphtheria," she said still staring into the ruins.

"You ain't got nowhere to go, then," he said.

She turned to him now and grasped a damp mat of blond hair tangled over half her face and tossed it back over her shoulder. "We have nowhere to go," she said, her bright blue eyes ablaze.

At that moment, Everett's belly churned the first time with that mix of fear and attraction that flowed up and down through him in a wave that weakened his knees and tugged his breath away. He starred down at her dumbly, and she looked at him as if drilling a series of holes all over his head for his brains to dribble out.

He must have looked a fright because after a time she asked, "Are you all right?"

He was started from this stupor and replied quickly, "Yes, ma'am. I'm okay. Well, look here then. I got a little place on an island on the St. Lawrence River two days from here. I got room for you and the boy 'til you find somethin' better."

"How do I know I can trust you?" she asked.

Everett scratched his head and puzzled over her question. "You don't know, I guess."

"An island?"

"Yes ma'am. Got pretty sunsets at night and a cool breeze that knocks down the mosquitoes pretty good. I can teach the boy to fish if he don't know already."

She looked toward the boy and raised her brows a bit in question.

The boy nodded yes.

She leaned down and started gathering pots. "Let's go, then," she said.

* * *

Everett dropped the heavy stone wrapped in rope that served as their fishing anchor. Early morning mist swirled slowly past and cooled the sweat on Everett's face after his three-mile row to a favorite spot where two channels converged at the edge of an enormous marsh. Everett and Jamie silently baited their hooks with minnows. The black water was smooth and silent, their rigs making an audible plop into the depths. Nearby a loon slowly cruised the edge of the channel, working the same edge that Everett and Jamie soon were plucking perch from nearly as fast as they could bait their lines. In the nearby marsh, mud hens cackled in staccato riffs.

"Them Frenchies scare you a bit?" Everett asked during a pause.

"Not me," Jamie muttered. "I ain't scared of them guys."

"Scare the shit out of me," Everett said quietly.

This brought a look of irritated puzzlement to Jamie's face. Not something he wanted to hear from the man who's supposed to be protecting his mother and him. He's bloody strange, Jamie had told his mom, and she offered no argument. He ain't like anybody we'd knowd, Jamie added, and his mother shook her head in agreement.

"What's so scary about them Frenchies, then?" asked Jamie.

"Too polite," said Everett. "Can't be trusted. Besides, I hate to see a boat handled so poorly. If that' s how they handle a boat, how do you think they might handle a gun? They might bloody shoot you just trying to be friendly. Now the Indians. You can count on them to know what they're doing."

"But, they're a whole lot more dangerous, you said so yerself."

"Yessir, they are," Everett concluded, yanking his line and pulling up a fat fifteen-inch perch.

"That don't make no sense," said Jamie.

"No, it don't," said Everett, not feeling that he had to make more sense of his fears than what he'd offered.

They worked the spot for an hour as the sun rose and burned the haze first from the blue sky above, then lower and lower until they sat in a bright, calm halo of thin fog and wispy mist.

"Your Dad like to fish?" Everett asked after a prolonged silence.

"Nossir, not that I know about."

"What did he like to do?"

"He liked horses and buggies. He built buggies. But he liked the horses better."

"Did he take you riding?"

"Yessir."

"I'll bet he was good with a horse, yeah?" said Everett.

"Yessir."

"You can call me Everett any time soon now."

"Yessir."

"I don't much like being called sir; yeah?"

"Yessir."

"It ain't polite to call someone by a name that they don't like."

"Sir ain't a name," Jamie countered.

"Oh? If it ain't a name, what is it?"

Jamie looked at him a moment while baiting another hook. "It's a surname," he said biting back a grin.

"Holy hell. Call me what you want, then."

"Yessir," Jamie laughed in quiet triumph.

"So long as it ain't profane or grossly disrespectful."

"Yessir."

"Yessir," Everett said.

"Yup," said the boy, suppressing a grin.

After a pause, Everett asked, "What exactly happened to your Daddy?"

"The British army took him to make wagons. He got shot fixing a wagon that got stuck in Lake George."

"Who shot him? French or Indian?"

"Don't know. Mama says it don't matter. She says it's the war that kills people."

"She's a wise woman, your Mama."

"I wish I knowd."

"Why's that. If your mama says...."

"It matters to me," Jamie said fiercely.

"Yessir," Everett nodded quietly, "And it would to me."

After a pause Jamie asked, "If you think she's so wise, how come it would matter to you."

"'Cause I ain't so wise as her," Everett said.

Jamie puzzled over that for a moment and then asked, "Is your Daddy alive?"

"Nossir."

"What kilt him?"

"Scurvy. My daddy was a fisherman, and one winter he went out on a boat and never come back. He died of scurvy which is something you catch on boats."

"Can we catch scurvy on this boat?"

"Nossir, not on this river. Just on the ocean. Maybe if we took this boat into the ocean, we could get scurvy, yeah?"

"If you say so," Jamie said.

"We'd more 'n likely flip over in a storm and drown first."

"Yeah?"

"I'm pretty good with boats, but this 'un a bit weeny for the ocean, so you don't need to worry about scurvy."

"Yessir."

"Pretty good fishin, ey?" Everett said setting his hook and pulling in a wiggling fat old perch.

"Yessir," Jamie squeaked, striking a fish of his own.

And so went the conversations between Jamie and Everett sharing the things that men need to share, taking things up to the edges of the unknown but usually stopping while it was still safe. Everett loved talking to the boy as much as he feared talking to Ella. She always was pushing from around some corner Everett couldn't see past. And as time went on he became more and more shy about appearing out and out foolish to her.

Toward mid-afternoon the wind quickened. Everett sniffed the air and looked skyward. Ordinarily he would have pulled anchor and started back as a precaution against an afternoon thunderstorm. But the fishing was unusually good, and Jamie was pulling them in as fast as Everett. It was good seeing the boy do so well. On many days Everett would catch two or three times more than Jamie until the boy turned downcast and discouraged. But today he was catching on, Everett thought, jigging the bottom with just the right snap and setting the hook so cleanly he hardly ever missed a bite.

There was no better teacher than success, he figured, so he stayed put until the wind shifted east and started kicking up white caps. Usually a shift to the east sent the fish on their way, but they just kept on coming, making Everett think it would soon turn west again, fish being smarter about such things than ordinary men. He watched Jamie set his hook and lift fish after fish, his face flushed with excitement and lips trembling with a self-satisfied grin.

After fishing without bait to make the boy feel even better about the day's break-through, Everett yelled out against the noise of the rising wind, "I've been meaning to ask a question, yeah?"

He watched closely as Jamie turned to listen.

Everett looked out over the gradually building waves, "You don't think I'm stupid, do you, son?" Then he turned quickly to see Jamie's response. Jamie didn't hesitate, but he did fight back that grin. "Nossir," he lied firmly.

Everett thought about trying to tease a little more out of the boy. Maybe ask him if at one time he might have thought Everett were just a *little* stupid or even if the boy first met Everett and were someone else, somebody important, that maybe on first impression that person might think Everett was maybe a little slow in the attic. Or maybe even if Jamie's mother thought him a bit dull of mind, sometimes. But Everett bit his tongue and fought back the urge to work the edges of his worst fears. *I may be a little dumb*, he thought, *but I ain't that dumb.*

Everett turned now and looked southwest at a bank of dark clouds on the horizon, the tops puffing upward into mean-looking thunderheads. The east wind kicked up another notch, and Everett pulled anchor and set his oars into growing waves. He cursed himself for waiting so long. It would be a long row into the wind and the sloppy, roiling chop cutting against the current.

Everett muscled the boat up the ragged slopes of the growing waves, pulling steadily and hard. The boy strained to see the island in the far distance, the wind soon whistling and yanking a light spray from the caps of the breaking waves. Jamie sat in the stern, holding the gunnel, the spray glistening on his tan, angular face, his eyes fixed on the distant island. Everett, his back to the waves and face-to-face with Jamie, watched the boy but didn't try to tell him there was nothing to be scared of because there was something to be scared of, and you didn't respect the river unless you felt that fear.

A large, off-angled wave broke at the bow and doused them both with sheet of water. "You get that bucket and bail us, son," Everett said with an edge of urgency, having to huff now from the hard rowing. And now Jamie could hear a bit of an edge in Everett's voice as the storm built, the bow raising at ever sharper angles and then plunging over the crests and slapping into the troughs with a shuddering splash of spray.

As he worked the oars, Everett called out between breaths, trying to keep up a conversation to quell panic in the boy. Fear was good, he knew, but panic could kill you, so he kept up a breathy chatter. "My daddy rowed the North Sea... in lots worse than this. My mum wouldn't let me go out with him... but she made sure I learned to swim. My daddy never learnt to swim," he said puffing. "Scurvy took him before he ever needed it."

"You come from England, then?" the boy yelled, his face shiny with spray.

"Yessir."

"You talk a little funny, I guess," Jamie said, keeping his eyes strained to the island and watching the waves rolling at them, marveling at how Everett seemed to see them even though he had his back turned.

"Yessir, a little of this and that. Americans think I talk funny, but them English straight off the boat... they don't mistake me for an Englishmun, neither way. We come here when I was ten," he puffed, "I can't say I know which I am or which I want to be, English or American or Canadian. But I ain't got a lick of French in me, for sure."

"You wouldn't want to go back to England?" the boy asked, looking at Everett for a moment and offering a bit playfully, "I don't think you'd fit in so good with all them redcoats and their wigs."

"They ain't all like that," Everett grinned. "They got some good lads, too. They sure as hell ain't proper, nossir. Don't let them wigs fool yah. Them Brits swear and curse so much, Americans won't fight with 'em." Suddenly his right foot slipped and the boat lurched to port. Everett cursed and reset his feet and muscled the oars hard to pull them back straight into the waves. "You ready to row, yet, son?" Everett snorted.

Jamie looked at him with horrified disbelief. "Not bloody well," he shouted, but feeling a glow of flattery just at the suggestion that Everett could trust him to the task.

Everett had no intention of giving the boat over, but he was glad to make his point and give the boy a bit of a boost. As much as Everett was taken with Jamie's mum, he knew the boy was ready for a lot more than she'd give him credit for. Above the whistling wind, thunder rumbled in the distance. The cloud bank was building fast, moving their way at earnest pace. Everett studied the dark mass looking for shards of lightening. He was glad the boy's back was to the storm. The clouds looked like swollen bruises, purple and brown and angry gray nudging upward and gobbling away the brilliant blue. Then he saw jagged rakes of lightning dance along the river's black horizon. Everett picked up the pace and heard the rumble and thud of the squall line closing fast.

The boat surged and crashed into deepening troughs of the channel waves curled back against themselves by howling gusts. A half mile from the island, the wind went suddenly slack and the air turned cold and damp. A huge dark shadow from the racing clouds raced over them. Two miles west, a wall of rain slashed the sky and a rolling mist sucked away the line separating sky and water. The waves quickly lost their skittery caps and rolled at them in undulating swells. Everett jacked up the pace in his losing race with a sky about to vomit.

"Gonna git wet," Everett grinned. "Here she comes."

Jamie turned and looked back. "Holy shit!" he gasped.

Huge drops of rain began slowly spattering around them. Lightning flashed and crackled as if racing down a hollow tube, then exploded with a percussive thud that popped their ears.

Jamie snapped around and grasped the gunnel, white-knuckled with fear.

Everett's heart pounded with a mix of dread and elation. "Hold on," he yelled just as wall of wind and driving rain swatted them, nearly lifting the bow straight out, save for Everett setting his oars and driving down the trough into a wall of green water that exploded over them drenching Jamie with a shock of cold.

For the next few minutes the rain roared down in a ferocious torrent. Gusts swirled and snapped and jerked the boat left and right, and Everett heaved hard right then hard left holding the bow into the wind, oars bending and groaning under the chaotic rip of wind and waves and surging river current roiling below, pulling them with silent, unrelenting defiance straight into the teeth of the howling wind. The sky flashed and crackled, lightning searing the air and hissing before each crunching thud.

In the far distance north of the island, Jamie spotted what looked to be the French patrol boat. He pointed, and Everett turned back over his shoulder, and then shook his head no, then looked again several more times, each time shaking his head no as the rain roared.

"Them dumb shits are in the channel," he gasped, "and heading down wind. Sure as hell going to broach. Ain't no way they can make it to the island."

Jamie stretched his neck and squinted against the steady spray trying to get a better look. He could see the oars plopping and chopping in that odd way they had, the French officer lurching as the boat heaved left and right, lifting and riding down the face of the growing waves. And then Jamie saw a wave lift and twist them. "Thar they go," Jamie shouted, Everett peeking back over his shoulder, shaking his head no. The boat rose to the peak of the crest, then lurched sideways down into the trough, the big wave flipping the boat over top, and in a moment the boat was nearly sunk, and arms flailed, slapping the water, the waves lifting four or five heads, and then they disappeared in the trough, and next time Jamie could see only three and then just one, and then nothing but the overturned bow section get sucked down the channel, a couple of oars stabbing out through the faces of waves before disappearing in the chaos.

Everett rowed hard, sneaking as many looks back as he could while attending to his coarse. "That's one hell of a swim," he called out. "Cain't believe anyone in that boat could swim that stretch, not in this wind. Not in that current."

Jamie had been around a lot of death in his life, but he'd never seen it happen directly, and it took his breath away and dried his throat and filled him with dread, watching those men slip away like that. He didn't want to believe it. "They can't be more than a half mile from the island," he called to Everett, straining for signs, for a dark head or any movement in the waves.

"More 'n that, boy. Distance'll deceive you on the water. Besides, ten feet is more'n any them lads could swim. Bloody shame to go like that," Everett called out through the wind. "You keep watch, but we're a good half hour from there, and we got our own problems, yeah?"

The wind shifted north, and the sun gleamed through a crack in the clouds and sparkled brilliantly in the froth as the deep blue water shimmered from a million violent slaps and tugs of the new wind twisting the waves in new confusion. Sweat and spray poured down Everett's face and arms as he pulled steadily, inching forward, slowly gaining headway toward the island's lee shore as the squall line raced past into a bilious eastern sky. As they closed to a quarter mile, Everett could feel the first sign of protection from the north wind, the island's huge trees undulating from the wind's force but absorbing its power. He knew then they were safe, and that in a few minutes the waves would all but vanish in the shelter of the island.

Exhausted from his hour of work, Everett asked Jamie to take over rowing. By now the waves were moderate, the wind tumbling over the island trees but spent in odd maverick gusts that pressed down on the water in swirly rushes. Jamie took the oars and pulled with relative ease now, the boat leaping forward with each hard stroke. Everett sat in the stern and turned his wet face to the brilliant sun. He took long, deep relaxing breaths, feeling his heart throbbing at his temples and ears. As they neared the island in the lee of the wind, the water turned strangely calm. Hundreds of leaves and tiny twigs torn from the trees floated buoyantly on the smooth dark surface.

Millions of moths shimmered and hovered in the calmness out of the wind, and above them wind swallows darted and dashed, filling their bellies with this concentrated bounty. When the swallows rose above the protection of the trees, the gale whisked them swiftly away. Shimmering black grackles, red-winged blackbirds, assorted pewees, warblers, finches, chickadees, creepers, and a half dozen kinds of sparrows cackled, buzzed, chirped and whistled greedily in the trees as they gobbled a multitude of disrupted insects driven to the southeast edge of the island by the wild squall and now the surging northwest gale.

For a few moments, Everett savored the sweet soft air, the gentle protection that would fool anyone that only a few hundred feet away, a northerly lashed the island point so hard a man could barely stand against the force of the wind. As they edged yet closer, the mosquitoes sang at their ears, and then Ella appeared drenched and swatting mosquitoes with a towel and glaring angrily at Everett.

"Goddamn you," she fumed, "you let that boy rescue you. You let him row *you* out in that madness... you bastard."

Jamie snapped around, the word 'boy' stinging his pride, hating her way of shattering his growing sense of becoming a man, making him cringe at even wishing it so.

Everett blanched. "No, ma'am."

"You stupid, lazy, ignorant fool."

Everett was struck dumb by the rage and conviction of her words.

Jamie released the oars, twirled, grabbed the bow line and flung it to her. "I didn't row none in the storm," he said angrily. He wanted to tell her he could have, but he was afraid of his anger, afraid he'd lash out at her with a venom that would wrench them apart. He could not do that. But he glowed with humiliation and watched her pale, desolate face as she pulled them to the moss edge, her blond hair drenched and dark and hanging limp and dripping at her neck.

Everett climbed silently out of the boat. He looked up at her as she backed up the bank. "I rowed, ma'am, 'til we hit the lee." But her hard look didn't change. He knew he couldn't say they weren't in danger. He should have seen the storm sooner, got back sooner. "Did you see them Frenchies flip in the channel?" Everett asked.

She lifted her hand to her mouth. Her fingers trembled. "Why were you out there? You could have saved those men if you'd been here where you belonged." Her eyes glowed with tears of anger and helplessness. "I saw five men drown..." then stopped and glared at Everett.

He and Jamie pulled the boat up the bank and pushed it into its hidden shelter, a tangle of brush and weeds, and raspberry bushes, and in a few moments you could never have spotted that boat even if you looked directly there and knew what you were trying to see.

They rushed silently up through the woods to the island's point where the wind howled and crashed against the rocks. The channel was empty of any sign of the French boat, the river empty except for the gleaming splendor of the waves, shimmering under the brilliant afternoon sun. The wind whistled through the giant willow, and the waves crashed loudly, spraying them with a warm river mist.

"That could have been you and Jamie," she seethed.

"No, ma'am," Everett shouted against the wind.

But he knew it could have been. If they'd busted an oar. Or if the wind got ten knots faster. Or if they got turned sideways in the channel. They were lucky they could hold into the wind that day, lucky the lightning struck just about everywhere but them. Sure, it could have been them, he knew, but it wasn't. They could have drowned, but they didn't. Still, Everett didn't know how to say any of this to her. He was afraid she was around some corner way ahead of him, and if he said anything more, she'd slice him open and find a coward and a fool in the center of his heart. And then she'd be gone.

So he stood there staring out into hard wind knowing the spirits of dead men were flailing in those waters, their bodies long since washed down river probably never to be found.

"Help me search the shore edge for debris," Everett said turning to Jamie.

"No," Ella snapped.

"Why not?" Jamie demanded.

She set her lips hard against the tone in his voice.

"Afraid we might find dead bodies?" the boy asked.

She looked now at Everett. She wanted him to tell Jamie to obey, but Everett just waited. He wasn't going to tell her to stop babying the boy, but he wasn't going to make it easy for her, either.

"You both make me bloody ill," she snapped. "Do as you please, then," she said turning and hurrying back to their hut.

Everett and Jamie worked the north shore of the island. Storms often washed up useful things... old logs, timbers, tables, chairs, tree trunks, much of it good firewood, some of it still good for timbering the hut walls and ceilings. The wind and waves from a storm spun these objects out of the channel where in calmer weather they would surge past far from shore. As they worked through the dense underbrush, powerful gusts swept crashing waves into the rocks and showered them with a cool mist. The shore line was a huge tangle of rain-shimmering vines, honeysuckle, blood root, stinging nettles, and a dozen other desperate weeds and shrubs fighting to the death over the steady spray and damp rocky soil. They wrestled through the weeds, straining to see objects rising or heaving in the breaking waves.

A few feet away, Everett saw two oars from sunken patrol boat and then noticed blue cloth and traces of a body clinging, face down in the surging waves. Everett crashed down through the shoreline underbrush, grabbed the body and flung it up on the shore. He yanked the oars out and flung them up, then climbed back, his body lunging clumsily from the power of the crashing waves.

"Grab that arm," Everett said, and they both pulled the body of the French officer up the rise into a clear patch. Everett then sat hard on the man's chest, then bounced a half dozen times until the officer coughed, then vomited and soon tried to get to his feet. Everett knocked his arm away, and the Frenchman flopped back down, gasping and vomiting again.

"Go get my pistol," Everett told Jamie.

He turned to the Frenchman, "You set and don't move, comprindey vooo?"

The Frenchman was too sick to protest. He gasped for air, coughing and thrashing weakly in a thick bed of stinging nettles. Everett knew the man was feeling less poorly when he started scratching at his hands and neck and face now growing hot red splotches from the searing itch of the island nettles. He recognized the officer now, the same inept chatterbox who stopped a week or so past and understood immediately why the bloat flipped.

With Ella a step behind, Jamie rushed back handing Everett the pistol.

"Well, help the poor man," Ella snapped at Everett and Jamie.

Everett handed her the gun. "Put a ball in his knee if he puts up a fuss," he said knowing first that she wouldn't do any such thing and second that it wouldn't be necessary. The man was slight and light as a feather. Everett grasped his tunic and lifted him to his feet.

"Ze men? Où sont des hommes?" the Frenchman muttered.

"Dead and drowned. Them oars probly saved yer ass, ey?" Everett said, holding the man's scraggly arm.

Though he staggered feebly, the Frenchman was too proud to be assisted and quickly shook off Everett's grasp and lurched weakly on his own toward the sod hut. Ella followed, the pistol pointed at the ground, hanging uselessly from her hand.

They sat him on a log in a patch of sun on the island point. They stripped off his coat and shirt. His ribs showed clearly through white, almost translucent skin. Ella draped a blanket over his shoulders. He shivered and breathed in pants through purple lips. But in a few minutes, he recovered enough to remove the blanket, folding it carefully, then putting on one of Everett's shirts which dwarfed his slight frame, the shoulders hanging nearly to his elbows, the Frenchman quickly rolling the sleeves.

"Good Christ, don't they feed you oer'n that camp?" Everett teased.

"Ils vous nourrit pas?" Ella said with a faint grin.

The officer regarded Everett for a moment, then Ella, and shook his head no emphatically. Then he smiled.

Everett held out his hand, "Everett O'Toole," he said.

"Henri Trouver," he said, "Merci. I owe for ze rescue, merci, Monsieur. I am en dette pour la rescue."

"My French is poorly," Everett said, "but, if you're offering, how about your life for our safety? You keep your mouth shut about us."

"Ne parlez pas de nous," she said.

"No pro-*blem*. I am done with ze soldiering, oui? I suis fini étant militaire. I am dead to them. They find da boat," he shrugged and coughed. "I am dead monsieur, oui? Je suis fini. No soldier ever again. I am sor-ry for ze men. Bon Dieu!" He shook his head no.

Everett regarded him skeptically but could not imagine this man ever being a threat to anyone. "Ain't yer fault. Ain't right sending a sorry bunch as you and them out'n this river. That ain't right."

The Frenchman shrugged mournfully.

Ella brought him some warm soup. "Merci," he smiled. Then drank it in ravenous gulps. "Ah, c'est très bon." he said, handing her the bowl.

"More... plus?"

"S'il vous plait," he said. "A most beautiful day. I die. I wake up een paradise being feed by ze beautiful widow and her kind guardien, I wake aux ce paradis pour belle femme et son aimable guardia," he exclaimed.

As much as he knew he should regard this man with suspicion, Everett was disarmed by Lt. Henri Trouver. The man's effusively friendly, buoyantly pompous, and mildly effeminate manner infected all of them almost immediately. He seemed utterly harmless. He and Jamie had to bite their lips at times to keep from giggling. "He seems just like a girl," Jamie laughed.

By early evening, Henri was offering Ella advice on her gardens. He picked a bouquet of wild flowers and offered to cook their dinner. "I coook, vary goot, très, très bien," he exclaimed.

* * *

Everett watched over the next days at how animated she became when Henri conversed with her and felt even more sluggish and ignorant than ever. Henri had read many books, Ella told Everett in a burst of excitement, and he knew all about theater and music. Ella was immediately taken with his vast knowledge and seemed constantly to exclaim with wondrous delight at his descriptions of plays and musical performances he had seen. Everett watched in depressed dismay as Henri captivated her with his charm, most of their conversations shrouded in French, punctuated by giggles and laughter at every turn. If this is what a woman wanted from a man, Everett thought to himself, then he would never have a woman—at least not one of Ella's kind. By comparison to them both, he felt dim and dull...as flat as the calm black river beneath a humid gray sky.

One night Henri cooked fresh perch in an elegant sauce fashioned from wild onions and mushrooms he and Ella picked. He told them about the misery and stupidity of the war. The French military became panicked about British expansion in North America but really had more to worry about in Europe where the war with Britain mattered. "Canada," he said scornfully, "geeve it to ze pushy geese," his favored term for Brits. So the French generals pulled people like Henri from their university studies and turned them into officers to send to North America. He was not even supposed to have been a combat officer. He trained in logistics, mainly food supplies. He hated boats and could barely swim.

"What did you study before?" Ella interrupted.

"Ah. Bot-anni. Ze plants. Scienteest. I 'ave studeed botanique, la science de legume. Dey tink I be goood coook," he laughed and twirled his fingers around his ear with a flourish of his wrist, "eediots, oui?" Then the British sent a Major George Washington to Fort Duquesne and attacked a large party of French scouts nearby. "Very bad... brutale mer-dur. Very, very blooody and what humiliation to ze French. Qu'est-ce-que humiliation pour France. Très mal. Very bad. Panique. Pan-eek, how do you say?"

"Panicked?" Ella offered, "the French panicked?"

"Ah, oui, and they send me," he said holding his hands flat to his chest, his eyes bulging in astonishment and indignation, "Moi! Mais oui!" he laughed.

They sent him to be a combat soldier, but his commanders realized quickly that Lt. Henri Trouver was not combat material. They sent him to an outpost on the St. Lawrence where they said they expected him to become a logistics officer of some importance when the war reached there. Henri wasn't sure if, perhaps, they lied to him. At the outpost he was told by his commander to head a river patrol. His crew, whom he regretted losing but detested thoroughly, were French Army regulars, not French marines who had been trained in seamanship. They hated Quebec, which was unimaginably cold in the winter and deathly hot in the summer. Everyone was always sick with diarrhea, malaria, and a thousand other fevers. His crew hated the water, hated not being at the frontline, hated not being back in France, hated him.

"Beeetch, beeetch, beeetch. Hopeless eediots. They can no row de bateau," he said gesturing wildly. "Fooocking eediots," he exclaimed, then raising his hands in surrender, "Pardon, madam. Oh, moi, very sor-ri, sor-ri, sor-ri, pardon."

Ella laughed. "I'm not offended, Henri. Please, it's okay."

"Ah, merci, madam. Merci." Then turning to Jamie, "Monsieur, pardon?"

Mouth agape at Henri's theatrics, Jamie just shrugged and grinned.

Turning to Everett. "I am sor-ry, je suis très naif, monsieur, pour ma mon elocution offensif."

"Don't worry about me, Henri," Everett said. "A few curses won't hurt me none."

Henri sat back in his chair, flung his hands out in surrender and sighed in relief. He would take this to be broad permission to swear at will.

So he and his crew rowed up and down the river looking for British soldiers or Mohawks fighting for the British, and mostly finding nothing but mosquitoes, black flies, no-see-ums, vicious deer flies, blood-sucking spiders, lunatic black bears, stinking skunks, hostile trappers, stinging ants, suspicious but mostly old and harmless local Indians, unfriendly French farmers and foul smelling fishermen who spoke an archaic dialect of French Henri could sometimes barely understand. He and his pathetic crew almost sank the boat a half dozen times. They knew nothing about navigation and couldn't figure out the weather patterns.

He had never seen such sudden, vicious storms or such periods of absolutely breathless, bug-infested calm. Neither he nor his motley crew could foresee nor adjust to such sudden, wild changes. They also didn't know the channels nor understand the currents, nor could he ever quite figure out how the wind affected water in every channel so much differently, nor how such large, sharp waves could emerge in minutes. Dozen of times they were nearly killed by lightning from squalls that howled across the river in bilious brown clouds. Henri made the hissing, crackling sound of lightening hitting water, then exploding in deafening thunder. He leapt from his seat, his face crimson, waving his arms and hissing and crackling and booming. "Mon Dieu!" he gasped, eyes bulging.

He and his crew were city men and farmers trained to march in orderly lines and be massacred by British soldiers also marching in orderly lines. The French marines fought differently, Henri told them. They hid behind trees and rocks like the Indians and shot the Brits in the balls and ran like hell. They were a nasty bunch and knew a few things about boats, as well. But not Henri nor his crew, and after a time, they grew to despise each other as they rowed pointlessly up and down the river, never knowing what horrors of racing wind and lightening and angry waves and driving rain might appear suddenly on the western horizon. And before they could row a quarter mile in soggy, listless pre-squall air on water still as a millpond, suddenly this vicious gale would erupt around them in blinding rage. It made no sense. "No, no. Not to me," he said sadly shaking his head, "Mon Dieu. Je comprends rien."

"First off," Everett offered slowly, "you don't ever want to git sideways to the wind or ass end to the waves, yeah?"

"Oui," Henri nodded.

"Me an' him's out there, same storm. Row into the wind. That's it, ey."

"That's eet, ici?" Henri shrugged approvingly.

"Go slow. Don't panic," Everett said, and Jamie nodded silently at his side.

"Ah oui. Not to wor-ry, no?" Henri smiled ironically.

Ella watched as they rattled on. Henri nudged and played and sometimes scoffed at Everett's simple offerings, but Henri also listened and nodded and helped her realize that Everett understood the river more expertly than she had yet appreciated. He had often predicted squalls and warned her about the currents and how the wind shaped waves. Much of it she took for granted as the casual chatter of a simple fisherman, but now as Henri described them—his horrific fears and puzzlement at the river's astonishing powers—she was forced to admire Everett some bit more and saw her son's admiration for him echoed in his nods and affirming squirms.

"It's the current flipped you, Henri," Everett said. "Warn't just the wind, nossir. Ain't nothin' worse than a channel current goin one way and the wind goin the other. That rip'll kill yah," he told a nodding Henri.

"How come *you* rowed in the channel, then?" Jamie asked Everett.

Ella turned and drilled Everett with a scowl.

Everett felt her glare but dared not look. "I was usin' that channel for speed to beat the storm. We come close, too. But them two channels ain't the same. That one Henri caught, that's a killer. Bigger, deeper, faster. Terrible in an east gale. Ain't never two rips the same."

Jamie and Henri nodded with narrowed eyes.

She watched these two men and a boy and felt oddly a touch comforted by them rather than merely frustrated, angered, baffled, and bullied as was often the case with men she'd known.

She wasn't sure what would become of them or if Henri could truly be trusted or if Everett could truly be counted on despite several months of what seemed even-tempered solidity and great kindness to her and her son. She wasn't sure if he and Henri could become friends, if Henri would stay and hide with them or flee to some greater wilderness, or if Henri might turn on Everett as an instinctive enemy and suddenly kill him. It seemed unlikely, but she had learned bitterly about surprises in her life. For now she was quietly encouraged by the respect Henri and Jamie showed this man she sometimes scorned for his leaden, convoluted platitudes. And she regretted her harsh scolding that afternoon of the storm. Perhaps it was her need for Jamie to learn about the arcane mysteries shared in the cloudy reaches of the male brain that softened her toward Everett this day. She poured them coffee and listened with bemused affection. Three boys, really, trading stories, punctuated by grunts and nods about the murky shifts of human fate.

"Yessir," Everett muttered.
Jamie nodded solemnly.
"Mai oui," Henri clucked. "That's it."

* * *

By late August, the nights had turned chilly and the days shorter. Everett and Jamie busied themselves catching and salting fish. Ella and Henri harvested vegetables. Henri expanded their harvest considerably with his knowledge of edible plants, mushrooms, and herbs. As fall approached, huge flocks of ducks gathered and fed ravenously before migration. Everett set nets in weed beds along several shoreline marshes. The ducks got tangled in his nets when feeding, giving him a large harvest of meat and feathers. The nets also allowed him to capture the birds live, clip their wings, and keep them until the weather froze enough to preserve their flesh.

Each day they scoured the shoreline for broken trees and errant logs they would dry and burn through the winter. Jamie was assigned to watch the channels for passing logs and to row out to rope those of any size and haul them in. They cut down old and dying trees and trimmed the branches of the healthy ones, but their most important source of wood washed down the river and would cease as soon as the river froze.

The cooler days and nights were a tonic for Henri, a reminder of France. He quickly settled into his new exile and tried to prepare himself for the dreaded North American winter, an ordeal universally hated by French and English both. Already by late August, some leaves began to turn bright colors and the grasses and marsh weeds slowly transformed to a soft golden glow. The days were dry, the winds more often whispering down from the arctic north, carrying a dry chill across the dark blue water.

One morning as Everett and Jamie arranged fish on their salting tables in the bright open sun at the western point of the island, three canoes of scruffy trappers pulled up.

The leader of six men was an immense creature with great snarled masses of filthy hair and beard dressed in greasy leathers. He climbed out of his canoe and up the bank, and from twenty feet away, Everett could smell the man...an acrid mix of burnt bacon, rotting flesh, breath equal to a hot blast from the outhouse, and sweat so old it stung the nose like a tub of lye. His right eye was blurred over with a whitish film and cast sharply to starboard.

Despite the horrific stench, Everett moved closer to the man to block further entrance to the island, to prevent his looking to see what they might steal or pillage in some later ambush.

"Yessir," Everett said, standing near to the man's height but just a fraction of his bulk and probable might.

The man spit a wet line of tobacco juice into the grass. His teeth were brown pegs, crooked here and there, a good half missing and the rest rotting and streaked with sharp, black edges of decay sharp and rough as a saw blade.

"This here yer island?"

"Yessir."

"Kin yah prove it?"

"Got papers," Everett said.

The man considered this a moment, looking around with his dull, bloodshot blue eye-the good one of the two-as the cloudy one darted oddly about as if on a separate inspection mission. He spit again and farted.

"Me and them be obliged to set traps."

"Nossir, can't be done."

The man rolled his eyes now in considerable agitation. If he had a dog, he'd have kicked it now. But lacking that he spit and started scratching at his chest with these long, yellow and brown fingernails that looked every bit as strong as bear claws.

Suddenly, from the path leading around the hut, Ella and Henri appeared with baskets full of vegetables. They stopped at the site of this astonishingly ugly man, and Henri twitched his nose in immediate recognition of the man's immense odors. With the appearance of Ella, the men in the canoes howled and hooted, and the immense man leading them grinned. His slippery wet lips glowed red, pulling away from these jagged pegs of teeth swimming in a brown tobacco slime.

"Why not?" the man grinned, apparently encouraged now by the howls of his fellow trappers.

Henri did not like this man's tone, put down his basket, and hurried to Everett's side with a wispy walk sufficiently springy to bring on a new set of howls punctuated by giggles, laughter, and muttered jokes.

"I set my own traps," Everett said with growing annoyance.

Ella picked up Henri's basket, which gave the men a bit of a peak down the front of her dress. They exploded with howls, and slapped the water with their paddles and kicked the ribs of their canoes. She stood sharply, turned her back and hurried to the hut door, but the clamor only increased as they sensed her annoyance.

"Shut ze feelthy foookin faces," Henri spit angrily. "Swine," he hissed. "Tu est filthy cochons qui merite d'etre dans des cages et mangent nos merde."

Everett tried to push Henri back, but Henri twisted away and approached the bank over the canoes and kicked dirt and stones at this motley swarm of hysteria. They laughed all the more uncontrollably. "Aller. Partez d'ici," he shouted.

The immense leader was growing less amused and increasingly agitated. He picked at his beard around his mouth, spit again, "Won't bother yer traps none."

"You won't bother 'em at'all," Everett said. "I'll shoot any man I see trapping this island, and any traps I see I'll toss deep in the river."

"This a free country, mister," the man countered quickly.

"Monsieur..." Henri began.

Cheers and whistles from the canoes.

"Shut-up, Henri," Everett growled under his breath.

"Monsieur, zis island ees not pour you, ey? Go. Go away," Henri shouted at the trapper.

"Shut yer fucking mouth you little shit," the man growled.

Henri turned sharply and marched quickly to the hut. In a moment he was marching back, a musket under one arm, and pistol held straight out in his other fist.

"Go," Henri shouted, "Go, go! Aller, aller!" He waved the pistol toward the men in the canoes, and they ducked and scuffled, grabbing at their paddles to escape. Their leader stood his ground, his face turning crimson with rage.

Henri hurried up to him and jammed the gun up under his hairy chin, "You t'ink I no shoot, monsieur?" Henri glared at the man, "Go," he shouted, Henri's face white as death. Then he jammed the gun hard into the man's neck. The man jumped back, turned, and rushed down the bank. He clamored, splashing, into the last canoe, and in a moment, they were gone, paddling frantically down channel heading east.

Everett frowned at Henri. "Yer a crazy Frenchman," Everett muttered, feeling his own heart thudding wildly with fear, thinking to himself the end was near that time, and they could all just now be splayed crooked, starring from dull-eyed blackness with musket balls through their heads.

"Merde," Henri smiled wanly. "Terrible men," he said, shaking his head no.

As they watched the trappers disappear down the channel, Ella appeared behind them waving a pistol at them. "I ought to shoot you both," she said in exasperation.

Everett and Henri turned. Henri shrugged his shoulders and lowered his jaw in mock surprise looking at first to her, then to Everett.

Everett was growing weary of her scoldings on this day and wished he had the courage to throw her in the river for a little cooling off. He didn't, at least for the moment, so he rolled his eyes and sighed deeply, glad to breathe another day.

"Don't you get fat-headed with me," she said, eyes flashing as she wagged the gun at them, all loose-wristed, her finger nowhere near the trigger.

Each man stepped back.

"That was just so stupid. You didn't need to pick a fight with those grotesque animals," she snapped. "I mean, why? Why do you do such stupid things?"

"Madam..." Henri began. "Zay are monstres."

"I'm talking to *him* right now," she said. "I'll get to you later."

Everett scratched his head in frustration. "Thar gone, ain't they?"

"Yes," she said, the color rising in her cheeks, "Yes, Everett; you are correct, but they'll be back, thanks to you two fools and your nasty threats..."

Everett turned away, growing impatient. "Ma'am," he said.

"Don't you ma'am me. Why? Answer my question. Why did you do that?"

"Madame..."

She silenced Henri with a look that could have burned flesh.

"Ma'am, excuse my crude ways," Everett said slowly, "but you ever seen the way mean dogs do things. They come on another dog's territory and piss on every bush. You let 'em piss on your bushes like that, and they think they own yah. They think they can do what they want."

As Everett explained, Ella looked at him with extraordinary intensity, bobbing her head yes, mocking his every word, blinking in disbelief with every new utterance.

"You cain't let mean dogs piss on yer bushes. You gotta go after 'em and you gotta be mean and ugly." He said watching her. "You gotta curl back your lips and snarl."

Henri nodded his head yes. " Oui, comme ze mad dog."

Ella nodded her head yes, as well. "And you two think this is how you keep people like that from coming back."

"Yes, ma'am," Everett said, pleased with his argument.

"Oui, madam," Henri nodded.

Ella closed her eyes, turned away and headed back toward the hut. Then she stopped, twirled around, wagged the pistol in their direction, and said, "But it's because you've threatened and humiliated these men, that they *will* be back. *We* are not dogs, and as disgusting as those men are, *they* are not dogs. They are people, and people do not like to be humiliated. It makes them angry and vengeful. Do you understand that. Do you both understand?"

Both men stared at Ella. They understood what she was saying, but they both knew her to be wrong. Each in his own peculiar way knew that ferocity was crucial for inducing another man's fear. They looked at her for several long moments across some deep elemental divide. Puffs of wind tugged at her hair, and wind rows of tiny waves flashed across the river.

They were startled out of this odd gulf of silence by the appearance of Jamie on the path from the rowboat. He carried several long strings of fish and greeted them with a cheerful hello, breaking the spell and sensing only momentarily that something was going on but preferring not to know. Henri and Everett congratulated him heartily for his catch, but Ella simply nodded and whispered, "Hello, dear," as she trudged tiredly back to the hut knowing that Jamie would soon be one of them, preferring bluster and threats over working things out sensibly and calmly. The signs were already there, she knew, and soon the dangers.

* * *

Everett laboriously rowed into the trading post dock towing his huge fish trap filled with live fish. He tied the boat, then sat to rest, sweat trickling from his temples and down his cheeks. He looked forward to seeing Lucy Desjardin and felt a tug of excitement anticipating a night in bed with this tough, rowdy lady-one of Everett's favorite people on all this earth. She, too, was a widow, but not a sad one. Her husband had been a terrible drunk who nearly ran the post into the ground. Everett recalled many times when he would arrive and both Lucy and Jimmy would be bruised and limping after one of their notorious fights.

Everyone suspected that during their last fight Lucy pulled a gun and shot her Jimmy square in the forehead, but she claimed a robber did it, not that anyone cared. They hadn't had a sheriff or seen a law man in years. People took care of their personal squabbles quietly and without any interference just so long as no one else got hurt and no innocent people got dragged into it. But Lucy would tell no one about her shooting Jimmy just in case there was ever a law man sent their way to clean things up. She wouldn't even tell Everett, and he was just about her favorite or at least that's what she told him.

Lucy kicked open the front door and emerged with two buckets of fish guts. Now this Lucy was a sight to behold. She had muscular, sinewy arms bulging with thick veins and wiry muscles. She had ink-black hair she acquired from her mother, a full-blooded Iroquois. As she walked down the steps with that hundred or so pounds of guts, Everett admired the muscles and veins in her neck and chest as they blended into the soft mounds of flesh of her breasts. Right down the middle of her forehead, another vein pulsed, and when she saw Everett, she winked. Her face was red from the strain, and had she not been carrying buckets of fish, Everett might have thought that from the shoulders up she looked like she might be fucking.

He loved her intensity and watched with a mix of growing excitement and bemused admiration as her strong legs wobbled from the weight. She hauled those buckets down the bank and at the dock, put them down and tipped the guts into the river where thousands of minnows darted in immediate, ravenous attack. There wasn't an ounce of fat on Lucy Desjardin, but she was built soft where it mattered, Everett knew, trying now to fix in his mind's eye the body he saw when she was prancing around naked during one of their wild flings.

"Well look who the cows drug in," she said, breathing deeply, her hands on her hips. Everett could feel in his memory the sharp curve of her waist where her hands rested, and now had to stay set or she'd see he was getting an erection.

"I guess you couldn't git enough from yer fancy new gal, hey?" she said.

"No ma'am," Everett grinned.

"She don't 'preciate your better points, ain't it so?" she smiled, revealing a missing tooth near the right front where she spit now, sending a sharp squirt into the river. Some people thought the missing tooth and all the muscles and a few emerging wrinkles were signs that Lucy was becoming just another river hag, but Everett liked her just as she was. Sometimes he'd notice her sticking her tongue in the big space where the tooth once lived, and it would send a delicious shiver up his spine.

"I don't think she figures I got any fine points," he said.

"That's her failing, then, ain't it?"

"Well, Lucy, I don't know about them things. I just cain't figure out what a woman wants," he sighed gazing out as a flock of gulls dropped down, squabbling and squealing, into the drifting slick of fish blood.

"You know what I want pretty good," she grinned. Then she spit again, just a clean fast squirt that kissed the surface of the river with the sweetest little splash Everett could imagine.

"Well, I got some good fish for yah," he said.

She studied him for a moment, figuring that he didn't get her little joke, that he wasn't yet thinking about sex. But she'd get that changed.

She moved over to his boat and leaned over to look at the fish, making sure he got a good look down the front of her shirt. She watched his eyes lock and then turn dark and swimmy. "Beauties, hey?" she said.

"None better in all this world," Everett said, looking at the full rich, pale swell of flesh down her inviting cleavage. He didn't know if he could survive until evening.

She stayed right there, her hands braced on her knees. "Help me take a load to Lachine," she asked. Lucy had a barge with a big section of the hold cut with slats open to the river so that fish could live during transit. It was two days of slow sailing down current, then several days of hard polling and rowing back up river unless she could catch an east or northeast wind and set her sail. "Or you too tied to that woman's apron strings?" she said turning a bit more directly Everett's way.

"I got a few days," he said, swallowing thickly. There just wasn't nothing better than spending a few minutes looking down Lucy's shirt. *Glory be*, Everett thought.

She watched his eyes slowly pull up to her own. She smiled. She had him now, she knew. She held his eyes which lolled all wet and dreamy. Then she turned away and spit, "I'll pay you good," she said.

Lucy's fish barge floated deep in the water like some huge old water-logged crate. A three-foot wide deck surrounded the enormous fish hold where thousands of fish swam lazily, held in place by netting below, preventing the catch from escaping through the open hull into the river. The deck extended on the stern to support a makeshift cabin fashioned of logs and timbers harvested from the river. Two rough-cut timbers in the bow and stern served as masts for patchwork sails that helped nudge the crude old vessel forward. Aft of the cabin was an enormous stern oar that served as rudder and propulsion whenever the wind didn't favor sailing.

Whenever Everett saw Lucy's old barge, he had to grin and chuckle. Her decks were so low to the water line that even a moderate wind kicked up waves that washed freely along the gangways and kept her perpetually slimy and treacherous for walking. Inside the cabin, the floors were often awash, making it necessary to sleep in hammocks and turning her ancient wood stove into an orange hulk of rust. Held together with rope and wooden pegs, the 'Old Bitch,' as Lucy called her, creaked and groaned with every wave and swell. But she allowed Lucy to deliver tons of live fish to the Lachine docks several times a year where they were snapped up by rich Montreal buyers catering to the elite French merchant classes, government dignitaries, military officers, and the city's finest restaurants.

They pushed off on a crisp September morning, reaching on a steady northwest wind, the sails billowing and flapping until Everett yanked in the sheet lines and watched them swell with wind and pull powerfully at the sturdy old masts pegged into the aft and fore decks. Lucy pressed the huge rudder with her butt, holding a northeast course that would take them to the main channel. From time to time the lurch of a gust and following waves would lift her clear of the deck where she would ride side-saddle before her weight brought her back to the deck as the barge settled heavily back on course.

It was a day of remarkable beauty. The sky was a deep, dark blue, the sun blazing, the water blue-black etched with flashes of white caps curling gently from a sprinkling of larger waves.

Everett lugged their small cannon out of the cabin and walked gingerly up the port deck. One slip here and they could lose their armor. Everett inched along, then once on the foredeck lowered the cannon into an elevated, notched crevice in the bow keel, then locked it in place, corking the barrel so that water couldn't dampen the powder.

They settled into their journey, picking up the channel and surging ahead for what looked to be an easy run down river.

"So tell me about this here lady you got out there," she said loudly against the wind.

"What's to say?" he said.

"She's good looking. I know that."

"She's a widow, Lucy."

"So," she shrugged. "Ain't we all?"

"She ain't got over her man. Besides," Everett lied, "I ain't interested. She's too smart and sly for me. Makes me feel like a damned fool."

"So, how come you let her stay?" Lucy said, not believing a word of this.

"Why not? She needed a place. She cooks good. I get pretty lonesome out there, Lucy. You ain't called for a visit for a real long time."

"Yeah, so," she said with growing annoyance.

"That don't seem to stop you getting your ass over here the minute you start growing horns."

"You complainin'?" he asked, starting to grin.

A gust tugged at them and lifted the oar and Lucy's feet several inches above the deck. She floated for a moment before Everett squeezed her thigh and guided her down again.

"What happens when she gets over her man?"

"How do I know?" Everett said, shaking his head in exasperation. "You jealous or somethin,' Lucy? Do I hear some jealousy, yeah?"

She rolled her eyes in disbelief. "Why would I be jealous over an asshole like you?" she said.

He stared at her. "Bloody hell, Lucy."

She smiled.

"That's not what you said last night," Everett snorted.

"I can take or I can leave any man," she said, leaning toward the stern and squirting a fine bullet of spit into the slow, swirling wake.

Everett wiped his brow and tip-toed along the port deck. He couldn't figure for the life of him what these women wanted from him. He tip-toed back to her side, careful not to slip on the slick, green deck.

"Would you like to git married to me, Lucy?" he asked.

"Not bloody fucking likely," she guffawed, growing irritated now.

He shrugged and scratched his head.

"Are you asking me?" she said, wanting to kick him in the butt.

"I'm askin yer opinion."

"That's good," she said derisively, launching a new squirt off the stern.

"So would you like to git married to *me*?" she asked.

"Well, if I was thinking of askin to marry you, Lucy, I'd want to know yer opinion?"

She looked up and studied his face a moment. He was a handsome man, steady, loyal, strong, and she hoped not quite as stupid as he thought he was and often seemed. She liked him, but every time she'd said she loved him, it was during one of their great drunken plunges into sex, and in the sober light of day, she wasn't so sure.

"I don't think you'd know how to ask," she said finally. "And to answer your question direct, I don't think you would ask, Everett. You ain't asked yet."

"Jesus Christ, Lucy. What do you think I just asked you back there?"

"Back where?"

He squinted into the glare of the water behind them. "Back by that old log," he said.

"You asked me if I would be interested in getting married to you."

"Yeah?"

"That ain't askin', peckerhead," she said in disgust.

Everett shook his head in total bafflement. He noticed the sail luffing a bit, and worked his way up the deck and yanked on the sheet line, then re-cleated it.

He yelled back, not even looking at her. "This conversation ain't makin a pig's ass worth of sense to me." He looked down at his white toes which were already starting to look permanently wrinkled. They were moving along good but he was sure this was going to be a long and difficult trip.

* * *

Henri stepped back from splitting logs, sipped from his coffee, and breathed in the crisp air. He looked down at the water's edge and watched Ella washing potatoes. He was glad to be rid of Everett for a few days. The man's strange way of thinking sometimes seemed to muddle Henri's own mind. He wasn't sure if it were the limits of his own English or some growing gulf between the European and North American minds or just what happens to a man living on an island alone by himself for so many years. But at times, Everett gave him a headache. Just talking to him could do it, but now his mind was fresh and easy.

"We have plenty for thees long winter, en?" he called to Ella.

She stopped her work and flicked back a lock of her hair with the back of her wrist.

"Henri, these winters are longer and colder than you can imagine. Do you see all that vast blue out there?"

"Oui."

"Can you imagine that being one huge slab of white as far as the eye can see? And no leaves on the trees and the wind howling non-stop?"

Henri shrugged. "We have some snow in France. A few."

She laughed. "It's the cold, Henri. Yes, we have snow, but it's the cold. It's so cold it burns your throat just to breathe," she said gazing out over the water.

"I no can wait," he laughed.

Then suddenly behind them, a shot exploded, and Henri felt an immense jerk as the shot smashed into the back of his ankle, knocking him onto his back, a searing burn snapping up his leg, blood spraying in the dirt.

The immense wall-eyed trapper staggered up the path past the sod hut. Ella scrambled up the bank to help Henri, but the trapper rushed between them, waving her away with the motion of his gun. Henri grasped his shattered ankle and moaned miserably. Ella backed away, the blood draining from her face, her heart pounding with fear and dread. The trapper leaned down and grasped Henri's shoulder, yanking him from his side to his back to make sure he was not armed.

Then he studied Henri's ankle, spitting tobacco juice into the dirt.

The trapper's crew hurried into the clearing but seemed as distracted and addled as before. They wandered about checking for utensils, shovels, and useful objects Ella supposed they would soon steal. The tallest and most alert, a stooped but skinny giant, picked up Ella's rifle, which was leaned against the stump on the point. The others giggled and clucked like nervous chickens as their leader motioned Ella toward the hut.

After gathering fillet knives, a garden hoe, two shovels, and a rack of drying, salted fish, they gathered around Henri who continued writhing in agony, blood oozing from between his fingers as he squeezed his shattered heal and ankle. Henri swatted them angrily away as they tried to touch his ankle. The tall one, whom they referred to as Bernie, dipped a wooden bucket into the river and doused the ankle with water. Henri swatted again, but these men were uncannily quick, alert to the snapping jaws of trapped animals and undeterred by Henri's sudden flailings.

"It's okay, mister," the bony Bernie said, squatting near the foot. "Let's have a look." He pulled an enormous hunting knife from his belt, stabbed it into the soil several times, then rinsed the blade in the bottom of the bucket. "Let me cut that boot."

With extraordinary speed and deftness, the tall trapper carved away the boot with his razor-sharp knife. Another of the giggling trappers brought a log and hoisted Henri's leg. Soon, they were all at work, bringing buckets, preparing a fire.

Henri was in so much pain he didn't fight them off. If they were going to help him, so be it. If they were going to torture him, it could hardly be worse. "Ma dit que je passera des journées a l'enfer," he groaned bitterly. Bernie heated his knife in the fire, and as he put it to flesh, Henri fainted.

Inside the hut, the trapper forced Ella to sit. He gasped and wheezed, his sordid breath coming in loud, hurried, stinking pants. Then he slumped down in a chair beside her, coughing from deep, deep in his chest. He swayed strangely as if in a drunken swoon.

"Whiskey," he demanded.

"Top left shelf," she said, pointing with her chin.

Slowly he lumbered over and pulled down a jug. He yanked the cork with a few brown, partially intact side teeth and took a long, deep slug. Then he slumped back down in a chair at the dinner table and wheezed, sweat dripping from his chin.

"What do you want from us?" she asked weakly.

"Where's the big 'un?" the trapper gasped.

"Fishing," she said.

His better eye moved nervously about, his bad eye turned down and to the side in a hazy, gray dullness.

"Didn't mean no harm to that little Frenchy," he said. "Missed the ground. Just meant to scare yas. I can't hit nothing. Can't see for shit no more."

"Are you here to rape me," she gasped.

"I ain't got no such plan, ma'am."

"Are you going to kill us?"

"No ma'am; I ain't considered that."

"Then what are you doing here?"

Then the enormous, fat trapper leaned forward and vomited on the floor. He coughed violently for a few moments, gasped for air, sweat pouring down his face in dirty rivulets.

"You're awful sick, aren't you?" she said.

He nodded yes and coughed again.

"Why did you come here?" she demanded.

His better eyed turned strangely up in his head, then moved slowly down, locking on her face, his chest heaving in rapid, panting.

"You was here, you was closest when the blood come up."

He leaned forward again, this time quaking with dry heaves. She could smell the rotting heat from his feverish body.

He lay his head down on the table. He panted like an overheated, exhausted dog, his better eye half closed and clouding over, slipping into unconsciousness. Ella rushed outside where the five trappers formed a circle around Henri, who lay unconscious. They had put a stick in Henri's mouth, and Bernie was sewing stitches up Henri's heal. Bernie looked up for a moment as she approached but kept at his work. The men were huddled around the fire cooking fish on sticks, eating eagerly as Bernie worked.

"Fixed a dozen sled dogs worse than this. Trapped 'em by mistake," Bernie muttered, talking to her as he poured straight grain alcohol over the wounds.

"That man's dying inside," she said.

"Cain't believe he ain't already dead," Bernie said. "He's had the fever fer a week. Said he wanted a sip of good whiskey and one more look at a pretty face before he went," Bernie said calmly. "Sorry he shot yer friend. There weren't no call for that. He was just trying to scare 'em a touch. Maybe it was the delirium. I'm sorry to say this man's gonna have a goodly limp," he said inspecting Henri's ankle.

One of the other trappers, a squat little man with brilliant blue eyes, held up a pair of crutches they'd carved during the surgery. She took them. The other trappers giggled as she bent over, but Bernie hushed them.

"It's broke pretty good, and the heel chord got pretty chewed up, but I got the bullet and chunks of bone out. Keep it clean, and he'll be okay. I ain't never lost a dog doin this."

"Bern's a butcher by trade," the squat little man muttered in grave admiration of the sewing job on Henri's ankle.

"It's gonna swell up pretty good. Have him soak it in the river for an hour in the morning and an hour at night," Bernie said. "That worked good fer the dogs."

He nodded to a trapper they called Pepper. Pepper walked with a painful stoop caused by getting whacked in the back by the boom of a navy frigate. He hobbled toward the hut, and in a few moments appeared at the doorway dragging the old trapper by the hair on his beard. "Gone now," Pepper grunted.

As Pepper dragged the dead trapper toward the river, Jamie appeared up the path with a string of fresh fish.

"Don't go in the house," she said to him sternly.

She leaned down to grasp the unburned end of a flaming log. She looked for a moment to Bernie.

"Yes, ma'am, I'd do the very same. I'll sink his canoe and pray the Lord we don't all git it just the same."

She walked to the door and flung the burning log onto one of the beds. Before long, smoke emerged in grey swirls.

She looked at Jamie and said gravely, "That man had the fever and retched inside." Jamie scratched his head, looking over at Henri and the strange band of ugly trappers. "We had an accident," she said, "Henri's been shot."

"Holy shit," Jamie muttered.

"Watch your mouth," she snapped.

Henri tried to rouse himself, his head throbbing nearly as badly as his ankle from the grain alcohol they made him drink before plunking him on the head with an oar. As he regained his senses, he puzzled at the smoke from the house, the old trapper being dragged to the river, the stabbing pain in his ankle. "Wot is 'appening?" he muttered. Soon flames licked out the door and acrid smoke swirled yellow brown into the air. Ella stood in dazed gloom as all she owned in this world simmered in a slow and stifled burn beneath the sod roof. By and by the roof collapsed and the flames curled up through holes and cracks.

Ella draped her arm over Jamie's shoulders and held him hard to keep from collapsing from weariness and a wave of arid despair. The trappers muttered their apologies and slunk down the bank to their canoes. A light gust twisted over the fire and momentarily wrapped them in a bundle of thick smoke before curling down the bank and scooting like some fleeing ghost across the water.

This was the second time in less than a year that fire destroyed her home, and she didn't know if she had the strength to start again. She leaned against her son and closed her eyes, remembering the fire at Lake Champlain. They might even been dead by now if they'd stayed, Everett had insisted. Now this time she torched her own on purpose, an impulse she now regretted.

That evening Ella sat on a log hugging her knees, her dusty face blank with fatigue as she starred out over the river. The hut had collapsed into its own hole, wisps of smoke from a few remaining smolders rising slowly skyward. Jamie was busily digging out Everett's cannon hideaway, their next home. Ella knew their new hut would take valuable time away from their harvesting and preparations for winter. Logs they had saved to burn would now have to be used inside for beds, tables, chairs, and framing to hold the roof and walls against the onslaught of winter storms. To the west a bank of clouds built and pressed toward them. Ella watched the cloud bank slowly build but could not move herself, could not budge.

Ella's prior certainty that this island was the safest possible haven against the uncertainties of the war slowly turned to doubt and confusion. No place was safe, she knew now. Even disease had found its way there. She tried to corral her energies and get back to work, but she was drained by these new doubts and weary from discouragement. She knew that she could not live this way, could not survive a collapse in spirit and resolve.

The river was smooth as glass, the wind absolutely still, the air heavy and damp. The setting sun had dipped below the huge cloud bank, yet above the sky remained blue and bright. Birds chirped in the woods. Wind swallows carved the air for the season's remaining bugs, fattening up for their migration south. Jamie's shovel clanked against the many rocks that made the dark, rich clay soil of the island a nightmare to cultivate, yet which held the island together like some stone and mortar fortress. Rarely had she witnessed such lovely stillness. Rarely had she ever craved sleep so deeply as on this evening.

But it was not possible for Ella to collapse. Some part of her knew that whatever suffering she may have felt now would be infinitesimal compared to a winter of starvation. She knew that her exhaustion now would pale in the face of watching Jamie and Henri freeze to death. They would be the first because they were the slightest, with the least fat to cushion them from the cold. Despite her annoyance that Everett was gone when they most needed him, Ella pulled herself together, and began pulling logs and salvaged timbers hidden deep in the woods up to the new hole that would become their winter home.

By the time the storm struck and the rain cascaded down in torrents, Jamie had dug enough into Everett's second hideaway so that they could all sleep beneath the lip of a ceiling of sod, laid out side by side on the hard, dry dirt dappled with rocks and bumps and ancient roots. Even Henri, whose foot throbbed horribly, dropped quickly away in exhausted sleep.

Outside, thunder boomed and roared, and the sky glowed a stunning purple-white from great flashes of lightning slashing the angry sky. Some of the strikes were so close, the ground shook and tiny particles of dirt and silty dust rained down on their faces from their sod roof. But they were dry, at least, and safe, water puddling near their feet and draining down two deep holes Jamie dug in the corners. Not even a desperate fool would be out on the river in that storm, so they were at least safe until morning.

Chapter 2

The Port of Lachine was a seething, stinking swarm of trappers' canoes, working skiffs stacked with chickens, fishing hulks rigged with oars and a myriad of homemade sails, two rough-hewed French gunships, a sprinkling of gentile sailboats, garbage boats, vegetable trows, grain barges, livestock haulers, and more. They criss-crossed in rancid green water floating with human waste and settlement garbage, wood scraps, floating lettuce, half-eaten apples, dead dogs, bloated cats, swimming rats, broken crates, and assorted swollen, dead fish.

Everett and Lucy slowly inched into the harbor. Despite the chaos of activity, most of these sailors, many of them drunk, were superbly skilled and could see that Lucy's barge was among the least deft of all the vessels. They made way, dodged, rowed or tacked out of her way, winking, grinning, waving and saluting as this woman stood boldly at the helm.

They edged up to the fish market pier, dropped their sails, and tied up. After a few minutes of haggling at the market desk inside the salting sheds, Lucy and Everett escaped to the fisherman's saloon while a half dozen boys netted her load of fish into massive holding basins built into the pier.

La Poisson Marchand was a smoky, dark cavernous saloon that reeked of dead fish, stale sweat, and fermenting alcohol. It swarmed with fishermen drinking away their profits in a desperate race to oblivion. The din of voices made normal conversation pointless. Everyone yelled. Most in French, some in English, some in Italian, Portuguese and Spanish. Lucy and Everett had more teeth than the entire collection of fishermen combined. It was a scruffy lot, the din of voices alternating between uproarious laughter and earnest, spittle-spewing yarn spinning.

They shouted their stories with arms stretched and waving to demonstrate the dubious sizes and girths of their recent and generously imagined catches. "Ca fus monstre poisson, deux mêtres et fat comme enceinte chevre, a feesh monster," yelled one fisherman, arms stretched wide, howls and guffaws erupting at this drunken tale. Except for barmaids and a few perfumed whores, Lucy was the only woman in the saloon. Everett detected the predatory eyes of a half dozen men checking her butt and breasts, inching closer, waiting for him to drift away. "Une mermaid pour moi. Oh to kees her mout'," a drunken fisherman yelled leering at Lucy as he staggered past. She slipped her arm around Everett's waist in the manner whores signaled a secure claim. She rose on her toes and spoke loudly in his ear.

"Sweet place, hey?" she grinned.

Everett eyed the place warily. In the far corner, men argued angrily, poking fingers in each other's chests. Behind him, a squat, powerful fisherman nudged close to him. "Indulge me monsieur to kiss her angelique derriere."

Everett snapped his head around. The man smiled, exposing pink gums, raising his hands as if to surrender. Behind Lucy, leaning against the bar, a tall, handsome bearded merchant sailor eyed her carefully as if inspecting a horse at auction. He ignored Everett's glare. In the east corner by the door, a teenage boy began playing a harmonica in long, mournful runs. Everett could barely breathe as the bodies and noise and damp fishy smells pressed at his face. He watched as Lucy downed a pint of ale in a series of eager gulps down her long, sinewy throat, rippling with muscles and an Adam's apple working as steadily as a well-worn pump.

"What the hell," he grumbled, and followed her lead, sucking down his own pint and within minutes reeling dimly from the astonishing punch of La Poisson Marchand's home brew.

The afternoon melted into blur of downed pints. A piano player dressed in rags and bowler hat pounded out an endless succession of weepy ballads sprinkled with frantic jigs. The boy harmonica player joined in from the corner, the two musicians chattering back and forth like all the rest except through their music, not a word exchanged between them.

"She is the one wot 'as broke my 'eart..." the piano player crooned.

"And t'rown me hoff ze cliffs of Normandie," the boy replied.

"Nevair to sing of mon amour again," the piano player howled mournfully amid a rapturous run at the keyboard and a chorus of derision.

Everett had to suffer Lucy's presence as he squeezed outside to urinate off the pier, so earnest were these men to pull her away the moment she eased her grasp on Everett's waist. Pint after pint, Lucy downed her ale with no discernible effect beyond an ever-deepening, vibrant glow to her sweat-glistening face.

During one furious jig, she yanked him to an opening behind the piano player and engaged Everett in a dance so frantic, he thought he might expire in a steaming heap. The next time he had to urinate, she made him hold her hands as she squatted, backside over the pier, skirt hiked to her knees, and she pissed with a long and audible dribble into the St. Lawrence River below. During this lengthy and blissful adventure, she locked eyes with Everett, spitting tobacco juice between her teeth onto his boots that were braced in vomit-befouled, piss-packed dirt at the dock's edge, a rising tide of hoots and whistles from boatman below happily distracted from their work.

After she was done, she straightened, turned, bowed to the boatmen now bumping and crunching into each other's boats in the day's first and only accidents. "Venez s'accroupir sur ma épaules, manquent. Hey cherie, come squat on my s' oulders," yelled one fisherman. They clapped and whistled; she turned, launched a spear of spit between her teeth across the bow of his quaking skiff eliciting a riot of admiring cheers.

"Bloody hell," Everett cringed, "You'll git us kilt."

But Lucy was on a roll.

By late afternoon the wind had shifted to the east, a welcome shift, though a bank of nasty clouds approached from the west. They would need that easterly to pull them upcurrent. But Lucy was now singing alongside the piano player, and drunken fishermen and sailors jammed the floor with their boots to the frantic beat of the music. Everett settled against the bar, slipping deeper and deeper into head-throbbing oblivion.

He could barely walk when Lucy finally dragged him out into driving rain and a gusty, thundery gale. Sheets of rain swept the dockside. Wind howled down the narrow quay, rain swatting and slapping the dimly lit facades of drying sheds and marine offices. Every few moments lightning torched the furious purple sky. Brilliant, glistening flashes lit a million racing droplets, frozen for a moment, then extinguished to the dim remnants of daylight shrouded in the roiling, purple-brown clouds.

When Everett leapt onto Lucy's barge, his feet skidded across the greasy wet slime, and he crashed to the deck, his head snapping against hard cedar. Bright sparks burst inside his head. He could feel his body slide across the deck and flop over the edge into the fish hold. He could feel the cold water envelop his legs, his body, his face, his head, but he could not seem to react. He felt Lucy's hand grab him harshly by the hair, and now this time the water peeled away from his flesh in exact reverse of time, as she dragged him back onto the aft deck and dropped him in a heap.

She rushed to the bow and rigged a small storm jib that flapped furiously. She yanked the bow line free and skipped along the slippery deck, stepping over Everett to set the aft mizzen. She leaned over the stern and yanked the stern line free, then heaved the sheet line to the forward jib. The sail puffed into a throbbing triangular arch. She cleated the line and set the mizzen, the sail erupting with a thud, full and throbbing from the force of the wind, the mast step squeaking from the sudden surge of force. The barge groaned and creaked at every joint, then slowly eased forward, Lucy straddling the tiller like a horse.

Everett moaned and hugged his throbbing head, a fist-sized lump emerging at the back of his head. Lightning flashed, and for a moment they could see scores of wobbling, swaying masts glow white in the glistening rain. Thunder crackled and hissed a moment later. In the sheltered port bay, the flat water danced and trembled from the wind, gusts swatting past, sweeping the water with frantic miniature waves rushing to find a place to build.

Quickly the waves grew as the port narrows opened to a broad sweep of widening river. Following waves crashed over the stern and yanked the rudder left, then right. Gusts yanked at the sails, from time to time snapping them from side to side in sudden, shuddering jibes that could have swatted either overboard or broken their necks had they failed to duck.

Despite the power of the wind, they made slow progress against the channel currents. Lucy eased toward shallower water. She sent Everett to the bow section with her sounding poll where he stabbed the water every few moments to gauge its depth. Darkness sank over them, the only light from bursts of lightning. Rain hurtled from the blackness above. Waves leapt and plunged from the blackness below.

"Yah crazy bitch," he yelled, partly to Lucy, partly to the barge, partly to the sky and river, partly to the raging storm. It was crazy trying to navigate the river in such utter darkness. They were doomed, he knew. They would die. But it didn't matter to him. Death would stop the throbbing and kill the chill. But he kept taking his soundings, ducking clear of the crazy, lurching sails. And he waited, knowing at any moment that they could move into shallows and not know which way to steer, go aground, and be smashed on the rocks by the relentless waves.

But Lucy knew. She knew that part of the river and scanned the horizon for the familiar tree line that emerged at moments with the glow of lightning and would tell her the bends and sways of the river she'd memorized from childhood. She gauged the wind in her sails, which was holding steady due east, pointing the way home. Her Uncle Joe, an Indian trapper, had taught her to navigate at night, a time when the other Indians feared the river spirits.

To navigate a storm at night was the safest time of all, safe from Indians, thieves, greedy soldiers, and competing trappers who'd kill without a wince of hesitation for a canoe load of furs. So Joe moved his furs on stormy nights and taught Lucy, often taking her as his second paddle, how to work the river in its fury, scaring her senseless every time.

Even by Uncle Joe's standards, this was a fearsome storm. Lucy's fears were considerably aided by her tremendous dousing of ale. She knew being drunk was an unnecessary risk, but she could return in one day on this easterly in what would take a three days in calmer weather. Still her heart pounded from fear. The waves built as they entered St. Francois du Lac and faced a series of emerging shoals. With the expanse of water, the wind kicked up huge rolling waves that crashed over the stern, each one threatening to break the rudder or catapult her into the river where she would surely drown.

She could hear Everett screaming out soundings now.

"Ten foot."

"Eight foot."

She needed at least six.

"Ten foot," he yelled.

And over that broad expense the wind picked up its force. Unbroken by trees and hills, the wind could race at full gallop, sucking the water with it into a furious, crazy chop that lunged angrily against the steady, unrelenting current.

Each time the numbers got smaller, Lucy's heart beat faster.

Jesus, God, she thought, *old Uncle Joe, let it deepen.*

"Nine foot."

A big storm like that dries the throat with fear and keeps it dry, but Lucy eventually began to relax and feel the rhythms and to trust a gust would reach a peak and not suddenly explode but would race by, leaving them in a momentary, dark lull before the surge of waves chasing that gust heaved the stern upward, pushing them homeward. For a moment after a gust, a momentary pause sagged the sails, and then the boat settled heavily before a new gust whapped the mizzen, then the jib, the boat lurching heavily forward. "Eight foot," he yelled, his voice barely audible, getting pulled into the wind as it rushed forward and skittered off the bow toward home.

"Louder," she said in an almost normal voice, her words carried to him as the wind rushed up the stern, across the decks, and up the bow deck, splitting off, some to his ears, some whapping into the sail where it would stick and push, then slither past in a swirl racing ahead of the waves.

"Eight foot," he shrieked.

Her heart bean to gallop.

"Seven,"

"Fuck off," she yelled.

"Six."

She wrapped her arms around the tiller and pushed toward shore, the bow slowly swinging, angling toward the center of the vast river.

"Six."

The barge scraped bottom.

She yanked the sheet lines, pulling in the sails to gather the wind to her new angle, a more efficient reach that groaned at the mast step, a new angle of force from the shuddering mast. The barge scraped and groaned, then broke free a moment.

"Seven."

"Bless you, Uncle Joe," she whispered, the tiller shuddering now as it cut the water, this heavy old barge leaping forward.

The worst angle in any boat was this following sea, dead aft. It plunged the bow downward and plowed them into river, digging, burrowing, pushing a mountain of water like a plow. But their new course lifted them, healing the old barge until the starboard deck slipped beneath the surface, the port deck lifting heavily but triumphantly like a grand frigate. She laughed at this sudden glimpse of grace from her hopeless old tub. Their glorious reach would be short lived, but she played it for every bit of speed.

"Ten foot."

"Fifteen."

And then his pole could not measure the depth as they ran the edge of the channel. She felt the bow lurch from the new force, the rudder suddenly pulling her with such force she had to set her feet against the rail. Now the risk was to be flung sideways by the current. She pulled with all her strength, feeling the water's shuddering power, feeling the water slithering like a hundred powerful snakes sliding over the surfaces of the rudder. She pulled and pulled and finally the wind pushed them leeward toward the shallows again, the rudder easing and now swaying as before from the odd lurches from following waves, back on their nasty old course. It seemed now to her that her Uncle Joe was guiding her, the boat and the wind, and the current and the waves transformed into Uncle Joe, ten years dead, guiding her home.

By morning the wind had eased but remained brisk out of the east. The black sky slowly eased to a dim, flat gray, but now she could see the silhouette of the shoreline trees, distant spires of cedars in familiar clusters marking the widest bowl of St-Francois du Lac, the first tangible reminders of home. In the far distance ahead, she could see the dim outline of the giant stone church spire of Ste-Anicet. Here the settlements thinned out. Cedars long since cut and burned within thirty miles of Montreal were now poking the sky thick as weeds.

With morning's light Everett could now brew up coffee and serve them chunks of day-old bread warmed on the cook stove. Lucy's hands were knotted, her knuckles stuck shut from grasping the tiller through the night. Now she could steer with her butt and knead her blistered, bleeding palms.

The wind tugged steadily at the dark, canvas sails, steam from their coffee twisting away in frantic twirls chasing the east wind west. Everett's head still throbbed, but he flung his arm around Lucy's shoulder and gave her a squeeze.

"Yer goddamned good, luv," he snorted, blowing ripples across the black surface of his coffee cup.

"Old Joe was with us," she said, "He kept us off the rocks."

Everett gazed at the dark stains of the numerous islands that sprinkled along St-Francois du Lac and reminded him of the corpses of ancient men laying in rest on their backs, profiles of faces and feet at each point, laid east to west, old ghosts asleep for the day but whose spirits awoke at night and rambled each island until dawn.

Huge trees crafted the bodies of these old men, stands of cedars like fingers raised to the sky, massive willows round shouldered, leaf-swollen basswood trees big as bellies. He knew the islands were haunted, knew the Indians were right about strange lights and great lurching movements at dusk on still nights. He loved those old men but feared them, feared becoming one of them. Old Joe was one of them, the master of an island they called Little Joe's, so there was no argument from him that Lucy got his help that night.

Everett wasn't ready yet, still wasn't enough part of the river to belong at rest, corpses floating at anchor for eternity. Most Indians knew and left the islands to the white settlers. In his ten years on his island he'd never seen an arrowhead, no sign of an Indian camp or burial mound or piles of mussel shells, the sorts of remnants that cluttered the shoreline.

On his island he'd seen just a few old camp stove parts, burned cabin posts, a table leg here or there, a patch of roofing tin from settlers who left probably from hardship or who fell through thin spots in the ice or died of disease and were buried in the river by fleeing families who'd had enough. Soon the ice would come and by February it would be a foot thick except over the channels where the ice was never thicker than an inch or two. He'd seen men go down. It was usually when there was snow, and you couldn't see the dark patches. It was very fast and very quiet. Footprints that just stopped, and in five minutes the hole was frozen over as before, and on most days, the wind silted over the hole, then the tracks, then nothing but a blinding sweep of white.

* * *

By the end of September, the island leaves had turned a blaze of colors and on many mornings ice formed on the water buckets. They woke shivering in their new hut on the island point but tried to preserve wood by making small fires they let burn for less then an hour. Each day Everett and Jamie traveled to shore to find wood. Henri waded the shoreline for logs, the cold water soothing the pain in his foot. Ella stacked, chopped, and split each morning until her back ached. Each afternoon they worked on the hut, shoring up the roof, stuffing cracks and crevices, building shelves, beds, tables. In some ways building the new hut was a blessing. It was bigger with more rooms and better storage. It would be drier, warmer, less cluttered.

Everett bought an old iron cook stove from Lucy as part of his payment for the trip to Montreal. Everett and Jamie showed up at Lucy's in the rowboat to pick it up.

"Ain't gonna fit," Everett muttered, looking at the old stove out on her dock. "Jesus God, she's bloody big."

"Got a raft you could use out back," Lucy offered.

Everett scratched his head, nodding yes.

Lucy's mule helped them drag the raft to the water. The mule's name was Harvey, and he loved making a racket hee-hawing. Harvey was motivated principally by apples and vigorous massaging around he ears.

"Ain't never seen a happier mule," Everett remarked as Harvey pulled and tugged that heavy old raft out of the woods. Everett rubbed around his ears, and Harvey hee-hawed and leaned his whole body into the task. After a few feet he'd stop, and Jamie would offer an apple. Harvey ate it, hee-hawed and gave it another vigorous pull for thirty or so more feet, then stopped.

Everett massaged his ears, and Harvey slobbered with pleasure, then hee-hawed and dug in, pulling for another brief stretch.

"Harvey's a good lad, yeah?" he said to Jamie.

"Yessir."

"Most mules is ornery and mean," Everett said.

"Not Harvey," said Jamie.

"Not Harvey. I like Harvey a good deal."

Harvey stopped and waited for an apple. Jamie offered it. Harvey grinned and took the apple and seemed very near ecstasy.

Lucy took the rope attached to his bit and tugged lightly, and Harvey set about his work. As they approached the gradual slope of the riverbank, Harvey had progressively longer runs. Then he stopped and wouldn't go.

Everett scratched his ears. Jamie gave him an apple. Lucy kissed his nose.

"I think Harvey knows his work is nearly done and it's done pissed him off," said Everett.

"Yessir," Jamie affirmed.

So Lucy leapt on Harvey's back and rode him around for a few minutes.

When she returned, they hooked Harvey back to the raft, and he got back to work.

As they edged into the water, Everett leaned against the dock. "I like Harvey 'cause he's only half smart."

"Kind of like you, hey?" Lucy grinned.

Everett blushed a bit. "Well if someone's too smart, they think they can always figure things out. They think they got all the answers, but the fact is, that people who are too smart git thesselves all a'cluttered and lose their common sense."

"Absolutely," Lucy nodded sardonically.

Jamie scratched his head in the manner Everett did when he was deeply puzzled. At those moments, they could have been father and son; they looked so much the same.

"Well, yah, by my way of thinking, Harvey's a mule damned near to having common sense. He's smarter than some men I know."

"Yes, he is," Lucy grinned.

They rigged a pulley atop a pole Lucy used for lifting satchels and supplies on and off the dock. They pulled the rope to lift the stove's front legs, and Lucy nudged Harvey into the water to pull the raft under the stove.

After they got it loaded, Lucy and Everett agreed that Harvey would have to ride in the boat and help them at the island. It wasn't that Lucy disliked Ella in any special way, but she told Everett he was on his own. She was too busy to come along, she lied.

"You 'an Harvey are cut from the same soul cloth," she said. "Besides, the boat will be full. You don't need me."

"Does Harvey know how to sit?" Everett asked, skeptical of this plan.

"He does."

"Sit, Harvey," Everett said.

Harvey, up to his knees in water, looked around as if to laugh.

"He ain't goin to sit in water, Everett. He ain't a fool," Lucy said.

"Why caint he just swim?" Everett asked.

"Not up current. He can swim back home but not up current to your place."

So they got Harvey into Lucy's biggest rowboat and got him to sit in the stern while Everett rowed and Jamie took the bow with a bucket of apples. It was a beautiful, calm day when they set out, but pulling that stove up current was slow and difficult work. Even though it was only a mile or so to the island, it took them most of the afternoon. When it looked like they were just about there, the wind picked up out of the northwest.

With the wind came waves, and with all that weight in the boat, the waves spilled over the gunnels, and the boat started to sway and rock.

Harvey started to get nervous. Jamie had to stand and lean over Everett to hand Harvey apples, and each time he stood, the boat swayed even more.

As they approached the island, Harvey decided to stand and shit. The boat tilted, a wave burst over the side, and suddenly they tipped and capsized. Harvey quickly swam away, heading home down current. Everett and Jamie slipped into the cold water and gasped. Fortunately, they were able to stand, and though shoulder deep were able to tug the boat and the raft slowly toward the island.

Meanwhile, on shore, Ella and Henri saw their plight and prepared to fling them ropes as soon as they were within reach. Henri was stiff laughing from the sight of Harvey first sitting, then standing to shit. Ella would have still laughed except for her worry for Jamie. Finally, they flung the ropes, and Everett was able to gain leverage enough to pull them in.

"Jamie! You get in here and get yourself dry," Ella snapped.

Jamie looked to Everett. Both their lips were blue, but Jamie was chattering from shivers.

"Do as she says," Everett said, "we're okay now."

So Jamie rushed in to get dry which meant the hard work would now fall to Ella. She waded out into the water and helped steady the swaying raft. The waves were building and pushing the raft into the island. But Everett had to right the boat or it would be destroyed on the rocks. He lifted one side, slowly tilting the water out, but the boat was too heavy to lift alone or empty by more than half. He pushed the bow toward the shore wedged it up on a mound of moss and tried to flip it over. His feet slipped, and he lost his grip.

"Ella, help me here," he gasped.

"The raft," she said, already breathing hard from effort.

"Leave it. The boat. We've got to save the boat."

"We'll lose the stove."

"It won't go nowhere," he groaned under the weight of the boat. "Come on. Now!" he said angrily.

She looked desperately toward the stove, let go of the raft and hurried over. The water was waist deep with waves breaking over their chests. She was surprised by the power and kept losing her balance as she plunged toward him. She grasped the stern of the boat. They tilted it sideways so the water could spill and then lifted. She could feel his body tremble from effort. Waves broke against them, and they lost their grip. The boat dropped in the water and immediately filled. Everett grasped her shoulders and held her, moved her closer so they could press against each other as they lifted. As they struggled to regain their grip, the raft surged toward shore. A wave lifted the raft. The stove slipped several feet, tilting the raft into following waves.

They began to lift, slowly at first to allow the water to spill and flow out. Even empty the boat was heavy onto the bank.

A large surge caught the already healing raft, and this time the stove slid all he way, the weight allowing the wave to lift and dump the stove into the water with a thunderous, clanking splash.

"Bloody hell," Everett groaned, lifting the rowboat bow onto the rocks.

Henri pulled the bow rope, and the three of them managed to slide the rowboat half way from the water before it tilted back and flopped, half in the water, half on the bank. Waves quickly poured over the stern gunnel. One more time, they had to tilt it on its side to empty the water.

"Git up there with Henri and pull. I'll hold the boat."

Ella scrambled up the bank.

"Now!" Everett yelled, and they heaved forward. Again the boat flopped over, but this time they were able to slide it far enough so that the waves could not fill it. Everett scrambled from the water, and the three of them pulled the boat up the bank to safety.

Everett and Ella gasped for breath.

"The raft." he said. "We pull it out across the point and set her to the lee of the wind and tie her."

So they plunged back into the cold water and pushed the raft into deeper water so they could float it around the point. They worked side by side, both of them leaning against each other to help their balance against the waves. Ella could feel her hands grow numb, making it difficult to gain a grip. Slowly they pushed against the heaving waves until finally they reached the point and could let the waves help them. In a few minutes, they were sheltered from the wind and waves, but on this side, where the current swept the island, the water was deeper and colder. Everett grasped the rope. They could barely touch. Everett's height gave him better leverage. Ella could feel the current pull her deeper. Her feet slipped away, weightless now in the deep water.

Everett grasped her by the waist and pulled her toward him. He lifted her a foot off the bottom, giving him more weight to fight the current. Holding her in one arm, the rope in the other, he lurched slowly toward shore. Several times he stumbled and they both fell, splashing like children romping. They began to laugh. As they gained ground, they still stumbled and slipped on the rocks, but lurched forward until they were safe in knee-deep water.

Breathless from the huge effort, they still laughed and sputtered. Everett realized now he held her but did not need to. She leaned limply on his shoulder, her body tilted against his, exhausted but still laughing. They were beyond cold now.

"My stove," she gasped.

Everett wiped his face and suddenly, inexplicably pushed the hair covering her face tenderly aside. "Let's git it now or we'll have to do this agin."

"Not again; no bloody chance," she laughed.

So they plunged back across the point into the waves and wind. Holding hands they swayed and leaned against the waves toward the old cast iron stove tilted on is side, rocking oddly with the force of the waves.

They soon discovered that the old stove was too heavy to move in one piece. Everett started taking it apart, and they formed a line. Everett at the stove, Ella at his side, up to her waist in water, Henri against the shore up to his knees. Everett removed each piece, swung it to Ella beneath the water where its weight was less; she swung it to Henri, and he flung it up on the bank to safety. Considerably lightened by the removable parts, all three were able to remove the main belly, the heaviest part, and coax it through the water and wedge it up the bank.

Jamie, now dry, made a fire in their little potbelly inside the hut, so they were able to recover from their worst shivers, and stood wrapped in blankets, teeth chattering. Henri gave them whiskey, and then hurried out into growing darkness with Jamie to secure the boat and drag the raft to safety before another wind shift smashed it on the rocks. They needed every pulley and stretch of rope to accomplish what Harvey could easily manage fueled by apples, ample massages at the ears, and an occasional kiss on the nose.

In the dim candlelight, both naked beneath their blankets, Everett and Ella inched as close to the stove as they could without charring. Every few minutes, Ella shook her head, her hair waving and flopping, a spray of droplets hissing as they landed, skittering across the rusty stovetop. Ella shuddered from the cold every so often, an assault of shivers gripping her.

"That was fun," she said softly, looking up at Everett. "That's the first fun I've had in two years," she smiled.

Everett nodded shyly and smiled as best he could manage, his teeth still chattering.

"Now didn't *you* think that was fun," she said bumping him playfully with her hip.

Everett giggled as she knocked him off balance. In truth, Everett knew it was glorious and could not erase from his mind or memory the pleasure he felt in holding her against him and how she just seemed to melt in some perfect fit he never before experienced. But he didn't know what to say. It was easy for him to crack jokes with Lucy and trade stories, as though she were a buddy. But Ella had him tongue tied even worse now than ever.

"Wasn't it fun, Everett?" she teased.

"Yes, ma'am," he said. In truth, he wished he had the courage to kiss her. He took a deep swig of whiskey. "I think we need to do that more often," he muttered lamely.

"Me too," she sniffled, staring down at the candle, her face aglow in the golden light, her hair glistening and starting to form a thousand wayward curls. "On a warmer day."

She wiggled her toes.

He wiggled his.

They both laughed quietly.

"For a minute there," she whispered, "I thought I was dead and gone."

"Oh, I wouldn't ah let that happen," Everett protested, shaking his head no, surprising them both with his vehemence.

"Thank you, Everett."

"Yes ma'am."

"Please call me Ella."

"Yes, ma'am. Ella."

"I don't want to hear any more of this ma'am stuff, yeah?"

"Sorry."

"Do you like me?" she said now, "or hate me?"

Everett shuddered and blushed.

She looked up at him, "Which is it?"

"Well, ma'am, I'd have to say I do like you. Most times. Today is good."

"Then just say it."

"Say what?"

"Say, Ella, I like you very much. Say it."

Everett was tongue tied yet again.

"Say it," she insisted.

He looked at her face, tilted and gazing drunkenly up at him, her eyes glowing with an irony he could not decipher.

He took another deep swig and handed her the bottle.

As she drank, Everett croaked, "Ella, I like you very much."

She did not look up but smiled to herself. She wiggled her toes.

"I like you, too, Everett. Sometimes. And sometimes not."

"Yes ma'am, I reckon mostly not."

"I'll fucking hate you if you leave us again."

Everett was startled by her profanity, all liquored up she was and more damned confusing than ever, he thought.

"I ain't goin nowhere. That Jamie's a fine boy," he finally croaked.

She turned now, rose to her tiptoes and kissed him gently on the cheek. She looked at him closely now. She did like him, she told herself. She wanted to like him very much. And he seemed to want to like her, too, but didn't have the slightest idea how, nor she a clue about how to show him.

Henri sat in the stern, Jamie on the oarsman thwart, the boat anchored in the lee of the island sheltered from the biting north wind. Dying leaves dropped from the trees swirling and twisting slowly before settling in the smooth dark blue water with a gentle watery whisper setting off delicate ripples. High above them the trees glowed in the bright sun. Henri had never seen such a rich spray of colors, a dozen brilliant reds and as many oranges and yellows splattered across gently swaying branches. The air hissed with the scratchy friction of drying leaves.

Henri watched with embarrassed gloom as Jamie pulled in fish after fish while Henri sat gazing helplessly at the vast beauty around him, jigging his long willow pole in awkward but fruitless imitation.

"Thees ve-ri great beauty," Henri muttered.

"Slower, Henri," Jamie offered.

"Oui," Henri blushed, slowing the movements of his pole.

"I tink I would die eef I have to leeve on my fish-ing."

"Yessir, I think you would," Jamie said suppressing a smile of pride at his own comparative skill. If Everett were with him, Jamie would feel nearly as helpless as Henri. But now he felt like the wise and seasoned guide, the skillful teacher, the deft, consummately efficient fisherman. "So how's the foot, Henri?"

Grateful for the distraction, Henri leaned forward, wiggled his ankle, and inspected his own movement. "Not so very goot," he said trying to be cheerful. "She hurts all ze time," he said shaking his head no, "and works like sheet when ah, when ze walk-ing, oui? Mon Dieu," he shrugged. "I don't tink it get bet-ter. I need ze crutch ah all ze day, for-ever, non?"

Jamie snapped in another fish, quickly extracting it off the hook, gently sliding it down into their floating bin, now swarming with the dark, glistening backs of two dozen perch. He quickly baited his hook with another worm and dropped his line.

Henri noticed Jamie's pink hands.

"Cold, oui, ze water ees more colder every day."

"This ain't nothin,'" Jamie shrugged.

"Ahhh," Henri shivered, "no, no s'il vous plait, no more cold."

"Oh yes, Henri," Jamie grinned. "In another month it'll make your snot freeze."

"Pardon?"

Jamie pointed to his nose, then simulated pulling a booger. "Your snot turns to ice."

"No!" Henri gasped, eyes wide.

"When you piss, you git froze to the ground."

Henri closed his legs and shuddered.

Jamie laughed.

Then Henri got a bite. He snapped his pole, yanking his hook in a wild arc, his worm flying free and plopping into the river out of reach.

Jamie laughed. "Easy, Henri. Give him time to take the hook."

"Oh, dear. Sor-ry. Not so goot, huh? Not so goot at thees fish-ing."

Henri fumbled with a new worm, his pink numb fingers clumsy and stiff. "I like France, et Paris more bet-ter. I mees m'h'ome," he said darkly.

"Do you want to go back?" asked Jamie.

"Ah oui, yes, yes, s'il vous plait. Vari nice, Paris, tres beauty, tres eleygant. And ze country and ze farm, vari beauti-ful. Vari warm. Vari nice. I like to go."

"Maybe next spring, Henri."

"Ah, thees crazy war. Mon Dieu, stupide, stupide," he spit, shaking his head no.

"Everett says they caint make you fight. He says yer ankle ain't no good."

Henri shrugged. "Oui, may-be. I tink yeah. But da winter ees vari,vari bat for me. Next spring I am dead, no?"

"Nooooo," Jamie scoffed, "You'll love the winter. It vari beauti-ful," Jamie grinned playfully.

* * *

Despite the cold wind sweeping off the water, sweat poured down Everett's flushed face and dripped from his chin. He raised that axe and smashed it down. Another log split, each piece flying.

Ella sat on a bench Everett had hacked from an old tree trunk. She gazed out over the dark water and burrowed further into her coat. The bright sky was a deep, deep blue. White caps licked the waves. Leaves hissed and swirled about them.

Everett wiped his forehead with his sleeve. He loved splitting wood. He could do it all day, building a stack, cord after cord.

He moved over beside her, sat, and worked his sharpening stone over the edge of the hard steel blade.

She moved closer to him to absorb his heat. She rocked with his sharpening motion and yawned with contentment. She was learning to enjoy his silence. They could be together for hours and never exchange a word, yet she felt connected to him as if they'd been chattering the whole time. After a time, he pointed across the river. On the far horizon, a French two-masted combat sloop inched eastward in full sail, healed to windward. She was a handsome sight, her sails puffed and swollen with wind, her 10 canons seemingly small as toys, arranged in soldierly precision on her golden deck. Despite the sloop's stately presence on this glorious day, her heart sank.

"Why don't they just go home," she said bitterly.

He stood and returned to his logs. He lifted the axe and smashed it down through the center of a log, each side splitting off with a crisp crackle. He leaned down, tossed the piece in his pile and set up another. He blew a bead of sweat at the end of his nose, causing it to fly away in a mist. He swung again.

"They ain't going to bother us none," he said.

But after a few more logs, they could see the crew lowering the sails and dropping anchor. Sailors worked the crossbeams like tiny ants.

"Caint figure it," he said. "This is a good wind. Why stop?"

In the shelter of the island, Henri and Jamie basked in the sun pulling in fish. The island hid the French warship from view. Henri dozed.

Jamie watched Henri's eyes droop, his head wobbling, then tilting to his shoulder. Jamie watched Henri's rod tip wiggle, then bend from the gentle tugs of a tiny perch. He smiled.

"Henri," he whispered.

Henri was asleep.

The tiny perch tugged from left to right.

"Henri!" he said more loudly.

Henri's eyes slowly opened and moved lazily from some distant place.

Suddenly a large fish snapped up the little perch. Jamie lunged to save the pole. Henri started, then grasped the pole just as it was teetering at the gunnel. With both hands Henri tugged frantically, hugging the pole to his chest. Henri's eyes bulged in excited panic. "Zis fish!" Henri yelped. "A mons-ter!"

For the next ten minutes, Henri held as the fish darted all around the boat.

"A muskie," Jamie shouted. "You got a giant muskie."

"Bloody hail," Henri croaked, his body jerking as the fish tugged powerfully, his willow pole bending over nearly to the handle. Henri stood and tugged back, laughing gleefully now, with one foot braced at the gunnel, flexing his muscles, the fish darting away and pulling Henri toward the bow. He fell over Jamie and crashed into the bottom of the boat, laughing. Jamie grabbed Henri's coat and pulled him back up, then guided him to his seat.

"Yer doin good, Henri. He's gonna get tired soon enough."

Jamie grabbed the gaff and peered over the edge of the gunnel into the shadow of the boat. An enormous four-foot muskie flashed past, this time nearly pulling Henri off the stern.

"Bring him back," Jamie said, lowering the gaff into the water. Henri tugged his pole toward the bow. The fish turned and flashed past. Jamie lunged, catching its side, the fish smashing into the boat. Jamie flopped back onto his seat, the gaff waving in the sky.

"Missed him," Jamie gasped. "Bring him back."

Henri, eyes bulging, puffing for air now, swayed his body back toward the stern. The big fish turned and swooped past the side of the boat. Jamie yanked the gaff, this time catching the gill. The power of the fish pulled Jamie over on top of Henri. They both laughed as Jamie held the wild, thrashing fish and Henri grasped Jamie by the back of his coat and tugged with all his strength. The huge head appeared now. The tail swatted the water, splashing them. Jamie grabbed the other gill beneath the huge, menacing jaws. The fish snapped, biting into Jamie's hand. Jamie pulled back, grabbed the gill again and tugged the fish over the gunnel into the bottom of the boat. It flopped and opened his jaws, rows of needle sharp teeth snapping at their legs.

"Whooey!" Jamie yelped.

"Mon Dieu," Henri cooed.

The fish flopped viciously. Jamie leapt away, grasped an oar and whacked the muskie on the head. Stunned for a moment, the fish eyed them, then flopped and snapped again. Whack.

The fish stiffened, his body shuddering with spasms.

Whack.

They watched, each perched on a seat, squatted down, studying the stunned fish.

New spasms rippled along its side, its eyes were glazed and unfocused.

Jamie clamored to the bow and pulled the anchor.

He set the oars in the locks, straddled the muskie's immense body and rowed feverishly for the island shore.

Jamie and Henri arrived in the clearing with the fish hung through its huge lip by a thick branch, each end hung on their separate shoulders. Henri held his crutch in one hand, the stick in the other and limped along behind Jamie. The tail of the fish dragged on the ground.

Everett stood, mouth agape.

Jamie laughed.

Henri grinned from ear to ear.

They muscled the fish to the ground, and the four of them formed a circle around it.

"Henri's catch," said Jamie.

Everett nodded wide-eyed at Henri and gave him a vigorous pat on the back.

Henri blushed and puffed his chest. "It was nah-ting. Je suis vari lucky, tres chanceux!"

"Oh, Henri!" Ella gushed, needling him a bit with a wink.

Henri pawed the ground with his good foot, feigning modesty.

"A born fisherman," said Everett.

"He was pretending to be asleep," Jamie offered. "He had this little perch on his line, and he just played that little guy waiting for the monster and than whap."

"You fooled 'em, hey Henri?" Everett said nudging Henri playfully.

"Simply brilliant," Ella said brushing her hand along the huge girth of the muskie's belly.

"It was ah, veri ah, oui. Brilliant!" Henri grinned. "Mai oui, but ah, Jamie was veri goot." He pantomimed the motion of the oar. "He eat us, no?"

"He nearly ate me," Jamie said holding up his bleeding hand, realizing immediately that he made a mistake.

His mother grasped his hand and groaned. "Whiskey."

"Sounds good," Everett laughed.

"Now, for his hand," she snapped. "Those teeth, damn," she said.

Everett fetched the whiskey bottle and poured it over Jamie's hand. Ella rubbed it vigorously into the wound as Jamie winced from pain.

Everett took a long drink and handed it to Henri. Henri tipped back and took a long, satisfying drink. As he handed the bottle back to Everett, his grin vanished and the color drained from his face as he spotted the French warship anchored in the distance.

"Ain't going to bother us none," Everett said.

Henri groaned with discouragement, the world he hated invading his moment of glory.

"They cain't make a cripple fight," Everett said.

Henri stared coldly at Everett. "Cripple?" he said bitterly.

Everett blushed.

"Celles non rendre an nui homme combats. They can't make you go," Ella said.

Henri chuckled derisively. "Ze cripple, he fight en France just ze same."

"They'll never find you," Everett offered weakly. We'll hide you."

"No hide," Henri snapped angrily. He turned away and gazed at Ella and Jamie, both huddled over his hand. He slumped heavily onto his crutch. "You take me to zis boat."

"Nossir," Everett said.

"Monsieur, Everett. I insist. I must go. Pleese," he implored.

"You let me think on it," Everett said. "Not today, yeah?"

"Tomorrow, then?" Henri said.

"I ain't gonna let you do something out of dumb pride and French stubbornness," Everett said. "This is a stupid, pointless goddamned war, and you got no business doin' more fightin'. You done yer duty. Ain't none of us gonna fight in this war. It took her husband and his father and that's enough. So you let me think on this."

For the rest of that day, Henri sat gazing out over the water, to his left the freedom of the great river, to his right the warship that could tear him away from his new found life. It was a ruinous but inevitable development. His sadness was inconsolable. Henri would not speak to anyone. "Je comprends vraiment, I really understand, Henri," Ella said, patting him fondly on the shoulder, but he did not move. Everett tried to interest him in more whiskey, then fresh fish. But Henri could not drink or eat, his depression deepening into a stunned, dark unutterable silence.

Inside, they cooked steaks from the muskie and ate until they ached. But that night they lit no candles and allowed no lights for the privy. The warship had probably seen them, but there was no point in encouraging a visit.

Henri slipped silently into the hut and took to his bed without a word.

They all realized now how much Henri had become a part of their lives. To Ella, Henri's demand to visit the ship was an agonizing reminder of her helplessness in the face of the bottomless pride of men in her life. She had lost her husband, could lose her son, could lose Everett, and would surely lose Henri. *For what*, she asked herself, angrily, tossing all through the night. The emptiness she felt that night made her crazy. They were all so helpless, she thought. Men helpless in the face of stupidity, pride, and arrogance; herself powerless to change their minds or hearts. For the first time in many weeks, she felt rage and helplessness begin simmering again in her heart.

The next morning they pawed listlessly at breakfast.

Ella had prayed that night for the gunboat to pull up anchor and leave at dawn, but it remained.

She told no one of her plan for fear Everett or Jamie might persuade her otherwise or even side with Henri and force her to respect the prerogatives of male gallantry.

She placed the pistol carefully in the muffin basket and covered it with cloth.

As the others ate, heads bowed and silent, she pulled the basket from cupboard, carried it to her place at the table, sat, and sighed deeply.

She carefully undraped the pistol, raised it with both hands, and pointed it at Henri's chest. She cleared her throat, and pulled back the hammer with a loud and decisive click.

They looked up, each astonished, initially puzzled. And then each slowly registered their understanding.

"Henri," she said in a firm clear voice, "believe me when I say I will shoot you if you do not obey everything I say to you. Do you understand? Je vous tire te si te n'obéissent tout je dire pour te. Comprends tu?"

Henri looked to Everett who shrugged and shook his head no, to indicate his own utter bafflement and innocence.

"Henri," she said sharply, "Tu comprends?"

"Oui, madame."

"The same goes for you, Everett. Do you understand?"

"Yes, ma'am."

"Jamie, fetch the rope. Everett, you tie his arms and legs and tie this cloth around his mouth."

Everett and Jamie hesitated.

"Now," she snapped.

"If you make any attempt to escape, Henri, I will wound you so severely that you will never lift a gun, never be able to fool anyone into thinking you can be a soldier ever again. I might even kill you in that attempt. Do you understand? Te volonté jamais soient militaire encore. You will not volunteer for the military ever again. Oui?"

"Oui, madam."

She held the gun on them as Everett tied Henri. When he was finished, she made him tie a whole new set of knots with more rope. When Everett was done, she ordered him and Jamie to drag Henri to the hiding tunnel. "Force him all the way to the end and lock him there."

The tunnel was long and deep. Even if he were to chew through the gag around his mouth, no amount or volume of screaming could be heard above ground or even inside the hut.

When they were finished, Everett tried to discourage her. "You cain't stop a man..."

"Shush," she said.

"This ain't right, Ella."

"I'll decide what's right," she snapped.

Everett stepped back, deferring to her anger.

"You gonna tie him up every time he wants to leave?"

"I'll blow both his legs off if I have to. Is there something I have to do to prove I'm serious about this."

"No, ma'am. I believe you're right determined."

"I expect your complete cooperation on this."

"Yes, ma'am."

"You can call me Ella again," she said a bit more softly.

Everett watched her carefully for signs that the turn was genuine. He'd had enough scolding and lacked confidence in her waving that gun around.

"You can set that hammer down now," he said reaching for the gun.

She lifted it sharply. "I can set the hammer."

"Easy does it, yeah?"

Using both hands, she nudged the hammer down, the heavy pistol wobbling.

"I can tetch you to shoot someday if you'd like."

"I don't *want* to learn to shoot," she said with an exasperated whine. "Don't you get it?"

"Well if yer gonna be wavin a gun around issuing threats and such, I'd prefer you knew a bit more about the mechanics of it."

"I know how to shoot a gun," she said. "My daddy taught me."

"I can see he did."

"Are you getting smart with me?"

"No, ma'am."

With a playful grin, she lifted the gun, wobbling and pressed the barrel beneath his chin. "Don't call me ma'am."

"Didn't' yer daddy tell you never to point a gun someone unless you aim to use it."

She lowered the gun again. "He taught me to use it only as a last resort, and that I will do," she said firmly.

"Yes, ma'am."

She scowled.

"Sorry. Ella. When I git scared, I resort to my best manners."

She gave him a good-humored push.

Their troubles were not over, however.

When they left the hut for chores, they spotted a patrol boat rowing their way from the armed sloop. The boat had drifted down river a bit, but Everett reckoned they were headed their way. They sent Jamie into the tunnel, fearing he could be taken as a cabin boy or crew. Everett set about chopping wood. They could do nothing, he knew, except carry on as settlers.

As the patrol boat neared the island, Everett went down to the water's edge and took their rope, guiding them around the point in shelter from the wind and waves.

A young officer stepped ashore, tipping his plumed hat, his crew sitting with their oars pulled in but their muskets nearby at the ready.

"Good day, sir," the officer said in flawless English. "Madam," he bowed. "My name is Lt. Gilles Chabert of the Royal French Navy."

Everett stepped forward and shook his hand.

The officer stepped up the bank and surveyed the island tip. "A glorious spot," he said.

"Yessir, I believe it is," Everett offered with a nod.

"You are settlers, I presume."

"Yessir. I'm a fisherman. She's a widow."

"I'm sorry, madam," he said removing his hat.

"Thank you."

"A casualty of this war?"

Ella looked at him steadily and nodded yes.

"A soldier?"

"No," she said. "A wagon mender commandeered by the British."

He replaced his hat and frowned. "An innocent?" he said, watching her carefully.

"He had no quarrel with anyone and never raised a gun."

The young officer studied her for a few moments, the turned to Everett.

"And you, sir?"

"I ain't a fighter for none other than her safety."

"But you are British, no?"

"Born British, but I ain't been there since I was a boy."

"American-British, then?"

"I been livin' here fer ten years, and I don't reckon anyone knows what I am. American, Canadian. It don't matter. I'm a St. Lawrence River man."

"Are there others on this island?"

"Nossir. She had a boy, but he got took by the fever."

"Diphtheria."

"I believe it was, but there ain't no docs out this way, and he went quick."

"And you burned your camp?" he said gesturing toward the charred beams that pierced the soil.

Ella stared down and willed the color from her face, thinking of her husband's death and dreading the possibility that someday Everett's story about her son could someday turn to truth.

The officer regarded her stricken gaze, studying her carefully. "I'm sorry for your losses, madam. This is wild and dangerous country and a terrible war. I have an equally beautiful sister at home and an infant nephew whom I may never meet. I take no glory or comfort from this war."

He turned to Everett, "But it is my unfortunate duty to request the inspection of your lovely paradise."

"Yessir, you ain't the first."

He motioned to the boat, and two marines no older than Jamie climbed smartly to shore and with pistols drawn, began an inspection of the island. When they disappeared into the hut, Ella's heart thudded. She stood in frozen dread trying with all her strength to appear impassive as panic stole her breath and utter helplessness drained her resolve.

She finally breathed when they appeared from the hut. She did not allow herself to look but gazed instead into the west, concentrating with all her might on licks of whitecaps flashing in the distance from an approaching line of increasing wind.

The marines walked cautiously down the path, and the officer returned. He walked past Ella, then turned.

"Your son's grave?" he asked, "I don't see it."

Ella groaned.

Everett stepped toward them. Rifles clicked. The officer held up his hand to calm his men.

"In the river, sir. The river takes our dead," Everett said.

"I'm sorry, madam," he said softly.

She nodded and moved away to hide her face.

Before long the marines returned and spoke to the officer in rapid, quiet French. When they were finished, the officer turned to Everett, "A bateaux, a canoe. You need both."

"The canoe is fast and light. And quiet. I hunt with it."

"Ah, yes," the officer nodded. He gestured for the marines to return to the boat.

"Then you can sell us fish?"

"Yessir. I have perch, live and salted both. I have muskie..."

"Muskie?"

Everett held out his hands to indicate its size. "Fresh steaks."

"I have 40 men to feed on board, 90 more in Port Lachine. Fresh fish for 130 men?"

"Yessir. I can bring them to your ship."

Ella shuddered, her eyes like knives thudding into Everett's heart.

"Very good, Monsieur. We will pay you well." He turned to Ella, "He will be safe. We are honorable men, madam."

The officer walked carefully down the bank. Then he turned and raised his hand as if to say he had forgotten something. "Monsieur, last night we saw through the glass two more men. Where are they?"

Ella's face drained again.

Everett smiled, "Enjoying a good sleep on shore after stuffing themselves with my good fish," he said.

"Ah, yes," the officer nodded, "you have satisfied customers, of course."

"You bet," Everett nodded, taking the bow line and holding the boat tight for the officer to step in. "Watch them rocks," he said pointing. "Take care at the channel rip," he said pointing further out. Wind's come up."

"Merci, Monsieur. We will see you and your fish in an hour, then?"

"Yessir, fair enough."

Everett cast them off and watched the marines set their oars and dig solidly into the increasing shop. These men knew their business, Everett thought, unlike Henri's motley crew. Within moments, the boat lurched briskly into the waves, the oars sweeping in precise unison on a course smartly windward of the warship.

Everett hurried with his fish traps, netting his catch and pouring them into the traps he secured to the stern.

"Why didn't you give *them* the fish," Ella said angrily. "Why the hell did you offer to take it to *them*, for God's sake."

"Hand me them muskie," he said impatiently, pointing to a wooden box filled with fresh cut steaks.

"Will you please answer my question?" she demanded.

"You gonna shoot me," he muttered.

"Everett," she snapped.

He stood in the stern and looked back at her. "I'm taken 'em fish 'cause I'm a fisherman. I'm taken 'em fish 'cause I was doin' my best to git the bastards off the island. I'm taken 'em fish 'cause sending them off with my traps woulda meant they'd have to come back or I would lose my traps. And it wouldn't made no sense to do nothing else, and that sonovabitch knew it. We'll know exactly what else he knew when I git out there. I'll thank you to let me carry on, then. Yeah?" he said glaring at her.

They both looked at each other for a moment. Then she lugged the last box to the gunnel and balanced it grim-faced until he stepped forward and heaved it into the stern.

"Cast me off, then," he said, "I ain't lookin' forward to this no more'n you, and the wind's building."

Her mood bleak, she tossed the rope into the boat and pushed hard with her boot as Everett curled out into the river, set the oars, moving with smooth, sure-footed precision. He watched her as he rowed away. He hadn't wanted to be quite so harsh, but the woman needed to learn that on some accounts, she had to trust he knew what he was doing even if he wasn't the smartest man alive. As he pulled away, he smiled thinly and she waved with tired resignation. She watched as her gaze broke away from him. She leaned against a huge willow branch, and he was softened inside as he looked upon her beauty cast sadly in the shadows of the old willow hunched over and seeming to embrace her rounded, downcast shoulders.

Everett repeatedly peaked over his shoulder as he approached the gunboat. She was massive by his reckoning, strongly crafted from local cedar, and deadly, her small cannons poked ominously past her gunnels. They threw him a line from the stern, then tossed over a rope, and lowered four giant hooks attached to pulleys as big as his head. Everett attached his fish cages, and in moments the cages were winched upward.

Everett attached the line to his bow and scaled the ladder. His rowboat drifted behind in the protective lee of the sloop's handsomely curved stern.

The captain greeted him along with the officer whom he'd met on shore. The captain was short, thin, and regally dressed in blue with gold trim. Everett shook his small, impassive hand. "Bonjour, Monsieur," the captain said sternly. "My crew will be very grateful. Mon équipage sera très reconnaissant," he said gesturing to the crates of flopping, shimmering fish.

"We meet again," smiled the young officer, "Bonjour."

Everett nodded and shook his hand. The young officer had a strong grip and large, powerful hands.

They escorted Everett to the captain's cabin in the stern. Everett had to duck to fit through the small, ornately carved oak door. The cabin was otherwise roughcut in red cedar with shiny brass fittings, and neatly arranged desk upon which were arranged navigational maps showing this section of the river. The captain handed Everett a small leather satchel swollen with coins. "For les poissons, merci," he said.

"S'il vous plait," the captain gestured toward the maps. "Inspect for us. Is thees accurate. The channel. The many hazard?"

Everett studied the map and its remarkable details. At first glance he was greatly impressed with the bottom contours. He noted his own island correctly named, Ile du Cedre, but quickly noticed the errant location of the two main channels north and south of the island and noted that the rocks at the point were not properly extended. The map showed deep water much too quickly. He followed the contours where the channels skirting the island should have been located. Perhaps they did not need that detail so far from the main shipping channel where they were now anchored. He studied the main channel, which seemed very accurate for its course and depth. But the map failed to show several rocky shoals running east-west several hundred yards south of the channel. He pointed to the contours. "Here and here are dangerous shoals. No danger to you but to a ship blown off course, these shoals could sink a boat of this size."

The first officer explained, "Ici et ici les banc peut couler le navire."

The captain handed Everett a pen. "Show thees shoals, s'il vous plait."

"I ain't no map maker," Everett muttered.

The young officer stepped forward. "Estimate for us. We can have the area surveyed. Please, draw for us your best estimate. It does not need to be perfect."

Everett drew several clumsy oblong shoals and wrote in six feet.

The captain nodded gravely and flipped to the next map. "Et ci?"

"And here?" the young officer said gesturing along the next section of channel.

Everett studied the drawings. He drew a circle. "There's a rock pile. Small but very dangerous."

"Danger?" the captain asked.

"Roches amasser," the first officer said.

Everett wrote in four feet. Then he circled another rock pile with a wider oblong and wrote in six feet.

"Deux metre, trois metre?" the captain asked the officer, cranking his head to read Everett's crude script.

"Oui."

"Maybe less," Everett said pointing to the center of the rock pile.

The captain nodded and then spoke very rapidly in French to his young officer. "Je veut que cet homme soit notre pilotte. Arrestation si il refuse." For a moment, the officer looked surprised, then turned to Everett.

"We would like to hire you to be our pilot."

"Nossir," Everett, "I'm a fisherman. I ain't no river pilot."

"We will pay very well," the young officer said.

"Besides, I don't know the river so good going west."

"But you know it east to Lachine, of course, where you take your catch. And surely you've traveled to Montreal and Quebec, no?"

Everett could now see his immense error at showing them the shoals and rocks. "Nossir, I cannot. I'm a fisherman, and I have the widow to protect."

The young officer turned to the captain and spoke rapidly. The captain spoke back, his voice rising toward anger. "Aux arrets alors. Maintenant. Aussitôt."

The young officer turned to Everett. "Sir, we will pay you enough to hire someone to protect the widow."

"Nossir."

"Would you prefer to be arrested?" the young officer said.

Everett was confused for a moment. Things were coming unthreaded. He needed to get out there. He turned to the captain, smiled thinly. "I have to go. The wind is coming up. Good luck with your travels. You have a great map. The channel is very good. Good bye. I have to leave." Everett hurried toward the door. As he opened it, three sailors armed with rifles pointed at his chest, awaited their orders.

Ella watched nervously from shore. Her heart fluttered and sank when she saw the sails drop from the yard arms and fill with wind, the crew rushing frantically in the rigging. In a few minutes, the gunship began inching forward. She could see Everett's boat trail out from behind. She waited, her heart pounding now with worry. The ship picked up speed, sailing west her sails now set and swollen with wind.

She watched for twenty minutes, a half hour, as the ship slowly grew smaller. Then she spotted what looked to be Everett's rowboat, but she could see no one rowing. It had been set adrift. It had been released at a point that a skilled seaman might calculate that with wind and current it would drift very near to the island. Jamie launched the canoe to rescue the rowboat. It drifted to within a few hundred feet northwest of the island until it hit the channel off the point and veered east where it would have disappeared had Jamie not towed it safely to shore. Ella was relieved only that Everett was not lying on the floor either dead or wounded. But they could find no note, no indication of what had happened. Still, Ella knew that Everett had been commandeered. They could use a riverman the same as the British could use a master wagon builder.

His safety now rested with the French, with his own willingness to cooperate, with God and luck, with his skill and usefulness to the French navy, and his capacity to swallow his pride and earn their respect. Ella knew that Everett's pride was his greatest danger, stubbornness both his greatest hidden enemy and his bravest ally. But mostly she was darkly depressed. She had seen the inevitable and could not stop it. She had felt a deepening caring for Everett that included more than her safety and more than a deep longing for comfort and security. As it grew, the more certain it seemed that it must eventually be shattered, and now it was shattered. All that she could foresee now was bleak hardship again. Yes, it was possible that he could escape; it was possible they would let him go. But it was more likely that he would be killed, more likely that she or Jamie would die before ever seeing him again.

Chapter 3

Henri blew on his cold, pink fingers and marveled at the size and density of snow flakes tumbling from the sky. Already the ground was coated with a thickening white dust. The sky glowed a brilliant but dreary grey. The still, black water absorbed the flakes slowly, forming a thickening gruel on the verge of coagulating into a vast field of iced mush. The island's trees were barren, the thick underbrush dead, grey, sagging. "It's gonna freeze over quick now," Jamie offered. "In a couple of weeks we can fish again."

Henri looked at Jamie with surprise at his eagerness.

"Ice fishing is good out here. Big ones."

Henri shivered. He raised the axe and swatted at log. Jamie dragged a long branch to the 'V' brace, braced it tightly, and sawed a short section suitable for the cook stove. Steam rose from his head and neck, his breath emerging in vaporous puffs and dissipating in the damp, thick air. He cut half way through, then stopped to catch his breath. The thought of eating another fish made him want to gag. He longed for a juicy beefsteak with an elegant French gravy.

"You think they'll let Everett go when the river freezes over?" he asked Henri.

Henri chuckled ironically. "Nossir," he said. He had been working on his accent, trying to pick up the local cadence. He had been quite amazed at how Quebec settlers had frozen an earlier, almost royal French into their own regional dialect. They spoke this oddly archaic form mixed with half-swallowed Americanisms and native expressions into a language soup which he had begun to enjoy imitating. He liked the Canadian-American dialect of English with its deep, soft tones and colorful simplicity. He had learned his English in Paris from fussy tutors imported from England, and they spoke with a rapid, chirpy impatience and shrill disdain. The North American dialect with its slow, flat, matter-of-fact mutter seemed a deliberate mockery of London English. It seemed to fit the English settlers here who walked with stiff, plodding steps and who talked with minimal movement of their hands. Even their lips barely moved when they talked. It was as if they devoted their entire beings to the most ardent conservation of energy. He was now beginning to understand why. In summer it was too hot to move and in winter too cold to breathe. Now that Everett was gone, it seemed to Henri that he must learn to speak and move as Everett had. Jamie was his best teacher, a passable mimic of Everett's speech and movements. He needed to be able to speak both a French and an English that placed him here and blended him into the immigrant populations. His life may depend on it someday.

"They ain't lettin' him go," Henri said in his practiced new dialect.

Jamie looked over at Henri. "They ain't goin' nowhere. They'll be froze solid 'til April.

"Yessir," Henri nodded, swung the axe and this time got it jammed in the end of the log. He lifted the heavy log stuck at the end of the axe and pounded it down on the ground. Nothing. He lifted it again and this time dropped it down on the immense old splitting log.

Jamie ambled over, dragging the sledge hammer. He lifted it and drove the axe deeper into the log. Then again. The log groaned and crackled. Once more he banged the axe with the hammer, the sharp, metallic ping echoing off the barren tree trunks. The log split, each side falling off with a clean squeak and crackle.

"Merci," Henri muttered and lifted another log onto the splitting log.

Ella watched through a marbly sheet of glass Everett had built into the kitchen wall before he left as a lookout to the west and northwest channel. Henri and Jamie worked like two small children, she thought, not unkindly. Everett could do both jobs in half the time. Still, they were making headway. She brewed up warm apple cider and sprinkled it with spices.

"It ain't so cold," Jamie said. "A cord of wood heats twice, you know."

"How's this?" Henri asked.

"It heats you when you burn it in the stove, yeah? And it heats you when you cut and split it, yeah?"

"Voila. That's it!" Henri laughed. "Heats twice."

"Yessir."

"Yessir."

They sat on logs when Ella brought them their cider. She looked out toward the channel. Always she looked for signs of Everett. And always she was quietly let down.

"It feels like a snow storm," she said, blowing on her hands and turning back to them.

"Nah," said Jamie.

"Nah," said Henri.

Ella and Jamie exchanged grins at Henri's Americanisms.

"It ain't gonna storm," Henri said, "Just gonna snow."

"So you're becoming an expert on North American weather," she smiled. "I'm much relieved."

Henri blushed a bit, then shrugged with his best French expressiveness as if to say in one brief flurry of movements, 'who knows, who cares, why does it matter, this is life, why to worry?'

She went back in for the cider pot. When she returned, she could overhear one of Jamie's lessons.

"No Henri. You put the accent on shit. 'No SHIT. No SHIT."

"No SHEET," Henri said earnestly.

"Not SHEET, No SHIT."

"No, SHIT!" Henri bellowed.

"Perfect."

"No SHIT," Henri grinned.

"Okay, so now some guy says to you, 'hey, it's a cold day, yeah. And then you say, no SHIT, Charlie. So are you ready?"

"Yessir."

"Hey, Henri, it's a goddamned cold day, ain't it?"

"No SHIT, Charlie," Henri said.

"Perfect. You're the nuts, Henri."

"I'm the nuts," he grinned. Then he blushed as Ella approached from behind the hut.

"Jamie, do you really think it's necessary to teach Henri profanities?"

"Oh, madam, thees Nort Americans, dey speak only da profanities."

She made an odd, bemused grimace, "I suppose that's true, but among yourselves, si'l vous plait?"

"Ah oui, pardon" Henri blushed.

She looked pointedly at Jamie.

"Yeah, mum," Jamie muttered.

By the next morning a foot of snow had fallen. Henri marveled at its extraordinary beauty. The trees, the ground, the rocks, the arc of the river bank all gently blanketed with soft, perfectly smooth whiteness of blinding silent brilliance beneath a late November sun. The temperature had dropped drastically, however, and Henri could feel ice crystals tug inside his nose as he breathed. The river that morning was a shimmering glaze of black ice as far as the eye could see.

"Extraordinaire," he said to Ella. "Thees is so beautiful. Ees very cruel, thees beauty, oui?"

"Oui," she said hugging her shawl around her shoulders.

Jamie dug into the snow near the water's edge and retrieved a small rock. He flung it out onto the ice where it bounced twice and then slid and slid and slid almost as far as the ice could see until suddenly it disappeared.

Henri turned, his mouth puckered in surprise.

"The channel," Jamie said.

"Ah," Henri grunted gravely. "I see."

"Very dangerous," said Ella.

"Yeah," said Henri.

"You learn those channels, Henri," she said.

"Ah oui."

Jamie dug up another rock and flung it north. They watched as it slid and slid across the glaze and then plunked into the depths.

"Watch here," said Jamie moving toward the south bank. He flung another rock, and this time it slid and slid and finally, very slowly, it stopped. That morning they worked the perimeter of the island, Jamie showing Henri the channels north and south. With a path of rocks flung further and further, Jamie traced the one safe route toward shore, a lazy arc to the south curling east to the bay and then to shore beyond Jamie's capacity to throw. By noon, the rocks all sank, the sun heating the rocks that baked a series of tiny holes. By evening most of the ice had melted and waves licked the shore again. But winter was near.

* * *

Lake Ontario was as much a mystery to Everett as it was to the French crew. But they welcomed his keen eye, and because he was shackled in leg irons that would prevent him from being able to swim, Everett had a heightened need to keep the warship out of trouble. As the weather grew colder, weed beds that thrived on shallow shoals died and drifted away. It was increasingly more difficult to detect signs of shallow water, so along with Gilles, the young first officer and Louis, the helmsman during Everett's watch, they each studied the maps with increasing concentration and dependence. Everett liked them both. Unlike the captain and others on the crew, Gilles and Louis treated him with respect and kindness.

But after his watch, which stretched over ten hours, he was taken below by marines and locked in the brig. The brig was dimly lit and stank of urine, vomit, and feces. Almost every day a crew member would be flung in with him after having been savagely lashed by the marines for what seemed to Everett minor offenses. Sometimes they sneaked an extra dram of rum from the ship's supply barrels or punched a crew member in an argument over a chunk of bread. Sometimes they returned late from shore leave after having consorted with whores. Sometimes they tried to escape the ship and were tracked down by the marines and whipped to a bloody pulp.

They told their pathetic stories in broken English often hissing and weeping from the deep cuts from the lash. "I foock ze whore. Thaas eet! Sixty lash. Mon Dieu."

When he had fresh water, Everett tried to help clean their wounds. But often they were too drunk and rolled their wounds in their own vomit, piss, and feces. Often Everett would awaken at night to the sound of a crew member pissing or shitting on the floor or just erupting in his own trousers with blasts of dysentery.

"Why do they risk their lives for a cup of bloody rum?" Everett asked Gilles during one cold watch, expecting a sensible answer from the amiable lieutenant.

"They are stupid men," Gilles snapped irritably. "What do you expect? They know the punishment. They know the marines love the lash. They know some men die from it. It's so stupid," he said, watching warily for marines who might overhear his scorn.

"Which is stupid? The men or the punishment?" Everett asked.

Gilles raised his brows and his eyes flashed with caustic anger, but he said nothing as a marine ambled up the gun deck and eyed them scornfully before turning away.

"I try to get you more time in the mess," Gilles said. "The brig is terrible, oui?"

They sailed across Lake Ontario on what seemed a pointless voyage and then a few days later were given orders to reverse course and hurry to Lachine before the ice locked them in some obscure port and crushed them. "The channel," Gilles said looking into the gray horizon, "does it freeze?"

"Sometimes. In some places," Everett said. On a following westerly, the warship swayed and groaned as they passed from the Lake into a section of deep narrows back into the St. Lawrence. "I've seen the whole river freeze solid, channels, too. This boat would be crushed like an egg. No boat can withstand the force," Everett said.

Louis spoke French to Gilles in an irritated voice, then included Everett, "Why de fook de lake. What we do-ing in de lake when de river freez-ing?"

Gilles shrugged. Everett shrugged.

"In Lachine. How do they protect the boats from freezing in the bay?" Gilles asked.

"They got crews who chop ice, stir the water. That's how they make a living, protecting boats from the ice."

Louis shivered. "Colda. Fooking colda."

Going to Lachine was good news to Everett. There he might escape and run the few miles along the rapids to Montreal where he could lose himself in the back streets and alleys. At Lachine the crew would drink the potent ales and consort with whores, and the chances for lapses in security would surely improve. For the first time in weeks, his mood improved. But he was not so sure they would make it. Already shallow sections of the river were iced over. He was sure St-Francois du Lac would be mostly ice by now except for the deepest channels.

That night the temperature dropped to 12-degrees f. Even in his fetid little brig, the snot in Everett's nose froze as he breathed. He shivered all night wrapped in his scraggly blanket supplied only at the insistence of Gilles. The next morning sheets of black ice peeled and popped like glass as the huge vessel plowed forward riding the steady westerly toward St-Francois du Lac. The decks were slick with ice, the ropes and lines stiff, icicles forming on every ledge and protuberance as they penetrated a strange, crystalline fog.

They posted Everett and Gilles in the bow and used bells to indicate Louis' course. Everett noticed the chill in Gilles' pale face, red at the nostrils and ears and chin. His fair skin was stretched too tautly on the fine bones of his handsome, angular face. His face would soon be frost bit, Everett knew. The ruddy Louis would probably be all right, but many of these French soldiers, even the marines, seemed too delicately constructed to survive the cold, as if the gray of winter light seeped into their skin and could penetrate to their bones.

Everett leaned over the rail and watched the shards of black ice rip and shatter as the powerful bow crushed forward. He was mesmerized by blunt power of the iron-like oak penetrating the delicate black ice, lifting whole sheets in great translucent arcs that suddenly snapped and exploded in a thousand shards sharp enough to penetrate a man. This was the beginning, this shimmering black ice of a quarter inch. In a few days it could be two inches, and then the hard oak would begin to chaff and sliver, and then it would be the power of ice that would begin to chew apart this seemingly robust vessel, and if it grew yet colder, the ice would carve the bow like sharp knives and then brutal axes, ripping it to shreds. But to stop would be even worse, to stop would trap them, freeze them, crush them, sink them.

In the gray fog that day, they followed the dark path of the channel, their coats turning to icy armor plate over their chests. The sails, puffed and full, hardened into glistening arcs of sheet ice, rigid as iron. By noon, the gunship groaned and crackled under the new, enormous weight of the misty ice. From time to time, gusts would crack the surface of the ice on the sails, and thin glassy sheets tumbled to the deck and shattered like glass.

By early afternoon, Everett warned Gilles. "You'd better lower them sails, or you'll break them masts."

But the captain pressed onward, and at dusk a sudden gust swirling out of the north twisted the sails, and sheets of black ice tumbled down, and not twenty feet from them, a sailor was struck by a huge shard that split his skull and ripped his shoulder from his chest. The man fell under the weight of the shattering ice, blood pumping in hot, steaming spurts from the base of his neck onto the glistening deck. The man groaned and turned to Everett and Gilles, reaching his fingers to block the spurts of blood but only causing it to spray in odd splatters over his blood-drenched face leaving only the white of his eye visible in the drench of glistening red. Further aft, a section of yard arm cracked and broke, tumbling toward the deck before yanking into a swinging arc held by a tangle of rigging lines like some doomed pendulum.

The spurts of the sailor's blood soon dwindled to an oozy flow, and then he was dead, his white eye looking off in dazed confusion.

Gilles persuaded the captain to lower the main sails, but the canvas was so stiff now that the sailors had to pound them with sticks just to soften them enough to tuck them out of the wind. Sheets and shards of ice shattered everywhere, cutting hands and fingers. Men slipped and fell, scampering helplessly on the ice-slicked decks.

By evening the temperature had dropped still further, and the ship now inched forward, ice crashing, shattering, and screaming against the hull. It was a race to Lachine across the emerging vast white of St-Francois du Lac where snow was now piled thickly on an enormous field of ice cut only by a jagged fifty-foot ribbon of black ice marking the narrowing channel. Everett was chilled to the depths, and only he seemed fully aware that this rugged craft was no better than a pile of match sticks should the channel close on them.

Snow fell in tiny dust-like flakes at dusk. In an hour it had begun accumulating on the thin layer of black ice, making it increasingly more difficult to see the channel. The wind had died, and the current was now trying to push the ship broadside.

"We need an anchor at the stern," Everett told Gilles. "A small one that slows us a bit."

"A sea anchor?" Gilles asked.

"No, the current will move a sea anchor faster than the ship. A couple of bateaux anchors just to drag the bottom, to keep the stern aft and into the wind. But we need to keep moving. Slowly. The current will keep us in the channel. Lower all the sails. We need to rely on the current. In an hour we won't be able to see the channel, and it's cold enough to keep freezing. If we turn broadside and freeze, we're fucked. If we're not crushed outright, the ice flow will turn us on our side, and then we sink. Do you understand?"

"Oui, yes. Can you make the captain understand?"

Gilles' body was trembling from perpetual shivers. He shrugged. "I hope."

Gilles climbed down the forward hatch. Everett waited. The ship turned further broadside. The temperature dropped until the snot in his nose froze as he breathed. Everett, too, shivered now. He could no longer feel his toes or fingers. His mind felt dull, foggy. Maybe he had made a mistake, he thought dimly. Maybe he would have his best chance at escape if they froze solid in the channel and in the chaos of being laid over, he could jump free and escape across the ice. Maybe it would be thick enough by then. Maybe not. He waited until finally in the darkness, Gilles appeared through the hatch. He handed Everett a steaming cup of tea.

"Yes, okay. The captain tells me for you to take the helm. You are the pilot. The ship is yours. You tell me. I give the orders, oui?"

Everett could barely hold the cup in his numb fingers. He squeezed it in both hands. He had never been so cold.

They climbed below decks and moved slowly through the hold where freezing men huddled in blankets, the decks slick with ice formed from the steam of their breathing. Listless faces gazed in vacant, sleepy indifference at their passage. Some of these men would die, but Everett was unable to gather himself to urge them to group together to amass their body heat. Even the marines-gathered in the mess around the cook stove-seemed dimly aware of the dangers. Their blood-shot eyes watched him impassively, jaws and teeth chattering. They were at least smart enough to gather around the heat. The floor here was wet. They would live.

The deck crew trailed several anchors they'd pulled from patrol boats and attached to the stern mast with stiff, icy ropes. They lowered the last of the sails and left them spread on the deck stiff as wooden floors. The ship slowly shifted, aligning itself with the channel as Everett had hoped.

By day break, the snow had ceased. At the bow, the sun glowed pink in the stark blue eastern sky. Slowly the ship crept forward, ice crunching at the bow, breaking now in sheets, spilling snow, exposing the black water of the channel.

Snow and ice several inches thick had accumulated on the deck and squeaked loudly beneath their feet as they moved. Everett could barely feel his own knees. His feet were like insensate wooden clubs attached to his aching knees. As the sun rose in the east, the pink blended into a brilliantly gentle gold that looked wonderfully warm yet offered little discernible heat for the first hour. But by mid-morning the sun and channel waters conspired to break up the snow and ice, leaving at first a small stream of water marking the channel, then widening nearly to the width of the ship. A breeze developed out of the north, and they pulled the anchors and set three sails that soon pulled them through the narrow strand of water.

Two dead men, frozen stiff were carried on deck. They were wrapped in white canvas shrouds, one hunched in a fetal position, the other with one arm stretched straight out through the shroud as if pointing in the distance. The captain, his pale face trembling, his nose red and running with freezing green snot, muttered a prayer through chattering teeth and commended them to the river. Two crew lifted the man in the fetal bundle and dropped him over the stern with a thunderous splash. They tilted the other man over the rail feet first, and the stiff outstretched arm caught the rail, and pivoted him with a loud clunk, and the arm swung as if pointing at all of them, and he hung there for several moments before a crewman pushed the frozen white hand with his own, and the stiff body swung over and splashed backwards with a loud slap into the dark water and floated like a white log in a strange twirl in the swirling wake.

By mid afternoon, they reached the center channel of St-Francois du Lac. Everett gazed sleepily at his island slipping past in the distance, a wisp of smoke from the hut rising and twirling eastward. He thought for a moment that he saw a figure moving at the point, but his eyelids drooped into exhausted slumber.

That morning they took him to the mess chamber and let him sleep in a corner near the cook stove. Gilles told them Everett had saved their lives, and if they reached Lachine alive, they would owe it to Everett's knowledge of the great river.

Amid the comforting clatter of cookery tins, Everett dropped into a deep sleep and dreamed of walking with Ella arm and arm along the path at the water's edge. It was spring in this dream, and the new leaves glowed greenish-yellow. All around them were small sailboats criss-crossing the great bay, a scene that he had once observed in a painting in the office of a wealthy ship owner from Massena who had purchased a load of Everett's winter furs. He had never seen so many boats or such small boats on the St. Lawrence, but he now saw them in his dream.

At some indiscernible point he and Ella were transported into one of these little boats, and Everett sailed it across the bay at a remarkable speed. It skimmed across perfectly flat water and then soared up over the island in a long, steady ascent which caused his heart to thud fearfully, yet Ella sat in the bow smiling peacefully. Then suddenly, whatever held the boat in the air gave way, and the boat plunged toward the water, and just before it crashed, Everett woke, sweat damp at his temples and neck, the clanking of pots and cookware and the busy procession of crew eating noisily eased him back to reality.

He opened his eyes a crack just to confirm where he was, but then quickly dosed, preferring not to let the crew know he had awoken, as if by closing his eyes he would be utterly invisible to them. In a few moments, his head was thick again with slumber, the hardship of the last few days seeming no more and no less real than the dream.

* * *

The day after the gunship passed the island heading eastward, rain poured down in vicious torrents. Ella forbid Henri to cross the ice during the thaw.

"We never find him," Henri protested. "We wait; I can't catch de boat."

"No," Ella said.

"The ice won't melt," Jamie protested.

"No."

So they waited three days until the torrent turned to drizzle, and then the sky brightened and turned bitter cold. On the morning of the sixth sub-zero day, the river was a huge silver sheet of ice, smooth as silk, as far as the eye could see.

Jamie pointed to the safest route to shore, but his mother forbid him to leave with Henri.

Ella called out to Henri as he set out kneeling on Everett's sled, poking forward with two knives, one in each hand to chip a grip on the hard, slick ice. "You say hello to Lucy for me," she called.

Henri waved one of his knives in acknowledgment, then leaned forward, set the knives into the ice, and plunged forward. The sled leapt forward and coasted noisily for at least fifty feet. He set the knives again, and in a few minutes he was cruising rapidly toward shore estimating the path Jamie had pointed out with its gentle arc southward. He crossed the channel at the safest point, but Henri could see the ice had darkened beneath him. He could hear a strange, hollow cracking and could see bubbles and the black water of the river perhaps no more than an inch below the ice. His heart thudded with fear, but he moved even more rapidly now, plunging frantically with his knives, recalling Jamie's warning that stopping on thin ice was to risk certain death.

Soon the ice thickened again, turning a deep opaque silver. He eased his movements, seeking a steady rhythm. The wind from his rapid pace across the ice burned his cheeks and chin, and in less than an hour he pulled up to Lucy's frozen dock.

Henri was relieved at Lucy's insistence that she would accompany him on their journey. They would sail to Lachine, she told him, and there they would find the warship docked for the winter.

"Sail, mademoiselle?"

"Oui. Le bateau a glace traverse la glace tres vite," she said.

Lucy had fashioned her ice boat from the carriage of an old buggy sleigh ordinarily pulled by horses. But she had removed the towing hardware and stepped a mast and triangular sail through the carriage seat. She fashioned a rudder from an old plow blade.

Henri circled this contraption skeptically. They spoke French.

"With this northerly, we can reach Lachine by sunset," she said.

"No," he guffawed.

"We'll sail faster than a galloping horse," she said. "We'll sail faster than the wind."

"Impossible. How can one sail faster than the wind, itself?"

"I don't know how, but I've done it many times."

"The ice. It is safe?"

"Oui. Especially at the speed we'll reach. The ice is not a problem."

"The great danger is to your face and hands and feet. You must cover everything with lard, or you skin will die and turn black from the cold and then it festers and grows infected, and if you are unlucky and have fair skin as you do, you may die a horrible, painful death."

"Oui, I wear plenty of lard. And the channels?" Henri asked.

"I know safe routes. In Lachine, the river splits, and we cross by barges. It is very safe. I have done this many times."

Henri marveled at this woman, who in all respects except her physical beauty, was as confident and rugged as any man he had ever met.

He watched with growing admiration as she rigged her ice buggy. He had never seen a women spit with such gratuitous alacrity, as if she were celebrating, with half a wink, her superiority over any man. He marveled at her fingers-strong, quick, precise, and impervious to cold. When she smiled, she set her tongue against a gap where she'd apparently lost a tooth making her look like a 12-year-old brimming with innocence, yet she swore with the ease of any sailor. And then with a quick pucker reminding Henri of a rabbit's sniff, she slipped a squirt of spit from between her tongue at that toothless gap, flung out into the air in an arc before penetrating the snow like a silent arrow.

He watched as she dabbed brownish lard on her face with the delicacy of a Parisian actress applying cream. Her fingers were long, thin, elegant, lovely. She moved over the buggy with the grace of a ballerina and the speed of a cat. She pulled the lines with hard yanks. She cleated the lines with lightening twists.

"Take a seat, Henri, and hold onto your ass."

"Oui, madame," he grinned, stepping onto this ungainly craft.

She raised the sail which flapped and slapped loudly at the wind.

"You will never get closer to flying than this," she yelled above the fluttering racket of the wildly luffing sail. She pushed the buggy onto the ice, jumped onto the wobbly seat, and yanked the main sheet. The sail made one loud clap, then puffed full, and in an instant they were off.

They quickly gained speed, the sleigh runners clattering across the hard ice. She set the rudder which cut into the ice sending up a fine spray of particles. Henri had ridden in horse drawn carriages at full gallop, but this quickly exceeded any speed he ever achieved short of jumping from a cliff into a limestone pool as a boy. Soon the runners were humming, the wind whistling. The carriage-which at first felt heavy and sluggish-now rattled and trembled with skittery hysteria.

"Whoooeee," she yelped, straddling the seat, holding the rudder in her left hand, the sheet line in her left, the whole contraption vibrating as if to explode.

Henri looked down and watched the ice streak past in a dizzy blur. Icy wind raced down his collar, up his sleeves, up his pant legs. In moments, he was trembling from the penetrating cold. But his face felt only strangely cool as if he'd dipped his face in a pail of water, the lard a cold but welcome mask. She faced the wind, her neck and hands exposed, her dark hair rippling, twisting, flying in the wind.

Had he been directing this thing himself, Henri would have been terrified. But she was so utterly moved to joy, he grinned and relaxed. He watched the shoreline trees rush past, the distant mountains slowly sliding westward. She was right. This was as close to flying as he could imagine. Henri was soon numb to the speed and the cold. The was a land of such desolation and starkness, the trees along the river banks so barren, too stiff to bend in the wind, too cold to sway. Everything was frozen white, frozen gray, frozen black. Stiff, lifeless, rigid. Henri had never witnessed such unrelieved starkness as if North American trees shed half their branches as well as their leaves just to hide from the cold. The sun, though brilliant, was a frozen crystal, the sky a piercing blue, the clouds great puffs rolling eastward desperately in search for warmth. After that hard rain, everything sparkled with diamond hardness, the snow so bright his eyes ached, the river a gleaming gorgeous, gaudy silver. They had now entered Lac du St. Louis, and the ice was extraordinarily smooth, the wind a bit lighter, the vibrations now transformed to a steady, crackly hiss. Lucy eased off the rudder. Their speed increased. They flew.

* * *

The "La Poisson Marchand" was steamy warm, a welcome mix of body heat baked to a near swelter by a wood stove so hot it glowed. Lucy and Henri took a table in the rear, and for the first ten minutes let the shivers rattle them free of the day's hard chill on the icy river. They each took enormous mugs of rum and gasped as it seared their throats and dropped into their bellies like hot coals. The saloon was packed with fishermen, sailors, merchants, boatmen, whores, and tradesmen, all apparently drunk on the brutal house rum. The piano player tapped out improvised and raucous versions of minuets, hunched over his piano as though he had never left from Lucy's visit months ago

"Your feet are okay?" She asked.

"Feet? I have not possessed feet for several hours."

"Let me know when they show up."

"Do you think they will let Everett off the ship?"

"Don't be foolish. Why would they? I think we'll find him on the ship if we find him at all."

Henri was mildly insulted. After all, he had been in the French Navy. It was not unreasonable to assume that the French officers would welcome Everett. But he was not ready to argue this with Lucy, goddess of the glace bateau.

"I think I will need my feet."

"We'll need to find the ship."

"Yessir."

She looked at him. "Are you mocking me?"

"My God, no!" he shuddered. "An expression. I'm working on my local English. It is a favorite expression of Everett's. I would prefer not to be identified as Parisian here or they'll send me off to the front."

"Or dump you in a dungeon."

"Ah oui," he said mournfully. "But, I will have flown first, yes? You are remarkably skilled at sailing your ice bateau. You are remarkably skilled at everything. If it were not for your remarkable beauty, I would have guessed that you must be a very gifted man."

She rolled her eyes skeptically. "You are really full of shit, aren't you?"

Henri snapped back in his chair and feigned great injury.

"Everett didn't tell me you were such a bullshitter," she said.

"Oh, my God, dear me," Henri gasped, eyes bulging, beginning now to flush with a touch of real injury. "What is your problem with me, mademoiselle," he said more sharply.

She looked at him with disarming directness, her eyes seeming to dance and glow with some inscrutable mix of scorn and amusement.

Her look was so direct that he cringed and held up his hands in defense.

"Are you a brave man? I mean, beneath this squirmy exterior, is there a brave man lurking, or are you a coward as well as a bullshitter?"

"Are you playing with me?" he snapped.

"My life may depend upon whether you have any courage, and if you'll excuse my bad manners, I just get the feeling you don't have any, and if that's true, I need to know so that you don't get us killed."

"I have great courage," Henri said with a pout.

"Please shake my hand, then."

She held out her hand. He grasped hers tentatively. She began to squeeze. He squeezed back. She squeezed harder. He squeezed back. Soon she was squeezing so hard Henri thought she might break something in his tortured knuckles. He tried to squeeze back, but she had clearly developed a knack for this form of torture.

Her voice trembled as she spoke. "Being able to endure pain around here is very important. One of the little tricks used by the Mohawks in these parts is to rip a captive's fingernails off with their teeth."

He could feel her arms and shoulders trembling from the effort. His hand ached horribly now and must certainly be broken in some aspect, but he tried to ignore the pain.

"The French navy will likely send their friends, the Abenakis, to hunt us down, and they can be horribly ruthless," she said, her voice straining as she watched Henri grimace with pain. "But they respect bravery."

She let go and looked at Henri with unrepentant skepticism.

"If an Indian ever squeezes your hand or pulls off a fingernail, stay perfectly silent. They like to see white men scream. It encourages their scorn and revulsion and makes them do worse things until they can make you shut up and suffer with dignity."

"Why are you telling me this? I have seen very few Indians."

She grinned and rolled her eyes. Then she leaned a bit and spit onto the floor.

"If we steal Everett off that boat, they'll probably put a bounty on our scalps. Everything is bounty around here. We're probably going to be worth a couple of hundred francs," she said.

She finished her mug of rum. "They usually pay a little more for a live capture. But, the Indians don't waste time keeping someone alive unless there's some use for them or maybe a barrel of whiskey with the bounty. If they catch you, you're probably better off getting your throat cut and scalped. It's better that way."

"Dead you mean?"

"Yeah."

"Torture is not the path you want."

"But, of course."

"If they're out of meat, they might eat you."

"Nooo," Henri protested.

She laughed. "Don't worry."

"You're fooling with me, then?"

"They don't eat people alive. You'd be dead. Although they might cook you before they kill you. They have a fascination for human reactions to fire."

"Jesus, God," he moaned.

"Hey, not to worry."

"Not to worry!" he protested.

"They won't run out of meat. They're damned good hunters."

"Thank God."

"They'll just cut your penis off."

"Oh, God, Lucy, must you?"

She laughed fully now.

"How do you know so much about the Indians?"

"My Uncle Joe was an Indian. And my mama, a very important tribal leader until she married my white daddy. My Uncle Joe was a very crafty warrior who taught me about Indian ways in the woods."

"You have Indian friends, then?"

"Oh, yes. Lots of friends. But, it's gotten all mixed up. This was a tribe-the Iroquois-that never fought its own. But the Mohawks broke off, and there's a lot of bad blood, and there's a lot of Mohawks hanging around here. And besides, if there's a bounty, then everyone'll be after us, and I don't have that many friends."

"Your mother was a tribal leader."

"Surprised?"

He shrugged, "Oui. Like a queen?"

"No, the Iroquois tribes are led by women picked by the tribe. It is a democracy. The Iroquois believe women are a whole lot smarter than men. More sensible, too. Less prone to dumb arrogant pronouncements and stupid threats than men. They send the men out to do battle. Hunt. Yank away the enemy's fingernails and take scalps. Men's work. They hunt, too. That's mostly all they do. They've been doing it for thousands of years so they've gotten awfully good at it."

"Well first, we have to deal with the French Navy. They aren't such pushovers, either," Henri said with a bit of resentful bluster.

Lucy grinned and rolled her eyes.

"I can see the courageous spirit of the French Navy in you, Henri."

"Yeah?" he said, flattered finally.

"And I'm not scared."

Henri nodded his deflated affirmation. "But of course," he muttered. "More rum?"

"Ah oui," she smiled, punching him lightly on the arm.

Lucy hurried from the apparel shop into the cold, early evening air and signaled to Henri. They walked gingerly, dodging frozen turds on the slippery, urine-stained ice coating the alleyway to their small boarding house.

Their room was small but benefitted from a heating grate directly above the downstairs woodstove. Lucy uncorked a bottle of rum, and each took deep drinks and hissed from the searing sting of this simmering street tonic. In an adjacent room they could hear muffled squeals and the quiet, rhythmic thumps of sex. As the evening progressed, Lucy thought increasingly of Everett and their last time mating in her room above the trading post. She loved the freedom she felt straddled over him, the heat of their sex rising until the autumn chill melted, and they flung their clothes and blankets to the floor, and steam puffed from their mouths and a mist lingered at their glistening skin.

As they became progressively drunker, Lucy nudged closer to Henri who sat huddled and still shivering on the edge of the bed. She unfastened her two top buttons and fanned her face with her hand. "How can you be cold?" she whispered.

Henri's eyes migrated to her neck and the hint of her cleavage. He swallowed more rum. "I think I am growing warmer," he whispered.

She nudged yet closer. "Listen," she whispered.

Bed springs creaked next door. A woman groaned in delicious, rhythmic shudders.

Henri eyed Lucy surreptitiously wondering if this were an invitation.

"When was your last time?" she whispered languidly, her moist lips brushing the edge of the rum bottle's opening, her mind filled with memories of the steam rising in that dim evening light.

Henri closed his eyes and swallowed. "I am a virgin," he confessed.

"Noooo," she cooed. "A man as handsome as you?"

She began unbuttoning his shirt. "I think you are too old and in too much danger to remain a virgin," she said in a low whispery voice as she alternated now between his buttons and her own. "I would not be able to live with myself if you were to die a virgin." She touched his lips and gently pressed him to the bed.

* * *

Lucy followed the young first officer Gilles as he stepped from the ship and headed along the icy walkways toward La Poisson Marchand. She followed him into the saloon, and after giving him time to order rum and warm his hands, she moved toward him and then Henri pushed her, feigning drunkenness. She stumbled and bumped into the young officer. He reached to steady her, eyeing Henri dismissively as he shrunk into the crowd.

"Pardon, pardon. I'm so very sorry," she said, "some rude ruffian pushed me right into you."

"Please don't worry. I'm glad you didn't fall."

"I owe that to you," she smiled warmly.

"Will you join me for some rum?" the officer asked.

In the world of Lachine whores of the time, Lucy feigned the part of an expensive escort, an officer's mistress, a gentleman's lover. Such women pretended to be quite respectable, and any notion of a transaction was handled very discreetly... virtually unacknowledged by both. A woman who was good at this game could expect return visits, loyalty, even a stable relationship to emerge with a select few men.

They soon left the tavern and took a table at the Grand Hotel. Here they were served fine wines and liqueurs and sat in a cozy corner lit by candlelight. She asked him about his life as an officer at war. She smiled when he told her how he hated the Canadian winter. "We very nearly froze in the channel only a few days ago. Our pilot saved our lives I am sure," he said.

"Your pilot? He is from around here?"

"Monsieur Everett. A very large man. Very strong. A bit of a mule head sometimes except about the river. He knows the river brilliantly."

She shrugged. "I don't know many pilots," she said.

"We captured him, actually. It is the war. We offered to pay him, to be one of us, to work for us, but he refused. So we arrested him. I like the man, myself. For me, he is honest and fearless, and he seems oblivious to the cold. It is quite amazing what he can tolerate."

"How can you be sure he won't deliberately wreck your ship?"

"He would die if we sink. We keep him locked in chains that are very heavy. He would not swim far in those chains. But, I don't think he would do this. I do not think he would try to kill us. He is not a soldier. The men like him. Men loan him their knives in the kitchen where we eat. He throws the knives at rats hiding in the food shelves. He has killed two dozen rats, at least. After the first several, the men began to wager. They give Monsieur Everett their knives and place bets on when he will strike the next rat. It is our only entertainment," Gilles smiled shyly, embarrassed now by his enthusiasm.

"How does this man throw a knife if he is in chains?"

"The chains are around his ankles and neck. One yank from behind, and even a big, powerful man such as Monsieur Everett is knocked painfully to his knees. I've seen men killed with a hard yank from behind."

"But he could throw a knife at one of your men."

"No, no. I know he would not. He has become my friend. I know he is not this kind of man."

"But he is too proud to join you, to work *for* you?"

"If he is free, he has said he would return to the widow and the boy to protect them."

"The widow and the boy?" she asked.

"He takes care of them," he shrugged, "on an island on the river. She is quite beautiful."

She must have flushed or betrayed her annoyance in some way.

"Not as beautiful as you, mademoiselle."

"Are they lovers?"

"No, no. This Monsieur Everett is not the kind of man to take advantage of a widow and her son."

"You admire him, this Monsieur Everett."

"Ah, oui. He is very unusual. I like him. I hope we can set him free."

"I'm very sure you will," she said.

He looked at her. "You seem quite certain of this."

"I can see that you are as honorable as he. That is what I mean."

"Merci. Yes, I believe very much in honor. I am not so sure my captain shares my view. More wine, mademoiselle?"

"Oui, merci. Please call me Lucy."

He poured more wine and toasted to her name. "A delightful name for a beautiful woman," he said solemnly.

Lucy took quickly to Gilles and found no difficulty in extending her affections. She had feared that her acting would fail her with some fat and pompous French officer, but with Gilles she did not need to act very much. Their first night in the Lachine Grand Hotel was really quite glorious, she thought, and at moments took her mind from Everett. But, when she returned to Henri the next morning, he pouted and sniffled and complained he was going to die very, very soon. "We must hurry; we must do the rescue soon," he said.

Lucy knew that morning that she had made a grave mistake making love to Henri and taking his virginity. He was sick, she knew, sick with jealousy. Love sick and now jealous of Gilles and soon to be jealous of Everett. Day after day his eyes followed her around the small room, not so much with lust, but with the desperate sadness of a lonely puppy dog. He wanted to hug her, caress her in the moonlight, adore her. She cursed her own drunken hunger for lust that night and thought of Gilles and Everett and told herself that she must not give in to Henri. She remembered her past confusion over Christian shame with Father Mercier's scoldings in the church at Ste-Anicet and her mother clucking quietly beside her on the hard bench when he spoke of eternal flames for the sin of lust. On their walk home that morning her mother said, "To love cannot be a sin. Do not let them scare you with all this talk of eternal flames."

"Then why do you go to their church if you do not believe them?" Lucy asked.

"Because Jesus forgives us and lifts our guilt," she said.

"Then what is a sin?" Lucy asked.

"Whatever makes you feel guilty, my dear child."

"But they are trying to make us feel guilty about so many things."

"They think that is their duty, but God has already given us this curse."

"I'm very confused," Lucy complained.

"It is *they* who are confused. You must learn to listen to your own heart. This matter of sex. It is not a sin unless it is done with theft in your heart. Only then you must ask for Jesus' forgiveness."

Lucy had not been to church or confession in many years, but she knew that what she had done with Henri had been a sin. She had been drunk, but her mother had warned her about how alcohol was really an evil spirit that stole away your guilt at night and returned it in the morning. It had always seemed such a wise warning, but her mother drank whiskey often and was drunk many nights as Lucy grew older. One of those nights when her mother was too drunk to cook, Lucy asked her, "If alcohol is an evil spirit, why do you drink so much?"

"It steals my guilt and lets me sleep."

"Doesn't it return your guilt in the morning?"

"I confess each week, and it is only three Hail Mary's."

Lucy tried to be kind to Henri, and several times crossed herself and began to say Hail Mary's but never finished, her mind wandering to Gilles about whom she felt no guilt yet despite her trickery.

Later that afternoon, she and Gilles walked along the stout wall guarding Lachine from British ships that might someday soon lay siege in their effort to eject the French from North America. Between notches etched for cannons, they leaned shoulder to shoulder gazing out at the frozen river to the west. A jagged strip of black water marked the passage of the crossing barge docked now on the distant southern shore. Chunks of ice floated in the thick, black water and picked up speed down river as they entered the Lachine rapids for a wild ride to Montreal.

She held her hands cupped almost as if in prayer. Lucy loved the great river and wished for a moment she could reveal herself and take Gilles on the ice boat flying across the vast sweep of ice faster than the wind. She wished she could show him the marshes in her canoe, show him the trees where the night heron roosted.

She sighed deeply and spoke softly, "In the spring the red-winged blackbirds sing mating songs, and the males puff their feathers and show their red patches to attract girlfriends."

Gilles smiled. "You like this river in the spring."

"I love this river all of the time," she said.

"In France I sail a little boat I built," he said.

"I love to sail," she said.

"Really."

"Oh, yes. So you built your own boat. Where did you sail?"

"At Le Havre, a fishing village where the Seine enters the ocean. It is a very beautiful place."

"I sail a canoe," Lucy said, "and in the winter an ice boat."

"Nooo."

"Yes, yes. I will take you some time."

Gilles reached his hand over and covered hers.

His hand was cold.

"How do you manage to stay so warm?" he asked.

"It must be the company."

He reached over and cupped both hands around hers. He shivered.

"It is not so cold in France?" she asked.

"Not very often. Usually it is much warmer than here although we think it is cold. But then we come here, and we learn what cold *really* is."

"It will be cold here until April, and then the ice will go, and the birds return, and soon you Frenchmen complain it is too hot."

Gilles laughed softly. After a pause, he asked, "May I ask you a question?"

"Yes, of course."

"Why do you do what you do?"

Lucy wished she could tell him the truth, tell him that she did not *do* what he thought she did. "Only in the winter," she said. "In the summer I fish and sometimes trade furs brought to me by friends."

"Your friends do not trap in the winter?" he said with surprise.

"Oh, yes, but I do not like the cold so much as you think." The sun peeked out from a row of angry clouds, and suddenly the harbor turned golden. "Besides, this is my last winter in Lachine. You've spoiled me," she said.

"Spoiled you?"

"Since I've met you, I have no interest in other men."

"I'm glad of that. This is not a good life for a woman such as yourself."

"Why do you say that?" she asked, unthreading her hands, and covering his with hers.

"I think that I like you too much to share with anyone else."

Lucy bowed her head. She could feel his body tremble from cold. She put her arm around him. He turned, and they hugged against each other. The sun dipped back behind the clouds, and the afternoon turned quickly dark and gloomy, the golden glow swallowed in gray. She pressed her face into the crook of his neck, and even here, his skin was cool.

"Let's go crawl under the covers," she whispered, "before you freeze to death."

"Ah, yes, yes," he laughed, "I am a very delicate boy."

Lucy opened her coat and pressed against him. She wished she could unthread her weave of deceptions. That she could not saddened her more each day as she realized how much she enjoyed each moment with this man. And as they made love these days, she no longer thought of Everett, no longer wanted to.

* * *

Ella jammed wood into the cook stove as Jamie shuffled from his room, his eyes puffy from sleep, and sagged onto the bench at the kitchen table. He had taken lately to sleeping late, and Ella was considering a reprimand.

She grasped the empty wood basket with an irritated scowl at her son and opened the hut door. She gasped with shock as Gordon, Everett's Indian trapper friend, stood not a foot from the door, his wrists crossed, two pistols forming a 'v' beneath his round and ruddy chin.

Ella stepped back, startled and speechless. Gordon moved past her and placed the guns on the kitchen table. Jamie gazed up in slack-jawed amazement.

"Gordon," she croaked, trying to be pleasant but not altogether sure his intentions would be friendly.

He nodded but did not smile. Instead, he turned and opened the hut door for Jean-Robert, his youngest son, in his early teens learning to be a hunter. The boy was tall and razor thin. He ducked his head and entered. He stood behind his father in awkward, rigid silence.

"Where Evert?" Gordon asked.

"Would you like coffee?"

Gordon nodded yes with one abrupt drop of his chin. "Evert not here," Gordon said. "No track."

"No, he's not here. He was taken by the French navy," she said grasping the pot and four tin cups, arranging them on the table. "He's been gone two months."

"You alone in de hut?" Gordon asked.

"Well, Jamie is here," she said gesturing toward her son, "but yes, we're alone."

She poured coffee into the cups. "Would you like to sit?"

Gordon shook his head no with a similar, single abrupt twist of his neck to the left. He raised the searing cup and drank deeply, oblivious to its scalding heat. He placed the cup down on the table. "Evert be soldier for dem?"

"No, they captured him against his will. He took them fish, and they kept him."

"Know de river good, dat's it, ey." Gordon said, his deep red-brown face glowing from wind burn and blinding sun glaring off the snow.

Gordon looked around the hut. "You no ready for some bad injun, ey. No gun. No knife, not-ting."

Ella blushed. "Well, yes, we have some guns..."

Gordon rolled his eyes and shook his head no. "I leave de boy. Good warrior. He stay wid you. Protect yellow hair. Evert, he come back, bring me de boy, ey."

Gordon turned to his son and spoke in his tribal tongue for more than a minute. The boy did not nod or react.

"Gordon, I don't think we need to have him stay," Ella said finally.

Gordon chuckled derisively to himself. "He stay. Be ready for de bad injun. Evert, he know. Now I go. Hunt de beaver, deer, bear. My people hungry. After de ice go, I find Evert. He come before then, he bring me de boy, ey."

Gordon was not to be deterred, and in a few minutes had all of Everett's weapons retrieved and was checking them for fresh powder and caps. He sent Jean-Robert to their canoe, and he returned with blankets, bow and arrows, and another flintlock rifle. He spoke to the boy again for several minutes, them hugged him silently, and left the hut without saying good-by.

Ella followed him out to his canoe perched on the ice at the point of the island.

"Gordon," she called to him as he pushed the boat away from the shore.

Gordon turned.

"I'll teach him to read, then."

Gordon nodded yes, then waved and began tugging the fur-laden canoe over the ice.

For the next few hours, Jean-Robert silently arranged the hut. His bed would be against the door. He placed guns in various positions for quick retrieval. He carved a hole low in the door where he could look out when in bed and another up high so they could inspect visitors before they were allowed to enter.

"You speak English?" Jamie finally asked.

Jean-Robert stopped and nodded yes with the same abrupt motion as his father.

"I'm Jamie, then," he said, holding out his hand to shake hands.

Jean-Robert nodded and reached for Jamie's hand, lifting it and then snapping it down abruptly as if shaking a dusty rag. "My name Jean-Robert. Pleased your met."

"And I'm Ella," she said, engaging in a similar hand shake.

"My name Jean-Robert. Pleased your met," he said.

Ella served them soup and asked them to retrieve more wood. She was pleased to see that Jean-Robert was quick and efficient, and by evening they brought a string of fresh perch they'd caught through a hole in the ice. By then the two boys were speaking in a steady chatter, and when Jean-Robert smiled, she noted his handsome teeth and sparkling dark eyes. For the first time since Henri had left, she felt optimistic again and glad for good company for her son.

* * *

Lucy brushed her hair in front of the elegant mirror. It was time to make her move, to test her plan. She would have preferred waiting a few more days. She loved their walks and the deep warmth of the their room in the Grand Hotel and was so much enjoying Gilles, a man of such very considerable charm and who possessed such a calm and gentle manner. Most native Frenchmen she had known were loud, arrogant, pushy, and always angling for advantage. She would have much preferred tricking one of them rather than this dear, kind young officer whom she liked as much as any man she had met in years. But she didn't dare wait much longer for fear that Henri would come unhinged and muck up the entire rescue in a fit of depressed and hysteric jealousy. Each day he was becoming more difficult, more moody. And each day grew more difficult for her, each deception more strained as her affection for Gilles grew.

That night with Gilles, she feigned a pouty, distracted mood. She pretended to be aloof and bored as Gilles read a newspaper. She looked at him through the mirror.

"You have a crooked nose, did you know that, Gilles?" she said finally in an exasperated tone.

He lowered the paper. "Does this bother you?"

"Well, I thought you were perfect, but now as I look at you through the mirror, I see that you aren't."

"Are you all right, Lucy?" he asked putting the paper aside.

"I'm bored," she said with a girlish pout.

"Is there anything I can do to assuage this *boredom* you are feeling?"

She turned now, brightening. She took an excited breath, then turned back to the mirror, "It's too silly a request."

"What could be too silly from you, my dear Lucy?"

"I am not so dear as you think," she said mournfully.

"What, Lucy? What can I do to assuage your boredom?"

"Take me to your ship."

"Well, of course. Why is that silly?"

"At night."

He nodded, "Ahhh, oui, at night, that is more dangerous." He paused and massaged his chin, deep in thought. "Perhaps it is possible. The captain is away for a week. But it is still risky. The marine guards dislike me. I would need to fool them. They would think nothing of betraying me."

She turned now, twirling her hair thoughtfully. "I would like to make love to you on your ship," she said.

His eyes widened.

"I knew it would be silly."

"This is not silly," he said solemnly. "It is dangerous."

"That is why I want to do it."

Gilles' pale face flushed.

* * *

Henri had objected strenuously to this part of the plan. Why was this love-making necessary, he protested. She countered, "To be sure he is disarmed. To be sure I have him in a completely vulnerable situation. To be sure we are entirely alone. To be sure he makes sure we are in complete privacy and that we are left alone. To be sure he eliminates all risk of danger. To be sure we have time to escape," she lied.

Henri rolled his eyes. "I think you are falling for this handsome young officer," he muttered sadly.

* * *

She knew, of course, that Henri's final words to her were true and that she must now, more urgently than ever, bring the plan to rapid completion lest she lose her will. She studied her own face in the nightstand mirror trying to see if her lies could be betrayed in her dark, reluctant eyes. This was the moment. Her heart beat loudly. She brushed her hair as slowly and languidly as possible but could feel her hand trembling. Gilles paced the room, caressing his chin, deep in thought.

Finally he stopped and turned to her. "Yes. Tomorrow night."

And for this she felt a shudder of guilt. Now the trap was set. She sipped brandy at her nightstand and recalled her mother's warnings. To love with theft in her heart.

"Will I meet your friend, Monsieur Everett?" she finally asked, struggling to keep her focus on the plan.

He looked at her, puzzled.

"If there is such danger, perhaps he should guard your cabin door with one of his knives."

Gilles laughed. "Actually, I would like to have you meet Monsieur Everett. I think he does not believe me when I have told to him I have met this beautiful Lucy. He thinks I am making this up to entertain him."

"You have told him."

"Do you mind?"

"No, no. I am flattered. Have you told him about... what we do?"

"Oh, no, no. I am not that kind of man. I do not reveal intimate secrets. A man who reveals the secrets of a beautiful woman is doomed to lose her."

Lucy lowered her eyes sadly. This was not a man she wished to betray, but she knew she must. It was either him or Everett. It must be him, she thought, it must.

It was a clear, crisp, bitterly cold day with a brisk wind from the north. The main channel was frozen, though still dangerously thin where the water rushed.

That afternoon they hauled the ice boat onto the crossing barge from the south shore and crossed the river to the Port of Lachine. A muscular, bearded crewman pulled the barge along rope pulleys the captain had rigged to polls across the width of the river. As they crossed the channel, Lucy studied the ice. "Comment épais est la glace ci? Dans le canal? How thick is the ice here? At the channel?" she asked the captain.

He held up his fingers to indicate a bit more than an inch.

"Est-il coffre-fort pour traverser? Is it safe to cross?" she asked.

The captain smirked. "Danger," he said, "Do not walk near here," he said pointing and moving his arm back and forth in the channel area west of the barge route.

"Is there a safe place?"

"To walk or for de ice boat?" he asked.

"Both."

"Go west along de boat basin on dis side. Two hundred meters dis side of de harbor entrance. Cross der. De current is slowed dere by de rock pile beneath de surface. Dat is where de ice fishermen cross with dere shacks."

"Auprés le vaisseau de guerre. Near the great warship?"

He thought for a moment. "Yes, it ees not far."

"Within cannon shot," she smiled.

"Ah oui," he laughed.

"Pour le bateau a glace. You must go fast for de ice boat. Très rapidement."

"How fast?"

"Très bon galop pour un cheval. The gallop for de horse," he said.

Henri shivered and rolled his eyes.

"Will the wind hold?" Lucy asked.

"Oh, yes. We have thees wind three-four days, may-be."

"At night?"

The captain puckered his mouth in thought. Then he nodded yes. "It ees okay at de night. Lots de wind. Très froid. Very, very cold."

Henri turned away and limped to the gunnel. He looked down at the mushy soup of broken ice and water sliding past. He turned to the captain. "How long does a man live who falls through de ice?"

The captain laughed skeptically and puckered. "Five minutes and den you sleep." Then he shrugged. "Eet does not hurt."

Henri stared at the man.

Lucy winked at the captain.

He smiled and patted her arm, then moved toward the bow to prepare for landing.

That evening Gilles gave most of the crew shore leave and ordered the marine standing guard at the gang plank to escort the bread lady to the ship's galley and notify him of her arrival. Lucy inched up to the ship hauling a satchel stuffed with fresh, steaming bread.

"Bon soir. J'ai le pain pour le capitaine," she told the guard.

"Oui, mademoiselle. Par ici, s'il vous plait," he said stiffly.

The marine shouldered the satchel and hauled it up the gangway to the galley door. He stepped through and squeezed the swollen satchel through the narrow door.

Everett was dozing in the corner of the galley next to the wood stove. He awoke to the staggeringly wonderful odor of fresh bread, and when he saw Lucy, his jaw dropped. But he quickly disguised his surprise to avoid the scrutiny of the galley's attentive marine guard.

"J'ai besoin de notifier l'officier. Ses pain sont arriver." Lucy's marine guard escort told the galley guard he would notify Gilles. He turned to Lucy. "Pardon. Moment, s'il vous plait."

Lucy snuck a look at Everett, then turned to the galley officer and held up a loaf. "Pain, monsieur?"

"Oui, Merci," he said. She tore a piece off and handed it to him. Then she turned toward Everett. "Pain, monsieur?"

"Celui est prisonnier. Celui ne parle pas Français."

"Un imbécile?" She asked the marine.

"Anglais-Américain," the marine smiled.

"La meme, the same," she said.

The marine chuckled and chewed his bread.

Everett rolled his eyes.

"Je donnera l'imbécile une morceau de pain," she said, tearing off another piece and tossing it to Everett.

He caught the piece and bit into it with savage eagerness, his eyes fixed on Lucy's impassive gaze. Clearly she was there to rescue him, but Everett did not know how this might be accomplished. He raised his chin so that she could see his neck iron. He pushed his feet out in front of him so she could see his leg irons and heavy chain.

"Good bread," Everett said.

She looked to the marine and shrugged.

"Peut-être il dit que le pain est bon?" the marine shrugged with uncertainty.

"Mais oui, of course," she said to the guard huffily, "You like da bread?" she said loudly to Everett.

"Yes, ma'am."

Lucy could barely resist laughing at Everett's familiar twang.

"You wait...ah... da few minutes," she answered loudly, "Den I give to you da special...ah..." she eyed the marine to see if he was following her English. To test him, she asked without looking at him, "Officer, would you like more bread?"

The officer ignored her, apparently not understanding her English. She walked over to the guard, tore off a piece of bread, handed it to him, and said directly to him, "In a couple of hours I will be back and you be ready."

The officer smiled and chewed, having understood nothing.

"Cough if you have understood," she said.

The marine chewed. Everett coughed.

When Gilles entered the galley, the marine stood sharply and saluted.

"Amener cet homme au brig," he told the marine, returning the salute and waving toward Everett. " Je payerais pour le pain."

Lucy eyed Everett but could see that Gilles was removing the guard so that he could smuggle her aboard. The marine pointed to the door, then gave Everett a harsh push. He stumbled through the galley door, chains clanking.

When the marine was gone, Gilles winked at Lucy, emptied the satchel of bread on the large galley table.

"Suivez moi," he said, ducking through the door and hurrying down the narrow galley way.

His room was tiny. They had to squeeze together just to close the door. Gilles held his finger to his mouth. "Shhh. Pas de bruit," he whispered. He took her shawl and hung it from a hook near his small bed sunk into an opening in the wall hardly larger than a coffin. Below the bed were shelves and single plank for a desk. He opened a cupboard above the bed, fetched a bottle of rum, and poured her a glass. He drank straight from the bottle. They whispered in French.

"Is this so dangerous for you?"

He laughed, "Ah, yes."

"I thought the captain was away."

"Yes, but the marine guards can't be trusted and are not easily fooled."

"Who was the prisoner?"

"That was Everett, the pilot I spoke of."

"Ahh."

"Later I will bring him to the galley again. The brig is very cold. I let him sleep in the galley by the stove."

"He can't escape from the galley?"

"Past the marine guards?" he whispered, puckering doubtfully.

"They never fall asleep?"

"The captain has them whipped if they even nod." He took a long drink of rum. "I'm sorry but there is not much room here."

She shrugged and finished her rum. He poured her more. They toasted, then kissed.

Later, when they were both abundantly drunk from the potent run, they made love in the tiny bunk. But she could find no joy, no lust, no desire that night and fucked in a distracted, sweaty tangle of bumped knees and elbows in his tiny bunk as she imagined a whore might fuck a desperate client lost in his own lust.

When they were finished, Lucy did not want think about the rescue. She lay in the dim candle light and wished Everett were not a captive. For a moment she considered taking Gilles prisoner so she could somehow redeem this tawdry night, but that would only increase the urgency and size of the search parties and bloat the bounties. She would miss him and wished she could confess her purpose and urge him to believe she cared for him. He would hate her after this night, *that* she knew.

"Will you return to France after the war?" she asked sadly.

He started from a doze. "Pardon, Lucy?"

"Will you go back to France after the war is over?"

"I think yes. But first I must survive the war. And before that I must survive the winter. And before that I must survive having smuggled you aboard!"

"These things you will survive. It is *us* that you may not," she said.

"Shhhhh."

They both fell silent and motionless as footsteps echoed in the passageway. Then passed by. Then Gilles wiggled himself out of the bunk, put on his pants, shirt and boots.

"Where are you going?" she asked as a bleak wave of fear and remorse rose up in her, the plan now beyond her capacity to reverse.

"It is time for me to make an appearance. It is my watch, and the guards change in a few minutes. I'll be back before long."

"What of the prisoner?" she asked, her heart thudding.

He turned and looked at her curiously. "What do you mean?"

"It is the coldest night of the winter," she said weaving her lie yet deeper into the depths of his trust.

"Ah, yes. He's in the brig, isn't he? I had forgotten. Monsieur Everett will owe you many thanks. I had forgotten about my clever little trick," he smiled. "His teeth must be chattering."

As he finished buttoning his tunic, she grasped his arm and pulled him down to her and kissed him softly on the lips, feeling him already tugging absently away from her thinking, of course, that he would return and perhaps make love again. But he would face, instead, a gun to his head, and she dreaded the look of betrayal she must face when he discovered she had tricked him all these nights.

* * *

Outside along the quay, Henri's teeth were chattering miserably as he waited for Lucy and Everett to escape. It had been three hours, at least, and the north wind scraped his face like a dull knife. His toes were numb, his fingers stinging with cold. *She is in there fucking the handsome Gilles,* Henri thought. *She is in there seducing the elegant French officer, le salaud. She has fallen for the man. She loves the man. And I am out here in the fucking frigid ice. It is as Jamie said. The snot is freezing in my nose. C'est comme çà. When we actually get this miserable boat going, it will be ten times colder, and they will be chasing us, shooting as us. Merde. I have to piss, but I have lost my penis to the cold. It has disappeared somewhere in my belly. Besides, my fingers are so cold, I could never feel it and then I piss all over myself and then it freezes and there is frost bite and my penis is forever gone.* But his stomach ached from the pressure to piss. The wind whistled from above the quay wall. Henri groaned miserably.

Finally he could hold himself no longer. He blew on his cold fingers and nudged up closer to the quay wall. At the edge there was a crack where water squirted up from time to time with shifts in the river ice. Henri put his hands down his pants. He let out a little chirp from the cold touch of his fingers on the last refuge of warmth in his body. He fumbled helplessly and unsuccessfully with the buttons. Then he pulled down the front of his pants and pissed on the quay wall. Steam rose from his projectile. *Bon Dieu. I have created yellow ice, my signature in yellow paint on the wall of misery. This is insane. This is hell. This is the seventh circle of hell, and she is in there fucking the handsome young French officer, and it is only a trick of fate that I am not there and he here.* Henri finally finished pissing and sat back on the ice boat. He sighed. *At least I won't die from a burst bladder.* He lifted the bateau seat and pulled out a jug of rum and took a long drink. He savored the stream of heat searing down his throat and dribbling into a lovely hot molten pool deep in his belly. He thought of Everett and looked forward to seeing him. But then Everett would enjoy Lucy's favors, and that would be a new form of torture. Why, he asked himself. *Why am I not her choice. We make love and she drops me like a cold turd and refuses me each time I beg her pathetically to let us repeat the grand beauty and splendor of our first time, my first time. Not her first time, la salope. Why do I know all these men who enjoy the favors of all the many promiscuous women of the world, and then I find one such woman, and she offers me the miracle gift of my virginity and then it is over, over, over. Finis. Pourquoi faut je souffrir?*

Henri could no longer feel his feet. Even his heel injury, always an aggravation, was utterly gone. It was as though he were walking on artificial legs made of wood from the knee down. It was as though these feet belonged to some other.

Henri tried to imagine Everett and Lucy making their escape. *What the hell are they doing, and what if they get caught? What the hell will I do with this crazy boat? And how do I rescue them both? If there are gun shots, what do I do. Should I raise the sails. Can I raise the sails?* He looked at the various coils of ropes in the dim light of street lanterns casting deep shadows along the quay wall. He traced the line to a pulley that would raise the sail. The other was attached to the end of the boom. It looked easy enough. Just like any sailboat. *Not that I am any good at sailing a boat*, he thought. He tried to imagine flying over the ice at the speeds they had attained coming to Lachine. *Yes, I can make this work if I must*, he told himself.

Then Henri heard Lucy call out to him from a distance. He pulled the boat out of the shadows and aimed it westward. Soon he could hear them running. He could hear other voices, yelling in the distance. They reached the quay panting breathlessly from their run. Henri could hear the clank of Everett's chains. He looked up and saw Everett climbing over the quay wall. Then he pushed himself and jumped, a fall of nearly ten feet. He landed with huge thunk and clatter of iron. The ice cracked and bled water. Henri hurried to Everett and dragged him away from the crack. Then Lucy climbed over and jumped. She landed on her feet which then slipped out from under her, flipping her backwards, her head slamming the ice with a hollow thud. She lay motionless for a moment. Henri hurried to her as Everett raised the sail which immediately set to flapping furiously.

Henri rushed to Lucy. "Are you all right?"

She groaned and held her head.

Voices called out still from a distance but closer.

Everett hurried over, dragged her by her coat, and lifted her onto the boat.

"Get in," he said in a loud whisper.

Henri jumped onto the boat, Everett snapped the sheet line, the sail filled with a thud, and the boat nudged forward. Everett pushed the ice with his foot. The boat inched forward a bit faster. Everett lifted Lucy onto the seat. She leaned forward holding her head. He patted her back.

"Hold on," he said.

The ice boat quickly picked up speed. It moved noisily along the edge of the quay. One of the marine guards reached the edge of the quay, raised his pistol and took aim. A flame leapt from the barrel and then a loud crack erupted, and a ball ripped through the sail. Another guard rushed to the edge and steadied his musket on a piling. He took aim, fired, the flame burst from the barrel, and the musket cracked loudly. There was a muffled thud.

"Fuck," Everett groaned, shaking his left arm.

"Ees a hit?" Henri yelped.

Everett held the rudder and set their coarse. In the distance the great warship loomed. They would pass by her, close enough for shots, close enough for the cannon. The loud scrape of the runners drowned out any other sound but Henri could see frantic movements on the deck. Several cannon barrels poked out from the ship's gunnels.

"Mon Dieu," Henri groaned.

By the time they approached the vessel, the ice boat was moving at ten or twelve knots. Within a hundred feet, Everett leaned hard on the rudder, and they veered out away from the ship. Henri could hear screams aboard the ship.

And as they passed the stern, angled diagonally away from the boat but still within a hundred feet, one of the cannon's erupted. Flames burst from the barrel, and a huge steel ball flew past their bow with an audible hiss. The huge ball skipped along the ice off their port bow and skidded into the distance. Then there was another burst, this time grape shot. The mast tore, and hot shreds of steel smashed into the ice boat hull. Rifle shots followed, but the sail held, and soon they were safely away from musket range. Henri watched off their own stern as flames leapt from another cannon, but the shot was far astern, and the huge ball clattered across the ice into the darkness.

"Everybody okay?" Everett yelled.

"Oui," Henri yelled.

Henri leaned over Lucy, his arm over her shoulder and spoke into her ear. "Are you injured, mademoiselle? Es te nui, Lucy?"

She raised her hand and waved them off, but held her throbbing head.

Henri watched in the growing distance as men from the ship rushed out onto the ice. Flames leapt from muskets, but the cracks were almost entirely overwhelmed by the loud clatter of the runners and rudder hammering the ice.

"Hold onto your asses, folks," Everett yelled above the clatter. "We're approaching the channel. Pray for fucking ice."

The ice boat was approaching twenty knots now, and the clatter slowly changed to a high-pitched frantic buzz.

Each of them froze in dread, their watering eyes staring into the piercing wind, trying to detect the dangerous black beneath the dim half-moon light. Their speed held, the vibrations eased as they crossed onto fresh black ice. For a few moments it looked as though they were flying above pure black oblivion. This soft, pliant ice caused only a whisper at the runners. Everett held his breath and braced himself for a sudden jolt that would send them tumbling into the frigid river. But soon the vibrations increased again as they approached hard ice on the far side of the channel. Everett breathed again. They had made it across the main channel. And unless they had the misfortune of hitting a roiling spring or upsurge from a lesser, unknown channel, they were probably safe from thin ice. But now he became aware of the deep burning ache in his left arm and the hot, slippery blood soaking the arm of his coat and flowing in narrow hot streams along his fingers. He had been struck in the upper arm. He flexed it and suffered a sudden searing pain. "Bloody fuckin' hell," he muttered, his head feeling dizzy and his eyeballs aching in their sockets. "Henri, take this fuckin' thing," he tried to raise his injured arm to point, but it hurt too much. Henri climbed over the seat and stood up against Everett.

"Take the rudder," Everett moaned groggily. He felt Henri's hand take the tiller, and in a moment, Everett fumbled forward and fainted in a heap on the seat beside Lucy.

Henri was not a skilled sailor, but he knew enough to maintain his course at the same angle of the moon on a very broad reach heading southwest. He watched as Lucy slowly tried to pull Everett into a more secure position onto the seat. She reached down Everett's neck pushing her hand down his sleeve. When she pulled it out, she turned and shouted up to Henri, "Take us to shore." Then she held up her bloodied hand and indicated a more southerly course.

Henri eased the tiller, and eased off the sail line, to follow the wind. For a few minutes on this course, it felt almost warm as the boat ran with the wind, absorbing its motion in almost perfect stillness.

As he approached the shore, Lucy climbed over the seat and took the tiller. There was danger at the shoreline-rocks, thin spots where springs flowed invisibly beneath the surface ice.

She lowered the sail several hundred feet from shore and let the ice boat coast. As they approached the dark shoreline, she lifted the brake lever. It scraped the ice loudly, ice chips and snow flying into the air behind and sprinkling them as the wind overtook them. Then she jammed the rudder and the boat spun around facing the wind.

"Hold on," she shouted. The boat's momentum carried them hard into shore where they struck a bank of snow. Lucy was thrown off the stern, and Henri and Everett tumbled onto the stern as the seat braces broke. But, they were safe, and after a quick inspection, Lucy flung the seat away. She and Henri pulled Everett up the bank. Their legs broke through a hard crust, but they managed to pull Everett to a clearing in a clump cedars.

"Find wood. We need a fire."

Henri did not bother to protest the wisdom of building a fire only a few miles from the ship. He could only hope that Everett would survive his wound. If they were caught, at least they would not freeze. They would be treated well by the French Navy. Surely, they would be treated well.

Lucy lit a fire and removed Everett's coat. His arm was drenched with blood. She ripped open his sleeve with her knife and inspected the dark, purple hole in his bicep, which she cleaned with snow. Everett woke several times, then fainted again and again. She made a bandage from Everett's sleeve and tied the wound tightly.

"I think he will be okay," she muttered to Henri who stood shivering helplessly over the fire, trying to block its light. The wind whistled across the river and up the bank, whispering quietly through the cedar branches which creaked icily from the sway of the gusts.

After an hour or so, Lucy kicked snow over the fire. It hissed and smoked and soon died to a few hot coals. She put Everett's coat back on, and the three of them huddled together, their backs to the wind, embraced against the cold.

By morning Henri was frozen to the core. His feet and legs were numb, wooden, clumsy. But, they were alive. Lucy gave Everett clumps of crusty snow to eat. He was pale, stiff, groggy but managed to move. Lucy dug up several rocks, and hammered at Everett's chains with loud metallic clanks that echoed in the frigid morning air. She and Henri took turns for over an hour until they broke the chain near his neck and at both ankles. They could not remove the thick, steel rings around his neck and ankles, but at least he could move freely. Henri and Lucy lifted him to return to the ice boat when they heard a loud click.

A trapper stood a few feet from the ice boat, his musket held on them as they appeared out of the trees.

The man was small and covered with a thick beard and long greasy hair. Bright blue eyes and red lips were all they could see through the tangle of hair and his clothing fashioned entirely of fur scraps. "I like dis boat," he said. "I tank you," he muttered, throwing a bundle of furs and several traps onto its deck. He pushed the bow onto the ice, and then sat on the stern holding his gun on them. He pushed with his feet. Slowly, watching them carefully and keeping his gun on them, he pushed the boat step by step deeper and deeper onto the ice. When he was a hundred feet or so away, he placed his gun on the deck, still angled toward them. His eyes flashing quickly between them and the tangle of rigging, he raised the sail and set a tack to the west. He secured the gun and held the tiller, and then waved slowly as the ice boat picked up speed.

"Fuck," Lucy muttered from lips and cheeks so cold she could hardly form words.

They watched helplessly as he headed west, then a mile or so out, he changed tacks and headed toward Lachine.

"Maybe he'll have a surprise when he reaches the ship," she said. "Come on. We've got a damned long walk."

Though wobbly at first, Everett was able to walk. After hammering at the chains, Henri could now feel his feet and hands and felt almost passably warm. He remembered Jamie's truism about chopping wood. He wondered what wisdom there might be about avoiding starvation. After a mile or so of wandering in the difficult crust, they found a firm trail heading west. Twice Lucy stopped to vomit and several times she staggered with dizziness.

"Is Mademoiselle all right?" Henri asked, patting her shoulder sympathetically.

"I feel as though a fucking bear has been chewing on my head," she groaned.

They walked slowly along the trail. By mid morning Everett had taken the lead. At one point he stopped, held his hand to stop them, then held his fingers over his lips to indicate quiet. He pulled Lucy's knife from her belt, and flung it.

A white jackrabbit squeaked several times, his hind paws digging wild-eyed at the knife sticking into its side. Everett hurried to the rabbit, lifted it by its feet, grasped its head, and snapped his neck. He brought the rabbit back to them, lifted it, cut off its head and held it above his head to drink blood from the arteries in its neck. He quickly stanched the flow with his thumb, moved over to Lucy who tipped back her head and opened her mouth. Everett released his thumb, and a thin stream of blood arched into her mouth. Henri never thought he'd engage in this sort of cuisine but did not hesitate as Everett raised the rabbit over his head. When the blood was gone, Everett handed Lucy the rabbit and rubbed his aching arm. She took her knife from him and skinned the rabbit, and in a few minutes they had ripped it apart and eaten it raw, their faces sticky with blood.

By afternoon they'd eaten two more rabbits, and the day had turned gray and warmer as they plodded along the path. From time to time, the path opened to the river. They stopped at one clearing and sat on a log looking out on the vast, bleak expanse, the snow a vibrant white beneath churlish dark clouds. Snow flakes as big as thumb nails swirled down from gusty twists of wind.

Lucy sat with her head huddled in her arms.

"You okay, luv?" Everett muttered.

She rubbed a huge lump at the back of her head. "What day is it?" she asked.

Everett and Henri shrugged helplessly.

"Where we been?" she asked. "How'd we git here?"

"I was hoping you'd remember," Everett said. "I got no fucking idea," he joked.

Henri stood and checked her head. He felt the bump and hissed. "The rescue. You remember? Souviens tu de la rescue?"

She shook her head no, then groaned at the movement. "I don't know where the fuck we are or what we're doing."

"What is your name?" Henri asked.

She looked at him blankly.

"Qu'est-ce-que c'est ta nom?" he asked again.

She looked at Everett, her eyes moving nervously over his face as if trying to read the answer from his eyes. She shrugged.

"I'll be fucked if I know," she said lowering her face in her hands.

"Mon Dieu," Henri muttered tiredly. "Thees is not good. Lucy?" he asked.

She did not move.

Henri turned to Everett. "She has the concussion from de head bang."

"She really don't know her own name?" Everett asked.

"Nossir," Henri said, watching the snow accumulate on Lucy's shoulders and hair.

"Thees concussion ees very danger. Thees not good all da walk-ing."

"We ain't got no other choice, Henri. We stay here we freeze, we git caught by them Frenchies. We got to keep going." He looked up at the sky, then down the path. "We got to go now or we lose the trail in the new snow."

"We to find a house, a shelter. She must rest, Monsieur Everett. She could die from thees bang on da head."

Everett stood, helped Lucy up. "Yer name's Lucy. Yer mama's an Iroquois tribal leader. Can you remember that, yeah?" he asked softly.

She looked at him helplessly.

By late afternoon, the path was a dim, soft outline in six inches of new snow. In a few hours there would be no trace remaining. Several times Lucy stumbled and had to position herself between Everett and Henri on the narrow path. By now her eyes were dim and droopy, her movements sloppy as though she were drunk.

As darkness fell, Everett spotted a clearing to their left. He lifted Lucy and carried her through the deep snow. At the edge of the clearing was an Indian long house, and as Everett turned to escape back to the trail, five Iroquois warriors moved in a half moon toward them, guns raised. The leader, an angular dark-eyed man in his late twenties motioned with his gun barrel toward the long house. The other Indians were boys in their mid-teens. No one spoke as they trudged grimly through the snow.

Henri felt an extraordinary bleakness rise through his exhausted body. He was so discouraged by now that his fear of torture seemed distant, abstract. He was too tired to resist, too hopelessly depressed to conjure an impulse to run. He felt himself to be utterly in the hands of Everett. He could only hope that Lucy would remember, that suddenly they would recognize her as some lost sister or cousin or family friend. Or perhaps they would have heard of the bounty and would return them to the French Navy. As he mulled these thoughts in his groggy, sluggish mind, he watched as if from afar, the lead Indian speak something to Everett.

"I ain't no Frenchie," Everett said.

And then the Indian snapped the butt of his gun into the side of Everett's head with such quickness that it seemed Everett had fallen for no cause other than exhaustion, and as he fell, the Indian grasped Lucy's coat and dragged her through the long house door, the last Henri would see of her. It occurred to him slowly that Everett's last words offered some possible glimpse of hope that these were friends of the French.

"Bonjour, merci, mes amis," Henri said trying to emerge from his gloom, trying to pretend delight and relief. " Je suis très content de vous voire. Ce trapper prenais moi ... peut-être peut-être pour me tuer."

The four boys circled around him. The tallest of them spoke, "Bonjour, monsieur. Il faut attend re ci."

"Oui." Henri said, affecting cheerfulness and a dim smile.

Chapter 4

Everett awoke groggily beneath a blanket of snow, his jaw and head throbbing. The snow had melted from his face, but he was otherwise covered by a foot of fluffy new snow. He could feel the warmth of a body at his belly and saw in the dim, pink dawn light a mound of snow curled from his knees to his chest. He assumed it was Lucy, and he lay still to allow her rest a few more minutes. He knew he must not move, in case he was being watched.

He moved his eyes to detect any presence near him. His right eye was swollen nearly shut. He listened for any sounds of the Indians inside the long hut. The stillness was profound. Maybe I'm dead, he thought. But why would I have a splitting headache if I was dead. He tried to press his jaws closed, and a piercing pain shot from his chin to the back of his ear. Something's broke for sure, he thought. He moved his tongue inside his mouth and could feel swelling along his lower jaw. He felt the sharpness of broken teeth. He became aware of the cold of the metal collar around his neck.

He prepared himself to jump to his feet. He would run to trees, then wait and plan his next move from there. He took a deep breath, leapt to his feet, and as he did so, the body next to him leapt up and growled. A dog. Everett was so stunned and confused that he stood there and watched as this large, gray dog shook off the snow, looked up at him and then wagged its tail. The dog stepped gingerly through the deep snow and peaked in the long house door. It was open. Tracks, covered by several hours of snow, formed the outline of a path south into the woods. The dog entered the long house, and as Everett studied the path, the dog re-appeared in the doorway, wagging its tail, perhaps in anticipation of breakfast.

Everett moved to the door and looked in. It was completely empty. He walked inside and held his hand over the coals of the fire circle. There was no heat. He touched the coals, and they were cold. He followed the concave outline of the trail toward the woods. He followed the trail for a few dozen feet, and then it disappeared. He made a large circle from the trail's end but could detect no signs of a new trail picking up deeper in the woods. He saw no signs of the indentations of feet, no disruption of puffy plumes of snow hanging heavily from branches all around him.

He returned to the clearing. They left him for dead, he thought. He reached to the top of his head to feel for his scalp. He had all his hair, all his flesh. He shrugged. They must have been in a hurry. They must not have heard about bounties or the escape. *Christ above, who knows,* he thought. *There's nothing to be done. I hope to hell Lucy comes to her senses. She can take care of herself as long as her mind isn't scrambled. But Henri, who knows? Henri will get his butt kicked three ways to Sunday. But who knows. They could make him a slave, torture him to death, drop him off in the next settlement, sell him to indentured serviture. Who knows what a bunch of Indians will do with a gabby Frenchman who walks like a girl and can't stand the cold. Wait 'til he sees how the Indians don't even feel it. Poor Henri don't know shit about the cold 'til he hangs around with a few Indians. Bloody hell,* Everett smiled to himself, his jaw screaming at the slightest movement.

He headed north toward the river, then turned west, sticking to the woods but keeping the river in view over his right shoulder. The snow was deep. Beneath the foot of new snow was a crust and beneath that another foot. It was slow, tiresome walking. The dog followed with two-footed leaps and lunges. From time to time Everett would reach down in a footprint and collect rocks. After a couple of hours of travel, Everett stopped and sank into a snow bank heaped over a boulder. He ate handfuls of fluffy snow and savored the cool, wet purity. The dog approached and sat beside him, leaning against Everett's thigh to share their warmth. Everett scratched at the dog's ears. "Yer a good girl, ey. Probly saved me from freezin' my ass," he muttered, scratching at the dog ears. The dog had a rope around its neck. Everett inspected the knot. It looked to be made of cedar wood which had strong, fibrous strings the local Indians favored for making rope.

Then he spotted a rabbit hunched in a gully. He held the dog's collar and reached in his pocket for a handful of stones. Slowly he stood, took aim, and flung the stones. The dog leapt toward the target. The rabbit, unharmed by the rocks, lunged through the snow. It was too soft for him to gain any speed, and in a moment the dog was on him. She grasped the back of the rabbit in her jaws and shook. Then the rabbit hung limply, and the dog plunged back up the gully edge to Everett.

Everett dug down in the snow and felt for more rocks. After a few minutes, he'd filled his pockets and finally found a sharp-edged rock which he used to rip open the rabbit's belly. He threw the innards to the dog, ripped off the skin, severed its neck and sucked the blood from its neck. He was unable to chew, but he sucked the flesh, and when he was done, held pieces for the dog. She growled and tugged, but Everett held on. The dog's teeth tore at the flesh which allowed Everett to pull off bits that he swallowed whole. He praised the dog and fed it the bones which the dog crushed and devoured in her powerful jaws. In this manner, they finished everything but the blood-soaked sack of fur. Everett could feel his strength return. He was lucky to have found that dog, he thought to himself.

They walked all day in the deep snow keeping to the river's edge but not daring to walk the ice which would have allowed much easier progress but would have made him too visible to bounty trackers. By late afternoon, Everett could smell wood burning. He heard dogs bark, and the ring of axes echoed through the woods. Everett figured this to be a French-Canadian settlement on the edge of Lake St-Louis. Indians never made such a clatter and trained their dogs to be silent. He wished he could stop there and perhaps find a tavern and a warm loaf of bread. His mouth watered with craving. And he knew a good lick of rum would take the ache from his jaw. But he had no money, and his iron collar would cause suspicion. When he reached the outskirts of the settlement, Everett was forced down to the river and walked onto the ice. He tossed a stick for the dog, trying to look inconspicuous. He and the dog made a large arc around the settlement whose homes and docks reached to the river's edge. As he and the dog walked, easily sliding along the fluffy snow on the slippery ice, the sun set to the southwest, draping the village in a golden red glow, smoke twirling from chimneys, a few windows glowing from indoor light.

"Oh, what I'd give fer a cozy stove, ey, girl," he said to the dog. "A cup of hot rum and a pipe. They made a further arc around an ice-fishing hut, their solitary tracks cast by dark shadows in a fluffy sea of pink-white snow.

As darkness fell, they eased back to the river's edge and then climbed the bank into the woods a mile or so past the settlement. Everett dug them a cave in the snow in a clump of trees. It was a clear night and growing bitter cold again. He and the dog hunkered into their little cave. Everett pulled branches over them, and with the dog huddled at his belly, they slept.

It took them three days and nights to reach the Ste-Anicet settlement and another two hours across the ice before the island appeared-a patch of scraggly, barren trees and ice-bowed cedars poking darkly from a sea of white. A trickle of smoke rose from the mound of their hut in he distance. Everett quickened his pace. It was a lovely sight, and he could now taste a bowl of Ella's stew and taste the hot rum and his desire for tobacco was nearly overwhelming. For the first time in months, he felt great cheer and optimism even though he feared that his island may soon be marked by bounty hunters.

Everett did not realize at the time that the French Navy figured him to be dead because the ice boat with the tattered sail had been spotted at dawn sailing across the ice toward Lachine and suddenly sank through a hole. The sailors on the gunboat watched its frantic captain, whom they believed to be Everett, clawing helplessly at the edge of the hole, then sink to his death just as the crew discharged their muskets. The return of the ice boat puzzled Gilles to no end, but he encouraged the belief that Everett was dead. This saved Gilles from hanging for treason by his furious captain and lifted the bounty before it was ever issued. Nonetheless, the captain threw Gilles off the ship for gross incompetence and treachery, banning him from the French Navy with a simple "décedé, par noyade" deceased, by drowning, in his command report.

Everett made large circles to avoid thin ice over the channels and approached the island from the north.

The Indian boy, Jean-Robert, spotted Everett first and cautioned them. Ella peeked from the window, and in a moment recognized Everett's stooped shoulders and oddly motionless shuffle. She rushed out the door in the snow and raced down the bank, slipping and sliding in the soft snow, and ran sliding this way and that onto the ice, tears of relief streaming down her face. When she reached him, she threw her arms around him and cried, so certain she had been that she would never see him again. Everett lifted her from her feet and hugged her with equal joy. "I tole you I'd be back," he croaked, not realizing the depth of his affection nor prepared for the rush of emotion he felt after so many months of deprivation.

And as they embraced the dog hunkered up the bank and wagged her tail at the boys as if she'd known them since birth. Jamie scratched at her ears and slid down the bank and gave Everett and his mum a relieved hug. It was as though he'd come back from the grave.

After a hot, steaming bath in melted snow and several mugs of hot rum, Everett settled at the kitchen table and sucked stale tobacco through his pipe. His jaw was feeling better, but his speech was still a bit crooked and slurred.

"So Gordon Eagle Bear left the boy, ey?" he said to Ella working over the grand old cook stove they'd plucked from the river last fall.

"They've both done great. We've got fish and duck and rabbit," she said with eager satisfaction. "I'm teaching Jean-Robert to read..."

"That part of the deal?" Everett asked with a wry chuckle.

"What deal?" she said with a touch of disapproval.

Everett sensed her irritation. "I ain't ever known Gordon not to have some sort of deal in mind. Offering a son for protection ain't somethin' Gordon would likely do for cheap."

"Well, he didn't say a word about some sort of price and teaching his son to read was all my idea. He's a very smart boy," she said.

"His Daddy's a very smart Indian. I'll bet the boy's good at numbers, yeah?"

"Exceptional. And he can already read the Bible nearly as good as Jamie."

"Hallelujah," Everett laughed derisively.

"Everett," she scolded.

"Sorry, ma'am," he said, wishing he'd been more respectful.

"Don't you blaspheme. Now that you're back in civilization, you'll have to watch your mouth," she said.

"I'm truly sorry."

"Now tell me about how Lucy and Henri rescued you."

Everett was glad for the change in subject and took another big slug of rum. He sucked on his pipe and as the smoke swirled from his mouth, he spoke. "Somehow Lucy git herself in with Gilles, the first mate I was tellin' yas about, the one who visited us from the ship last fall. But I caint tell you an awful lot 'cause we was hardly a couple of minutes off the ship when she falls and bangs her head on the ice, and from then she caint remember nothin', don't even know her own name. It made a hell of a thud and then she's puking and the Frenchies are shootin' at us with their cannon and muskets and Henri who ain't been worth a bucket of lead in a three-legged race has to sail the iceboat when I lost all the blood there. I guess he done good, tell the truth, 'cause he got on to shore and it weren't his fault we got picked clean by a little trapper no bigger'n a muskrat. And then we got caught by the Indians, and they whacked me in the head with his musket, and next thing I know I'm waking up buried in snow with this here dog, probly kept me from freezin' to death, and they're gone, all of them, Lucy, Henri, the Indians. I woulda tracked them but there weren't no tracks. Lord knows how they got Henri not to leave a trail-probly carried him-but they was gone, clean as a whistle. So I caint say for sure how she sprung me loose other than I reckon she seduced the lad. He was took with her real good and now will pay the price, maybe at the end of a rope."

Ella stirred a pot of vegetables and asked, "What's going to happen to them?"

"Caint say. If Lucy don't regain her senses, she ain't goin to be worth much to no one and about all Henri can do is cook and talk. They could probly try to get a bounty from the British troops, but how they gonna convince anyone Henri was ever a soldier?"

At that point, the boys and the dog came in from outdoors with fresh perch.

Everett peeked at the mound of white filets, "Gonna be awful good. I ain't had a fresh perch in quite a spell. You boys just catch 'em."

"Yessir," Jamie said. "Jean-Robert is a darned good fisherman."

"I expect he would be," Everett said, motioning for the boys to take a seat. Jean-Robert remained standing. "You can set here with me," Everett said to the Indian boy. "I know yer Daddy, and he's a good man and an honest Indian."

The boys sat.

"So, did yas have some visitors while I was sailin the deep blue seas?"

"Yessir, we did," Jamie said.

"And who might that be?"

Jamie looked over at Jean-Robert and scratched his head in thought. "Well, there was Gordon. He come for the furs and scairt hell out mum."

"Jamie, no cussing," Ella scolded.

"Sorry ma'am," he cringed, "and there was the priest. He come by with the Bible there..."

"I guess that explains why ever one's got so pious," Everett said.

"He was Catholic," she said irritably.

"Did he dunk you in the river," Everett said to Ella.

"Of course not. He was very respectful..."

"He wanted to dunk Jean-Robert," Jamie said.

"I told him Jean-Robert was a Methodist," Ella said, fetching a loaf of bread from the oven.

"You lied to a priest," Everett grinned.

"It was not a lie."

"You a Methodist?" Everett said to Jean-Robert, who squirmed uneasily and shrugged.

Jamie continued, "The priest told us he don't think the French can win the war. He says the British have a huge fleet of warships down to New York and Philadelphia and that they're makin' Americans join the army, and they got all the Mohawks drinkin' whiskey with some British guy at Lake George..."

"A man named Johnson," Ella offered.

"That's it. Johnson," Jamie added. "The priest tells us this Johnson is real smart and how the French have messed up the Indians..."

"More like the Jesuits have chased 'em all off into the woods," Everett chuckled.

"And Johnson has got the Mohawks ready to fight the French and come next summer the war'll be over 'cause Quebec City is a sitting duck."

"So I guess that priest is a little nervous, ey? Probably heard how they treat priests in England, ey?"

"How's that?" Jamie asked.

"Cut off their heads and mount 'em on sticks above the entrance door. So who else come to visit?"

"Well, there was the traveling medicine guy with a boat load of cures for what ails you," Jamie grinned at Jean-Robert.

"You buy any of them quack concoctions, Ella?" Everett asked.

"She got some beauty creams," Jamie smiled.

Ella blushed.

"I'll bet he was after more'n yer money," Everett grinned, dizzy with drink.

Ella was turned crimson now. She moved quickly over to Jamie, grabbed his ear and lifted him, "Kindly fetch some wood, Mr. Jabbermouth."

The boys retreated giggling out the door.

"He didn't try to warm up to yah, did he?" Everett asked, his foolish daring fueled by the strong buzz of rum in his roiling brain.

She stood, her fists braced hard on her hips. "I'll have you know I can take care of myself. We've done just fine in your absence."

"That's good," Everett muttered, "I'm sure that priest was giving you the eye, too. They ain't so holy, you know. They're just ordinary men when it comes down to it. I heard stories about them Jesuits and the Indians girls."

Ella returned to the stove. "The priest was a perfect gentleman."

"Young, weren't he?"

"Yes, but he's a priest."

"I seen him last summer down there at the church in Ste-Anicet." Everett said recalling the priest's lean, angular face peering out from a great fluff of beard. "I wouldn't trust him to hold the door," Everett snorted.

"The peddler was a truly disgusting man, " she said.

"I'll bet he offered to help you apply them beauty creams," Everett said.

She rolled her eyes and shook her head, tolerating his wagging tongue in the boys' absence. "His ears were gone. He had just two holes in his head and not enough sense to grow his hair long. And he didn't have a tooth to his name," she said, frowning at her memory of this grotesquely stricken man.

"Probly tried to sell the Indians a bottle of cat piss, and they cut off his ears and busted his teeth in the bargain. You have trouble getting rid of him?"

"The boys escorted him off the island," she said.

"So he had his eye on you, yeah?"

Ella looked over at Everett. She decided to challenge him at his randy little game. "He surely did. If eyes were hands, I would have been in deep trouble," she said.

Everett blanched at her boldness. "Well, thank the Lord eyes ain't hands," he said.

She took a sip of rum and brought the bottle to pour him more. She allowed her hip to touch his shoulder. She leaned over him and poured, allowing him just a quick peek down her neckline. "In the case of that horrid man, I'd say amen," she said. She stood and waited to see if Everett would muster up some courage to push this turn in the conversation further.

He sipped. "Thank ye," he said, "I caint say I blame these fellas for stopping by and all."

"Oh?"

"A nice lookin' widow settin' out here all by herself," he said, feeling the color rise in his face.

"Well thank you, Everett. I thought you'd never notice." She moved back toward the sink, "Did you ever wish your eyes were hands?" she asked, head tilted with a playful, ironic grin.

Everett rubbed his chin, then took another long drink from his rum, then cleared his throat. "Well, to tell the truth? You askin' me to be fresh?"

She rolled her eyes, laughed, walked over to the table and leaned down across from him, bracing her hands on the table exposing her wrists and her neckline. "Yessir," she said.

Everett sat frozen for a moment, his eyes awash over her throat and neck and the smooth white bulge at her collar bone where the cloth pinched at her breasts. Then he lowered his eyes and said, "Well, yes, ma'am, to tell the truth I have at times had that wish."

"In my company?" she said boldly.

"Tell the truth, yes ma'am." He scratched his head and croaked, "I confess I have, indeed, and I'm sorry to offend you, and now that yer even more in a pious way than you was, I ain't proposing to turn a sin of thought into a sin of deed, but you asked, and even though I ain't a pious man, myself, I'm duty bound to tell the truth."

With that, the boys came kicking through the door with arms full of fresh cut wood, and Everett took some relief in helping them stack it near the stove. He would have done better having his fingernails yanked out one at a time than to have continued that conversation. He couldn't understand it, but she scared the hell out of him bad as ever. Having her turn that little flirt of hers on him was enough to damn near have strangled him dead. He took the cold wood from the boy's arms. Life was a funny thing, he thought, he could let loose with Lucy like they was buddies from way back when, but Ella had a way of grabbing his throat and reducing him to a whimper, three sheets to the wind notwithstanding.

* * *

Soon after the capture, the Indians stole Henri's boots and after carrying him in a sack for a few miles, set him down to walk barefoot in the snow. They tied a rope around his neck and tugged him along, yanking him harshly whenever he slipped which happened with greater and greater frequency once his feet went numb.

They were more respectful of Lucy whom they cooed over as though they'd found a great prize, although they spoke Indian, and Henri couldn't understand a word. At midday the Indians stopped, made a fire, and cooked a dog's leg over a makeshift spit. They offered Henri some charred scraps but giggled knowingly when he refused. He was chagrined when he saw Lucy take a few bites. Henri had heard about men eating dogs at the fortress at La Presentation, but he wasn't prepared to indulge in such desperate cuisine. "J'imagine I am nex on de menu," he muttered.

"Shut-up," Lucy growled. "They won't eat you."

The Indians giggled, and the leader poked Lucy with a stick to shut her up.

By the way they sized them up and felt their muscles, Lucy knew from soon after the capture that the Indians were planning to sell them back in Montreal. They owed one of them to the Jesuits, she heard them mutter, and she hoped that would be her being that the next best market was for prostitution. She did not reveal to them her Indian heritage partly because she did not know which tribes may have recently betrayed these men, nor what tribe she has once belonged to, her memory of the past still as foggy as the night before. She knew that Indians were quick to exact revenge against their enemies, and if she spoke of the relatives of the wrong tribe, they could cut her throat. If she guessed the right tribe, on the other hand, they might well adopt her to replace their dead-a common custom that would only lead to greater hardship and with all the inter-tribal warfare in the last few years, would probably end in death. It was a complete puzzle to her how she could know these things yet not remember the facts of her life. But she knew lying to the Indians or inventing facts about her past would be very dangerous, worse even than being an indentured whore.

As they squatted around the fire eating the dog, the leader asked Lucy in French what things she was good at, and she said attending to priests and preparing them for mass had been a recent vocation, and they cooed approvingly. They turned to Henri, and he refused to answer.

"He is an excellent cook and barman," she told them.

Henri scowled and turned to her. "Dey make me cook you next, Lucy," he said bitterly in English.

The leader swatted Henri's head with his stick. " Assez Anglais, monsieur," he snapped.

The Indians conferred with each other in whispers, and she overheard the words 'Monsieur Fourmet a La Taverne Canard Noir' amid a tangle of Indian phrases she could not decipher, but later on the trail she whispered to Henri that he would be sold to the Black Duck Tavern, and if that were the case, not to protest.

"A slave?" he asked indignantly, getting another yank at the neck.

"A servant."

"The same," he said, and this time the Indian boy behind him yanked him to his knees. "Ferme la bouche," he snapped, grasping Henri by the hair, pulling his knife, and threatening to scalp him on the spot.

The others stopped, the leader scolded the boy, and Lucy heard the word francs and knew they would probably be safe from injury by the Indians provided they could earn hard currency in exchange.

The Indians led them back toward Lachine but instead of entering the port, they took an icey, well-worn path along the Lachine rapids down river toward Montreal. As they neared Montreal's fortress walls, the leader told Henri that if he made any attempt to escape, he would drive a spear through his back. He removed the rope from his neck, and the small band entered the city walls after a brief exchange between the leader and a French marine guard.

At the Black Duck Tavern, Monsieur Fourmet ushered them to a back room. Fourmet was an enormous man with an immense belly that hung like two sacks of jelly over his belt, divided strangely in the center by his deeply sunken naval. The Indians offered him either Henri or Lucy, and when Fourmet discovered that Henri was an excellent cook, he grabbed Henri by the shirt and yanked him over beside him.

"Qu'est-ce que tu peut cuire?" Fourmet demanded.

Henri recited a vast menu including, "tout les fruits de mer, poisson, cabillaud, morue, saumon, truite, hareng, palourdes, moules, huitres, scampi, calmar, et volaille, poulet, dinde, canard, viande, boeuf, rosbif, bifteck, porc, jambon, saucisse, agneau, cervelle, langue, tripes, et toutes avec bearnaise, Hollandaise, Normande, Provencale, garni tout les legumes et tout les soupe, bisque... delicieux, magnifique... encore, Monsieur Fourmet?"

Fourmet grinned. "Tres bien," he said and handed the leader a fistful of coins.

The Indians and Lucy left after a brief exchange of paperwork. Fourmet told Henri that he could earn his freedom in three years and would be allowed a small allowance.

"You can't do this to me," Henri said.

"Bloody hell I can't," Fourmet shouted and pounded the table. "I just bought you your life. Now you pay it back, and if you can't cook all this great list, I'll sell you to the street cleaners, and you can shovel shit for the years. Comprenez vous?"

The man had a point, he thought to himself looking around at the filth. "Oui, Monsieur," he said. "I will make you de most popular taverne in Montreal."

"La taverne le plus populaire à Montreal, voire," Fourmet grunted skeptically. "My only patrons are pathetic drunks."

"If I make you the most popular taverne in Montreal, I am a free man in two years. D'accord?"

Fourmet grinned and shook Henri's hand with an immense, puffy hand. "Gladly," he grunted.

* * *

Lucy awoke slowly as if from some groggy fog in a tiny, cold, candlelit room. She lay on her back beneath wool blankets, a statue of Jesus nailed to the cross hanging from the wall at her feet. The walls and ceiling were stone. Beside the bed Father Raymbault prayed with a steady, quiet hiss, pale pink hands folded on his lap. His eyes were closed, or mostly so. She could detect a slit of white between his eyelids. As she gained her senses, she became increasingly aware of the slow, hard throb of a terrible headache.

She drifted off again, then awoke some time later to the missionary's voice.

"You have suffered a head injury. Our physician has taken your blood several times, and he believes you will recover. We have prayed for you and lit many candles and said two masses for you."

She looked up at him as if stuck half in a dream and trying to awaken. She dozed in and out as he spoke softly to her. "The savages brought you here and have left you in our care. You are with us now, and you are safe and with God, and when we feared you may die, we baptized you because Father Germaine believes you are an Indian and may suffer eternity in Purgatory, so we have said an Act of Contrition over your soul, and if it is God's will that you should die, you will ascend to Heaven and be saved as a innocent child at the right hand of Jesus Christ Our Lord. You are with grace, my child. If you live and recover you will stay with us and serve the Lord through us until such time that you decide-if that is in your capacity and your will-to venture forth again into this harsh world."

Lucy had drifted in and out of consciousness for more than a week, and each time she awoke, the young man in monk's garb was at her side praying or speaking softly. From time to time she was awoken by a gentle, insistent nudge by an ancient nun who helped her with a bed pan. When she tried to sit up, Lucy was overcome by dizziness and would frequently faint and be gone in this strange swirling darkness.

One morning she awoke to the sound of her own blood trickling from her wrist into a shallow pan held by the ancient nun. The physician was a little squirrel of a man with a roving left eye and several long, plume-like hairs growing from his hooked and crooked nose. When he saw she was awake, he spoke to her, and attending his words was breathe as foul as fresh sewage. "Yes, dear, you are doing better. Your fevers are down, the flushed glow at your cheeks now diminished. You see this blood. It is no longer so dark."

In the background she could hear the young monk praying in Latin.

Lucy recovered slowly and learned that the young monk was really a priest who sometimes irritated his superiors by donning the modest garb of monks or sometimes wandered around in tattered woodsman's clothes, so modest was his sense of self importance. He invited her to call him Father Ray, a simpler version of his pretentious name and told her upon her recovery that she had been assigned to assist him on his next mission to a Huron village. He was praying for her recovery of strength, he said, because mission work was extremely hard and very physical.

They had assigned a woman to Father Ray, in fact, because they found his humility so grating and his popularity among the Indians an irritation causing them such jealousy that they secretly wished him failure or at very least a bit more challenge.

But Father Ray was delighted to have Lucy with him because women were so important in the tribes and a key to persuading their women first and then their men to turn to Jesus. This is what he told himself, in any case, and when his mind drifted to thoughts of her pretty face, he prayed to the Virgin Mary and whispered the Lord's prayer quietly beneath his breath, thanking God that her life had been spared and a pleasant friendship finally delivered to him.

Chapter 5

Father Raymbault strode along the path with his usual earnest rapidity, his black robe swinging with his long strides during a welcome late-February thaw. He spoke earnestly to Lucy in French.

"Vous serez ebahi tout à fait à leur dévotion à Satan et ses plusiers manifestations. You will be quite amazed at their devotion to Satan and his many manifestations, and some of the most devoted of these zealots are women who we must persuade, because they are pervasive influences of family and tribal life. These women are so promiscuous and refuse utterly... they utterly refuse," he said, waving his arm, "to join with God and honor Him and honor their husbands." He stopped then, and twirled to face her.

"Pas tous d'eux, bien sûr ... not all of them, of course. Some of them have acquiesced to baptism and are quite cooperative and are really quite pious and pray with us and take communion and confess their sins which are really quite remarkable." He crossed himself, indicating to Lucy that evil thoughts or images has just crossed through his mind. His eyes turned upward, he twirled and again strode down the snow-packed path.

Lucy could still not now recall her own most recent sins of promiscuity, but for a moment her mind flashed with vivid pictures of Everett. As she pondered these visits with Satan within her, she crossed herself and took several half skips to regain the gap between herself and Father Raymbault.

Still, she was not altogether convinced that God disapproved so very much about lust or that given all the other horrible things people did to each other, why lust was such a problem. So she asked, "Father Ray, why does this concern you so much when there are other things of greater magnitude such as, well, torture and cannibalism, murder and all forms of violence?"

"Are we speaking of lust, Lucy?"

"Yes. Isn't it natural...isn't it...."

"Well, yes, of course," he said without turning back or breaking stride, "but it is allowed only for the purpose of procreation, and beyond that," he said, again hurriedly crossing himself, "beyond that... I mean, as an act of pleasure as an end in itself," he said crossing himself, "no, no, no. That is a sin, and of course out of wedlock it is a mortal sin or with the husbands or wives of others, it is a mortal sin, the sin of adultery."

"But why lust?" she asked. "I understand why adultery with another's husband is a mortal sin, but why is lust out of wedlock such a terrible thing?"

He stopped, twirled, swallowed thickly. "My child. It is because God says so. C'est les mots du bon Dieu."

"But why do you think He thinks it's a sin. I mean, what if you and I stopped right here and engaged in lust."

He crossed himself, his eyes jumping wildly left and right, steam rising from his hot, flushed face. He turned quickly and strode down the path muttering the Lord's Prayer twice before answering.

"I have taken a vow of chastity."

"But what if you hadn't. What if you were an ordinary man. Besides, breaking a vow is not the same kind of a sin. The vow is not the act itself. So, yes, you break the vow, and that is a sin, but what of the act of lust. What if you love someone and feel only charitable things toward them, only kindness and concern and care..."

"You marry that person," he said sternly.

"But then you are only allowed to experience lust for procreation purposes..."

"Quite right."

"So if you make love for purposes only of lust for your wife or husband, that is a sin?"

"But of course." He crossed himself again.

"Do many married people confess this sort of lust."

"I cannot divulge what I hear in the confessional."

"I'm not talking about a particular confession. I am asking if this is a commonly reported sin."

He did not answer for quite some time, but then stopped and twirled about. "No, it is not. Because there are more grave sins."

"C'est la convoitise, donc. So, you are upset with these Indian women because they are filled with lust?"

"No, because they are filled with the devil. Their lust is merely a manifestation of the devil within them."

Lucy enjoyed tormenting Father Ray with questions about sin. She supposed her own enjoyment was, itself, a sin, but he was always so eager to answer, and sometimes he even thanked her for testing his knowledge and resolve, even the fabric of his faith. In any case, she had become very used to carrying on this discourse as a way of passing the hours on their treks between villages or during the long, boring days at the monastery.

They arrived at Father Raymbault's most promising Huron village in time for lunch. Lucy suspected that in the long houses yet to be converted to Christianity that they may be dining on human flesh, an activity she, herself, considered to be a sin. But, they dipped into a Christian-friendly long house and enjoyed venison after a lengthy blessing during which everyone bowed and muttered through the acrid haze of smoke.

Among those at the lunch was Mary Tall Tree, a young, fiery-eyed skeptic Lucy learned to both admire and fear. Mary Tall Tree refused Baptism by Father Ray, but wanted to be present at his ceremonies and prayer services. In Lucy's view, Mary was a spy who stared at Father Ray with such intensity, Lucy could not tell if she harbored lust or torture in her heart. Her skin was a lovely beige the color of deer skin, and her hair long, coarse, and brilliantly black. Her eyes were a luminous black, so dark they blazed with light from every source-the fire, the doorway, the candles. She was a startlingly beautiful creature who moved with fluid grace except when near Father Ray. Near him, she stumbled and spilled, bumped and staggered.

As they ate, Mary sat cross-legged, exposing her womanhood to Father Ray and delivered her usual commentary in an intense whisper. "You are the devil, the demon. You have brought your devil's disease, and as we eat, the pox has befallen our long house as it has each year you have visited us."

Father Ray prayed audibly, and the other men and women around the table prayed with him, but they had so far refused banning Mary. "Notre père qui est dans le ciel..."

"You have not cured a single Indian with your all-powerful Jesus God. And we have cured many, praying to our Grandmother as she looks down at us from her tree of life, and yet each person here has betrayed our Grandmother, and you have cursed us with your false blessings."

Everyone prayed louder and with more intensity, including Lucy.

"You have turned our men into cowards who now beat their new wives after your hollow marriage ceremony as if the ceremony is the devil's permission to ruin our lives and cast us into humiliation. You convert our warriors to your all-forgiving God and turn them into soldiers to do your killing for you in the white God's name. Your promises that their deaths as white men's soldiers will send them to a glorious place you call heaven is a lie of such horrible cruelty. How can you call yourself a holy man, a man of medicine? Vous êtes un démon malin."

Father Ray did not answer her torments but simply prayed and bobbed his head indicating his forgiveness and bestowing on her blessings. Two weeks ago he tried to sprinkle holy water on Mary's head, but she kicked flames from the longhouse fire into his lap, burning large holes in his black robe.

"God forgives you, child," Father Ray chanted, then spoke the Lord's Prayer in French, then Latin.

That afternoon, they worked busily at constructing his mission at the edge of the woods on a slight hill overlooking the longhouses. Father Ray removed his robe on such occasions, and Lucy was struck at how sturdily built and how wiry this man was beneath the robe. He pounded nails and trimmed logs with the skill of a master carpenter, moving about the frame of the building with the ease of a squirrel calling out orders and directing the work as if it had been his life's work. His face, which seemed a bit chubby and cherubic when bundled by his robe, was actually quite chiseled when his long, naked neck was visible. His face was ruddy, even rugged, not nearly so boyish as when dressed for his church duties.

Lucy, too, could set aside her robe when working and welcomed the freedom. Father Ray watched her with admiration wielding an axe or hammer... whatever tool as required, with her strong, angular hands, pale at the wrists. When contrasted to the Hurons at this mission, Father Ray noted that Lucy was fair-skinned, her hair a bit lighter, her brown eyes more pale. She was a good worker, he noted, gazing upon her and crossing himself several times. From time to time, they all stopped and took drinks and smoked tobacco which the Indians handed around in their sacred pipe. Father Ray's face trickled with sweat, his armpits, back and chest damp and steaming in the damp February air.

While adverse to most of their pagan rituals, to refuse the pipe was considered an insult of such depth that even he dared not pass it by, and before the mission was even half built, Father Ray looked forward to smoking the pipe. He took a deep draw and handed it to Lucy who sucked deeply and resolved to ask Father Ray if they could get their own pipe for use at the monastery. She was amazed at how quiet and gentle the Christianized Indians had become, and it was not through any discernible force on Father Ray's part except for his constant reminders about the fires of hell for eternity. Lucy wished for some rum, but knew Father Ray would become distraught at the Indians if they brought rum or even wine to the day's proceedings. These were sinful temptations, he said, which afflicted the Indians even more to the extreme than their white brethren.

After passing the pipe several times, they returned to work on the mission. Later that afternoon, Mary Tall Tree and several young warrior friends sat on a log in the near distance and observed the work. They frequently broke into uproariously laughter, causing all of the workers but Father Ray to look up and frown disapprovingly. No one seemed to notice when Mary Tall Tree's gang finally grew quiet. One of the warriors drew a bow and arrow from behind the log and set aim at Father Ray still working on the roof. The warrior yelled out a war cry; everyone turned; and the arrow released and flew in a swift, slightly wobbly course to the roof and penetrated Father Ray's upper arm between the bicep and bone, barely missing penetration into his side.

The warriors fled into the woods with Mary Tall Tree, and Father Ray climbed down and strode on a wobbly path toward Lucy. A few feet before reaching her, his flushed face turned a bleak white, his eyes rolled up in his head, and he fainted in a heap in the muddy, melting snow. Lucy rushed to him, snapped the arrow and pulled it out of his arm.

"Those little bastards," she muttered angrily as the converted Indians formed a circle around her. They helped her carry him to the longhouse where they heated water. After a few minutes, an unconverted woman in traditional leathers entered with a wooden bowl of brown paste and stuffed the wound thoroughly, jamming the paste deep into the wound with a small stick. She spoke Indian prayers in a tongue unfamiliar to Lucy, then turned to all of them and spoke, "If you wish him to live, pray with me in your native way."

The Indians then formed a close circle around Father Ray and emitted a steady, rhythmic chant cast toward chasing the evil spirits from the arrow poisoned by rattlesnake venom and a paste squeezed from assorted deadly mushrooms. The brown paste was made from chewed snakeroot mixed in a mussel shell with herbal antidotes and human urine. After their prayer, she commanded them to remove Father Ray from their tribal grounds immediately. Several of the converted men quickly secured Father Ray to a sled and escorted Lucy and Father Ray quickly into the woods. Before they were far and out of view, Lucy noticed a glow in the darkening afternoon stillness. She looked back to see flames rising above the trees, the mission set fire. An hour later as they moved through the woods, Father Ray muttered in delirium. Then in a garbled mix of Latin and French, he shouted the most profound obscenities about his burning need to enter Lucy's privates and evacuate a lifetime of lust into the core of her being. The Indians giggled as they pulled the sled swiftly through the woods, forcing Lucy to run just to keep up.

Father Ray suffered through several feverish days and nights. Only the doctor heard any repetition of his obscenities about Lucy, causing only the mildest chuckle. The presence of the priests was perhaps so overwhelmingly sobering that Father Ray was able to perceive through the dim light of his rapturous delirium that to be caught speaking in such ways would surely cause Lucy to be banished from the monastery. The murkiest depths of Father Ray's confused mind somehow understood the perils of her banishment, and he lay quietly in their presence as the priests prayed over him twice daily, his partially open eyes peeking groggily from crusted lids yellow and runny with pus. The priests ignored Lucy's vigil of muttered prayers, slumped on the same wooden stool used by Father Ray during her own prolonged recovery. The old nun, sickened by the smell of his festering wound and foul tinctures, left Father Ray's bathing and cleaning chores to Lucy. And as she washed him gently, she watched his eyes brighten and knew that even if he died, he would have realized at least some small fraction of the stormy lust that lurked so deeply inside him.

By the time he recovered, Lucy knew that inside this man was a caged beast of incredible hunger and need. When his fever broke, she smiled and patted his forehead with damp cloth and pushed back his snarls of dark hair. He smiled back, touched her hand, and whispered weakly, "Bless you, child. Bless thy healing hands and heart. May God lift your soul."

She wondered what, if anything, he would remember of those days and nights, but was certain that if he returned to his former piety, God would forgive him for his sins, because it had been *her* caresses that had eased the pressure of his tormenting lust and not his conscious will. She had given him relief. She had entered into his delirium. She had released the poisons of his need. Would he ever know their sin, she wondered.

He did not remember the arrow, the loss of the mission, or the raucous laughter of Mary Tall Tree and her warrior friends.

"You were delirious for nearly a week," Lucy told him.

"Did I say anything to disturb the priests," he said fitfully.

"No, they heard nothing. You were quiet whenever they visited. Do you remember them praying over you?"

"No, no. I do not remember. May God bless them," he said. He turned to her, trying to brace upon his elbow, but falling back onto the pillow. He grasped her hand and squeezed. "And may God bless you, Lucy. You have become such a very dear and trusted friend."

Lucy smiled and squeezed his hand in return. "Yes," she said quietly, "and now you must rest. You'll need all your energy very soon."

* * *

On the day of his fifth lashing Gilles wished for death. His back was torn with four hundred cuts, many of them now festering from being smeared with shit and piss where they flung him unconscious on the brig floor. Each morning he awoke shivering uncontrollably as they grasped him and pulled him out on the deck where the marines carried out their lashes in full view of the crew and captain. Every few minutes when he lost consciousness or appeared ready to faint, they doused him with buckets of ice water. On this fifth day with still five more to go, he vomited with dry heaves before the first crack of the lash. His legs were so weak, they had to tie him hard to the mast, and as he hung there, his feet turned out in strange angles as if broken at the ankles. Each new day more people came to watch from the Lachine quayside, some of them exchanging bets on when he would die-on what precise lash his body would cease twitching and the buckets would no longer cause the horrible gasp and snap of his neck.

On this morning he appeared so close to death by the fiftieth lash that a fight broke out in the quayside crowd. It took five buckets before he finally gasped and twitched, and from dockside cheers erupted as his ankles flopped strangely when he appeared to try to run. Steam rose from his soaked body, and diluted blood rain in streams down his torn back. At the seventieth lash, the captain ordered him cut down and brought to his cabin for medical attention. The three marines who shared the lashing duties glared angrily at the captain, but cut him down amid boos and hisses from the quayside crowd. Several crewmen took their popular lieutenant by the arms and dragged him to the captain's quarters.

Gilles lay face down on a sheet over the captain's table as a physician dressed his wounds with a plantain poultice. When the physician finished his work, he told the captain that more lashes would surely kill the man. The captain handed the physician several coins and ushered him out. He closed the cabin door, poured whiskey into a cup and helped Gilles sip from it.

When Gilles had drunk enough to take away a modicum of the pain, the captain helped him sit, then threw him a shirt from his sea chest. Gilles tried to button it, but his hands trembled too much from cold and pain and the chills of dysentery.

The captain took whiskey for himself in a tin chalice and stared out the small stern windows.

The captain spoke quietly, not looking at Gilles. "In a few minutes I will call for a stretcher and have you taken to the undertakers where they will leave you for dead. I will record you as lost to drowning in the ship's log and will include that in my ship's report to the command. I see no need to humiliate your family back in France. You will have died honorably if not heroically in service to your country. I am doing this at some risk, so I strongly suggest that when you make your escape, you head out of Lachine and lose yourself in Montreal or into the wilderness."

"Why are you doing this?" Gilles gasped.

The captain did not turn. "I see no point in killing you, and five hundred more lashes would surely kill you. My marines would be gratified, but I would not. But I cannot reduce your punishment-surely you must understand that. I cannot have discipline if I reduce your sentence, so I will pronounce you dead myself. So, unless you wish to receive the rest of your punishment, I want you to lay down on your back and remain absolutely still."

Gilles lay back down, closed his eyes, and waited. The captain came to his side, lifted the sheet over him, and quickly stitched it closed in the manner recommended for corpses by the French Navy. The captain opened the cabin door and called for a stretcher. Gilles soon felt himself lifted from the table and lowered gently to the stretcher on the floor. He felt the cold air penetrate the sheet as they took him outside, and as they hoisted him across the quayside, one of the crewmen slipped and nearly dumped Gilles between the dock and ship. But they grasped his arms and wrestled him back onto the stretcher, then carried him in stride down the quay.

At the undertakers he was lowered into a wooden coffin and was carried to a corner for storage before being scheduled for transport to a mortuary in the cemetery where bodies were stacked for burial until the ground thawed. When the ship's crew members left, the undertaker pounded nails into the top of the coffin. His mind feverish from dysentery and infection, Gilles was not certain he was not dead and that what was happening was not some strange death dream. The pounding felt as though he were stricken directly on the temples. The undertaker kept nailing. Up one side, down another. Then after twenty nails or so, the pounding stopped. Gilles gasped for breath, and when he tried to move his arms to open the burial shroud, discovered that the coffin and shroud together confined his movement and may have paralyzed him altogether.

He tried to calm himself, tried to think what he should do. He listened but could only hear his own desperate, claustrophobic gasps. He tried to move his arms but could gain no leverage against the strong fabric. He heard the loud slam of a door. He waited and tried to calm himself. Slowly, he was able to stop gasping. He waited for a count of five hundred. He heard no other poundings, no more door slams. Slowly, using his fingers to claw up his own sides, he was able to join his hands. He found the seam where the captain had stitched the shroud and forced his hands up through the seam opening until he could plant his palms against the coffin lid and push. The top of the coffin bent in a gentle arc, but this only pulled the sides in tighter.

Gilles released the pressure and moved his hands up the shroud toward his face. He broke one stitch at a time until he was able to wedge the shroud away from his face. In the darkness of the coffin he could see cracks of light where the cover fit over the box. The cracks were thinnest, even entirely dark where nails were driven. Between the nails the cracks widened, but not by much. Once again, he pressed to see if he could widen the cracks, and when he did so this time, he noticed straight above him, almost behind him, a sliver of light widen as he pushed. The end piece was not nailed through the top piece. Gilles wedged his hands past his face, found the crack and pressed with all his strength. The wood groaned, the crack widened, but the nails would not budge. Drawing from his experience building boats in his youth, he reconstructed the coffin in his mind's eye searching for a weakness, the most likely break point. The end piece had to be weakest, he surmised, because it was the only part of the box not nailed on all four of its sides. If he stretched himself out, he could touch the bottom of the box with his feet and the top with the hair on his head.

He lowered himself with squirms and wiggles, then wedged his forearm between his head and the end piece, making himself taller in the box. Then he pushed with his legs. The wood groaned, then a nail squeaked. He pushed until his whole body trembled and his arm seemed ready to break, and then the end piece cracked down the center. Soon he was able to wedge out half the end piece, then yanked and pulled until the other half loosened and finally broke free. He pulled himself out the end, the nails clawing at his ragged back, but he was free, gasping the cold air as he wiggled and lurched and squirmed out of the box, tearing away the burial shroud, then yanking it out of the box to wrap himself for warmth.

Though weak and exhausted from the beatings and illness, Gilles staggered out of the coffin barn and soon found the path along the Lachine rapids. The sun blazed in the southern sky, but it was as cold as it was bright, the river roaring down ice-capped rocks, huge icicles hanging from narrow cliff sides, a mist casting the path with a film of ice so slippery Gilles tumbled on his hands and knees most of the way to Montreal, still not altogether certain he was not dead and now plunging aimlessly toward even deeper and crueler depths of hell.

Gilles stood panting and gazed at the rows of snow-covered boats at Le Petit Bateau Bâtisseur boatyard. Maybe this could be work, he thought. Maybe. He brushed his fingers through his tangled hair, buttoned, and tucked in the shirt the captain had given him. He grasped snow from the ground and washed his face, then wiped his face clean with the burial shroud and tucked it beneath a stack of canoes on a rack beside a long work building.

He entered the front door and breathed in warm air for the first time in several weeks. Dozens of boats were spread out in various stages of construction. Some canoes, some bateaux, several larger fishing boats, mostly in skeletal stages of framing. A half dozen men were spread out and stooped over their work. Gilles walked toward a row of four bateaux being worked on by an older man with a stooped back and immense, hairy forearms. The man moved a plane slowly and smoothly along the joint where the stem and keel were fastened. Fine curls of cedar billowed above the blade and tumbled from time to time to the floor. Gilles watched the man who looked up briefly but continued working without comment.

After fifteen minutes, the man stood and arched his back, his face grimacing with pain. He rested the plane on the upside-down keel of the next bateau in line and gingerly lowered himself to an uncomfortably stiff sitting position on a stump beside the boats.

Gilles fought back shivers from his fever and walked as steadily as he could manage to the bateau with the plane. He lifted the plane and flipped the shavings on the floor, then set his legs wide and began a smooth, even planning motion as he had learned in his youth. The blade was sharp and cut fine, smooth curls of fragrant cedar. Gilles ran his hand along the joint, then resumed planing. In a few minutes he lowered his face to the keel and eyed the curve of the wood down its length. Then he moved to the next boat in line and began planing a much rougher joint this time. The plane squeaked over a knot, and Gilles stepped back and worked his hand over the knot, then adjusted the blade to take less of a cut. He resumed his smooth easy motion, using his legs and body in a gentle swaying motion.

After a time, the older man, Monsieur LeBlanc, stood and felt the joints that Gilles had planed, then lowered his face and eyed them along the length of the keel. On the third boat, he tapped the stem with his knuckles and raised his brows as if to say, 'Here, fix this one. It is not so good.' He said nothing, but Gilles hurried over and found the slightest bump and carefully planed the imperfection away before returning to the fifth boat.

LeBlanc returned and moved his large, knarled hand over the spot and nodded yes.

As Gilles worked LeBlanc shuffled away, and in a few minutes returned with a box of tools. Then he fetched planks and laid them beside each bateau. When the planks were in place, LeBlanc lifted one end of the plank and muttered, "We measure and cut," nodding for Gilles to lift the other hand and help him position the plank for measurement. They worked for several hours exchanging remarkably few words. At the end of the day, when the other men began to leave, LeBlanc dug in his pocket and gave Gilles coins for his day's work.

"Come back tomorrow, ey?" LeBlanc asked.

"Oui, of course," Gilles said quietly, sweat pouring down his face and dripping silently into the sawdust.

"You have built boats, I see," LeBlanc muttered.

"Ah, oui," Gilles smiled.

"You like?" LeBlanc asked, his face dour.

"Oui, very much. I built boats when I was a boy."

LeBlanc nodded yes. As his men passed by him for the door, he raised his hand in a weary, almost motionless wave.

LeBlanc shuffled across the large floor for his coat and was surprised to see Gilles still at work. He stopped and studied the young man.

"You have no place to live, ey?" LeBlanc asked.

"No, Monsieur. I am new to Montreal."

"Sleep here, then. Have the fire going by six."

"Merci, Monsieur, merci," Gilles said, feeling profound relief and gratitude constrict his throat. He turned away, nearly overcome by emotion.

"Bonne nuit, Monsieur," LeBlanc muttered and shuffled out the door, leaving Gilles alone in the cavernous barn. Later Gilles rushed out and bought a tub of stew and fresh baguette, then returned, stoked the huge stove, sweeping piles of sawdust into a warm corner where he sat, close to the stove, swabbed his back with the shroud drenched in steaming water. Later he sat and dried his wounds with his back to the hot stove. He sipped the stew, devoured the large baguette, and wondered about the woman Lucy, wondered if she had really cared about him, wondered if he would ever see her again.

* * *

The first week in January was one of the coldest Everett had ever experienced, his thermometer never reaching above 20 degrees below zero. Despite the cold, he and Jamie made the rounds of their traps. Under orders from his father, Jean-Robert refused to venture further from Ella than his eyes could see.

Ella could not understand Everett's obsession with furs. On the coldest morning of that coldest of weeks, Ella questioned him.

"Why do you risk your lives for furs? I'm not allowing Jamie out there today. It's fifty below zero," she said cooking flour pancakes on the glowing stove.

Jamie looked up from his work wrapping his feet in swaths woven from wool and reed grass. "Look, mum, it's not *that* cold..."

"I'm not talking to you."

Everett wrapped his own feet and thought about his answer. He knew she did not like the idea that he should repay Gordon with pelts. "It'll warm up quick when the sun rises," Everett muttered.

"Why are you so obsessed with furs. We don't need them to survive. Gordon did not ask for furs. I am teaching Jean-Robert to read. That is repayment enough."

"You don't understand Indian ways," Everett said, not looking up from his work.

"This isn't Indian ways. This is good old fashioned British gratitude; buying your way out of guilt."

"I ain't British. I got nothing to do with British. I ain't guilty about nothing."

"Then what is it?"

"It's what a man's got to do. It's what I got to do. It's what I do. I'm a trapper and a fisherman, and the coldest days of winter are the best days for trappin. There ain't no better fur than January fur. There ain't no worse fur than March fur. Come March I fish. Right now I trap. I don't give three shits how cold it is."

It made Ella furious hearing Everett muttering his little speech, his face buried in his wrapping ritual. She wanted to grab his ear and make him look her in the eye. What is the matter with this man, she wondered angrily.

"I'm goin' with Everett," Jamie muttered from the same, absolutely identical posture.

She walked over and planted herself between them. Even just a few feet from the fire, she could feel the frigid drafts. The wind whistled at the doorway.

"Look here, young man," she said.

"Boy's gotta learn," Everett said leaning back and looking up at her from his stool.

"I'll decide what my son will do and won't do, thank you very much."

"The boy's of age. You caint shelter him. You caint wrap him in your apron strings. He's *gotta* learn."

"He's learned enough."

"No he ain't. You caint learn January trappin' settin' around a hot fire sippin' warm milk."

Ella was furious. "What the hell is the difference between January trappin'," she spit, mocking Everett's speech, "'an February trappin'?" She rolled her eyes in disgust.

"Cause it's cold, goddammit, woman."

"Don't you call me *woman*," she snapped. "I'm not some kind of milking cow."

"No ma'am, you ain't for sure. That's God's own truth."

"Gordon does not need furs. I am teaching his boy to read."

"I'll decide what Gordon needs."

"Then do it without Jamie."

"No ma'am. I need the boy."

"Take the bloody dog."

"I plan takin' the dog, and I plan takin' Jamie, and I don't want to hear no more'n about this, yeah?"

The pancakes were burning, and she rushed over and flipped them angrily on a plate and flung them on the table.

The truth was that Everett was accounting for the weather with great caution. They needed to cast a far wider area for their traps, but he wasn't going to risk staying nights in the woods until the cold snap broke. But as soon as the temperature rose, they were going for a week or more, and she'd bloody have to get used to it. He tried to contain his anger and wasn't getting into a verbal battering with her because she'd surely win any battle involving words. Still, he could barely contain himself. What goddamned business did she have telling him what to do. And it sickened him the way she tried to pamper the boy. Someday the boy's life would depend on him being tough and knowing how to survive the cold and a thousand other dangers.

* * *

Jamie ran the point of his knife starting at the beaver's rectum and slicing to its gullet. Its innards rolled into the snow and steamed. Everett reset the trap and looked out over the beaver pond where a half dozen mounds remained cemented in ice.

"Gonna be one more here," Everett said, "maybe two." His steamy breath twirled from his mouth beneath the blazing sun.

The dog licked at the innards, then dug at them with her claws and began gobbling down the heart and liver.

Everett held the beaver by the eye sockets, and Jamie sliced carefully at the scalp, grasped the fur, and they both pulled. The skin and fur peeled back over the steaming pink body, and before the dog could get at it, Everett slashed off the legs and stuffed them in his satchel for lunch later on. He tossed the small, naked body to the dog, and she ripped the flesh from its bones, her lips curled back from her strong, sharp teeth.

They worked the traps all day with little luck. They took a total of two beavers, one otter, a half dozen muskrats before settling in a clearing for lunch.

Everett started a fire, and Jamie dragged back branches of dead wood frozen so stiff they easily cracked when they stood over them and plunged down with their weight. In a few minutes, they had a goodly fire. They cooked beaver legs on a spit made from green cedar branches that hissed and smoked but refused to burn.

"That mother ah yers don't quite git the picture, son, but she's a fighter, ain't she?" Everett laughed, sucking on his pipe.

Jamie squatted down and poked a stick into the hot coals. "She's just scairt," he said, applying the flame at the end of the stick to the end portion of the beaver leg not quite cooked by the flame below.

"She's gonna be hotterin' a half boiled weasel when I tell her you 'an me goin' off for a week. We cain't stay here. Ain't nothin' left but rats."

"Scairt of her own shadow," Jamie said shaking his head no.

"Cain't blame her none, son."

Jamie looked up at him.

"She ain't scairt for herself. She's scairt for you."

"I ain't scairt," Jamie said.

"You gonna go with me, then?"

"Yessir."

"Gonna be hard damned work."

"Yessir."

"Cold as bitch at night."

"Yessir," the boy said.

"Dog'll keep us warm."

"She will. She's a good dog. She pulls the sled real good."

"Hell, a mouse could pull the damned thing with all the furs we got this week."

"She can pull me and Jean-Robert."

The dog trotted over and sat, leaning against Everett's leg.

It was so cold the snot froze in their noses, and the snow squeaked when they walked. It was so cold it didn't feel cold, so cold and dry you couldn't hardly work up a spit, and their lips cracked and split from the moisture sucked out of them by the air.

"Yessir," Everett muttered, scratching at the dog's ears, "She's a good dog. Strong for her size."

"Think she's the runt?" Jamie asked.

"I figure. They ain't gonna leave behind nothing but a runt. But they learnt her a lot, just the same."

"Maybe she learnt from the other dogs."

"Yessir, maybe so."

"Jean-Robert says once you got one smart lead dog, you ain't got to train the rest. They learn from the lead dog. That's how the Indians teach 'em."

"Yessir, I reckon."

"It's the truth."

"Yessir, that boy would know."

Everett pulled the stick off the spit, and they both bit into juicy, steaming legs of beaver.

"Ain't nothing better'n this," Everett said.

"Nossir," the boy muttered as he chewed.

On their way back that afternoon, Everett and Jamie shuffled across the frozen river following the dog who pulled the sled with barely a lump of furs strapped to the sled's deck. The sun was quickly drawing down on the horizon, casting hundred-foot shadows of two immensely tall, skinny skeletons ambling along the river ice beneath wispy patches of snow and row upon row of dune-like drifts that formed like waves frozen in time.

Everett enjoyed talking to the boy as much as he feared talking to Ella. The boy was learning fast and could now set traps, skin a beaver, catch strings of fish, shoot a duck in full flight, and keep pace with Everett under any conditions without complaints. Often they would walk or work for long stretches without saying a word, without needing to-the true measure of a good companion. The boy was growing up, Everett knew, and could talk about the things men talked about, the things that made a difference to men and managed to pass the time and take the edge off the long hours, the cold, the aching hard work, and the long bouts of tedium. The boy was learning how to think ahead, too. They could work a trap site without a word.

You could tell him something once and that was all he needed. You never had to tell him twice. He could spot a rabbit or fox and had a sense for when to be cautious. He could hear the silence in the woods indicating a predator nearby. He could hear the blue jays call out in alarm. He could spot a pheasant or partridge in a thicket. He could identify animals and birds by their tracks, and he could move without a lot of noise and ruckus. He was ready, even if his mother wasn't.

* * *

Father Ray's recovery was swift after the fever broke, but his arm remained partially paralyzed, forcing him to rely heavily on Lucy in their missionary work. Lucy persuaded him to avoid the Huron mission.

Instead, they visited a Seneca encampment where as many of the Indians spoke English as French and were divided in their loyalties as well.

Father Ray would not sleep in the long house because the Indian lust was so public and sometimes raucous that he could not concentrate on his prayers. So he and Lucy and several Indians build a hut dug into a hillside. By evening of their day of arrival, they had a tight encampment with two warm bear furs to soften and warm the floor. The Indians helped them fashion a stove...a tall circle of rocks with a wide opening for cooking and above it a sheath of maple bark tied to form a pipe hanging from the roof that captured most of the rising smoke. The Indians provided them with venison and a jug of wine, then left giggling into the darkness.

That evening Lucy poured wine into wooden cups. She fashioned a spit of cedar branches and put the venison to roast at the opening atop the pile of rocks. She knew Father Ray to have a fondness for wine but that night he drank abundantly. As they ate their venison, his eyes sparkled, and his cheeks glowed.

During the night she was astonished when she awoke feeling Father Ray's hand caressing her body and then yet more amazed as he crawled silently beneath her blankets. But she was not surprised by the abundance of his passion as they made love in the darkness with an ardor she had never experienced in her memory.

The next morning Father Ray was up before dawn gathering firewood. He made a fire as she feigned sleep. He whistled hymns as happy as a child, and busied himself making tea mostly with one hand, having to compensate for the numbness in his left arm and hand. After finishing a cup, he knelt and said his usual prayers for an hour. Lucy could not imagine what to say or how to behave now that she and Father Ray were lovers. So, she decided to pretend nothing out of the ordinary had happened. Sensing the end of his prayers was nearing, she sat up, bundled in her blanket and sipped groggily from her cooling cup of tea.

"Good morning, my child," Father Ray said cheerfully.

She muttered her hello.

"Yes, I think these Indians will be quite difficult. Their divided loyalties will surely make things tense."

Lucy rubbed her eyes. As always, she was amazed at how silly some of his notions were, especially early in the morning. "Do you really think they care that much about the white men? Do you think their loyalties to whites are deeper than to each other?"

Father Ray considered her words. He smiled and seemed almost to debate with himself within his mind as if Lucy had not yet woken. "Of course, of course, how stupid of me," he finally said, looking at her as if she had just suddenly joined him.

Father Ray's handicap almost proved a blessing. It was now more necessary for him to enlist the help and support of the Indians and to persuade them to build a mission, the house for God who loves you all very deeply, he would always tell them. He began with projects, such as the mission, to get to know the Indians, their tribal habits, power relationships, loyalties, and leaders. He would then increase his teaching, always beginning with heaven and how Jesus had come to live on earth to save mankind and escort them after death to this wonderful paradise filled with deer and beaver and fields of corn, free of all disease and war, perpetually warm but free of mosquitoes and snakes. Lucy spoke these things in English and for those who did not understand, she labored with her childhood remnants of Iroquois that were quickly joined by the members who understood English or French and took her clumsy translations in hand and filled them out until all eyes grew large and bemused. Lucy always thought that even those who converted believed only a fraction of Father Ray's stories, and like her mother, picked and chose what they wanted to believe-mostly that Jesus was a kind-hearted fellow who forgave all of them their sins and wished them full bellies and peaceful fun in the white man's version of heaven.

On this second day at the Seneca encampment, they began building a log mission on a hillside overlooking a lovely lake tucked in the Adirondack Mountains. The weather turned cold and windy late in the day, and that night snow fell in a howling, snowy gale. Exhausted from their hard work, they drank wine and cooked beaver legs, and fell asleep quickly. Deep in the night, the wind whistling at the openings in their hut, Father Ray again crawled into her covers and mounted her with the same abundant passion, his tongue caressing every crevice. His numb hand seeming to recover its lost memory along the smooth curves of her body.

* * *

Everett, Jamie, and the dog set out for a two-week trapping trip in mid-February at the first sign of thaw. They pulled their canoe on the ice up river to the St. Regis River tributary, then south along the creek bank toward the Adirondack Mountains and into the heart of Iroquois country.

In less than a day, they began seeing more beaver dams and hutches but forged onward buoyed by the knowledge that the deeper the wilderness, the more beaver they would encounter. On the second morning, Jamie took out a bow and arrow made for him by Jean-Robert. He had learned to be a passable shot, and Everett preferred the quiet of an arrow to the blast of his musket.

They spotted dozens of fresh deer tracks at a brook entering the river and tipped the canoe on its side downwind of a rocky shelf overhanging rushing water where the deer had not long before gathered to drink. They hid and waited, and in less than an hour a half dozen does and an enormous buck arrived at the shelf.

Everett lay on the ground peaking through brush covering the stern of the canoe. Jamie sat hidden behind the boat, threading an arrow onto the string. Everett raised his fingers to indicate the deer count. They waited until the deer settled and set to drinking. Everett signaled him with a thumbs up.

With his heart pounding, Jamie burst upward, pulled back the arrow in the bow. For a moment, the deer froze, then suddenly broke with huge leaps. Jamie sighted the lead doe as he'd learned from hunting with a gun, and smoothly following the motion, let the arrow fly. He could hear the wet thud of penetration, the arrow piercing the deer's neck. The deer darted, seemingly unhurt, into the woods. Everett held the dog. They listened. Blue Jays cried out in an audible pathway of panic as the deer plunged deep into the echoing woods. When all was silent, Everett and Jamie rose and set the dog on a lead. They quickly found blood and followed the trail marked by the hard-pulling dog.

In less than a mile, they came upon the deer. She lay gasping beside an old birch, blood glistening and wet, flowing in a steady ooze from the shaft of the arrow. When she saw them, her left eye turned back-huge and horrified. She struggled to her feet, staggered, and collapsed, front legs first, then her haunches tipped unsteadily and her legs buckled. They could hear the rasp of blood and air burbling in her throat. Everett let the dog go. She lunged to the rear of the deer, and as she tried to turn, Everett plunged forward, grasped her head beneath his arm, and slit her throat. Blood burst from her neck for a few moments, then her eyes dimmed, and her body sagged.

They worked quickly and silently, the dog tied to a tree. Jamie ran his knife up the smooth skin of her belly, and the large sack of innards rolled, steaming from her belly. They tied her legs to a tree, hoisted her, and skinned her. Everett reached into the slippery mound of innards, cut out the heart and liver and flung them to the dog. Everett chopped at the hip and leg joints, then cut away the best meat and stuffed it in his shoulder bag. In less than a half hour, the deer was butchered. They took the skin, the best meat, and left the rest for the Indians or wolves, whoever came first.

When they neared the canoe, the dog growled quietly. Everett and Jamie crouched and approached from behind dense tangles of underbrush until they saw three Iroquois men inspecting the canoe. Everett walked into the clearing. The Indians watched him carefully but were unalarmed. Everett waved his open hand in a display of greeting and good will. They returned the identical movements.

"Hello, my friends," Everett said quietly.

The men nodded and separated a bit. They watched Jamie emerge, the deer skin slung over one shoulder, his bow wedged over the other. One of the Indians grinned slightly and nodded at Jamie. He was thin, almost slight, with a handsome, angular face and a bold tuft of hair raised atop his head like a brimmed hat. All three were similarly built, but the other two had long, braids tied behind. Each wore leather trousers and English woolen coats.

As Jamie approached, Everett took the deer skin from Jamie's shoulder and flung it to the tufted Indian, who caught it, sniffed it, and nodded approvingly.

"The boy shoot dis one?"

"Yessir," Everett nodded.

"Ees a good boat," The Indian said, indicating the canoe.

Everett lowered his shoulder pack into the canoe and nodded his agreement.

The dog slinked carefully at Everett's heal, growling quietly.

Everett swatted at the dog's ears. "We come as friends to trap a few beaver. Then we leave for the great river," he said pointing north.

Everett reached into his pack and removed a leg, offering it to the Indians.

The tufted man took it, smelled it, and nodded his thanks.

"Are there waterfalls ahead?" Everett asked.

They looked puzzled.

Everett signaled with his hands, showing a long flow downward.

"Three leagues dat way. Big water," he said, making a similar motion with his hands. "Take de trail," and he made a loop with his hand. "Then ees good," he said, making a paddling motion. "Many beaver. Very beeg." Then the tufted Indian drew a map in the snow showing the falls, and the loop around it."

Everett nodded his thanks. "There's more deer meat in the woods," he said pointing to the leg and then to their trail through the trees.

The Indian nodded and spoke to his partners in their own tongue. They prepared to leave.

"Are there any soldiers or war parties ahead," Everett said pointing up the narrowing river.

"No, no. Not da war here. Dat way and Dat way, but thees not good for de war," he said pointing east and west, then making a large circle and pointing his fingers in the shape of mountains. "Thees no good for da war. Da soldiers, dey not like da beeg hills."

Everett nodded his thanks and made the greeting signal again. They returned his gestures as in a mirror, and strode quickly into the woods to retrieve the meat.

Jamie sighed deeply. When they were out of view, he asked Everett, "You think they'll be back?"

"Don't know."

"You think they'll track us?"

"Don't know, son."

"They wouldn't steal our skins, would they?"

"We'll need to keep a sharp eye. Keep watch on the dog. She can smell 'em long before we can. You smell 'em, son?"

"Yessir."

"Don't forgit that smell."

"Nossir."

"They ain't likely to bother us if we're ready. They ain't stupid. They don't want to take losses. They ain't gonna die over a few beaver pelts."

They gathered scraps of wood and made a fire to cook their meat. Everett fashioned a spit and set some steaks above the fire. He squatted down and lit his pipe. Birds chirped now in the near distance. The damp air hung heavily, holding the smoke around the fire. The brook flowed rapidly over a rocky ledge into the St. Regis with a steady burbling.

"Them Indians is like wolves," Everett said.

"Yeah?" said Jamie, poking at the fire with a stick.

"They attack men who are drunk or sick or not paying attention same as a wolf takes the sick deer or the young ones don't know better and ain't ready. You won't see a wolf take a healthy deer. It's too risky. One hoof in the mouth, and it could fester and kill 'em and they know it. Same with us. You saw me go for that deer when the dog had her attention. They got sharp hoofs. They'll bite yah, too. Got to be careful, and when you go for 'em, you got to go strong, and twist hell out 'em and slit the jugular quick. Otherwise, leave 'em be and let 'em die slow or stand your distance and shoot 'em. I took her that way 'cause I wanted to be quiet and git on with it. She could ah lived another two hours. It don't pay to get injured out here. The wolves know it, and them Indians know it."

"Them Indians scare you?" Jamie asked.

"Scare the shit out of me, boy. But you don't want to show it. They think you're scairt, and that's a sign of weakness. They'll come back if they sense a weakness. They drawn to weakness same as wolves. It's bred into 'em. Ones who cain't smell a weakness is long since dead and gone."

Jamie considered that in silence and wondered if the Indians could smell his fear.

"You scairt, boy?" Everett asked, twisting the meat on the spit.

"Nossir."

Everett looked at Jamie for a moment and knew he was lying, but he wasn't going to tell him it was okay to be scared. "Them Indians was wearing white men's coats," Jamie said.

"Yessir."

"Where'd they git 'em, you figure?" Jamie asked, poking the fire at the edges and putting on more sticks.

"Maybe they traded for 'em. Maybe they stole 'em. Maybe they kilt for 'em. But I didn't see no blood or holes or chars. I reckon those boys traded for 'em or stole 'em. Looked damned near brand new, dandy as could be."

"Yessir."

Everett considered the possibility that those Indians had followed them up the river. Maybe they were after the bounty and had come from Montreal.

"We just got to be ready, that's it. There ain't no other way. You caint out think the bastards. They got a thousand reasons to hunt down white men and only one reason not to."

"What's that one reason."

"They don't want to git killed. They don't even want to git hurt. Them Iroquois are smart sonsabitches. Smart as wolves."

"They probly learned from the wolves, ey?"

"Yessir. And from foxes and otter and bear and wolverines and the whole damn lot of 'em with all their goddamned tricks. Them's Indian ways. They think most white men are idiots, but they're smart enough to figure which ones are and which ones ain't, and they leave the smart ones be. I'll tell yah, though. I'm glad we got this here dog. She's one ah them, and they knew it, damned for sure."

"Yessir. She's a good girl," Jamie nodded.

Everett took a lower leg bone from his pack and tossed it to the dog. She grasped it and took herself close to the fire, sat down and chewed.

* * *

Jean-Robert kept a spear leaned against the wall in a spot he could find in the dark. He carried a large, razor-sharp hunting knife at his belt. He kept a pistol hidden on a shelf in the kitchen. He kept a musket outside hidden beneath a skin between two logs. He kept his bow and arrow at his side nearly at all times and could set an arrow and fire it with deadly accuracy in less than a second. He slept with his eyes slightly parted. His hearing was so acute he could detect the change in splashes at the shore's edge if a canoe or boat landed. He knew the cries of danger of every bird.

He could hear and feel people walking up the path from the lower island at any time of day or night. His Indian name meant Waiting Night Heron, a tribute to his patience and acute sense of movement. On the island he was comforted by two night herons who roosted nights in two great birches overhanging the river. When a night heron was disturbed by movement of any kind up to a mile or more away, they let out an odd and ugly squawk. They were equal to any eagle or hawk in their profoundly acute hearing and vision. They could see at night as well as during the day, an attribute shared by Jean-Robert from the early days of his youth.

It was not clear to him why a young warrior of his skill was needed to protect the white woman, Ella, but he did not question his father's assigned mission nor did he allow himself a moment's complacency. He liked her very much. She was always kind and showed great patience with his readings of the Bible book. Unlike the women of the tribe, Ella was most often quiet and would spend many hours reading from several score books. The women from the tribe were always joking and laughing and played many tricks on their children. He missed their cheerful ways but was relieved not to have to be on constant watch for some trick or prank that would set his mother and his aunts into great spasms of laughter. The white women, Ella, did not engage in any pranks and was not given to much laughter, but she often smiled kindly and spoke with double meanings and an edge to her voice she called 'sarcasm' or sometimes 'irony.'

"I'm sorry to be ironic," she said often to him, "I know it must confuse you."

She did confuse him at times, saying something that really meant something else, but she had reserved most of this for Jamie. "You are so neat and tidy," she would say to Jamie, and Jean-Robert knew that it was the opposite, yet he needed to listen carefully for the little edge to her voice that signaled her irony and warned him she had another, nearly opposite thought in her mind.

When Everett and Jamie announced they were leaving for the beaver hunt, Jean-Robert was deeply jealous, but he knew it was his duty to stay. And with Everett gone, he knew he must be doubly careful and alert. While the white man, Everett, was large and sometimes clumsy and could not see or hear as well as an Indian, he was a worthy warrior. His father told him that Everett was a powerful force who thought in the wild with the clarity of an Indian and was as honest a white man as they would ever know. His father told Jean-Robert that it was necessary to cultivate their Iroquois friendship with these whites with as much care as they would tend their garden. His father had had a vision in his dreams that white men would someday come and take all of their land, a vision experienced by many wise and powerful Indians, men and women alike. The white man, Everett, would save their lives someday, his father, Gordon White Tree, told him, "It is in my vision."

The greatest danger on the island, however, was not other white men, but patrols of Huron warriors seeking out English whites on behalf of the French-speaking army. Each year more English trappers and traders moved to the Iroquois region. The English were tough and crude and badly behaved. They treated the French with contempt and scorn. For many years the Iroquois had chased the Huron further north and west, taking their trapping lands. So the Hurons and French shared a common hatred for the English and their Iroquois partners. Someday, his father said, their enemy would be the English more so than the French, but now it was the French and the Hurons who posed the greatest threat.

Jean-Robert did not worry greatly about the French. They would not kill Ella nor himself, but the Huron patrols were far different and beyond the control of the mannerly Frenchmen. They were a desperate people in need of revenge and replenishment who hated the English and the Iroquois with equal rage. "If they come upon you," Gordon White Tree told his son, "you must attack them with a fierce and wild charge that will remind them why we have conquered them. You can scare the Huron warriors if they believe you are inhabited with the evil spirit of the Iroquois. You can defeat ten of them at once, but you must transform yourself into a banshee."

So each morning Jean-Robert applied war paint and plucked hairs from his head except for a fearsome spike of hair at the very top and middle that dared any Indian to take his scalp. He painted his face with red and black and made white lightening bolts on each arm.

"Why do you do this each day, Jean-Robert?" Ella asked him one day.

"Do I scare you?" he asked.

"Yes. Yes you do, indeed," she said with sudden animation.

"I do this to scare our enemies so that they will think I am the devil."

"I'd rather you didn't," she said.

"It is my father's command."

"Your father isn't here. This is my home, and the devil frightens *me*."

"I must obey my father," Jean-Robert said fiercely.

"Well if you must," she said, "But you are quite a sight, reading the Bible in your war paint looking every bit the devil." And then she laughed and patted him kindly on the shoulder and said, "It's okay. I'll try to understand."

But sometimes she would turn, when her mind was absorbed by cooking or mending, and see this extraordinarily quiet boy, bare from the waist in his fearsome colors and give herself a start. She did not like the word "savages" used by most white men at the time, but on days or nights like this, a cold chill raced down her spine. He could sit for hours without moving, perched on a bench watching the door, waiting as if ready to pounce, and she could not help thinking that very word herself. Often he would pace, checking the small window, peeking out the cracks, walking outside in the bitter cold without a coat or shirt. And if the wind gusted, he was like a sprung cat, leaping to his feet, grasping his bow and quietly escaping outside to see what, if anything, was within a telescope's range of the island.

It was, then, a breathtaking surprise to them both when one morning, as she turned to place fresh bread on the breakfast table, the door slammed open, and a Huron warrior, his spear held tightly beneath his arm, charged at Jean-Robert and drove his spear into his chest with this horrible crunching thud, and drove the boy back against the central beam holding the roof, the spear piercing through Jean-Robert's body and pinning him against the beam. Jean-Robert's face was aghast with surprise. He grasped the spear with both hands, but could not budge it loose. He looked to Ella, stricken with horror, blood gushing from the fatal wound, and in a moment, his eyes flattened and sagged, and his body slumped and hung limp, pierced through the heart.

Ella screamed and covered her face and fell trembling to the floor as a half dozen Huron warriors rushed in, ripped open the bedroom doors, stole blankets, whiskey, clothes and found her musket and Jean-Robert's pistol as if they knew every inch of the place. Ella gasped for breath and quietly prayed for her soul, expecting at any moment for a spear to burst through her back and end her life. She prayed that God lift Jean Robert's soul into heaven and asked that God grant him peace. She prayed that Jamie would live to ancient years and remember their happy times. Then she heard the unforgettable, haunting sound of skin ripped from bone, as they took Jean-Robert's scalp, followed by a deep and mournful howl.

The Indians flung their findings onto open blankets they spread on the floor, and then tied them, forming swollen sacks that they quickly seized and took out doors. They threw the final blanket over Ella, bound it with rope, covering her entirely, and lifted her over the shoulder of an Indian who rushed her out the door into the startling cold. She felt her body bound and bounce as this small Indian with slight shoulders ran down the path and dumped her into an enormous canoe capable of carrying twelve warriors but stuffed with heaping blankets and the stunned and horrified Ella.

It took less than fifteen minutes to accomplish their raid. Ella felt the canoe lurch as the Indians grasped ropes and pulled the loaded canoe out over the snow onto the ice of the river. Soon they glided along with a loud scraping as the Indians pulled her as fast as they could run. Perhaps a mile or so from the island, they slowed their pace to a walk and spoke in their own language-perhaps about their raid; she did not know.

Nor did she know that her safety was assured, that she had become one of them, a replacement for an Indian lost to an Iroquois raid, a replenishment, as the Jesuits called these strange kidnappings by the savages they could never understand.

They dragged the canoe most of the day with Ella tied inside the blanket and jammed in a heap with the other satchels.

Finally they stopped and a young warrior, whom she later knew as Falling Feather, released Ella from the ropes. It was late afternoon, the sun glowing dimly behind thick slow-moving clouds on the southern horizon across the river. They had pulled the canoe into a frozen stream on the north shore. Falling Feather helped her out of the canoe and steadied her like a newborn calf in a patch of wet snow. He turned her and poked her legs and arms as if inspecting her for dinner. He was tall and thin with fingers as hard as sticks, his long dark hair pulled back and tied in a tuft behind his head. His face was a deep, reddish brown with taut wind-burned skin stretched tightly over sharp, angular cheeks. He touched her neck with his cool, hard fingers, then pulled her hair up over her head with both hands, admiring the golden color.

Ella had resigned herself to a half dozen fates-the worst being cooked and eaten. Each time her heart began beating wildly with fear, she began praying in an attempt to shut out all thought from her mind. Her next worst fear was being tortured and raped. It did not easily recede to the words of her muttered prayers. Falling Feather handed her one of Everett's leather coats. She put it on and tried to remember things Everett had said about dealing with Indians. Do not show fear. Do not be rude. Be direct. Do not assume the worst until it happens.

"Why did you kill the boy?" she asked him as clearly and forthrightly as her fear would allow.

He looked at her with complete puzzlement.

"Pourquoi vous avez tuer le garçon?"

"Il aurait nous tuer." He said, simply. He would have killed us.

"Why have you taken me from my home?" she demanded. "Pourquoi vous m'avez prise de ma maison?"

"Vous êtes une de nous maintenant." You are one of us now, he told her. He handed her a rabbit leg, lightly cooked from a fire already crackling near the stream's edge.

For a few minutes, she held the meat and felt waves of depression pass through her. Then she ate the meat, vowing to maintain her strength and preserve her determination. It would not do to become weak or ill, she thought. He gave her another leg, and she ate that as the other warriors spoke quietly in their native language and ignored her.

"What does this mean: Une de vous êtes nous maintenant?" she asked.

He again frowned in his puzzled way and seemed to search his mind. Then he shrugged and pursed his lips in that strange, exuberant way French Canadians used to express their bafflement. "*Vous êtes une de nous*," he said more emphatically."Tu vivra entre nous comme l'esprit choisi de une de nos filles tombé." You will live among us as a chosen spirit of our fallen daughters. "Vous es safety. You be safe-tee?" he said.

"I'll be safe?"

"Oui, yes. Inglash not so very good. Mon français est meilleur."

"You will not kill me?"

He looked at her strangely. "No, no. You have dead enough."

"Pardon."

He searched his mind again. "Vous avez eu assez de mort. Ton esprit est retourner avec nous." You have had enough of death. Your spirit is back with us.

Ella felt a disquieting mix of relief and dread. She understood him to be saying she would taken among them as a hostage to replace one of their dead, at least that was a custom Everett had described. They are not unkind to such hostages, he told her, but the Indian life is very hard. He had told her that it was an insult to refuse their offerings of food. *'At least they have good manners,'* she told him. *'Human flesh is sometimes tough to swallow,'* he said with a great laugh. *'Never,'* she said. *'You must,'* he smiled.

She ate another piece of tepid, bleeding rabbit leg and regarded Falling Feather cautiously.

He smiled, revealing several broken teeth, severed at odd angles. His lower lip was lightly creased by a thin, white scar. He was a handsome creature, she thought. She had heard that Hurons were a handsome people favored by the Jesuits because of their almost European features. Perhaps the Jesuits believed they had larger souls. Ella gazed down the stream to the expanse of the St. Lawrence and thought that she may never see the great river again in her life on earth. It was not such a loss. It had obviously been such a huge mistake to have left Lake Champlain. She had fled the war only to find herself lost at its fringe. She thought of Jamie and asked God to protect him. Then she asked God to protect Everett so that he could aid in protecting Jamie. Then she had a shudder of dread as she imagined that Jean-Robert could have been Jamie or that Jamie could have been there that day. She thanked God that Everett was so obstinate and insisted against her wishes that Jamie go with him. She prayed that God would rejoin Everett and Gordon. She prayed that Gordon's suffering be brief. But she did not dare pray to God that they come rescue her because she knew that would bring Jamie with them.

The eldest of the grandmothers, Whispering Cloud, greeted Ella at the village with a warm hug and made her a bed next to her own in the cabin closest to the stream that ran past the Huron village. The first night, she ate with Whispering Cloud's family. They sat in a circle around the fire in the long house and ate from a large, common bowl carved from wood and filled with a mix of grains and strips of cooked meat. Ella tried to find her appetite, but was too exhausted and depressed to rekindle her spirit. She noted that each adult Indian and each child took nearly identical portions, and when Ella only took a nibble, Whispering Cloud held the bowl before her and shook it until Ella ate an amount equal to the other adults. When they were finished, Whispering Cloud's son lit a pipe and handed it around the circle. His wife smoked from it, then their two sons and three daughters. One of the oldest daughters-a girl of ten, perhaps-handed the pipe to Ella. She did not smoke from it, but attempted to hand on to Flying Turtle, Whispering Cloud's daughter.

Everyone's faces grew stern, and the mother of the children stood and took the pipe angrily. Whispering Cloud and the woman exchanged words.

"It is an insult to my family. You must smoke from the pipe. C'est une insulte à mon famille. Tu dois fumer la pipe," the mother said to Ella.

Ella took the pipe and sucked on the wet mouth piece. As she breathed in the smoke, she coughed. The children laughed. Ella smiled thinly and handed the pipe back to the mother who nodded sternly. Whispering Cloud nodded and rocked her body forward and backward in meditation. The others followed, and Ella imitated their movements. The mother nodded her approval to Ella. Then the Indians chanted quietly in the circle, their bodies swaying to the rising and falling of their voices. Ella did not chant, but closed her eyes and swayed in unison, silently praying to God for forgiveness for practicing heathen rituals.

That night Ella slept next to Whispering Cloud and Flying Turtle. Their beds were slabs of bark spread on the dirt floor covered by thick bear skins. Exhausted and dispirited, Ella fell quickly to sleep and dreamed of her childhood home, a cabin overlooking the Hudson River. She and her mother cooked a huge bowl of turkey feathers. During the dream, Ella tried to warn her mother than they should be cooking the turkey, not the feathers, but her mother merely nodded and smiled and continued laying feathers one at a time in the cooking pan until they formed a large mound. Ella woke in a sweat of frustration, and for a few moments was lost in the darkness of her new home without any memory of where she was. As she gained consciousness, she felt herself falling deeper into darkness and fought, as if swimming, to reach the surface until finally she remembered where she was and grew miserably depressed again.

The next morning more than a dozen women from the long house escorted Ella to the stream where several warriors smashed at the ice with hatchets until the ice was broken in a wide circle. They flung fragments of ice to the opposite bank until a dark pool of frigid water was exposed. Flying Turtle and another woman pulled Ella into the water up to her waist. Ella gasped from the penetrating cold. They tore her dress from her shoulders and began washing her naked body with harsh, painful strokes from their rough, callused hands. Dozens of Indians from the village stood along the shore and chanted prayers. After a few minutes of this washing, Ella's legs ached from cold, and her feet turned numb. Then the two women pushed down on her shoulders.

For a moment, Ella resisted, assuming that they would now drown her, but she soon collapsed under their strong arms prayed silently for

God's mercy and a speedy death. But they only dunked her briefly, then lifted her gently, rushed her from the water, and a group of other women threw blankets over her and rubbed her entire body vigorously as they escorted her back to the long house, and dressed her in a long leather skirt and thigh-length shirt. They built up the fire until her shivering stopped and her face glowed pink from the heat. They then left her alone with Whispering Cloud who hugged her for several minutes. She sat Ella down and dried her hair with a wool blanket and tied braids decorated with beads, bone fragments, and tiny feathers threaded to the braids with the coarse hair of a deer's white tail.

Whispering Cloud sat beside her in front of the fire holding Ella's hand and sang a long and intricate song in her native tongue. After an hour or so of this song, Whispering Cloud explained to Ella that she had been cleansed of her white flesh and had now been adopted as the reincarnation of Whispering Cloud's daughter who had died at the hands of a Mohawk raiding party as a young child many summer seasons ago. "I welcome you back, daughter," the old women whispered, "and from now on you will be known as Morning Glory." Later Ella would learn that Whispering Cloud's daughter had blue eyes, like her own, and for this highly unusual attribute, had been considered to be a sacred person in the tribe whose radiant beauty bloomed each morning with the rising sun and brought joy and optimism to the long house. The child's death caused Whispering Cloud to lose her voice and her own eyesight for two years, and for the next twenty years, the mother refused to consider replacing her daughter and regain her wandering soul.

Then she learned only a few weeks prior to Ella's capture that a radiant woman with blue eyes lived with an Indian child on an isolated island. Whispering Cloud knew this to be her daughter, and the raid was ordered. The boy was to be stabbed through the heart to avenge Morning Glory's death, and the blue-eyed woman brought back to the village to rejoin her mother for the rest of her days on earth. The boy's scalp was fastened to a long poll decorated with beads and feathers and stabbed into the soil near the long house door as a reminder that no Indian's death was ever forgotten nor left un-avenged.

After welcoming her daughter back that morning, Whispering Cloud presented her to the tribe. All through the day and night there were celebrations and a great feast of deer, beaver, bear, squash, grains, and corn bread. The women painted her face and neck with a deep red-brown paste, rubbing it deeply into her skin so that it actually stained her the color of the Indians' flesh and made her bright, blue eyes glow wondrously in contrast to her darkened face. Each month thereafter, they repeated this application until her facial pigment had become permanently darkened, and save for her bright blue eyes, Ella became indistinguishable from other women in the tribe.

* * *

Henri quickly discovered that the Black Duck Tavern was a stinking, seething sewer of such unimaginably poor quality that only Montreal's dregs bothered to visit and only they because it offered the cheapest ale, rum, and food in the settlement. Monsieur Fourmet's recipe for Black Duck stew included chunks of rabbit, horses, alley cats, dead dogs and any other festering meat he could pick up for free at day's end at the quay-side market. He cooked kitchen rats who fell into the stew vats and simmered to death. He tossed in anything he could find, dead or alive.

Henri first set about cleaning the place, a job that took more than a week.

"I will not cook in such filth," Henri told the bemused Fourmet. He doused the floors with lye and washed every nook and corner, every shelf, every pot and plate until the acrid stench of urine and vomit vanished. He bought two fine cats bred for their rat and mouse slaying skills. He put up signs pointing to the privy out back and included warnings that anyone caught urinating or vomiting inside the tavern would be banned for life.

He generated a list of demands and a plan for restoring the Black Duck Tavern.

He presented his plan one cold, gray morning.

Monsieur Fourmet read the lengthy document, frowning and burping. When he was finished he sat back in his chair, his belly settling over his belt like two giant fleshy pumpkins. He sighed deeply, and Henri prepared himself to issue a tantrum.

"Oh, oui, très bien. We will close for three weeks, and the work will be done. But these food and drink prices, Monsieur, they are very high. We will lose all of our customers."

"That is precisely the point, Monsieur Fourmet. We will begin anew. The Black Duck Tavern must re-open with a completely new face."

Fourmet regarded Henri skeptically over his spectacles. He scratched his beard. "Tres bien, Monsieur, but if this fails, I will hang you by your balls until you die."

"Agreed," Henri said. "When we are within a week of re-opening, I will advertise all over town and we will serve the finest Parisian meal this forsaken wilderness has ever experienced. Moreover, we will hire a bouncer and allow no bums, no drunks, no stinking fisherman nor rancid trappers. We will cater to French officers, merchants, established property owners, government dignitaries, Jesuits, ship owners, and wealthy farmers."

"And if they don't come?"

"Promise me a month after we re-open. If we are not making as much money as you make now, you can have your bums back."

"Très bien, nous verrons."

The next Monday, Henri hung a *Ferma pour le Dépannage* sign on the door and welcomed the crew of carpenters Fourmet had secured for the work.

They tore out the festering floor and brought in new planks. They rebuilt the kitchen, tossing out old, rotting table tops and sagging cupboards. Henri ordered new plates, pans, cooking pots, utensils, table cloths, candles, lanterns, and replaced everything. He ordered a new sign, *La Taverne du Canard Noir*, a grand black duck, carved and painted and hung on wrought-iron over the door. He replaced the door, itself, the tables, chairs, windows, and had a grand bar built across the full length of the far wall. He had the privy dug out and rebuilt, a four-holer-two for women, two for men, each with silk-lined seats over the holes to offer comfort in the cold.

He generated a menu and had it printed on fine paper pressed with a water mark with an image of the carved Black Duck sign over the door. As the date for re-opening approached, he shopped the quay-side market for the finest black duck, turkey, beef, and vegetables available in the region. He ordered French imported wines, fine ales from Britain, and a rich selection of brandies, after-dinner drinks, and Champagnes.

Fourmet groaned and muttered but issued the notes and payments from the considerable wealth he'd accumulated over the years feeding people with virtual garbage and selling spirits diluted with raw grain alcohol and river water.

Henri hired waiters and a tailor to make them all fine new clothes, including elegant suits for both himself and Fourmet. He scoured the docks for a man big enough and strong enough to serve as bouncer and found a man named Picquet, newly from Paris who had worked as a lion tamer in a gypsy traveling circus and had worked between acts as the circus barker. He was as handsome as the statue David, and his deep, resonant voice could be both scary to raucous gate crashers and awe-inspiring to welcome guests.

As the carpenters finished the renovations, Henri began training his crew, soon discovering that he would need an assistant chef.

"You are the bloody chef," Fourmet boomed angrily.

"Mai oui, Monsieur, but I must be everywhere."

Fourmet gave him a paltry budget for the assistant chef, so Henri found a young woman who worked as second assistant in the kitchen at the Grand Hotel. "If you are good, you will be head chef in two years," he told her.

When Fourmet saw the prospective assistant chef, his resistance melted. Though not beautiful by Henri's refined standards of female elegance, Mademoiselle Renée Gaston was a sturdy, handsome young woman with strong hands and a crooked smile that set Fourmet's knees to trembling. When it appeared that she would not leave the more secure job at the Grand Hotel, Fourmet increased the salary offer to more than twenty times the token allowance he had granted to Henri.

Mademoiselle Gaston agreed to the job of assistant chef and shook their hands and smiled crookedly, her head tilted oddly to the side, the right lid of her startlingly light blue eyes slightly more shut than the other, giving her a somewhat sleepy visage. Her eyes, combined with her soft, almost whispery voice, perhaps suggested to Fourmet that she was a bit doltish and an easy target for his bed. But Henri had questioned her extensively and watched her at work after sneaking into the Grand Hotel kitchen in the guise of stove repairman. She cooked with rapid, confident hand movements and offered precise, exacting orders to her own assistants and waiters. She spoke softly but was in complete command, a manner that Henri preferred over the semi-hysteria that governed so many Parisian restaurants. And her timing was exquisite, and what could be more important in cooking, Henri asked himself, than perfect timing. It was one of his own best traits, after all. He noted, as well, that she kept her calm when her own chief chef yelled obscenities and scolded everyone, including her, for his own frantic errors.

"You are not like my chief chef?" she said to Henri before their interview with Fourmet.

"No, no, no," Henri laughed. "I do not yell and throw tantrums and abuse people."

She looked at him cautiously, then nodded. "That is good because someday I would cut off the fingers of that horrid man in a terrible accident," she said softly.

Henri opened the door for her to the Black Duck Tavern. "A terrible accident for a chef," he said, taken aback.

"These things can happen around sharp knives, yes?" she said.

"Ah oui, but yes. I'm am not one of those tyrants, not at all," he said.

And so, the Black Duck Tavern was transformed, and the afternoon of the grand opening party, Henri sat at a new table by a new window peeking out at the street and sipped from his imported brandy. He watched a small group of Jesuits hurry by on the way to the church and wondered how things had gone for Lucy and Everett. He had been so busy in his new life, he'd almost forgotten them.

* * *

Everett and Jamie followed the St. Regis River deeper and deeper into the wilderness until it narrowed into a rushing stream that carved deep gorges into the emerging mountain foothills. Each day the dog stopped several times and sniffed the air, growled quietly and raised hers hackles like porcupine quills at the back of her neck. Although neither had ever seen them again, Everett figured that the Indians they'd met many days back were following them. One afternoon, the blazing sun blazing casting sharp shadows across the snow, Everett and Jamie came upon the first of a series of great ponds created by immense beaver dams.

"This be beaver heaven, my boy," Everett said squinting into the sun.

"Yessir, that's God's own truth," Jamie smiled.

As far as the eye could see were lines of beaver dams and hundreds of beaver lodges poking through the ice. They set about setting traps, working the entire afternoon until darkness. They made camp on a cliff overlooking the river, and Everett cooked venison he'd shot the previous day. They flipped the canoe and set it as shelter, using greased deer skins as bedding to prevent snow melting and penetrating their clothes and blankets during sleep.

Everett dragged a log to the edge of their fire and sat. They both shared rum and tobacco as their meal cooked.

"This'll be our camp for the next week or so," Everett said, glad to be able to add rest to their long trek.

"Must be a thousand beaver down there," Jamie said.

"I reckon."

"Keep your eyes and ears open, son. Them Indians'll be close by."

"You think they'll attack?"

"Don't know for sure. Not yet, they won't, I don't think. They'll likely wait 'til we done our work. 'Til we got us a load. We'll put out beaver meat for 'em. Could be that they're following cause we leave a trail of meat. But when we git done, we'll have a heap of furs. Good as money to 'em, so I reckon they'll try to hit on us 'bout when we're ready to leave."

Jamie felt a flutter of butterflies just thinking about an attack. He'd never shot a man and didn't know if he could. He turned to Everett and asked, "What do you aim for when shootin an Indian?"

"Go fer the body. Whatever's the biggest presentation. We got five guns before reloading. Better if we don't have to use 'em all at once. Better that we reload as we go along. Like I says, they ain't likely to be reckless. They can hunt and trap better'n us, so they ain't desperate and we been feeding 'em good. We just caint show 'em any weakness. Whatever you do when and if they come, shoot to kill. A nicked Indian ain't nothing but dangerous. A wounded Indian comes at yah to avenge his own death. Ain't nothing that can discourage him short of death or a mortal wound. If they get past the guns, keep your head up and your eyes open. They come at yah with arms flailing, screaming and hollering. Don't pay no attention to all that flutter. Take yer axe or knife and draw a bead on their shoulders and neck, and get yerself ready to attack so it's just one motion. Don't close yer eyes for nothing. Watch that blade sink in. Watch it same as you squeeze off a bullet in the gun. You flinch or close yer eyes at the last second, and you'll miss and that's all she wrote."

Jamie's heart pounded with fear and excitement as he imagined an Indian flying at him.

"They're quick and strong, but they ain't big. Yer already bigger than any Indian we're likely to see. Them boys we seen warn't big. They look skinny and light as a feather. They was all that but they're gonna be quick, and all that yelling 'd scare the shit out of a mama bear. Don't pay no heed to the noise. It ain't nothing but show."

"What if they come silent?" Jamie asked.

"Same deal, but I think they'll come 'a screamin' cause white men get the notion that there's a lot more of 'em than there really is. Most white men'll be lookin' all around like there's a goddamned army, and that's when you get hit first. Don't look at nothing 'cept yer man. Same as hunting a herd ah deer or flock ah ducks. You take the lead animal if you can, but you take just one and don't worry 'bout the rest until the one you targeted drops. As soon as that's done, mind yer ass 'cause at least one'll be comin' from behind."

Everett stood now with his hatchet held tight in his fist. "Git that arm cocked and ready. Don't hold it low 'cause that means yah got to raise it, and that's lost time. Git it cocked right here just behind yer ear. Git down in a crouch, feet wide and be moving back and forth sideways." He crouched low and moved left and right. "Don't give 'em an easy target, and don't fergit that one behind yah. They're big swingers, most Indians, and that means if yer moving good, they might miss or just nick yah. And *you*, you don't need a big swing. A good sharp snap of the wrist, and that hatchet does the rest." Everett could see the boy's face grow pale in the glow of the fire, his eyes sharp with fear and alertness, picturing an attack. "Let's hope there's just three or four, and we can shoot 'em. Now, git up here and pretend I'm an Indian comin' at yah."

They worked over several attacks, Everett giving Jamie pointers on his crouch, his side movement.

"Git that hatchet up to yer ear. That's it."

As the darkness fell, their bodies cast a long shadow into the woods that no one could ever tell from the real thing if shadows were all they could see. One big man rushing at a smaller man crouched low and skittering to the side and the sudden flash of an arm and hatchet coming down quick, and the big men dropping to his knees.

"One more hard on the head, then step away and spin and be ready for the next sonvabitch."

After fifteen minutes of this-movements they practiced at every meal from then on-they sat on the log and ate in silence, both envisioning an attack and maybe the last moments of their lives on earth.

The dog growled quietly, her nose held high.

"That be them," Everett said.

"You don't reckon they'll come tonight?" Jamie asked nervously.

"The dog won't smell 'em the night they come. Or the morning. Or the day. When you don't hear the dog growling and sniffing, you got to be most careful. Ain't nothing more dangerous than silence. You can relax when she's growling, but when there ain't nothing, you gotta be awake and ready. Some say Indians won't attack at night 'cause they lose their spirits if they git killed in the dark. I know for a fact that ain't true with Indians that learnt to fight against white men."

Now that they'd set their traps, Everett knew the Indians could attack at any time soon, so they slept in shifts. Jamie took the first shift awake, and hugged the dog the whole time, feeling her low grumbling and hoping to God it did not stop.

Chapter 6

Father Ray was able to convert many Iroquois to the ways of Jesus and after several weeks had completed the new mission building. Each morning he said mass in the new log structure, and each passing day, more Indians came to worship. It was clear to Lucy that Father Ray had a gift for gaining the trust of the Indians and deserved his growing reputation as being among the most effective missionaries in New France. This new mission was an indisputable and quick success, yet she could tell from his constant muttering of prayers that he was troubled and growing restive.

The men of the tribe gathered after their February feast and prepared to embark on their winter hunt. Rumors circulated that the warriors were really planning to join the British army at Lake George, but they did not want to irritate Father Ray or express disloyalty to him by signaling their allegiance to the British and their Mohawk brothers. One morning Father Ray and Lucy awoke, and all the men of the tribe, even boys as young as 11 and 12, had vanished, leaving only the women and a few older men. Most were converts, and Father Ray's work was really done, so he sent word to the monastery at Montreal to send a young monk to the new mission to serve on a permanent basis.

The thaw continued late into February, leaving the snow drab and dirty. Each day was gray, damp, and threatened rain, but it was usually only foggy or sometimes drizzly. After mass one morning, Father Ray sipped coffee and stared out the window, his eyes moving in nervous snaps and jumps as if observing a wild panoply of events outside rather than a few motionless pine bows refracted through the dim, bubbly glass in the small parish window.

"You seem troubled," Lucy said cautiously.

He looked at her, surprised that she would read his thoughts so easily. He shook his head no, and said a hurried Hail, Mary to expiate his small sin of lying. In truth, he could not take his mind off the Huron mission. He had failed them and needed to return to finish his work there, but his struggle was not so much with failure as with fear. And this fear drew him as a moth is drawn to flame. It was as if God were calling him back, not so much to continue with his work as to confront his loss of courage and dwindling faith.

"As soon as the monk arrives, I am going back to the Huron mission," Father Ray told Lucy.

"Father Ray, that is a very dangerous choice," she told him, sipping her coffee from a hot copper mug.

"You do not have to accompany me," he said.

"The danger is not to me but to you," she said.

"It will not be so dangerous. I did not handle my leadership of the Huron people properly," he said, praying again to the Virgin Mary and asking for guidance in telling small lies that may serve a larger purpose, perhaps even in saving Lucy's life. Surely this could not be a grave sin, he thought. Nothing compared to adultery. Nothing compared to his sins of doubt.

Lucy knew that returning to the Huron mission was dangerous, and that the leaders of the tribe would not necessarily protect him if he returned. "The Indians do not obey a single authority as we do in the white world," she reminded him quietly. "Anyone is free to kill his enemies. You know that to be true, Father Ray."

He looked at her briefly and shrugged. "We were so very close to converting them all. I cannot give up on those people," he said, blessing himself and regretting the deepening web of tiny lies he was forced to tell her. But it was not for her to really know why he must return. And yes, there was some truth that he did not manage Mary Tall Tree well, and it was not fair to the other Indians at the Huron mission that he not return to finish his work.

Lucy regarded his preoccupied silence and pressed him, "Then please promise me that you will request Indian guards from the monastery to accompany us."

Father Ray kneaded his bad arm and absently ignored her question. Recently he had regained some of the movement and sensation, but he told her it often itched and tingled in a most annoying fashion. His brow was knit tightly, forming two deep creases between his eyes at the bridge of his nose. Lucy did not know that part of his renewed commitment to the Hurons had really to do with his deepening sense of guilt for his sins with her. He could not tear himself away from her. He could not repent. He had fallen in love with her and for his penance he must at least put himself closer to God's will. If God were angry with him, He would make his will known at the Huron mission. Father Ray knew that in the absence of repentance, he must place his fate in the hands of God, and to stay at a safe and secure mission as this one would only postpone his confrontation with God's true will and postpone a full test of his own faith.

"Will you promise me that you will request Indian guards," she said more earnestly after a long silence.

"Ah, Oui. For you I will do this, Lucy, my child," he sighed. "If you insist on going, I will do this for you."

"I insist," Lucy said.

Lucy did not believe she had fallen in love with Father Ray, but she was certain she had grown to love him in a special way. She had never met a man who cared so deeply and so gently about the lives of people. He never spoke to her about their nights together. She wasn't altogether certain that he even knew what he did. He never spoke to her or whispered to her during their moments of lovemaking. It was as if his delirium returned in the complete darkness of night and that what happened was as much a mystery to him as it was to her. She did not dare speak of it, in any case, for fear that if she did, he would end their relationship and probably flee from her forever.

Several days later, two converted Indians arrived at the new mission with a new, young monk, and Father Ray prepared for their journey back to the Huron mission to the north. The Indians wore white men's clothing and had allowed their hair to grow out so that they looked like French-Canadians with sun-burned skin. The young monk was very short with a huge, bushy beard and balding head. He spoke in a nervous, high-pitched voice that Lucy knew would amuse the Indians.

Later that evening, Lucy tried one more time to discourage Father Ray from their journey. They walked along the dark pathway to their hut in the woods.

"This new monk is not respected by the Indians. They are already laughing behind his back."

"He will learn," Father Ray said sharply.

"They won't give him a chance," she insisted.

"It is God's will, Lucy. It is in God's hands. It is not for us to judge. It is not for us to predict the future."

"But, this is not the future!" she pled.

"Enough," he said sharply, the first anger at her Lucy had ever witnessed from Father Ray.

Then she heard him praying quietly, and she knew that soon they would leave.

Early on March 1, 1760, Father Ray, his two Indian guides and Lucy set forth with a sled and a small cache of provisions. The sky was a thick gray, the air damp, and the temperature dropping.

"It's going to snow?" he asked the Indians.

"No, no," the oldest said pursing his lips and giggling, shaking his head no as if to say what a foolish notion.

They moved briskly northward on well-traveled trails, now hard and slick from the lengthy thaw. As the temperature dropped, the path hardened to ice. By early afternoon the sky was a deep, purple gray. Snow began falling, and the wind picked up considerably. By late afternoon, the wind howled, and snow felt in a hard slant, stinging their faces.

They stopped and made camp. Father Ray and Lucy dug a cave into the hollow beneath the thick canopy of a large spruce tree. They tucked slabs of birch bark on the snow cave floor to insulate them where they would sleep.

The two Indians found a hollow at the base of a nearby limestone outcrop and fashioned a canopy using the sled and pine boughs.

"S'il vous plait, a fire," Father Ray called to them as the Indians began settling into their shelter.

"Ees too wet, monsieur," said the older Indian.

"Des absurdités," said Father Ray irritably. "I've seen Indians make fires in driving rain. S'il vous plait, fait nous un feu. Immédiatement!"

The younger Indian wrapped himself sullenly in his blanket and looked away.

The older Indian stood. "It is too wet. C'est humide," he said defiantly.

Lucy moved up behind them. "Give me the flint and steel," she told the Indian.

He looked at her, then at Father Ray.

"Immédiatement!" Father Ray snapped.

The Indian turned and leaned down, rummaging through a pack on the sled. He turned, handed the flint and steel to Lucy with a sneer, and plunged into his shelter, covering himself with a blanket.

"I'll gather wood," Father Ray said. "Before you get comfortable..." he said to the Indian. He leaned down and grasped the largest supply satchel and pulled it out of the sled. The Indian spoke sharply in his native tongue, causing his younger friend to snicker. Father Ray glared at them, then plunged into the woods in search of wood.

Lucy dug below snow for dry grass and twigs. Soon she had a small blaze, and Father Ray placed a bundle of larger twigs and small logs on top. After hissing and puffs of smoke, the fire caught, aided by the strong wind. Lucy looked up at him. "Making the dinner fire is squaw's work," she said, "maybe that's why they're so pissy."

Father Ray shrugged.

They cooked slabs of venison, and then snuggled into their snow cave for the night. The wind howled and whistled though the trees, snow falling so rapidly that had it been daylight, they could not have seen more than a few feet. By morning, a large drift covered them entirely. Father Ray dug out of their snow cave, and in the dim dawn light saw the sled had disappeared. At first thinking it was the depth of the new snow or a large drift that covered the sled, he continued clearing around his and Lucy's cave. But when Lucy appeared, he turned again to the hollow where the sled had been, then approached with a growing sense of alarm. He plunged to the spot and swatted the snow. The sled was gone, including the provisions and the musket. He peeled away the boughs. The Indians were gone as well.

"Ils ont allé. Des disparus. They've left us," Father Ray said angrily. "The storm has buried the trail. The sled is gone. Everything is gone. The gun. Everything. Tout est allé."

"We have this," Lucy said, raising the large satchel of venison. "And we have this," she said, leaning down and grasping a tiny hand-sized pistol from a pocket in her boot.

"Where did you get that," he said.

She shrugged coyly. "I found it."

"Lucy, it is a sin to tell lies."

She grinned. "Then bless me, father, for I have sinned."

He regarded her with solemn skepticism for a moment, then smiled. "Tous êtes pardonné. I'm afraid we're lost, in any case. Too much snow has fallen."

Lucy was less worried about being lost than staying alive. They were standing in a blizzard miles from shelter. It was going to get worse, she suspected, much worse.

* * *

The March blizzard of 1760 lasted three days and nights. The temperature dropped to zero degrees, and the wind howled out of the northeast, dumping more than five feet of snow. Everett and Jamie built a shelter beneath the boat. After the first day, the boat was buried, and by the third day, it was nothing more than rounded puff beneath a great mound of new snow. They spent most of their time during the storm dozing inside their shelter and made small fires for cooking their dwindling supply of meat. On the morning of the fourth day, Everett dug out from under the boat and watched the sun rise, at first glowing a glorious pink, then casting a golden glow on trunks of trees and casting a million brilliant sparks on the wondrous blanket of snow. Everywhere, thick puffs of glittering snow hung like cotton from branches and pine and cedar bows, bending them beneath its weight, smaller trees bent over entirely, their top branches buried in canopies of snow.

They spent this gloriously beautiful day searching for beaver lodges which were now mere mounds in the flat new fields of white. Even the stream was buried and silent, thin spots and open rapids were covered and impossible to detect. Their traps were buried, as well, so Everett and Jamie waded through the deep snow searching for lodges with their feet. When they found one, they dug away the snow, and with hatchets, smashed the lodges, dug inside and captured the beavers, grasping them by their hind legs, pulling them out, then snapping their necks over a log they dragged along with them for that purpose.

They spent the morning and afternoon employed in this wreckage until they had nearly four dozen bodies piled on a blanket they dragged through the snow.

As the sun dipped in the southern sky, long shadows fell like prison bars across the snow. Jamie could barely lift his hatchet as they began smashing the final lodge of the day. Each time he looked up, the sun blinded his eyes so forcefully, he had to turn away. Both of them breathed heavily as they took turns swinging. Branches cracked with their blows. As Jamie swung his hatchet downward, he felt a sudden, sharp blow to his shoulder as an arrow struck and tore through his coat and penetrated the muscle above his shoulder. Had the arrow arrived a moment earlier, it would have penetrated his heart.

Jamie cried out, and Everett looked up, saw Jamie falling, grabbed the two muskets, and leaped over the lodge, dragging Jamie with him for what meager shelter the smashed lodge would afford. Everett heard screams and war cries, but as he looked toward the screams, the sun blinded him. He tried to shield his eyes with his trigger hand as he raised the musket to his shoulder. The dog growled ferociously, barring her teeth, readying to leap into the sun.

"Shit, bloody hell," Everett groaned.

Then, out of the corner of his vision, a shadow fell over him a moment as a warrior charged over the bank toward them. A moment later, he could see nothing but blinding shafts of light. Everett looked into the sun and shot just to its right of where the shadow passed. The musket ball smashed into the right side of the Indian's chest; his breath leapt from his throat, the blow standing him up straight, and then as if only momentarily startled, he again plunged forward in the deep snow. As he approached the beaver lodge as though swimming through the deep snow, Everett lunged from his squatted position, and with his musket held in both hands, smashed the gun butt into the Indian's face with all his power. He felt the nose and bones give way, and a cascade of blood sprayed over the lodge, splattering hotly on Everett's face. As the Indian sagged leftward, Everett grasped his knife from his belt and jammed it up through the man's chin, feeling the bone and cartilage give way, the blade crashing into his brain, freezing his eyes in a wide stare at the sudden arrival of death, his body slumping but propped upright in the deep snow, his head tipping onto his right shoulder, blood oozing from his mouth.

Everett pulled the knife free and jumped back over the lodge where Jamie lay gasping for air, holding the musket tucked beneath his wounded shoulder. As Everett strained to see back into the sun for the next Indian's charge, the second musket erupted, the cap hissing, then exploding, and before he could turn, an Indian landed on Everett, the dog leaping at the Indian's throat.

Everett snapped around, flinging this small, limp man and the snarling dog backward, a single hole oozing blood at the bridge of the Indian's nose, dead instantly from Jamie's shot, the dog shaking the man's neck in his jaws. Everett frantically reloaded the muskets while trying to see through the shadows. "Good shot, Jamie," he whispered, "scream bloody hell if you see another." He handed Jamie the flint-loaded pistol and hurriedly rammed powder and a ball down the barrel of his own rifle.

There were no new attacks, and in a few minutes, the sun dipped below the tree line, and Everett could see no movement, no sign of the Indians, nor any sign of the blanket with their load of beavers.

He inspected the arrow lodged mid-length in Jamie's shoulder, the arrowhead having penetrated and emerged through the flesh.

"I gotta break this thing," Everett whispered, his breath coming in deep pants and his heart thudding in his ears.

Jamie's groaned miserably as Everett tried to stabilize the arrow with his knee as he bent the shaft. In a quick movement, the shaft snapped, and Everett pulled both ends free of the wound. He pulled Jamie's right sleeve free and packed snow around the wound with his own trembling hands.

"Hurt some?" Everett gasped.

"Not so bad," Jamie lied.

"You sure as hell saved us, boy," Everett said washing the wound with the snow. "I got tricked by the sun and failed to follow my own advice."

"He come from behind just like you said he would," Jamie said as bravely as he could. His mind was a blur of fear and horror at having killed this man who would have killed him in less than another second. His shoulder burned where the flesh tore, and deeper inside ached with stabbing throbs metered to the racing thuds of his heart.

"I got froze by the sun. I couldn't see nothin' and it happened same as if they'd been screamin' bloody murder," Everett muttered angrily, furious at himself for his careless obsession with the blinding sun.

"Dog saw him first," Jamie said. The dog had now let go of the Indian's neck and was licking blood from the hole in his head.

"Yessir," Everett said taking a deep breath, trying to calm himself. "That would be down wind coming in that way. They must have been hungry, them Indians, must be their village is hungry, or they'd've finished us. They took a risk in that heavy snow, but they chose their spot and used the sun, goddammit, and they suckered me for sure." Everett shook his head no in self-disgust, then helped Jamie to his feet. Let's git back and clean this proper.

Everett was relieved that the Indians hadn't destroyed their camp or stolen the boat or any supplies. He made a fire and melted snow in a small cook pot. He washed the wound in steaming hot water, and heated an iron shaft he carried for just this purpose. He made Jamie drink as much rum as he could stomach until the boy's eyes glazed over and his speech grew slurred. He had the boy rumple his leather glove in a ball and put it in his mouth.

"This may hurt some, but we gotta do it," he said, giving the boy scant warning before cauterizing the wound with the glowing iron shaft.

Jamie shrieked, then passed out, and while he was mostly out, his head lolling and his eyes half open but dimly cast, Everett poured more steaming water over the wound and dressed it with clean clothe he carried for these purposes. He found a willow tree at the edge of the river and peeled off branches which he crumpled and boiled. He placed the cook pot in the snow to cool it, then poured some of the willow tincture over the dressing and the rest he gave to Jamie to drink.

The boy was pretty drunk by then, and soon after sunset passed out entirely.

At first light Everett dug the boat out of the snow, loaded the pelts they'd accumulated, and had Jamie lay down on top of the furs inside the canoe. Everett tied on snowshoes he'd made last summer and rigged a line to the dog. She had to leap through the snow, but she showed surprising strength and was aided by her large webbed feet. They began their journey down stream, dragging the boat over snow piled thickly over the ice. At mid morning, they spotted a deer struggling through the woods. It was chest deep in snow and having trouble moving, weary from lack of food and hampered by its sharp hooves penetrating so deep in the thick snow. Everett shot him through the neck, and the exhausted deer bled to death, blood spraying across the snow in steaming spurts from its gradually failing heart. He spoke to the boy who lay dazed and vacant-eyed, weakened by the wound and the rum which Everett forced him to keep drinking.

"Ain't no reason to be quiet no more," he said as if needing to justify the gunshot to the groggy, bleary-eyed boy. "Them Indians know where we're headed. They'll come if they want," he said, figuring they might be back to avenge the deaths of the two warriors. They ate venison raw and pressed on as the weather turned warm again. Everett knew they'd have to travel day and night, so he and the dog pressed on. By midnight rain fell in torrents, the wind blowing it sharply into his face, the cold rain burning his cheeks and drenching his growing beard.

By noon the next day the weather cleared and turned cold. Branches sagged from the weight of the rain absorbed in the snow. Everett stopped and made a fire, and decided to wait for an hour or so to see if it would crust up. He cooked venison and bathed Jamie's wound in steaming willow juice.

"Hurt some?" he asked.

"Some," the boy groaned miserably.

"Your mama's gonna be bloody pissed off at me, ain't she?"

Jamie smiled thinly. "Yessir."

As the air drew bitter cold, the wet snow turned to ice. Branches cracked and fell around them. Whole trees snapped in half. Each crack, sharp as gunfire, startled Everett from his growing exhaustion. They ate until they were stuffed full. A crust had begun to form on the snow's surface which made pulling the boat easy but walking more difficult, the crust breaking and catching the snow shoes and forcing Everett to stumble with nearly every step. Everett finally had to put the dog in the canoe after her shins were torn raw from the edges of the crust.

By midnight the crust was hard enough so that Everett could walk easily on top. The canoe skidded easily along, and Everett's was able to run clumsily, the boat gliding so easily it bumped his heels. By morning he was able to remove the snowshoes and trot easily on the crust alongside the dog. He hoped the crust would trap so many deer the warriors would have to stay back and hunt. They could stock themselves until spring, and couldn't risk doing otherwise lest many of the deer would die of starvation and be consumed by wolves.

On the fourth day Jamie insisted that he no longer ride. They ate venison and gazed out over the widening St. Regis River.

"Once we git to the St. Lawrence, ain't no Indian gonna bother us," Everett said.

"How much further."

"Sunset. You think you can run some?" Everett asked. "We gotta use this crust while we can."

"Yessir, I can surely run faster than you."

Everett smiled. "How's that shoulder."

"Just a little throb; ain't nothing."

"Good boy. You keep good watch now. When we git near the big river, them Indians'll have to hit us if they're ever gonna."

"The dog ain't smelt 'em," Jamie said.

"She ain't gonna with a north wind," Everett said.

"Yessir, I shouldda knowd. But if they curled out ahead, she'd smell 'em."

"Yessir, she would. So that tells you to keep an eye back there, cover our asses."

"Yessir."

They trotted all day, dragging the boat over the crust, slowing only to break up the crust and to eat fistfulls of snow to keep them fresh as they moved. As the sun dipped close to the tree line, the St. Regis widened and marshes appeared at the edges, making it more and more difficult for Indians to hide. With the sun behind them, casting their huge shadows to the north, they entered the St. Lawrence River where Everett knew channels and thin spots as well or better than any Indian. Over the channels, only thinly covered by ice and the layer of crust, Jamie and Everett got in the canoe and had the dog pull them. They crossed a half dozen treacherous thin spots before nightfall, so that anyone tracking them would risk falling through the ice. For most of the night, a three-quarter moon shown brightly, casting a shadowy purple light for miles on every side. This made travel easy for them and impossible for any trackers to follow them undetected as they headed downstream mid-river en route to Ile du Cedre. "We're okay now," Everett told Jamie.

"Yessir," Jamie muttered, his mind so thick with sleepiness he could barely put one foot in front of the other.

"Ain't no Indian gonna touch us now."

* * *

Lucy and Father Ray stayed in their snow cave for three days as the storm raged. When it finally cleared, they had no snow shoes nor a river to follow, and soon lost the narrow path. Lucy knew to keep the sun behind them, and to travel in the direction pointed by the moss on the trunks of trees. She could recall the face of her Uncle Joe, but was still trying to piece together the details of her former life, especially her deepest past. She remembered her lessons from the old Indian, and now that Father Ray was lost and fumbling in the wilderness, she felt her instincts and memories bubble upward within her mind. She wasn't sure how she knew, but she felt she'd been on this path before-not this exact place-but lost in a blizzard, trying to find her way home to the great river. During the worst of the blizzard, she opened her clothes to warm Father Ray who began shivering the first day and trembled from cold until they finally were able to begin moving again days later.

On the first sunny day, they came upon a yearling doe with an injured rear leg. The animal could not push off and clawed at the snow with her front legs as Lucy approached. She walked slowly and carefully, knowing a deer had powerful, sharp hooves and could even leave a nasty bite. Lucy found a hefty branch, and inched closer until the deer's eyes glared wildly and she kicked frantically to escape. Lucy moved within striking distance, her steps like climbing a muddy cliff-exhausting, frustrating, every inch a struggle in the chest-deep snow. She swung the branch striking the deer on the side of the head, dazing it. Then she plunged forward, her knife drawn and sliced its throat. Blood squirted into the snow, and Lucy saw the deer's horrified eyes soften almost as if to thank her, the blood from her artery pumping in decreasing spurts until the deer's eyes turned dim, and then flat as her head sagged nose-first into the snow.

They cleared a spot in a tight cluster of pines where only a foot or two of snow had accumulated. They built a fire and cooked venison, their first big meal in several days. Father Ray soon began shivering again, and Lucy smiled at his thin French blood and trembling vulnerability.

"God didn't make you for wilderness travel, did he?" she teased.

He looked at her, jaw trembling, huddled inside his blanket. Glumly he shook his head no.

"We'll be okay," she said patting his hand. "It's already warming, can't you feel it?"

He shook his head no, his face blank with misery.

Later that day when the rain began, Lucy stripped the bark off a dead poplar and formed a tiled roof on a snow cave she built around the up-turned roots of a fallen tree. She made another fire and kept it well supplied with hissing, crackling wood, but despite its warmth, Father Ray shivered.

"How far?" he asked.

"Two days, maybe three," but she knew, as Everett did, that the rain might bring a crust, making it possible to walk much more quickly and easily.

Though not a frail man in appearance, Lucy began to worry that Father Ray might succumb to illness. She frequently touched his pale brow for signs of fever, and tried to cheer him with fantasies about chocolate cakes dipped in brandy. She offered a running monologue about food to take their minds off their soaked misery. "And now I'm thinking of cream whipped into a small mountain and dribbled with steaming chocolate sauce, heaped over our cake with an giant spoon we can both lick," she said, pretending to lick an imaginary spoon.

Father Ray smiled dimly and shuddered from the damp, penetrating cold.

* * *

Everett suspected something was wrong several miles before they reached the island. He could see no smoke rising from the chimney but hoped, perhaps, that they were still too far away. As they drew closer, however, Everett knew there was no fire. He said nothing of this to Jamie, but his heart beat rapidly, fearing the worst of calamities. When they were a few hundreds yards away, Everett stopped.

"You stay here. Keep the dog. Cover me," he told Jamie.

"What's wrong?" Jamie muttered, then quickly sensed urgency in Everett's voice.

"Ain't no fire. Ain't no paths I can see. Something ain't right."

"Maybe they left," Jamie said nervously.

"Maybe so," Everett said readying his pistol and musket. "You hear any shots, any shouts... anything, you turn and run like hell and don't stop."

"Yessir," Jamie said lowering himself behind the canoe, his heart thudding with fear.

Everett trotted to the island and scooted up the bank, noting the lack of tracks even around the hut doorway.

He moved carefully to the door, listened, then plunged quickly through the door where he saw Jean-Robert slumped, frozen against the beam, dark brown streams of blood frozen over his face, a pool of frozen blood between his oddly crooked feet, the spear jammed through his chest and holding him upright. Everett groaned and rushed to Ella's room, stripped bare of blankets but a chaos of clutter from having been ransacked. He looked everywhere for signs of her and was relieved he didn't find her dead. But a huge wave of discouragement passed through him. He heard a gasp behind him, turned with his pistol to fire and saw Jamie standing slack-jawed and astonished at the sight of his friend. Everett raised the pistol and eased off its hammer, refraining from scolding the boy for disobeying his orders.

"She ain't here," he said to Jamie.

Jamie stared at his friend, moved slowly toward him and wondered strangely if he'd been scalped before or after being run through by the spear. Jean-Robert's eyes were wrinkled and sunken, his mouth sagged open in an expression of puzzlement obscured by streams of frozen blood. Exhaustion washed over Jamie completely now, and he staggered a moment to keep his balance. His heart thudded rapidly in his chest, but he could not muster an ounce of energy and stood paralyzed as Everett kicked through the clutter on the floor and pulled the spear from the boy's chest, catching the stiff body as it teetered toward the floor. Everett lay the Indian boy down gently, closing his eyes with thumb and index finger.

"You stay here," he told Jamie.

Everett let the dog loose from the canoe at the river's edge, then inspected the pathways and docking bay. He could see no signs of movement, no tracks, no objects, the dog catching no scent.

He returned to the hut to find Jamie knelt beside his friend gazing blankly at the wall.

"We gotta get the boy to Gordon," Everett said lighting an oil lamp and stoking the woodstove. "Ain't no sign anywhere. He must been kilt before the big snow. Ain't no tracks. Ain't nothin." Everett lit the fire, and soon after it began to roar, he laid his coat over the Indian boy. "We gotta eat good and then take this boy to Gordon. If anyone gonna find your mama, it be Gordon."

Jamie sniffled and fought back tears, hiding his face from Everett.

"Yessir," he whispered.

Everett busied himself preparing meat to cook. They both ate in silence, taking their food with listless indifference. The reality of the death of Jean-Robert passed over Jamie in a series of waves. One moment he was chewing venison, feeling this deep and voiceless sense of dread, and then the fact of his death rushed over him anew, making his stomach turn with emptiness. It could have been me, too, he thought vaguely. If I'd obeyed her wishes, I'd been just as dead. But fear of his own death did not erupt any impulses in him-not fear nor anger nor a sudden surge to run. Rather, he sat in utter listlessness, until a new wave of recognition of his friend's death passed over him with in-utterable bleakness.

Everett knew Jamie was weakening, but for the moment saw little point in trying to arouse the boy. But his own mind was filled now with preparations and plans, the need to prepare the canoe for proper presentation to Gordon, the need to move fast out of respect for the father's loss, the need to gather what few clothes and possessions that remained in the camp to help keep him and Jamie warm and to present the remainder as gifts to Gordon.

"When an Indian dies," Everett said, "his friends and kin give him things to help him in the next life. When we git done eatin', you see if you can find some gifts outta this clutter."

"Yessir," Jamie muttered.

"Anything useful. The Indians don't see no difference to speak of between this life and the next. More hard work. More survival. Ain't much rest for an Indian the way they see it."

"Nossir."

"Take up whatever things the boy kept here that ain't ransacked or stole."

Jamie nodded.

"We lay the boy in the canoe. We give 'em the furs."

Jamie looked at Everett and nodded again.

"You finish that steak. We gotta lot of work."

* * *

Lucy and Father Ray followed the moss back of trees north, walking the crust by day and sleeping in snow caves by night. The underbrush and thorn-tangled shrubbery, normally impassable, was partly buried by snow, making movement easier as the cold held and the crust thickened. Still, their progress was slowed by scores of dense thickets, broken trees, and hanging brambles that they lacked tools to cut, forcing them in long circles and detours that ate up long hours. They finally bumped into Plum Brook, a stream that meandered northward to the Raquette River. They followed paths along these waterways until they merged with the St. Lawrence. At a trading post where the rivers met, Lucy and Father Ray stopped for coffee and a few supplies.

They were greeted by a young man-not yet 30- with prematurely long greasy silver hair and a pointy beard of the same color but stained yellow from tobacco and dribbles of spilled food. He was sitting reading a newspaper with his boots crossed on a round table.

Father Ray warmed his hands by the man's roaring fire and asked cheerfully, "Bonjour, Monsieur. Quel sont les nouvelles du mond dans votre journal?"

"Me French ain't so good, come again," the young man said peaking over the top of the paper.

"What's in the news?" Lucy asked.

The man sat up and inspected her body carefully. He scratched his beard, lay down his paper, and replied, "Frenchies shot General Wolfe in the nuts and kilt him dead." He pointed to the story for Lucy to see and tried to peek down her neckline when she leaned his way.

She studied the paper, and her eyes widened. "Quebec is lost, it says. Québec capitulait."

"Yes, ma'am. Ain't gonna be long 'fore them Frenchies git their asses kicked here to Sunday."

Father Ray turned and spoke over his shoulder, "Ees surrender, Québec?"

"They say the British fleet's headin to Montreal," the bearded man nodded. "You better watch yer ass, mister. Them Brits got a bunch ah wild injuns they'd scalp you clean and feed you yer balls fer dinner." Then he grinned, showing a mouth of black-stained shattered teeth.

Father Ray did not understand a word, but Lucy pulled back and glared at the impudent cracker and wished him the same fate.

"You are Eenglis, monsieur?" Father Ray asked pleasantly.

"American, I am. Gittin to be more and more of us up in these parts, thank Gawd."

Father Ray looked puzzled.

Lucy translated, "Il est américain. Il dit qu'il y a de plus en plus des Américains dans la region ici. Il a dit que l' escadre Britannique sont arriver dans le Québec."

"The war be over soon," the man said.

"La guère soyez sera fini bientôt," Lucy said.

Father Ray sighed deeply and spoke to her in French. "Cela est folle. (This is so crazy. If the British win, all the missions will be burned, the priests banished or killed. What are we doing here?)" he asked. "Pourquoi?"

Lucy shrugged. Nothing made sense to her. Why did the Hurons need saving by French priests, she wondered. Why were Indians fighting for white men of both sides? Why were the white men fighting each other? Why was everyone risking life and limb? For what? "Porquoi," she said dryly.

"What can I git fer yah?" the man said standing.

"Tobacco, wine, bread, oats, squash, a small tub of lard, and a little ammunition," Lucy said dryly brushing her hand softly on a thick wool blanket in British redcoat crimson.

"Hey, lady, don't I know you from somewhere?" the man said.

Lucy turned sharply. "Do you? Do you know me?" she said with such sudden mock enthusiasm that the man thought she was flirting. As much as she craved meeting someone from her prior life, this was not the man.

"I just thought I seen you somewhere before?" he winked.

"Where?" she demanded. She turned to Father Ray and said, "Il pense qu'il me connait."

Father Ray turned and regarded the man who was now scratching his beard and rolling his eyes to the ceiling. Father Ray wished he could be more charitable, but he felt a sudden rush of jealousy toward her other life. He closed his eyes and mouthed an *Our Father* and tried to empty his mind of his growing contempt for this churlish American worm.

"I swear I seen yah, but I caint say where?"

"Montreal?" she asked.

He shrugged.

"Lachine?"

"I was prob'ly drunk." He shook his head no.

"In church?" she said mockingly.

"No chance of that," he grinned, exposing the wreckage of his mouth.

That night she and Father Ray drank rum and ate tin tubs of rabbit stew in their room at the trading post. Father Ray had not been so drunk since he'd been a teenager. As he let her into the room, he thought about perhaps trying to kiss her. Perhaps it was time to break their silence, to shatter the darkness of their secret nightly meetings. Perhaps he should acknowledge his love for her, and stop here. Walk away from the church. Then he scolded himself and tried to muster a prayer.

"So why are we doing this?" she said sharply "Why are you insisting on saving people who have not asked to be saved?" she said in growing exasperation, knowing she was angry at the very kindness and dedication that drove her admiration for him. She knew also that it must come from him.

Father Ray was astonished by her sudden scolding. He tried to finish his prayer. He did not like to start a prayer without finishing it, and certainly didn't know what to say to her even if he did stop.

Lucy very nearly broke her silence. Here was this man who had been fucking her for months now spewing prayers, incapable of caring enough about her to save them both, incapable of even listening. But just as she was trying to frame another suitably shocking accusation, Father Ray dropped to his knees and prayed even more earnestly now.

He was not sure if it were a loss of nerve-simple cowardice-in facing her or his unwillingness to challenge God in a well-lit room. He asked the Virgin Mary to give him guidance, buried his face in the edge of the bed, and muttered seven Hail Mary's, pressing his fingers harshly into his eye sockets.

Lucy slumped down on the bed. Despite how pathetic he seemed to her just then, she could not humiliate him. She turned away, suddenly exhausted by their travel.

By the time he had finished his prayers, Lucy was snoring softly.

Father Ray covered her shoulders with a blanket and thanked God for having answered his prayers. He crossed himself and gently lowered himself beside her. He blew out the candle and vowed that he would not violate her that night in her sleep.

They arrived the next evening at the Huron mission. He and Lucy were invited into the primary long house. The converted Indians among them were glad to see him and passed the tobacco several times in celebration.

They told of the harshness of the winter and how, until very recently, they had run very low on food and could only eat squash and left-over grain for many of their meals. The chief spokesman of the tribe told of many dreams. The white priest had returned in these dreams and this time he built his church from stone and mud. Several men and women, sitting around the fire, nodded earnestly. They did not tell the rest of the dream, however, because they did not want to make Father Ray nervous about his dark future. Tonight they would celebrate his return, they said. Tomorrow they would worry about the prophecies.

They ate a small feast of bear that night, and Father Ray and Lucy were invited to sleep along the side of the long house with the other Indians.

The next morning Father Ray was awakened by the harsh hands of several warriors who lifted him from his bed and took him to an open area between several long houses.

"What's the matter?" he asked with growing alarm. "What are you doing? Qu'est que vous fait?"

They did not answer him or acknowledge him in any way. The men's faces were painted with red grease, so he would not have recognized Mary Tall Tree's friends nor did he see Mary Tall Tree watching from the edge of the woods as she carried buckets of water from the creek.

They forced Father Ray's back to a tall cedar post, then tied his hands behind him, in effect, locking him loosely to the post. They tied his feet with a rope manacle, allowing him enough movement to stand and even circle about the post but not enough slack to kick or cause injury to the women or children, the first of his tormentors. As they tied him, Father Ray prayed and moved his head to the sign of the cross, blessing each of them. He had heard many stories of Indian torture and knew that in the very end he could die and could face at least several days of excruciating pain. The Indians muttered to each other as they secured him. Then the tallest said to him, "Vous êtes le diable. Nous devons tuer le diable. We keel de devil." Father Ray's heart sank yet further, and fear began roiling from deep in his belly. He soon was breathing faster and faster, almost gasping with fright.

He searched the emerging crowd, trying to spot Lucy. Perhaps she could save him; perhaps she, too, was doomed. They had tied her to another post but not in the same way. She was manacled at both her hands and feet but was allowed to move about in a ten or fifteen-foot radius. Father Ray prayed that she would be spared after his death, asking that she be adopted by the tribe, the only possible alternative to torture and death. When they had finished tying him, they moved away and left him to stand alone. They also moved back away from Lucy so that both he and she were facing each other surrounded by a large ring of at least 100 Indians who now began to chant and raise their faces and hands to the sky. Even when she was injured, Father Ray had never seen Lucy so drained of color, her face stricken, stunned, her jaws slack, her eyes starring blankly at the ground. Had she not been standing under her own power, Father Ray could have mistaken her for being dead. As the chant grew louder, two women grasped Lucy's face sharply and forced her face to the sky. She tried to pull away.

"Do as they say!" Father Ray shouted. "Obey everything they tell you!"

The crowd hissed angrily at his interruption of their prayers, and in a moment, stones flew at him, bouncing off his body and face. One fist-sized stone smashed into his forehead, stunning him for a moment. Blood gushed down into his right eye and over his lips, then dripped to the ground. Then the chants resumed as the Indians again looked to the sky.

Lucy gazed blankly at the sky and felt the deepest, most numbing dread of her life. She wished she could have died in the night and cursed herself for not having fought Father Ray more adamantly at his insistence that they return to this Godforsaken mission. What else could it have been, she asked herself. I knew what would happen. Why didn't I break his leg? Why didn't I fight. I knew if they turned on him, it would be this. Unspeakable misery, torture and death. Part of her was infuriated at her own passivity, part of her was paralyzed with a fear so great she could barely stand, barely breath.

Father Ray tried to collect himself, tried to gather his thoughts and muster his courage before God. He knew that he faced a preview of eternal life, knew that the hell fire he had described so often to the Indians was absolutely familiar to them because each of them had inflicted it on their enemies dozens, even scores of times, and when he had spoken to them about the fires of hell, they nodded knowingly. Father Ray tried to tell himself that what was soon to happen had happened to many, many men, and that those of them who were good men and proper Christians would pass from this hell to eternal peace in heaven and that those who were sinners would die in this living hell and pass to a hell even more furious where they would writhe in agony for eternity.

But his fear was such that he could not muster himself to ask for forgiveness, could not admit to God that what he had done with Lucy was not only a mortal sin but one he committed over and over without once having asked forgiveness, without having once confessed. He could not admit to himself or to God that what he had done was even wrong. He could not admit that his sins invalidated his life as a missionary and obliterated his holy covenant, making him, in effect, an ordinary sinner pretending to be priest, pretending to hear confessions, pretending to offer absolution and penance, while receiving the body and blood of Jesus and carrying on as if he were forgiven when he had not yet even asked.

Father Ray tried to organize his thoughts, tried to reach below the hollow words of an Act of Contrition which he had mouthed so many times since he had met Lucy but had never meant, never felt in the depth of his being with the necessary sorrow. He looked out now, his knees weak with fear as the chanting stopped and swarms of women and children began circling him with rocks and stones and sharp sticks. And though he wished he could say he was sorry, he could only look over at Lucy's drawn, dazed face and say to himself and to God, I am not sorry. I am not sorry. Then began the fusillade of rocks which struck his face, his body, his eyes for perhaps ten minutes until he was stinging and bruised but not yet really hurt. He knew and they knew he was not yet hurt, and he gazed out at them, his right eye already caked with blood, his left eye stinging and swelling shut, and as he prepared to smile at them, to forgive them-he could do that; he could still forgive them-a large rock flung by a teenage boy crashed into his mouth. The rock jarred his head, shattered teeth and tore his lips. Suddenly a new wakefulness was aroused in him, a new alertness, a new and dreadful fear.

As the blood washed down from his mouth and face, the crowd cheered and screamed and celebrated his first reaction to pain, his first astonished look of fear, his benign smile torn away with a flap of his lip, exposing his lower teeth in the very first inkling of the grimace of death. A half dozen women came forward now with sharpened sticks, chanting in a soft almost loving voice while nearby other women ignited an enormous fire. The women with the sticks came to him and dabbed his blood and tasted it delicately with their tongues and then closing their eyes and looking skyward prayed to their Great Spirit, then patted him softly, soothing him. Then forming a line, each came forward and inserted her stick into his flesh pressing the sticks in at odd angles close to the surface of his skin so that the outline of the sticks could be seen in grotesque relief.

Father Ray prayed now, prayed as he often did simply to close his mind to all thoughts and sensations, felt each stick penetrate and after a moment of sharp pain, slide beneath his flesh. In a few minutes he had sticks pressed beneath his chest and arms and thighs, and the half dozen women moved back to the fire and another half dozen came forward and lit the ends of the sticks with large burning logs from the fire. Father Ray closed his eyes and prayed that God spare him the pain, knowing at the very moment that he must not be sparred, knowing that he and God had to reckon with this, had to accept this pain, but Father Ray was unable to accept. Please God, spare me this pain, he said over and over, and this time the Indians allowed him to close his eyes-they knew; they understood and waited, and when the first flame burned to his flesh, Father Ray's eyes opened wide, and they saw now the second sign of terror and called out gleefully and began to dance around him. Then the second and third of the sticks burned to his flesh, and his skin hissed and then it began to burn, and Father Ray screamed.

Lucy dropped to her knees and fainted, and soon after, the blood running down Father Ray's face stopped flowing, and he turned white and fainted, slumping oddly and sagging, the large post holding him at a strange and awkward angle. Then young boys rushed at him splashing him with copper cook pots of freezing water, and his breath returned and his dazed eyes regained their focus, and everyone cheered.

Lucy recovered in a pool of her own vomit, for a moment dazed and inchoate, not knowing where she was or what was happening and feeling only this deep sense of relief which then evaporated. She looked up and saw women now bringing hot coals from the fire using tongs they'd cut from green willow. She could hear Father Ray gasp, could hear his skin hiss as they pressed the coals against his flesh until they burned holes deep enough so that the coals stuck in his skin in dark, smoldering, smoking lumps.

Two women held his trembling hands and with their mouths pulled at his fingernails, and each time they yanked one free, Father Ray screamed and moaned in a single, horrible sound for which white men had no single word but which the Indians knew as kasma. When his fingernails were gone and his trembling fingers hung limply, dripping with blood, the women and children slowly approached in a moving line and licked at his blood and patted him gently and with reassurance. After each had tasted his blood, three women dressed in white leather brought buckets and clothes and began bathing him with extraordinary care and gentleness, cleaning his charred and purple wounds.

Father Ray could barely breathe now. He panted and cried as a wounded child would, his mind now dazed and exhausted from this first stage of his ordeal. Lucy lay crying, and women from the tribe came to her and patted her softly and wrapped her in a blanket and urged her to drink water, and Lucy sipped in stunned silence, already trying to accept his death, trying within herself to skip ahead to the arrival of death but knowing that it would get worse. In a deep recess of her mind, she prayed to some strange mix of God and the Great Spirit that Father Ray show his bravery, prayed that the warriors would come forward and kill Father Ray mercifully and that time race forward, but her prayers were not words, not even formed thoughts so much as a deep and filmy wish for peace and deliverance of her friend and lover.

* * *

Everett and Jamie spread beaver furs on the bottom of the canoe and placed the body of Jean-Robert gently into the bottom, trying to bend his head and legs-stiffened from so many days slumped against the post. They twisted and pressed his arms and legs in a way that looked like peaceful slumber, then covered his body with a deer skins and blankets. All around him they tucked objects from the hut, more than 60 gifts as was the custom of a death so profound as a warrior's son. They then covered the gifts and everything but the boy's face with carefully arranged stacks of beaver skins and set out for Gordon's village.

Jamie's shoulder had already begun healing, but on this day he refused to show any signs of discomfort from the steady, throbbing pain. Using both hands and arms, he pulled his side of the canoe, and they proceeded out across the snow-crusted frozen lake. Everett set the muskets and pistols to the ready half wishing they would be attacked rather than to have to face his friend and deliver his youngest boy for burial.

When they reached Gordon's village in the late afternoon, Everett's and Jamie's grim faces betrayed their mission, and when Gordon saw them, he began his first deep groan of mourning before he had even seen the boy or learned of his death. Gordon cried out in a wolf-like howl when he saw

Jean-Robert's face, and even before Everett could explain what had happened, Gordon began building a ten-foot platform and before darkness other men lashed together a bark coffin, and just before darkness, they raised the body of the boy onto the platform, draping it with Everett's furs and gifts and adding many of their own. All through the night Gordon cried and moaned in a strange and guttural chant inside the long house, attended by his own grandfather, the shaman of their village.

At midnight he stopped and asked Everett for the details.

"We found him stabbed through the chest inside my hut, his hand still grasping his bow and arrow fallen at his feet. He died bravely trying to save Ella who was captured and taken away. Me and Jamie was huntin' beaver."

"She is gone," Gordon nodded gravely. "I will find her in my dreams. She be where de spirit of my boy wander. I find him."

Gordon did not ask questions or criticize why Everett and Jamie had been away and accepted his explanation fully.

"He die bravely as great warrior," Gordon said softly. "His mind spirit is with de yellow-haired woman, am sure, and we will find dem both and avenge hees death and bring back hees mind spirit to hees body spirit home and return de yellow-haired woman her home and leave hees killers twisting in der own blood," he said calmly.

Gordon turned to his own stooped grandfather, then back to Everett. "Now is time to see my dreams," he said, and the grandfather nodded.

Everett got up to leave but Gordon made him come back and gave Jamie and Everett a place to sleep on bark pads along the long house walls. Theirs was the only fire remaining in the hundred-foot long house; other families were now asleep on bark pads along the walls the entire length, a half dozen other fires smoldering and glowing in the growing darkness. Everett and Jamie quietly moved to their beds, and Gordon covered each of them with thick bear skin furs.

Gordon returned to the fire and sat crossed-legged with his grandfather, closed his eyes and moaned quietly until they slept.

* * *

Gordon, Everett, Jamie, Gordon's two other sons and three nephews stood in a circle inside Everett's hut and inspected the spear that had killed Gordon's son.

"Wendat," Gordon said using the Indian name for Huron. "It is as my grandfather say. It is as I saw in my dream. She Wendat now."

"She ain't kilt or tortured?"

"No, no," Gordon said, "They treat her as sister now."

"You know where them Wendats are at?" Everett asked.

"No. Dere are many, many Wendat villages now. Since all de disease, dey break up many long houses and go all ways, and dey be traders and move all de many times. Mohawks, dey stay one place. Wendat, dey move too many, and I not see in my dreams," he said shaking his no.

"I thought you said you saw them in your dream," Everett said.

"Yes, I see dem. I donn see where," Gordon said glumly.

Everett was angry at himself for pressing Gordon and patted him kindly on the back.

They looked carefully along the island pathways and at the boat bay where they always launched. They dug in the snow looking for tracks or lost objects that may have been layered beneath recent snow but found no other signs.

Gordon walked out on the ice and looked west. He pointed west, then north. "Dat way, I know. Dey always live de river or de stream."

"Could be hundreds of streams," Everett said.

Gordon nodded. "We no hurry. Dey treat de yellow-haired woman good. She work hard. She get tough an' strong." He looked at Jamie staring out blankly over the ice. He walked back to the island shore, leaned down in his canoe and retrieved Jean-Robert's bow and arrows.

He approached Jamie and handed him the bow and arrows. "For you. My son he friend to you. He want you dese."

Jamie took them, and Gordon patted him hard on the shoulder. "You be warrior now."

Jamie nodded.

"We find yer modder. We bring her."

Jamie looked at Gordon's brown creased face and dark, sparkling eyes. Gordon smiled, exposing a tangled assortment of brown and broken teeth, his cheek bones so high, his smile closed his eyes to tiny slits.

Jamie smiled thinly in return, not sure what to make of Gordon just yet.

* * *

Gilles frequently stayed after his long days at Le Petit Bateau Bâtisseur to work on his new boat design. At first Monsieur LeBlanc was amused at the notion of anyone building a 12-foot covered canoe, especially one that supposedly would weigh 35 pounds and sailed with two masts and a bowsprit. He scoffed at the usefulness of such a small craft. "Who would buy such a boat? And for what?" he scoffed. "A toy schooner to move a cargo of singing ants?"

But as mid-March arrived, and the river ice began to break up, LeBlanc grew eager to see the boat finished and launched. "Sa soit un beau bateau, très beau," he told Gilles that evening. LeBlanc brushed his strong, rough hands over the smooth and delicate wood and smiled. He had grown to respect Gilles and counted him among his best and most promising workers.

"You see how strong she is," Gilles said grasping the gunnels and squeezing. "The deck makes her very strong. Très fort. But it is very light wood, finely hewned. Her strength is in her angles; in the right placement of her members."

LeBlanc nodded and lifted the bow end. He whistled at her lightness. "Elle est comme une plume. Like a very fine and delicate woman with exceptional teeth."

"Ah oui," Gilles laughed.

"But you have too many sails."

"No, no. She will fly. Believe me. She will paddle or sail faster than any canoe a man could ever build."

"But why would a man buy a boat such as this?"

"Because she is so easy to portage, so easy to lift from the water, so easy to store, and she carries 300 pounds. Besides, this is a boat for fun. For fishing. For sailing on a summer's day. Très romantique, no?"

Gilles brushed his hands along her smooth curves. She was made entirely of wood, smooth-hewned quarter inch pine planks slightly lapped to give her strength with the tiniest, most delicate ribs LeBlanc had ever seen. She included no bark, a primary building material at Le Petit Bateau Bâtisseur. She had double ends fastened at an oak keel that curved up to form a daring rake that would make her turn easily under sail and maneuver deftly in rushing shallows.

"When did you *first* learn about building boats?" LeBlanc asked.

"As a boy in France. I built little models. Très petits bateaux."

"And your first real boat?"

"A little rowing skiff. I rigged her to sail. She wasn't much, but I learned the principles of sailing and boat design. Each summer for three or four years I rebuilt her. I tried big skegs and little, centerboards, leeboards, at least two dozen rudders of all sizes and shapes, dozens of sails, two masts stepped fore, aft and all points between, a bowsprit, a mizzen. I tried everything to make her better. But she was fat and heavy, too beamy for much speed."

"A strong boat don't need to be heavy," LeBlanc offered.

"And you, Monsieur LeBlanc, when did you learn about building boats?"

"I learned from an old Indian when I was just a young boy. He built me my first bark canoe. A boat no bigger than this," he said, patting Gilles's boat, "It took him two days. That got me started. After a couple of years I built my own. Then I built an eight meter and sold her to a British trapper who didn't know shit about boats. She floated and was dry, and you could have put a horse in that boat. After that I built a dozen or so canoes. Sold 'em all. Then I opened the shop and did a lot of repairs for the French Navy, and then they finally got the idea that the best way to get around these parts was by canoe, and they ordered a whole fleet of them. And skiffs and patrol boats and traditional wood bateaux. Couple of years back I built 'em a gunship sloop that they still use on Lac du St-Francois."

Gilles was tempted to ask if this were his former naval ship, but decided to let it drop, in the event LeBlanc were a fervent nationalist.

"So what brought you to New France, Monsieur Chabert?" LeBlanc asked.

"Adventure, fame, and fortune," Gilles smiled.

"You won't make a fortune building a boat like that. She's pretty but she takes too long to build. But a few rich buyers could make your boat famous enough. Some of those captains. The mayor. Some bankers. Make yourself a half hull model, and hang her at Le Canard Noir Taverne. That's the best these days. Might get yourself some orders. Build 'em at the shop here, and I'll take 20-percent off the top, the rest is yours."

"Le Canard Noir Taverne?" Gilles asked.

"Used to be a pig's pen but they got this Parisian chef now. They say it's the cat's palais for rich folks. Too fancy for me, but that's your market for a boat like this," LeBlanc said, patting the boat softly.

"Yes, I will give your idea a try. Merci. Merci beaucoup."

Gilles built himself a fine little half hull mounted on a deep purple slab of cedar. He polished both to a high wax sheen, and early the next morning took the model to Le Canard Noir. He was let in by Mademoiselle Renée Gaston.

"Monsieur Fourmet is quite ill, but if you wait, I will bring Monsieur Henri Trouver, le directeur."

Gilles looked around as he waited. He was impressed by the fine carved wood at the doors and windows and over the fireplace. This had the look of a very fine tavern, indeed, Gilles thought. He inspected the tables, each made with fine maple and nicely polished. The joinery was precise-strong but delicate. Each chair was carved and similarly polished.

Henri did not like being disturbed when doing the books, but had developed a strong affection for Renée Gaston, and was incapable of being irritated at her even for a moment. But upon entering the tavern bar, Henri made quite a clatter to show he was a busy and decisive man.

Gilles turned quickly. "Ah, I am Monsieur Gilles Chabert. How do you do, Monsieur Trouver?"

"Bonjour," Henri said hurriedly. "You have a request of me?"

"Ah oui. I build fine boats, and I have this model I would like to hang over your mantel."

At first Henri only thought Gilles Chabert was a familiar face-perhaps one of his many patrons. He stepped forward and took the half hull. "Hmmm. Très bon." He walked to the window and held it to the light. "Très beau." He looked back at Gilles, trying to place his handsome face.

Gilles moved to his side. "Do you know boats, Monsieur Trouver?"

"Only enough to avoid them when I can," Henri said. Then the light caught Gilles' face, and Henri knew him from the island visit last fall. He paused for a moment to consider if there might be a danger in revealing who he was. "Pardon moi, but why do you want to decorate my tavern?"

"To sell my boat to your customers."

Henri tapped his foot impatiently. "Please, who are you?"

"I am Gilles Chabert, a boatbuilder at Le Petit Bateau Bâtisseur, and I am told this tavern is the city's very best with patrons who might very much appreciate a boat like this."

"What if I suggested to you that you are not a boatbuilder but an officer in the French Navy. What would you say to such a suggestion?"

Gilles blanched. He turned away a moment to collect himself, then cleared his throat. "I would say perhaps I was once an officer but no longer. I would say there are many such men in Montreal."

Henri stepped back in shock. The French Navy had tracked him down. Astonishing. An enormous gloom flooded him. He slumped into one of his chairs. "What do you really want from me?" Henri said with sad sigh.

"To hang my model over your mantel. That is all."

"Are you still an officer in the French Navy?" Henri asked forlornly.

Gilles was surprised at how theatric a negotiation had evolved over so simple a request. What choice do I have, he thought, but to tell the truth. "Yes, I was an officer, but I was removed for an error in judgment by a captain who was a rigid ass."

Henri considered the man's story. He would need to test him further. "Does the name Lucy mean anything to you?" Henri asked.

Gilles turned, his heart suddenly racing. "Yes."

"Does the name Everett mean anything to you?"

"Yes. Please, yes. What can you tell me? Do you know them?"

Henri sat back suspiciously. This could be a trap-a very dangerous one, he thought. The French Navy could hang him for associating with Lucy and Everett.

"No, I am not going to tell you. Hang your little boat if you please, but I know a clever trap when I see one, and you French officers are not going to fool me. Cut my balls off if you wish, but I will not betray my friends."

Gilles took a seat across from Henri. "Please, they are my friends, too. Lucy is...I just miss her so very much. I think of her every day. What has happened to her?"

Henri rolled his eyes.

"Look, I love this woman. Please, Monsieur. Believe me, I hate the French Navy. I hate the bastards. Monsieur Everett was my friend. I saved his life; he saved mine. I let them escape, do you understand. I am lucky that I was not hung because I let them go in front of the marine guards."

"That is treason," Henri snapped. "This could not be true. They would have hanged you."

"My captain took mercy."

"So he was not a rigid ass," Henri said.

"He sentenced me to death by drowning."

"You are a very handsome dead man. All the drowned men I know are a bit puffy at the jowls," Henri sneered.

"You do not believe me, obviously," Gilles said slumping back in his chair. "Look, the captain took a small mercy. He banished me from the French Navy and recorded me as a drowning victim. That is my official fate. He saw no purpose in hanging a young man or beating me to death, as he almost did. But please. Tell me of Everett and Lucy. They are not dead? The officers reported they shot Monsieur Everett in the Lachine channel and he fell through the ice and perished. He was trying to sneak back to Montreal on his ice boat. But what of her? He was alone in the boat, they told me."

"Where were you during this supposed shooting?"

"In the brig. But I was told, of course."

"Do you think Everett would have sailed back past that ship?" Henri asked.

"I don't know. Why not? Monsieur Everett was not easily daunted. But he is alive? Is she alive?"

Henri pushed back from the table. He rolled his eyes skeptically.

"Please, Monsieur, I beg you," Gilles said desperately. "I will swear on the Holy Bible. I am telling the truth. I have no reason to lie, and perhaps I can help them. Perhaps if they have been captured, I can help them escape."

Henri turned away. He remembered Lucy's affair with this young man and knew she loved him almost from the first day. Henri recalled Lucy fondly, but now that he had met Renée, he was no longer jealous or angry with Lucy. After all, Lucy had shown extraordinary loyalty. She had sacrificed her life and her love for this handsome man to rescue Everett. She could have been killed. She put her life on the line. Henri wondered of himself if he could do the same for his two lost friends. Henri stood and walked to the bar.

"Monsieur," Gilles pled.

"Fermez ta bouche," Henri snapped angrily. "I am thinking." He walked behind the bar and selected his very best brandy and two glasses. He returned to the table and poured them both to the brim. He sat and held his glass and nodded to Gilles. "I will ask you to drink a toast to the truth. A toast of two gentlemen, two former officers of the French military."

"You, Monsieur?"

"A lieutenant in the army. I drowned as well," Henri offered acidly.

Gilles raised his glass. "I swear as a gentleman. What I have told you is the truth."

They touched glasses and sipped deeply.

Henri lowered his glass and sat forward. "I was in the ice boat that night. We survived your crew's inept marksmen, but Everett was wounded and Lucy fell and banged her head on the ice. She was badly hurt and could not remember a thing about herself. I had to sail them myself, and we were forced to shore. The next day a trapper stole the ice boat. Perhaps it was he who drowned; a great surprise for him, no?

"And soon after we were captured by Indians. I think Everett may have been killed by them. They smashed his face very badly and left him to freeze."

"He would not freeze, that man."

"Perhaps not. But I have not seen him since. The Indians took Lucy and me. They were interested in ransom and sold me to the proprietor here, Monsieur Fourmet, for a hefty price. I told the Indians that Lucy had served the church hoping that they would ransom her to the Jesuits, but I am not certain what happened to Lucy. The Jesuits would pay well for her freedom, and she was not well. The Indians could have sold her to prostitution, but she vomited frequently, and the Indians are not fools. It is better to do business with Jesuits than pimps, yes?" Henri touched the tips of his fingers to his lips and sighed. "This is all I know."

Gilles sipped from his brandy and leaned closer to Henri. "Now that we are telling the truth, you must tell me. She was pretending to be my mistress. This was all a ruse, no?"

"She cared for you very much, Monsieur. I can say that with certainty. I was not certain at all that she could carry out the rescue of Everett. You see, I cared for Lucy at that time and was quite madly jealous of you. She was a woman in love."

"You are not jealous now?"

"No. I have found the woman who is right for my soul."

"Mademoiselle Gaston?"

Henri sat back. "Oui, it is my hope."

Both men sipped from their brandies. Henri poured two more glasses.

"What would you do in my position," Gilles asked.

"I would go to the monastery and ask for Lucy. But you must prepare. She may not know you. She may not be there. She may be an invalid. She may be a prostitute. She may have been kept by the Indians. It is possible she is not alive."

Gilles's face sank.

"Monsieur, you should know, however, that Lucy is very, very tough and resourceful. Très résistant."

"Oh, yes? Tell me more of this," Gilles said more optimistically. "She did not seem so rough to me."

"Ah, mais oui. She owned a trading post near Ste-Anicet. She knows boats and handles them better than most men. She is strong and fearless. She can shoot. She can hunt and fish, and spit farther and straighter than any man I know."

"Spit?" Gilles laughed in amazement.

"Oui. The soft Lucy you met is not the real Lucy. The real Lucy swears like a sailor and could cut your throat in an instant. She is part Indian, and is oblivious to unbearable heat and bitter cold. She can walk or run all day," Henri said with a slight grin, then raised his finger in caution, "if she is healthy, Monsieur. If she is alive and healthy, Lucy is a remarkable woman."

Gilles sat back, his eyes searching his mind for pictures of this woman he'd not yet glimpsed. "She said she loved to sail," Gilles shrugged. He lifted the half hull from the table and pointed to small letters carved in the bow of his little boat. "Lucy...you see I have named my boat for her."

Henri squinted and saw the tiny, finely crafted name. "Voilà! Oui. Lucy"

The door opened from the street, and a finely dressed lawyer, Frederic de Montegron entered with a packet of papers.

"Excusez-moi, Monsieur Dumas. L' avocat est ici. The lawyer for Monsieur Fourmet; we have a meeting. What we have said today. It is between us."

"Oui, of course," Gilles said standing and shaking Henri's hand.

"I wish you the greatest luck. And please, come back and tell me what you discover about Lucy and Everett. I will try to help, if I can. And, yes, please come by for dinner. It is my gift whenever it pleases you.

I am the chef, and the food, it is very good. It will make you weep for France."

Gilles smiled. "Merci beaucoup, Monsieur. I will talk to you soon."

A few minutes later Henri, Frederic de Montegron, and Mademoiselle Gaston were standing solemnly at Monsieur Fourmet's bedside. The man who only months ago was fat and pink was now sallow, gaunt, yellow-faced... barely able to lift a hand, only capable of brief whispers.

The lawyer spoke softly, peeking over spectacles balanced on a long nose crooked severely to the left. "We are here at the request of Monsieur Fourmet who has completed and signed his last will and testament. He has no family, no living relatives, no heirs, and has decided with sound mind to bequeath 95% of his tavern and quite considerable fortune in equal parts to you both, Mademoiselle Renée Gaston and Monsieur Henri Trouver. The remainder, five-percent, he has left to me, his attorney of sixteen years."

Fourmet waved his finger, beckoning the lawyer to lean down. He whispered to the lawyer for a few moments, then sagged back in his pillow exhausted but with the faintest smile.

The lawyer dug through a packet of papers, then cleared his throat. "Monsieur Fourmet wishes me to say that the indentured contract signed by you both, Monsieur Trouver, is now null and void and that you are now retained as head chef and chief accountant of the Black Duck Tavern for the highest wage of any chef in Montreal." de Montegron tore up the old contract and continued, "Mademoiselle Gaston is henceforth promoted to general manager of said tavern at an equal wage. Monsieur Fourmet would like to thank you both for serving him the last few months with the very finest food he has ever tasted."

Fourmet smiled wanly from his pillow and bobbed his head feebly.

"Merci, Monsieur," Henri said softly, his eyes bulging with tears.

Renée Gaston squeezed Fourmet's knarled and trembling hand, and smiled kindly. "Bless you, kind sir," she said with a sniffle.

The lawyer handed Henri a copy of the will and ushered them from the foul smelling room. In the hallway, he turned and spoke again. "The doctor tells me it is only a few days, perhaps a week. Monsieur Fourmet's liver is failing very badly, I am told. You will see that there is much land... many, many hectors of farmland southwest of here along the river. And great wealth in banks here, in Paris, and New York. I am, of course, at your service in continued management of this wealth, and as executor, I will release to you his cash accounts immediately upon his passing so that you can continue the tavern without interruption while the estate is litigated. If you wish to retain someone else after..."

"No, no, Monsieur," Henri said trading hurried nods of agreement with Renée Gaston. "We would like you to continue, of course."

"Very well. My fee is five-percent a year. I will prepare a contract when the time comes."

By week's end, Monsieur Fourmet had, indeed, died of liver failure. Henri, Renée, the lawyer, and a motley dozen of previous customers were the only people at the funeral. When it was over and the casket placed in a stone vault until the ground had fully thawed, the lawyer handed Henri and Rene packets with checks that could be drawn on personal cash accounts in the Montreal Bank of Paris for 5,000 francs each. A third cash account of 15,000 francs could be drawn on by the tavern in either's name, the lawyer de Montegron told them in his quiet, solemn voice. "I will see you in a few weeks about the estate. The French government will take 40% or so in taxes. My fee is five-percent." He shrugged and added, "But this leaves more than you could have ever wished. And the land. There is no better farmland in the world. Congratulations, Monsieur, Mademoiselle. You are among the wealthiest people in New France." He looked up then from his hunched over posture, "Could you have ever imagined such a thing just a month ago?" he said with a faint smile.

Henri and Renée returned to the tavern and took brandy in the corner table, both stunned into dazed silence by their sudden turn in fortune. Henri nearly wept as he gazed at the tears streaming down Renée's face. He reached across the table and patted her glistening cheeks with a crisp cloth napkin. She touched his hand softly and smiled bravely. Henri knew, of course, that this sudden turn in wealth could be lost to the British who took every opportunity to torment their most hated enemies, the French, at every turn. Everyone knew Montreal would fall within the year and all his patrons' recent talk of burying their money in the countryside took on new meaning. For a moment he remembered his 'English' lessons from Jamie and smiled to himself in fond memory of the boy and wondered if he could fool the British into thinking he was an American. Then he stiffened and vowed never to betray Monsieur Fourmet.

He reached over and squeezed Renée's hand. "It is a miracle," he said.

"Oui, Mon Dieu," she whispered through her sniffles.

"If the British come, we will stuff them until they burst. They are so used to eating their own shit," he laughed, "they will not be able to resist our cooking and will suffocate on their own fat!"

Renée giggled approvingly and wiped her tears.

Henri raised his glass to her, and they toasted silently to a better future.

Chapter 7

Her fingers numb from icy stream water, Ella lifted the bark water barrel to her head in the motion shown to her many times by her Indian captors. As she stepped to the muddy path, her foot slipped, and she fell, the barrel landing on her head, smashing her cheek into the hard mud, icy water splashing over her shoulders and down her neck. Though a bit dazed, she quickly struggled to her feet. Flying Turtle, Whispering Cloud's widowed daughter who had now befriended Ella, rushed to help her, and hissed at several other tribes women who giggled at Ella's clumsiness. Ella blushed and shuddered at the cold water rippling down her back. She had long since learned to bite back her tears and to accept her status as object of derision whenever her clumsiness merited. She knew the giggles were not intentionally cruel. It was part of a shared amusement at human folly, Flying Turtle had explained. "We enjoy thees little misfortunes, and we each see ourselves in your struggle. We laugh because we are glad we are not de one suffering."

Flying Turtle gently cleaned the mud from Ella's cheek with a soft leather cloth. "You okay?"

"Yes, fine. I'm okay," Ella said, "Thank you, Flying Turtle."

But Ella had still not learned to laugh at herself-an important sign of a mature woman in the Turtle clan. During her weeks in captivity, Ella learned that the Indians laughed a great deal at what white people considered life's humiliations and indignities. It seemed at first to be a childish sort of humor-ill mannered, embarrassing, girlish, and silly. In an English family such indignities were either ignored, scolded, or were cause for apology, but always were a source of shame. Ella could not shake that training in her own childhood. But she came to welcome the absence of shame in others and gradually was less flustered by her own foibles. She envied the Indian women for their capacity to find hilarity in their own stumbles and goofs. If you could laugh at yourself, she saw, you could gain untold amusement and sometimes joy in the otherwise grim hardships of an Indian woman's life.

Ella had never considered herself lazy or frail. But she had never seen women work so hard or so long under such difficult conditions, and she had never worked like this ever in her life. Squatted at the stream's edge, Ella grasped the bark water barrel and dipped it into the current. She had learned not to dip too deeply. During her second day of captivity, she had dipped the barrel too deeply and had been pulled into the frozen stream. Every woman burst into hysterics. Had it not been for Flying Turtle, Ella may have been pulled under a ridge of ice and drowned. But Flying Turtle had grasped Ella's arm and held her until the other women, still laughing gleefully, were able to lend a hand and pull her to the stream's edge. Ella had never been so humiliated in her life. The women quickly stripped her naked in full view of men, women, and children and sent her to her cabin fire. As she pranced tippy-toe and baby naked up the icy path, laughter spread, and Ella was mortified by her public ridicule.

Now she dipped more carefully and filled the barrel with a smaller bark bowl they made for her until she gained the strength to fill the barrel properly in one motion. It had taken her many days to learn to lift the bark barrel properly so that it did not spill, fall off her head, or collapse from improper positioning. The Indians made it look very easy, but the barrels weighed 80 or 90 pounds. Though neither small nor weak in the world of English or American women, Ella was a frail weakling among these women, and even after weeks of practice and strengthening, lifting the barrel to her head still caused her heart to beat in anxious trepidation. Already having slipped in the mud and fallen this morning, Ella positioned her hands nervously as she had been taught, and in one smooth, fluid motion, hoisted the barrel to her head. It slurped and swayed and splashed her shoulders for a few moments, but she steadied it, and this time took smaller steps, watching the path carefully. She stopped at their cabin where Whispering Cloud helped pour a portion into a much larger water container, and then she took the rest to the long house where a huge communal bark barrel provided emergency water for all to share in the event of the a deep freeze or for the many ceremonies and meals they took in the long house together.

Ella learned that the tribe had begun living in cabins a few years ago at the time of the last migration of the village to fresh farmland. They had once all lived together in long houses, but when the white men's diseases decimated the tribe only a few years ago, they were told by the tribal shaman to build two dozen cabins. Shaman Turtle Cloud, who had studied for a time with an American doctor, explained to the tribe that ghosts of white men's diseases thrived in the warm air of the long house. When outbreaks occurred, they needed to live separately so that the diseased spirits could not ride the warm air from family to family.

Ella now lived in a cabin with Whispering Cloud and Flying Turtle and her three daughters and one son. Flying Turtle's husband had been killed in a Mohawk raid two years ago, and now that her mourning was complete, Flying Turtle would soon marry again. Ella was speechless when Whispering Cloud told them she hoped for a double wedding and urged Ella to keep an eye out for a desirable man when the warriors returned from their winter hunt.

Ella learned that the women of the tribe enjoyed considerable power and control. They owned the land, and while they were expected to do all of the farming and most of the hard domestic labor such as cutting wood and clearing farmland, such squaw's work was considered an emblem of their power and prestige. While men were important political leaders when dealing with other tribes and white leaders, women held the votes and chose the men who led them. Whispering Cloud was the most powerful woman in the village and had to be consulted for all treaties and important agreements. It seemed remarkable to Ella that a woman of such power could behave with such child-like innocence. It often seemed to Ella that the women were like the large groups of pre-adolescent girls she had known from church in her own childhood. They giggled and gossiped and played jokes on one another, and seemed to live much of their lives in innocent, girlish delight. They played with their children as if they were fellow siblings, seldom scolding or punishing them. Sometimes Ella had to bite her lip to hold back her temptation to reprimand Turtle Cloud's exuberant children. It seemed to Ella that they were like an enormous family without parents, yet, when it came time to work, they all pitched in without complaint, including the children.

When the warriors were away, some of the women, most boys over six or seven, and the male elders participated in hunting and trapping. But there were many mouths to feed and after a few weeks without warriors, their food supplies wore thin, and they resorted to many meals of mashed squash and cornmeal bread.

Nearly every night, Whispering Cloud told stories, and gradually Ella learned of the great hardships these people bore year after year. Whispering Cloud, herself, had had four husbands, all of them killed in tribal skirmishes or in combat with the English or French settlers or troops. "War ees a condition of ar lives," she told Ella.

"But you sign treaties," Ella protested. "The Iroquois are admired by white shamen as a people of sustained peace."

Whispering Cloud shrugged. "Thees was a short time. Ees over now."

Ella was surprised to learn how few deer and bear and beaver remained in the tribal wilderness. It seemed to her that wildlife prospered but remembered Everett complaining of how difficult trapping had become.

"Ees not da same," Whispering Cloud said. "When I am de child, deer everywhere, a nuisance. Ees easy to kill. And de beaver, everywhere. De pond everywhere. Flood de stream. Flood de river." She rolled her eyes in remembrance of the annoyance of beaver floods. "Then come de trapper. And de wampum. And we de Indian, we buy de gun wit de wampum. We trap. We de best. We shoot de deer, de bear, de beaver. But ees not so easy no more," she said solemnly, her sparkling dark eyes searching inward for memories, her wrinkled old face creased by dark shadows from the cabin fire.

One night the old women spoke about wars she had experienced, and Ella interrupted at one point to inquire about the brutality. "Why do the Indians take scalps."

"Ah. Better to take de head. Always. To bring back the spirit of the warrior, we cut off de head. But too many heads. Sometimes too many heads. So we take de scalp. Ees easier to carry. And then de white man. He want de scalp. De more de scalp, de more de gun and de more de whiskey for de Indian. Ees change too."

"White men have told stories of Indian torture," Ella said. "Are these stories true?"

"Could be. Why yes maybe. De Indian not use de word tor-ture. Not our word. Ees a ceremony. A brave man, he die crying, ees not so brave, ey? A coward, he die wid de clear eye. He brave man. Ready for de spirit place. A brave man wid de clear eye. He endure beeg pain. Ees a great warrior, ees ready for de spirit place. He come back to us. Ees wid us and in our hearts. Ees not enemy no more. Ees broder, ey?"

"Have missionaries ever come to your village?" Ella asked.

"Ah, why yes. De one, I am de young woman. De missionary come and we see he ees de witch. Ees de devil. Everybody sick and die. He do ceremony," she said waving her hands to pantomime the sign of the cross and other blessings. "Dey die. All dey die. Each time. Babies. Modders. Warriors. Old men. Old woman. All de ceremony. All dey die," she said shaking her head sadly.

"So we cook de missionary. Not brave dis man. Cry, cry, cry. He go to hell place. He tell us 'bout de hell place where dey cook for many,

many moons." She smiled, "we start him to cook. Cry, cry, cry. He know. Before he tole us. Cook de hell. He know. Cry all de way der."

"You think he was a witch."

"Ah yes. Eees de witch. He say cook de hell," she shrugged, "he tell de way, dat man."

"I can't imagine being cooked like that," Ella shuddered.

Whispering Cloud leaned toward took Ella's hand in her warm, leathery palms. "We no cook you. No cook," she smiled. "We marry you, ey? Better dan de cook," she giggled with playful wickedness and traded nods with Turtle Cloud, and they all smiled, Ella more thinly than the others.

* * *

Before embarking on his trip to find Lucy, Gilles returned to Le Canard Noir Taverne to consult with Henri about Lucy's affliction.

"The Jesuits told me she was very ill and almost died," he said to Henri at the same table where they had sat two weeks ago.

"But she is better now?" Henri asked.

Gilles shrugged. "They said she recovered and was an assistant for a missionary. They said she was free to go anywhere she pleased, but that she chose to help a Father Raymbault at a Huron mission. They said it was very dangerous, and they urged Raymbault to go elsewhere, but he insisted, and Lucy insisted on going, as well."

"Lucy?! A missionary? No, no. That does not sound like the Lucy I know. Her memory is still gone. This must be," Henri said, shaking his head with a frown. "Look, I want you to buy two good horses and all the supplies you need. Guns, ammunition, food, warm clothes. And whiskey. Take extra guns and whiskey, so that if you have to, you can buy her from the Indians."

"I have no money, Monsieur."

"I will pay."

"But you said you were indentured..."

"Monsieur Fourmet died last week," Henri said. "He gave his money to Mademoiselle Gaston and me. I have so much money, I feel tortured by guilt." Henri reached in his pocket for a satchel of coins and plunked it on the table. "Buy everything you need. Do not hesitate to get the very best."

"Merci, Monsieur, but..."

"Henri. Call me Henri, s'il vous plait."

"Oui, Henri. But what if she will not come with me? What if she does not remember?"

"Bring her here, and Fourmet's doctor will care for her. He is the best in Montreal."

"I will not capture her against her will," Gilles said firmly.

"Return this afternoon at three, and I will have the doctor here. Perhaps he can help. Perhaps he can help you jog her memory. But if this is a dangerous place, you may have no choice but to capture her. This may be her only chance.

Gilles frowned skeptically.

"Look. Don't fuck around with this. Get going. God only knows what will happen, but since my capture, I am told this happens all the time, and I am lucky to be alive. Capture is a way of life with the Indians, but that most people end up dead. Now go."

Gilles went that morning to the Montreal trading post and bought two fine horses. He packed one with whiskey, guns, and food. For himself and Lucy he bought two flint lock rifles and four pistols. He returned to the tavern at 3 pm, but the doctor was not there.

"He had emergency surgery on the mayor's daughter," Henri told Gil, holding the edgy horse's rein. "Go now. He told me there is not much you can do except tell her about her trading post, tell her stories about Everett, about the hotel. It will take time. She will remember your face but perhaps not know who you are. Now go. I do not like this. You must hurry," Henri said releasing the rein.

Gilles spun the powerful, spirited horse and fought him to a slow trot through the slippery Montreal streets. At the edge of the river, Gilles gave his horse a spur, and they galloped down the muddy trail, the smaller mare straining to keep pace through a cascade of mud kicked up by Gilles' massive stallion.

After an hour of hard riding, Gilles slowed the pace and let the stallion cool slowly. By evening he was nearly a third of the way to the Huron mission by reckoning of the Jesuit's hand-drawn map. Despite Henri's urgency, Gilles took the horses off the trail and made camp for the night at the edge of a small stream. He dug through the snow, exposing grass for the horses, and hobbled them. He knew that having tired horses upon his arrival could be very dangerous and had no way of knowing that tomorrow was the third day of torture for Father Ray.

The sky only dimly lit by predawn light, Gilles chewed jerky as he broke camp and headed west. If his map were accurate and his journey were without incident, he knew he could arrive perhaps even before darkness. He held the stallion to a brisk walk until the sun rose, then let him loose for a gallop along the snow and mud-strewn path. Then he slowed the pace again, aiming to keep the horses fresh and injury free. His face and clothing spattered with mud, Gil looked a strange and frightening site mounted on the huge and wild-eyed horse. It took every bit of horseman's skill he'd acquired during his youth in France just to keep the steaming beast from racing wildly down the river path.

* * *

They led Father Ray back out to the post. Despite their attempts to revive him and cleanse his wounds, his legs were wobbly and his will spent. He prayed that God take him quickly, but his fear rushed new energy to his racing heart as they packed sticks and logs around his feet. He looked on through swollen eyes with horror and fear for Lucy's life as they forced stones into her hand and dragged her to the circle of Indians forming around him. She kept dropping the stones, and each time the woman guiding her yanked hard on the rope around her neck, knocking Lucy first to her knees, then yanking again upward.

The stoning began. Father Ray closed his eyes but held his chin high not so much in defiance of the Indians but in deference to his God. The Indians screamed at him to open his eyes, but he refused until an old woman came forward and wedged small sticks inside his eyelids, holding his eyes open. In a few minutes tears streamed down his face, and his eyes rolled desperately as the stones smashed into his face and body. He saw through the murk of those tears, Lucy being pushed forward.

They forced her to throw, but her heartless fling went wide, and the Indians hissed and forced her to throw until a stone struck his cheek a glancing blow and there were cheers. By midmorning, frozen and numb, slipping in and out of consciousness, Father Ray felt hands rip at his privates, and he shuddered in a spasm of pain as they tore away his sinfulness, and Father Ray called out to God for forgiveness, blood streaming down his trembling legs. They raised their arms to the sky and chanted earnestly for nearly an hour before they all came forward and patted him softly and kindly, and removed the sticks from his eyes.

During the afternoon they inserted sticks beneath his flesh and set them afire as they had the first day, but as the sticks burned down and broke off, the sticks at his feet began to smolder, and Father Ray prayed for absolution. He could hear the crackle of burning sticks and felt the heat, at first a comfort in the freezing air, and then he set his broken teeth and battered jaw as the fire burned his legs, and the wind gusted suddenly. In a few minutes the small fire exploded into a wall of flames, and Father Ray's body spasmed as his skin hissed and crackled, and he looked out through the flames one last time and gasped deeply, breathing in the wall of flames and lost consciousness, sagging to his right and dying behind the wall of fire.

Lucy sagged to her knees and vomited as she saw Father Ray's last desperate look swallowed by the flames. Her stomach was knotted so severely she could only gasp before a sudden blackness swept over her, and she fainted. They dragged her limp body away from the roaring flames and left her in a heap in the mud. She awoke dazed and listless, laying on her side alone. Father Ray was gone, the charred post tilted strangely in a bed of smoldering logs. The sun had dipped below the tree line but cast a red glow across the mud, strange shadows wiggling and dancing from the brilliant sunshine shimmering through the sway of barren branches. The tribe had gathered in a circle a hundred or so feet between Lucy and the darkening sky. They chanted and prayed, and consumed the remnants of Father Ray, all of them dressed in their ceremonial clothes.

She turned away and tried to breathe smoothly, but her stomach was knotted and painful from vomiting, and her body trembled from the cold. She gazed blankly at the shadows dancing across the mud, and then her eye was caught by a man and two horses standing motionless for a moment at the edge of the clearing. Then, as if gazing through the lens of a nightmare, she saw the man and the horses break toward her, and felt the huge thud of hooves from the enormous horse, and saw a wall of mud and chaos flying and splashing in all directions and the black face of a man drenched in mud, the whites of his eyes and bright pink of mouth shouting "Get up, Lucy. Get up. Get to your feet, Lucy!" She did not know what this apparition could be or why, but struggled to her feet in dazed obedience, staggered and tried to steady herself and watched as the horse and rider thundered toward her, and now she could hear the howls of the Indians behind her, but could not take her eyes off the rider who pointed two pistols held in each hand, and for a moment felt certain that he was aiming at her, and that this man was an Indian, and she was now going to meet Father Ray, and her whole body glowed with the most profound relief as she readied herself to absorb the bullets from the immense fifteen-foot storm of flying mud and chaos.

The guns exploded, and Lucy braced but felt nothing, and then the huge horse set his immense hooves and mud flew in a wall at her. The horse and rider curled around her, the second horse galloping into the crowd of rushing Indians.

Gilles grabbed Lucy under her arm and twirled her up and behind her, and she grasped him just in time to avoid being flung completely over the other side. She heard the man yell, "Hold on, Lucy, Hold on," and the huge horse twirled and Gilles set the spur, and the powerful stallion leapt back along the tortured path where he had just galloped, and in a moment they were at full stride heading into the dark tunnel of the rapidly approaching woods.

When the Indians saw the black and crazed fiend thundering toward them on the enormous horse, both so mud-splattered they looked to be one beast with four wild eyes, most screamed and fled in every direction. Several were knocked down by the trailing mare which zigged one way, then the other. The mare set her hooves to a halt just before crashing into the tribal fire. She flared to the side, and one of the warriors lunged for her reins and held her as she tried to escape the screaming chaos. Two other warriors charged her, grabbing her neck and she slipped and fell. More warriors jumped on her, pinning her to the ground, as a fifth hobbled her front hooves. As the horse gasped, they quickly climbed off as she wrenched herself to her feet, they steadied the horse and calmed her with whispers. The Shaman stood behind the fire raising his hands in a circle, chanting loudly. Other Indians near the horse quickly stripped away the bags of supplies, guns, and whiskey, and before long the rest of the Indians returned to celebrate the gifts from Father Ray sent to them from the spirit place and delivered by his charred apparition on the equally charred and massive horse. They gave thanks that they had been able to give the mixed blood woman in exchange, and that the Great Spirit had rewarded them for bringing out the bravery from the missionary many of them already knew was a special man whose walk on the muddy winter earth was strong and brave.

After two hours of hard gallop, the horse slowed to a steady trot, and Gilles felt Lucy's arms loosen as she fell asleep against his back. He tucked her wrists under his elbows. They rode through the night letting the big stallion find his own pace along the river trail. As the sky lightened before sun up, Gilles stopped and slid carefully off the horse beside a quiet feeder stream at the edge of the St. Lawrence River. He pulled Lucy off the horse, and she woke. Gilles washed the caked mud from his face in the frigid water and looked up at Lucy who stood dazed and swollen-eyed.

"Do you remember me?" he asked.

Lucy nodded yes, but struggled to place him in the scrambled sequences of her slowly returning memory.

"Are you all right?" he asked wiping his face with his sleeve.

She nodded yes again. But she was not at all sure any more what 'all right' meant. Though her neck was burned and sore from being yanked repeatedly by the Indian's rope, she was not injured. But she felt as though her insides had been torn out and her emotions left in the pools of vomit she'd deposited at the Indian village.

Gilles handed her jerky which she chewed quickly and swallowed. He gave her more, then more again, then water from a brass cup. She squatted at the stream's edge and gazed at the steady flow of dark water.

"Do you remember the gunship?" Gilles asked.

She looked at him and shrugged.

"What happened back there?"

She closed her eyes and looked away from him. He seemed both kind and familiar, but she could not place him. She was comfortable in his company and would let him take her where he wished. He seemed in her memory to feel as comfortable as she had felt around Father Ray. She shuddered as her memory of Father Ray's last look through the flames formed a vivid picture in her mind. In order to erase that picture, she turned back to Gilles.

"Tell me who you are," she said in a flat, hurried voice.

"Do you remember Henri?"

She shook her head no.

"Everett?"

She shook her head no.

"Then you probably don't remember the gunship. Everett and Henri were your friends. Everett was being held on a French warship against his will. He is a fisherman and trapper who lives on an island near Ste-Anicet where I am told you own a trading post."

She looked at him in puzzled confusion. "This isn't making much sense to me," she said.

Gilles let the horse drink from the stream and fed him from a head satchel of grain. He spoke as he worked. "Look, you and Everett were friends for many years. We forced Everett to serve as our pilot on a French gunship. He was our prisoner, and you and Henri decided to rescue him. I was the ship's first officer, and you befriended me in order to gain access to Everett. You rescued him one night, and you fell on the ice and injured your head. Do you remember the ice boat?"

She shook her head no.

"You were captured by Indians and ransomed to the Jesuits at the monastery."

"I remember the monastery. I was very sick," she said quietly. "Father Ray helped me recover."

"Father Ray? Is that Father Raymbault?"

"Yes. I called him Father Ray. I traveled with him. I was his assistant."

"Is he still back at the mission?"

"No, no," she said, the picture of Father Ray returning again. "He's dead. They tortured him, then burned him alive."

Gilles stepped away from the horse and squatted down beside her. "You saw this happen?" he asked quietly.

Tears welled up in her eyes. She nodded yes.

Gilles patted her shoulder. "I'm sorry."

She closed her eyes tightly and felt the familiar constriction of her stomach. She tried to breathe deeply. "I should not have let him return to that mission," she whispered bitterly.

"Surely you cannot blame yourself. They told me at the monastery that no one could persuade him otherwise. He was a missionary. He felt a duty to God."

Lucy pressed her lips tightly. Tears dripped down her cheeks into the snowy mud. "Yes, he felt a duty to God," she said with arid irony.

Gilles knew then that there was more to this, but he did not press. "We must go," he said, lifting her shoulders.

She shook him off. She did not need help, she thought. She did not need sympathy. She straightened herself and set her teeth hard in her jaw. A moment after Gilles mounted, she held up her arm, grasped his elbow and swung up on the horse behind him. She settled herself and upon a familiar impulse, she spit over her left shoulder as the great horse spun and broke into powerful gallop down the river path to Montreal.

Tears welled up in Henri's eyes when he saw Lucy astride the great horse. She swung down on Gilles' arm, and Henri rushed to her and hugged her with trembling gratitude.

"I'm sorry; I'm sorry," Henri croaked, "you must think me crazy, Mon Dieu! You don't know me, but I am your friend," he said hugging her fiercely as she stood puzzled by this other familiar face, a man she knew but could not place in the fragments of memory. "Merci au Bon Dieu, vous etes revenu," he gasped.

Henri finally stepped back and rushed them into the warm tavern.

"Renée, cela est mon ami Lucy," he said to Renée Gaston.

Renée nodded and smiled. "Welcome, Lucy. A friend of Henri's is a friend to me. I will make up a room for you."

Renée helped Lucy draw a bath and that night brought her dinner and wine. She gave Lucy a satchel of clothes Henri had ordered from their seamstress in anticipation of her return. It seemed to Renée an odd selection with a silk blouse and velvet trousers, but Henri had explained that Lucy favored men's styles and would scorn fancy dresses. Renée explained to La Couseuse that she required a suitably feminine admixture until Lucy, herself, could speak for herself.

During the next few days, Lucy developed a liking for the steady and firm-minded Renée Gaston, a woman of quiet, understated good humor who clearly felt great affection for Henri and who handled him with bemused good will and a firm resolve. Lucy returned to the monastery where she reported to the priests the fate of Father Raymbault, and after attending a solemn high mass and funeral service, left the monastery for the last time. She visited Henri's physician who prescribed several weeks of rest and recommended she spend as much time with Gilles and Henri piecing together the facts of her past and then urged her to visit the trading post she was told she owned on the presumption she would find people and places that could help her regain her lost and scrambled memories. He explained to her that her concussion might leave her with some permanent loss of distant memory, but that since her recovery in the monastery, she seemed to have excellent recall of recent events. "Some people recover completely. These events are still there, Mademoiselle," he said giving her salts and a package of pills, "you have damaged the means to find them."

* * *

By early April, the ice was broken up and drifting down the great river, and Lucy felt rejuvenated and for the first time in a long time, very well fed. Several times each week, Gilles visited, and they dined in the

Black Duck Tavern. Several patrons ordered boats similar to the half model on the tavern wall, and Gilles told her he was building a boat for her.

"You told me you loved to sail," he told her in the soft, evening glow of candlelight at their corner table.

"Did I?" she said, "and what else did I say I loved?" she asked, seeing his eyes melting with affection when he gazed upon her, sometimes for such prolonged periods that she blushed uncomfortably.

Gilles turned away in embarrassment. When he composed himself, he turned back to her and took her hand in his. "In time you'll discover for yourself," he said. But he dared not say, 'I have my hopes; I have my hopes.' Instead, he raised his wine glass and toasted, "To our first sail on the great river."

* * *

For the first several days of their search, Everett and Jamie brought up the rear. Gordon and his raiding party ran everywhere, keeping up a steady, unrelenting pace. After leaving the island, they headed up river dragging their outsized canoe through increasingly slushy ice. Everett and Jamie tried to keep pace, but Everett soon fell back. Rather than leave Everett behind, Jamie stayed with Everett and both alternately ran and walked as Gordon's party soon became specks on the gray horizon.

"I guess we're a sorry pair," Everett said panting.

"I believe we are," Jamie said.

"And of the two of us, I'd have to say I'm the sorriest," Everett gasped and broke to a walk. "These bloody bastards. They say a good Indian can outrun a horse, and I don't doubt it."

"Me neither."

"Nossir."

"They'll think we be lily white sissies," Everett said with a huge sigh.

"They'd be right, I'd say," Jamie grinned.

"Well shit, boy. I don't hear you pantin' none."

"That's cause I ain't."

"You ain't winded?"

"Not hardly. I'm just keepin' you company."

"That's a sorry story."

"Well, I'm sorry to tell it, then."

"I gotta say I'm hard pressed to think of a single goddamned thing I can do better'n some Indian," Everett said mournfully.

"You can sure as hell fish as good."

"Not a chance. Them Indians is as much better at fishing than me than you are better'n Henri."

"I don't believe that," Jamie laughed.

Then they sloshed through the slurpy river ice in silence beneath the lifeless gray sky.

"Springs ah comin'," Everett said finally, "I can smell it."

Jamie nodded, then turned and asked, "What do you suppose happened to Henri?"

"Kilt more'n likely, I'm sorry to say."

"That don't seem fair," Jamie said quietly.

"Trouble with Henri was he ain't no good at nothin' cept cookin' and entertaining chatter. I just caint see what a bunch of busy Indians would do with a gas bag like him 'cept run a spear up his ass. I don't mean no disrespect 'cause I happened to like the man, but it's the God's truth."

"What do you think they'd do with us if they caught us?" Jamie asked, breaking into a jog and urging Everett with a wave of his hand to keep pace.

Everett rolled his eyes and lumbered forward in a lifeless shuffle. "Well, son, they already tried stoving in my brain and probly didn't have time to figure my head's hard as granite. Why they kept Henri is a mystery to me 'cept maybe they figured he was so small, he couldn't cause no harm. They just ain't have heard him talk yet probly and when they did, they probly right away cut his tongue off and fed it to him for dinner."

"They wouldn't do that, would they?"

"Oh, hell. That's a common practice. Tongues and ears; first things to go."

"How can they be so cruel?"

"Yer askin the wrong man; why don't you ask Gordon?"

"Are you kiddin? Ask Gordon; are you crazy?"

"Truth is, it's been goin on a long time. The Bible says so, don't it? An eye for an eye, an ear for an ear?" Everett was beginning to pant again.

"Yessir, the Bible does say it."

"Well, when pushed to the dark corners of fear, men do terrible things to each other, and this land ain't nothing if it ain't a constant bundle of fear. A day don't go by when I don't practically shit my pants thinkin about some horrible possibility." Everett then staggered to a slow walk. "If I thought I could save my own life by cutting off another man's parts, I wouldn't hesitate a whisker. Not a whisker. That's all it is, boy. Fear. It'll make a man desperate. And a desperate man'll do anything to save his own ass."

"Well how is it that some men just freeze up and git their throats slit without a fight?"

"They prob'ly think it'll prolong things a little. How come a rabbit freezes when you git it trapped just right? It's gotta be thinkin' that runnin' is even more dangerous. There are men out there who somehow think if they don 't fight back, maybe whoever's tryin' to kill him will change his mind. Who's gonna kill a wimperin' rabbit, they think? Truth with all men is that there ain't no such thing as no danger. Indians learnt that from each other first, then from white men. A live enemy is always dangerous. That's their way of life, and it all boils down to fear, and they understand it better'n most of us. And they better understand it, 'cause all these white men pushing west- all these white settlers, French or English don't matter. They're all bringin' fear and desperation with 'em. I heard many a settler say the only good Indian's a dead Indian, and they're sayin' it outta fear. All that hate and cruelty. It's fear. Simple as that, son, nothing more."

"You afraid of Indians?"

"Scare the shit out of me, son. Scare the living shit out of me."

"I ain't see you do nothing cruel."

Everett laughed. "Ask them two dead'uns back there at the Regis River."

"But take Gordon. He's your friend. Are you scairt of him?"

"Gordon scares the shit out of me. I'll bet I scare the shit out of him, too. We're friends now 'cause we both agree on the same thing. The minute we want something different or start'n to disagree on who gets what, that's when the fear creeps in. The day me 'n Gordon git our asses in a snitch over something we caint agree on or share fair and square, then him and me start gettin' a little bit scared. When one t'or other thinks he's getting fucked by t'other, that's when the big fear starts buildin'. Truth is pretty good men can git hatin' each other real quick, and then the fear turns 'em wild. I truly hope that don't ever happen 'tween me and Gordon, but it's always there. He knows it and so don't I."

"What you're sayin' is pretty mean and ugly," Jamie grumbled.

"You don't have to believe it, son, but it's the sorry damned truth from the life I'd lived so far. You can measure it in my life. In most ever life I've known so far, yup. Ugly's the word.

By early evening Everett and Jamie finally caught up to Gordon and his raiding party camped at the edge of the St. Lawrence where a stream entered from the north. They had a good fire going with fresh venison sputtering on a spit and a jug of whiskey passing hand to hand. The dog sat near the edge of the fire circle chewing on the innards of the fresh-killed deer.

The Indians grinned and muttered jokes in their native tongue as Everett and Jamie approached.

"Here comes the rear guard," Everett joked, "Me and the boy been covering yer asses."

Gordon smiled and nodded. He offered them the jug of whiskey and prepared a pipe.

"You got a man gone missing," Everett offered before tipping back the jug.

Gordon looked to the others and grinned. "Dat man ees scout up de crik," Gordon offered, trying to muffle his chuckling.

Everett hissed at the hot raw whiskey and handed it to Jamie. "Take a sip, son."

Jamie lifted the jug and drank. He swallowed the searing liquid but before it reached half way down, his throat erupted and he spat it out over the fire where it exploded in a blue flame.

The Indians all laughed, and Jamie turned crimson with embarrassment.

Everett pounded his back and grinned.

Gordon saw the boy's tears-swollen eyes and moved over a bit to make a space for him to sit. Jamie coughed and took a seat beside Gordon who reached his arm over the boy's shoulder and patted him briskly. He eyed the other Indians, and they all wiped the grins quickly from their faces. They drank and ate as darkness swallowed the expanse of river and thick forest behind them and embraced them like the walls of a black cave. The fire lit their faces a red-golden glow, and Gordon told stories in his throaty, Indian voice.

"My grandfadder live in de mountains. He friend to de bear and de beaver and de Mohawk peoples all de one wit da Iroquois nation. Da white trad-ders come an grandfadder show dem all de beaver and trade all de many pelts for de guns and de whiskey and de wampum. My grandfadder have de dream. De white men grow de wings an' dey come down like de crows to eat de dead bear. De bones of de bear rises to de sky and make wings and become de great eagle bear and go away in de sky.

"Ees not da good dream, ey?"

The other Indians shook their heads no and grunted their agreement.

"My granfadder, he go wid da Engleesh and fight de Frenchmon in de King Willam War. He fight de Caughnawaga Mohawks, brodder against brodder and dat is how da great Iroquois nation ees break up bad."

"My granfadder say dis how de crows eat de bear. My fadder he go wit da Engleesh an da Caughnawaga brodders dey go wit da Frenchmon. All de same, ey? Ees the same today. Ees one family keel de odder."

The other Indians nodded from time to time, their bright black eyes shimmering from the fire light. Gordon told of the Wendat and how they and the Iroquois were bitter enemies over many generations and that tomorrow they would enter Wendat territory. "Ees more danger. Ees great prize fer dem de Mohawk scalp. Ees great victory for dem."

The next morning they broke camp at sunrise and headed north up the creek. Before they left, Gordon told Everett they would move more slowly now and to stay closer to the raiding party. He said the Wendat hunting parties would still be out. "Very danger," he said.

They departed from the creek trail into an immense tangle of swamp and bramble. The warm weather had softened the layers of crust, making every step a struggle into murky muck. In the absence of trails, they were forced to wrestle through huge masses of vines, thorn bushes, prickly pears, and underbrush so thick it sometimes took an hour to move a hundred feet. Even the Indians gasped, pink-faced and flushed, sweat dripping down their faces as they trudged through the dark mire.

That night they camped without fire and ate venison raw. Gordon forbade the drinking of whiskey and set watches through the night. The next morning they emerged out of the swampland into thick, dark forest alternating with swamp stands and criss-crossed by streams swollen with melting snow and beaver ponds. Everett and Jamie labored to keep pace, shivering and numb from the constant wet that soaked their feet and legs and chilled them to the bone. They gobbled jerky to keep their energy and plodded forward in exhaustion, often oblivious to anything more than a foot print in front them.

At midday they broke into large clearing of charred homes, a white settlement strewn with charred and bloating bodies, men, women, and children scalped in an endless variety of contorted poses freezing in time their moments of death. Gordon inspected the fires and bodies and concluded the raid occurred a week or so earlier, the work of the Wendat enemy. Before leaving the vulnerability of the clearing, he took Jamie aside and spoke to him.

"You see dis. Dey kill wit no mercy. Dey kill fast." He pointed to a bearded man laid in flailing pantomime on his back, his throat cut, his skull scalped, blood blackened into dried crust, his eyes shriveled and mouth agape as if still screaming in horror. "Dis man kilt in one, two second, thas it. He run and de Wendat catch him and slash de throat and scalp him. Thas it, one, two second. Dey come at you, no hesitate. You shoot. Attack, shoot, stab, fight like hell. No run. Wendat very fast run. If you run, no see Wendat. You face da Wendat. Be ready. My boy not ready," Gordon said, eyes drilling into Jamie's. "Too slow, dat's it, ey? You unnerstand?"

Jamie nodded, his heart thudding with fear.

That afternoon they broke into a clearing fresh with new tracks. At the far end at the edge of the woods stood a long pole, and festooned at its top was the mangled head of Gordon's advance scout. At that moment, the hunters became the hunted. Crouched at the edge of the clearing, Gordon motioned them back where they had come. Jamie caught Everett's eyes, and they traded fear. Jamie could not detect the same fear in Gordon but saw a new alertness, and for the first time the dog growled quietly and her neck fur spurred and her lips curled. Gordon orchestrated their movement now with his hands. They moved east in a circle with his best warrior following the group walking backwards into new swampland where Gordon felt he had the advantage against any man.

They moved like cats hunting, each step slow, precise, silent. There was no need to hurry, no urgency beyond terror. To hurry now was to hasten death, to fall into a trap, to make telltale noises, to scare birds, to send a rabbit fleeing, a fox scurrying. They all knew the Wendat were ready for the hated Mohawk raiding party. Gordon stopped and held them motionless. Birds chirped and buzzed. The wind whispered through stiff winter branches. Branches crackled and groaned near and far. A blue jay preened on an upper branch not thirty feet before them. They froze and barely breathed.

In the distance -a quarter mile at least-another blue jay called out in alarm. The bird near them stopped preening and cocked his head. Then it leapt into the air, its wings swatting the air, heeding the warning. Gordon motioned slowly for them to lower themselves into the swampy murk of melting snow and tangled bramble, and there they stayed, motionless for three hours, the wind whispering through trees and shrubs until every groan and crack, every chirp and chattered bird song, every scratchy long dead leaf seemed to Jamie a startling cacaphony of signals and warnings in a world of constant, unrelieved dread.

* * *

The Indian village prepared for the return of the hunters. Ella and the other women collected huge mounds of sticks and logs in preparation for the feast of new meat and the arrival of their men. They built these into fire mounds ready to be lit and cut large spits of green cedar. They tapped huge maples and captured sap, then boiled large copper pots day and night into thick syrup that they tasted with their fingers.

An air of excitement and whispery urgency spread throughout the village. The women prepared their beds with fresh thatch they dug from the melting snow at the swamp edges. They dug open caches of squash and beans stored through the winter and soaked the beans and boiled them into soup that simmered into a thick, pasty gruel. Ella, along with the rest, fasted for days at a time sipping sweet water laced with syrup. The games and laughter diminished now. The Indians turned inward, solemn, largely silent but worked with feverish intensity speaking only when necessary in whispery voices and clucks.

The days grew longer, the sun rising higher each day, and warm winds melted snow leaving them in a sea of mud that sucked at their feet and wrinkled their toes. On some days now the sun baked down hot on their faces. Red-winged blackbirds arrived one morning calling out for lovers, the males swelling the red mounds of their shoulder feathers, puffing their throats with scraggles of dark feathers and scratching the air with mating talk. Mosquitos and swarms of bugs erupted from the nearby swamps, and green shoots of swamp grass nudged from the brown-gold graves of last year's growth. The trees, once stiff and crackling, swayed easily now, and fat buds throbbed with nascent urgency, swollen with the urge to burst.

The nights were often cold, the mud hard and crusty until mid-morning before glimmering wetly beneath the sky's new heat. The ice at the stream's edges melted and plopped into the rushing water, and hungry trout nudged the evening water where moths and gnats hovered to mate. On some days the rain poured down through thick fog which rolled and tumbled along the stream and rose in wisps from clumps of still unmelted snow. The rain hissed and splattered in the deepening mud, forming a thousand footprint pools, and the south latrine from where the wind seldom traveled began to fester and stink from the winter's frozen droppings.

Spring flowers began blooming first at the stream's edge, then in upland patches where the sun beat strongest and nudged huddled tufts of green growth that erupted like thin green fingers from tangles of gnarled and matted grass beaten down by the winter's snow. To Ella, this was the loveliest time of year, each day teasing with the possibility of spring. Although she did not yet feel she belonged in this place, she knew now that she could survive among these people and often find rich moments of enjoyment and good will. Her body was now lean hard, her hands calloused and strong. She could now chop wood and lift water nearly as well as most of the Indian women. When she stumbled or struggled to learn something new, she could now tolerate the giggles and nudges from the other women, could see how the very same gestures she once felt as humiliations were acts of affection. They did the same with their own daughters, with each other. Laughing at their own foibles and mishaps, each stumble part of some shared reservoir of discomfort and amusement, a childlike glee as relief against such perpetual hardship.

But at other times she would wake at night in the cold and smoky cabin and long to see her son again, only to be reminded that it may never happen except when both were dead. She wondered how he and Everett were doing and pictured them both huddled in the warm hut on the island doing their best to cook, tromping off together with identical huddled shuffles to catch fish or set traps. She hoped they thought of her and hoped for their own safety that they never tried to find her. While the urgency to escape had lost its desperate edge, she knew that over time she would learn from the Indians all the skills that would be required.

She could already read the sun and the tree moss, and find her way in the wilderness, at least for short distances. She knew all running water ran south to the St. Lawrence, and the great river ran east to the ocean from the unexplored reaches of the west. The Indians taught her that the greatest danger in being lost was traveling in circles. They showed her how moss always grew on the north of aging tree trunks, and if she ever got lost, she should travel due opposite until she reached the great river and then wait until they came for her. She was learning what wild plants the Indians ate and could fast for several days without ill effects. She could now walk at pace with the Indians most of the time, and had gained such strength in her ankles and legs that she could run along their paths and stay close to the Indian women. Oddly, they did not seem to mind when she was off alone harvesting acorns in the woods. They seemed perfectly adjusted to her assumption of her Indian identity, convinced fully that she was their sister now and would chose to stay with them.

* * *

Gordon picked up the tracks of the Wendat along a glacial ridge running parallel to the great river. They were headed west but could be counted on to circle back any number of times. "Dees track no hide. Ees many trap," he told Everett and the others. "Dey split. We go nort. Make beeg, beeg circle."

To fool the Wendats they started south leaving tracks until they found a small creek. They walked in the creek back north, the rushing water swirling quickly around their steps, destroying any evidence of their tracks. After a few minutes, Everett and Jamie's feet were so numb they could barely walk. They stepped into the same places as the Indians in front of them, their feet so numb they couldn't feel the slippery bottom.

They followed the stream for many miles until it was little more than a trickle. Then they headed west in a single line, Gordon going last to hide their tracks. At the next creek, they headed north again, sometimes walking in thigh-deep water that surged powerfully over slimy rocks and threatened to sweep them off their feet. They walked north this way for the rest of the day, and as dusk approached, they stepped out of the creek and headed west again. They found a cave in a ridge and huddled together around a fire to warm their feet and dry their clothes. They cooked scraps of venison and melted snow still thick at the bases of pine trees and drank a bitter herbal tea that made Everett's heart pound rapidly in his chest and heated his body until he broke a sweat.

"You figure them Wendats still got our scent?" Everett asked Gordon.

"Don't know," he shrugged. "Could be yes. Could be no."

"Tell me true, Gordon. If you was them and them was us, could you follow our tracks to where we're at?"

Gordon chuckled and grinned at the other Indians. "Yessir, Evert," he smiled, "yessir."

The others grinned and nodded yes.

Everett looked around then at Jamie and scratched his head. "Bloody hell," he moaned.

Jamie leaned toward the fire and asked Gordon, "Why would them Indians follow us all this way?"

Gordon sat back a bit and slowly passed his fingertips over his lips over and over in the deepest thought. Then he leaned forward and looked directly at the boy.

"All thees time. All de hours. All de work, de cold water. Ees not-ting to me. Ees not-ting to de Wendat if he be dead, ey?"

Jamie looked at him in utter puzzlement.

Gordon sat back and wiped his fingertips back and forth over his lips, and then sat forward again, his face even closer now to the boy's. "You wan die to save tree-four hours, ey? Indian warrior very patient. Walk two, tree, four, ten days in de stream, ees nothing. Me, I walk thirty day, one year, five year, ten year in de stream. Ees not-ting to save my life. Unnerstand?"

Jamie looked at Gordon's dark glimmering eyes and slight hint of a kindly smile.

Jamie cleared his throat and said, "Yer sayin' that it don't matter how long or how hard you suffer so long as it keeps you alive. And if you don't do it, you end up dead, and if yer dead it don't matter how long it took or how much it hurt. Is that what yer sayin'?"

Gordon looked at Everett and the other Indians and then back and the boy, and he nodded yes. He leaned forward and patted Jamie's hand, and for a moment Jamie thought he saw tears in the Indian's eyes, and they all knew for a few moments that Gordon was looking not only into Jamie's eyes but into the eyes of his own son. The other Indians bowed their heads and nodded with Gordon and then broke into a quiet chant in honor of his living spirit.

* * *

Lucy's heart quickened as she saw Gilles and Monsieur LeBlanc carrying the two tiny boats down the catwalk at Le Petit Bateau Bâtisseur docks.

"Tres beau, ey?" LeBlanc grinned as they lowered the boats into the water.

Gilles tied them, and all three stood gazing down in admiration. The boats bobbed light as corks in the dark blue water, the hand-rubbed golden decks glowing softly beneath the warm blaze of April sun. As Gilles and Monsieur LeBlanc lowered and packed supplies and paddles beneath the decks, Lucy waited nervously. Henri and Gilles had convinced her she knew how to sail but she had forgotten so much else, she was not sure now if she would remember. While the day was hot, the river remained barely warmer than ice despite the passing of its massive spring melt.

Gilles showed her how to sit on the dock's edge and quickly transfer his weight to a sitting position on the floor pad of the tiny craft. He got out by leaning his shoulders over the gunnel onto the dock and pushing with his arms as he rolled to a sitting position. He demonstrated one more time, then Lucy followed into her own boat. Although her mind could not remember handling a boat, her body knew exactly what to do.

Instinctively she tested the balance and stability of the tiny boat, dipping her paddle and worked it in a circle and feeling its extraordinary responsiveness.

LeBlanc untied them both, and they paddled up the shore a few hundred feet.

"You okay?" Gilles called to her.

Lucy smiled and nodded yes.

"Shall we set sail, then?"

"Why not?" she said, then set her paddle and pivoted hard, feeling the entire boat snap smartly to her paddle's command. They glided into the dock, and in a few minutes Gilles set the sailing rigs.

He handed Lucy the lines to raise and control the sail, and then soon paddled back into the river.

Again Lucy's heart fluttered nervously. Gilles raised his sail; it fluttered in the wind until he tightened the sheet line. The sail popped softly and filled with wind, then leapt forward as Gilles shifted his weight to hold a steady reach on a soft northerly. Lucy followed, raising her sail and cleating the halyard with quick twists of her wrist. The sail fluttered. She sniffed the cool air off the water and yanked in the main sheet line. The sail popped and puffed, and she smiled as this tiny craft surged forward. She adjusted her weight to port then starboard and noted how the boat changed coarse with each shift.

LeBlanc watched gleefully knowing it took a good design for a boat to track forward on a goodly reach absent a rudder, deep keel, or leeboard. He watched them come about digging their paddle for a brisk result then carving a half decent tack angled into the wind, running in parallel together handsome as could be. He could detect Lucy's slight edge in speed and smiled to himself knowing Gilles would have his hand's full keeping pace with the lighter craft. He'd never seen a woman take to the water with such ease and figured she must be lying through her teeth, claiming she hadn't never sailed.

They circled past the docks one more time, and Gilles yelled to LeBlanc that all was well and now they'd be off to Ste-Anicet.

"Bon voyage," LeBlanc shouted and waved, then sat on the dock rail as the two nimble covered canoes crossed the channel angled such that they neither gained nor lost on the current but moved south briskly, and once in shallower water dashed smartly up river westward.

Lucy soon gained the feel for her small craft and grinned mischievously as she fell back a bit spilling wind until she dropped behind and to windward of Gilles' swift sailing twin. She tightened her sail and lurched forward, then shifted her weight a touch until her boat began inching up his starboard shadow. She felt the cool spray from small waves spitting from his hull, then winked at him as she pulled even, and then his jaw dropped as he saw she was moments away from stealing his wind. Then his sail luffed, and she skittered past him with a burst, laughing gleefully as his boat swayed off its heel and bobbed heedlessly until she passed and he regained his wind.

He chased her nip and tuck to the Coteau Rapids where they pulled the boats upcurrent from the well-worn path at the river's edge. Past the rapids they set forth again this time Gilles sneaking up to steal her wind, but just as he approached, she broke away, tacking 90 degrees to the northeast. As he reached the south shore and ran out of river to hold his tack, he came about and followed her. He looked to have a solid lead on her as he approached the channel but soon realized his illusion when he saw her cross his bow on her new tack west. By the time he tacked back to follow, she had a two-boat lead, a solid whupping by any standard when measuring two boats of identical design and rig. She looked back as they headed upriver again and thumbed her nose and made girlish faces, both of them laughing beneath the bright sun heading into the broadening waters of St-Francois du Lac.

It may have been that afternoon as her mind and body clicked into some level of memory that had wandered off course from the narrative of her former life and now, through her body and senses, she discovered she lost nothing but blocks of time that now would begin stumbling back into place. She saw the tree line along the lake and knew she was heading home. While she couldn't yet put a name or face to Uncle Joe, she sensed his presence as she had so often before and knew this patch of river as well as the creases of her own hands.

Perhaps it was just fresh air and a coincidence of healing, but it almost seemed to her that her vivid memory of joy flying before the wind on the great river in the cusp of spring proved the turning point, the beginning of her re-acquaintance with the moments of her life that took the form of pictures and words. Perhaps when she took that fall and bashed her head on the hard ice, part of her was already wrecked by disappointment she must betray a man she loved, and through a web of lies, rescue a man who was her lover, yes, but more a friend.

Late that afternoon she raced shoreward in a quickening wind against a growing spray, just half a boat length ahead of a man she would remember with a gasp as they kissed in the shadows of the cooling sun standing pressed together, breathless and wet-faced at the edge of the river she loved. It did not all return to her that afternoon, just the certain knowledge that this man, Gilles, she knew, and this time she would not betray him again.

She knew as well the soft skin of her aging mother's cheek at the trading post and knew the smell of fish and whiskey and the damp warmth of the fat cast iron stove inside; she knew she was home and safe again, and from then onward began putting together pieces of memory. Not all of it would ever fit perfectly together, and her days and nights with Father Ray reared themselves as shattering nightmares that felt at times more real than the shadowy memories of her deeper past. Many times she would awake at night trembling and drenched in sweat, and even reaching for Gilles and feeling his solid warmth, she could still not for a few horrible moments wrench herself free from the cold mud as she gazed up at the flames that swarmed over his face.

* * *

It would have been easier to have rescued Ella while the Wendat warriors were still away hunting, but Gordon needed her to identify his son's killers, and he needed the element of surprise.

"No can rescue yellow-haired woman, den come back 'an kill de Wendat," he told Everett, gazing into the twindling flames of the evening fire. "Kill de Wendat first, den rescue yellow-haired woman.

"That puts her in greater danger," Everett said as calmly as possible.

"Yessir. Ees danger. You wan no danger?" Gordon asked.

"I'm just thinkin', that's all."

Gordon nodded and turned a stick in the fire. "Ees danger, my friend. Great spirit, he be wid us."

Everett had long since given up on the idea that God or the Great Spirit took a daily tally of the strange activities of men, but he wasn't going to argue Gordon on that point. It was going to have to be a shared risk, Everett knew. Whether an Indian's revenge or a white lawman's arrest, there wasn't going to be any kind of justice without risk of life and limb. Everett looked up at Gordon and asked, "You got a plan?"

Gordon stared into the fire and nodded his whole body back and forth. Everett took that to mean Gordon was working at it. But in straining his own brain every which way, Everett saw no way to rescue Ella and punish the killers that didn't almost guarantee certain death for several if not all the members of the raiding party. He knew Gordon to be a good deal more skilled in the ways of war than he was, but he wasn't so sure that Gordon was enough more clever than Everett to get them through this alive.

They both gazed into the dim fire, pondering their own thoughts. Finally, Everett got to his feet and looked down at Gordon. "Okay, then, you're the boss."

Gordon didn't answer, didn't even acknowledge Everett's acquiescence, perhaps because the Indians didn't recognize the notion of a boss in the same way. Gordon knew himself to be the leader but understood each man with him to be of free will. He had to prepare a plan that would work with all of them or none but himself. It wasn't the same as the white men, either the soldiers or lawmen, who could give orders, no matter how bad, and expect blind obedience or be shot as a deserter. It was not an act of shame for an Indian to walk away from a stupid plan or a losing cause, and that made Gordon's position even more difficult.

The raiding party assumed the role of a hunting party. In case they were spotted by a Wendat scout or hunting party, this would give them a story and some bargaining power. They set about making traps, and in a couple of weeks they had an impressive cache of skins and furs. Each day, Gordon traveled by himself to find the Wendat settlement and learn its every detail. Once he found the village, he began digging holes along the top of a moraine overlooking the stream and the rear side of the village. Each new hole would be a position for one of his own warriors to hide when it came time to strike. Each would then become a booby trap for their escape. The moraine was well situated to the south of the tribal latrine and refuse area down wind from the village, and in the event of a rare south wind, the latrine offered cover of his own smell from dogs and especially skillful Wendats, some of whom claimed to be able to smell an Iroquois from a considerable distance. The latrine offered other advantages Gordon planned for the night of the raid.

Each morning two hours before sunrise, Gordon dug himself into one of his holes and watched the movements of the tribe. By the time the warriors returned from their hunt laden with fresh meat and furs, he knew every routine, every inch of ground in the village. He memorized every tribal member and traced Ella's movements each day. He watched her gather water and laugh with the other women. He watched her wash clothes, work the fields, chop wood, build fires, and attend to her personal habits. On several occasions he could have snuck up on her to warn of the raid and tell her of his plan, but he knew it would be better if she knew nothing so that she could not mistakenly reveal any change in her behavior that might warn the Wendats.

Gordon's raiding party moved frequently in the manner of trappers. They shaved the heads of both Everett and Jamie and clothed them in deer skins. Each day they rubbed both white men with bark pigment so that they looked like Indians. The boy looked the part and learned to move like an Indian, but Everett would have to pass as an adopted Indian captive if they were ever discovered.

"We call you 'Wandering Muskrat,'" Gordon told him one night around the camp fire amid giggles from the other warriors.

"Ees good in de water, ey?" Gordon smiled. "No so good on de land."

They all giggled, and Everett smiled wanly.

"Yellow-haired woman, she strong wid de Wendat way. Lift de water, chop de tree. Ees good," Gordon reported.

He described the Wendat village and drew pictures and maps in the hard soil around the fire. He showed them where the holes were and how the traps could be quickly set during their escape. He explained what each warrior could expect on the night of the raid and how each was to escape without regard to Gordon's own fate. "I keel de warrior dat keel my son. Ees mine. Den I come."

He went over the plan several times and made each person in the raiding party explain the plan and draw the maps until everyone knew exactly what to do without thought or hesitation. They gathered around the fire that night and applied red grease to their faces and chanted in celebration of victory.

* * *

The Wendat warriors returned to the village, and for several days they prepared for the great feast signifying the end of the hunt. Ella learned that although there was great excitement and anticipation among the women, it was also a time of difficult transition. The men returned in a wild state, filled with swagger, irreverence, and short-tempered menace.

She was soon gratified that no men lived in their cabin. She discovered how badly they stank from lack of bathing. Rather than hurry to clean themselves, they drank rum and whiskey through the first days and nights, and re-created their hunting experiences with wildly exuberant stories of their own prowess and bravery. Several times a day fights broke out as warriors argued over who took which bear or great buck, who was the best tracker, the best shot, the fastest runner, the best with a knife, a bow and arrow, and so forth, endlessly huffing and puffing with male vanity. She feared in this atmosphere that she might be assaulted and raped by one or several drunken Indians, but to her surprise none seemed interested either in her, their wives, or the young, unattached girls coming of age that winter.

"Ees part of de fool in dem," Whispering Cloud muttered the third night. "Come back, get drunk. Stink up all de place. Fight like de bad boys," she said rolling her eyes.

"Tomorrow dey take de bath. Get ready for de feast. Dress handsome. Not so drunk. Take de place in de village. Be good boys. Den we choose de hus-band, ey?" she smiled. "Dey start behave, ey?"

Flying Turtle smiled and nodded, echoing her mother's explanation. "You need to look for husband. Modder gets first choice for us, but we have to be quick."

Flying Turtle and her mother then mulled over a list of the warriors that Ella should check out right away. Ella sat at the fire in helpless astonishment at their offerings.

"Running Snake, he ees good warrior. Lost de teeth. But ees good wid da children," Whispering Cloud said.

Flying Turtle eyed Ella cautiously and shook her head no.

Her mother sniffed indignantly at Flying Turtle's snub and tried another.

"Laughing Fox. Ees beeg and strong. He help de women sometime. Children like heem very big..."

Flying Turtle shook her head no and rolled her eyes. Her mother huffed and tried again.

"Summer Bear, ees da one who bring you here from spirit world, very, very brave warrior, very strong, many man afraid de Summer Bear..."

Flying Turtle raised her brows in approval.

Ella's heart dropped knowing that Summer Bear was the warrior who drove the spear through Jean-Robert and led the brutal raiding party against her home. She shook her head no.

"Ees good warrior," Whispering Cloud said more emphatically.

"He's one of the best," Flying Turtle said, turning and nudging Ella.

"No," Ella said sharply. "Look, I'm not ready for another man. I'm still in mourning for my late husband."

Both women frowned and squirmed uncomfortably at the reference to Ella's former identity as a white woman.

After a long silence, Flying Turtle patted Ella's back softly. "You must choose. Women without husbands are often thought to be witches. They can be driven away, even killed. This would be great dishonor to Whispering Cloud and very danger for you."

"Not Summer Bear, then; someone else," Ella said finally.

The mother and daughter exchanged relieved looks.

"Little Wolf?" Flying Turtle said to her mother.

Her mother grinned. "Oh, yes, yes. He perfect."

Flying Turtle raised her brows skeptically but turned to Ella nodding her tentative approval.

Whispering Cloud smiled broadly and said, "Ees very small. You bigger dan Little Wolf," she said, holding her hand to Ella's shoulder. "But he very strong, very brave. Win all de fight. Love de children. Very kind."

Ella turned to Flying Turtle. "Does he have teeth?"

They all laughed gleefully.

"Yes, yes. He have teeth. Many, many teeth," Flying Turtle giggled. "We show you, ey?"

They hurried out to the village center, staying close to the long house to avoid drawing attention to their spying. The warriors variously sat, lay in heaps, staggered, or shuffled around the fire drinking from huge jugs of rum and whiskey. Some of them spoke, standing and waving their arms in extravagant oratory. Others listened attentively; others slept or appeared utterly disinterested.

"There," Flying Turtle said, pointing. "The one with the big spear."

Sitting on a rock, both hands grasping a spear jammed in the ground, his chin resting on his wrists, listening attentively was a small, thin, angular man with sharply etched features and large, scowling eyes. His black hair was formed into a dozen or so thick spikes that pointed in all directions and gave him a look of surprised and extraordinary alertness.

"The one with all the spears in his hair," Ella asked

"That's it," Flying Turtle giggled, "That's him."

"He's just a boy," Ella said softly.

Flying Turtle shrugged. "Better they be young. Easier to kick them in the ass."

Ella turned away. He looked dreadful, a squirrely runt of a man, but she could not stop herself from laughing. How could she possibly marry such a scrawny little creature and make love to him, no less, in their crowded little cabin. It all seemed so comical to her, so bizarrely out of the blue. She turned back to inspect him again. "What about the one who's talking? He's not so bad."

"No, no," Flying Turtle blushed, "he's mine."

"Oh, sorry. Maybe he's got a brother."

"Yes, Summer Bear. They are brothers," Flying Turtle said enthusiastically.

"Oh, no. Not Summer Bear. Let me look some more."

They watched the men for a time, and Ella noticed an older man with a limp. "What about him, with the limp?"

"He's married," Flying Turtle said sadly.

"The one with the white man's hat. Who's he?" Ella asked.

"Winter Eagle." Flying Turtle said turning to her mother.

"No good," Whispering Cloud said emphatically shaking her head no.

"What's wrong with him?" Ella pressed.

"No children for him. Iroquois cut hees parts. No good."

"That's too bad," Ella said.

Both other women nodded solemnly. "Very sad," Whispering Cloud said. "I like heem, too. Very handsome, ey?" she said nudging Ella.

"Oh, yes," she fibbed, "Very." In truth, he wasn't so bad, but his handicap seemed to be well known, and Ella knew that having children was very important. She turned to Whispering Cloud, "He can never marry?"

She huffed her shoulders and pursed her lips in the way that indicated maximum scorn. "No. Ees all done for him. Very sad. Cover with piss all de time. No live in de cabin. Drip all de place. No, no!"

So it looked as though Ella would be stuck with Little Wolf, for better or for worse. She watched as he stood and waved both arms in a round arc and began his story of the hunt. Some of the men watched and listened but most drank and fiddled idly with their weapons. Ella turned away, and the three women returned to their cabin. Ella tried to tell herself that maybe he would be okay once she got to know him. And maybe it would be better, after all, to have someone whose ass she could kick.

* * *

As darkness fell Gordon broke camp and led his raiding party down the now familiar path toward the Wendat village. It was a frosty night, the sky crowded with stars and a slivered moon that offered scant light in the northern woods. They formed a single line with Everett and Jamie wedged midway. For three hours they moved with a precise urgency and quiet through tangled brambles and lowland swamps. The only sounds were the hushed pants of white men breathing and the occasional brush of branch against leather that brought them to a halt to listen for any counter movement of fox or skunk or wolf or man as Gordon gently held the dog's throat for any trace of vocal warning. Sometimes they waited for ten minutes or more as Gordon listened and held them frozen in place until he sensed the night whisper of the woods had returned to an ambiance insentient to all but nocturnal hunters and their trembling prey.

Jamie's throat seared dry with fear, yet he moved with determined faith in Gordon's silent path. He felt each pricker, each bump in the path, each patch of ice, and after an hour could match the pace of movement and breath that radiated from Gordon through each warrior and himself. The only asynchronicity in this hushed rhythm came from Everett whose labored breaths and heavy steps seemed increasingly to Jamie like the clumsy rumblings of a fatted bear. Only weeks ago Jamie had held Everett's wilderness skills in awe; now he could sense Everett's clumsiness, his lack of fit and now his threat to the safety of Gordon's raiders, his threat to Jamie's own survival in this dangerous quest, and he wondered now what made Gordon bring his friend along at all, what made these fine-tuned warriors risk their lives in the company of the fatted bear.

There must be a reason, Jamie knew, so deep was his faith in Gordon's wisdom in the wild.

More than five miles from the Wendat village, they could see the glow of the ceremonial fires and hear the drums thudding, and as they approached in a wide circle from the south, they could smell the acrid stench of the latrines carried by a gentle northwest breeze softer than the quietest whisper. They moved now very slowly, timed to the steady thuds of the tribal drums. The dog-never more than inches from Gordon's heal-growled quietly and with one swat from Gordon held silent.

They crawled the final half mile and dug into Gordon's soft pits the shape of graves, covering themselves with soil and soggy leaves on the moraine overlooking the glowing fires. The Wendat warriors formed a large circle around three fires and danced slowly to the steady pounding of their tribal drums. They chanted in one low, rumbly, haunting voice, the women and children forming a second circle, sitting cross-legged and swaying to the drumbeat and rifts in the warriors' chant.

Jamie's heart thudded now, and fear washed over him in waves until Gordon reached over from his adjacent pit and squeezed his arm steadily. As though Gordon held him directly by his heart, the thudding din in his own ears slowed and grew quiet. Then Gordon placed his hand in front of Jamie's face and pointed his finger, and as though siting down a gun barrel, Jamie saw his mother, her eyes closed, her body swaying amid the women, dressed in white leathers.

They watched for many hours as the Wendat celebration built toward a fever pitch. They watched them feast on giant slabs of bear and venison, and Gordon nodded as the jugs of rum and whiskey were passed from hand to hand. The Wendats drank deeply, and the slow rhythms from the drums increased in tempo, and warriors now stood and danced and sang their stories as flames licked the dark sky, while others smoked tobacco and mushrooms and smoldering herbs concocted to elicit vision dreams and horrific demons for the bravest warriors to conquer in the final nightmares of the winter hunt.

As midnight approached and the celebration lurched toward chaos and crescendo, Gordon led the raiders crawling on their bellies into the pit of the latrine. There gagging in the searing, steamy stench, they covered themselves with coal black septage, and emerged like snakes on the other side and then stood and formed a wall, and then to the very same cadence of the drums, the raiders danced slowly out of the darkness. The women first saw this ghastly apparition, this wall of tremulous mire and dung, emerging from the night shadows, and there were screams. The women stood and collected their children and then broke in all directions at once, and then the Wendat men saw the apparition. Some mind-wrenched by drink and nightmare visions fled screaming while a core stood and grasped their ceremonial spears and faced the howling mirage as it danced slowly toward them.

Gordon stepped back behind the line exactly as per plan, the line merging instantly, as Gordon lowered himself and scooted back into the shadows and raced behind the long house where the path to Ella's cabin crossed, and as she rushed down the path, Gordon grasped her, yanking her into the shadows. His hand over her mouth, he lifted her and ran back along the shadow of the long house, and as he did so, he whispered loudly in her ear. "I Gordon; I Gordon; we come rescue; we come rescue; point the man kill my son; point the man who kill my son."

He knew she understood when her wild kicking relented, and he felt her nodding, and as they broke into the bright light of the clearing and dashed through to the shadow behind the wall of his raiders, Gordon growled, "point now; point now," and he burst through the line. Not fifty feet away stood a line of six warriors.

"It's Summer Bear," she pointed, "with the red spear."

Gordon pushed her back through the wretched line, took his own spear from Jamie, and charged screaming in a voice curdled with blood and rage and a ferocity never experienced in a Wendat village.

At that moment the raiders took aim with pistols and fired a volley, a thunderous staccato spewing smoke and sparks, then charged with tomahawks at the startled line of Wendats, all but two tumbling away with wounds. Summer Bear stood his ground and braced his spear but was not ready for Gordon's extraordinary quickness. Gordon rammed his spear through Summer Bear's chest and knocked him backward in a burst of bloodspray, and as Summer Bear's brother raised his tomahawk to strike Gordon from behind, Everett jammed his second pistol into the brother's jaw and shot.

Blood and brains burst from the back of his head, and the man flipped over Gordon's back, dead before he hit the ground in a splayed and rubbery heap. From the shadow of the long house came an horrific wailing which Ella knew to be Flying Turtle, and now wrenched free from her new home in this torrent of chaos, Ella staggered numbly until she heard Jamie's voice screaming, "Come on, mum; come on!" She turned and saw his blackened face and gasped wordlessly as he dashed toward her, grasped her wrist and tugged her into the shadows.

The escape path worked as Gordon planned, several Wendats having fallen into grave-like traps and shrieked as they were pierced by sharpened sticks carved by Gordon and set before they left. Screams and howls of chaos echoed through the woods as the raiders ran south for several miles then looped northwest toward their old camp. There they lept into the cold stream, stripped naked and let their stinking leathers drift downstream in the roiling spring melt.

They dressed in dry leathers and in the dimmest light of early dawn, Jamie could see that neither Everett nor Gordon was with them. After dressing, they set off again following the paths and wading creeks mapped by Gordon. They ran at a fast and steady pace that seared their lungs and cramped their bellies. When they stopped to rest and chew on jerky, they could only gasp, too exhausted to talk. Ella squeezed her son's hand several times and was startled as his height and strength. He ran like the Indians she had learned to know, taking long, even strides wherever it was dry, then short rapid steps in muck and snarly underbrush. In the streams, he lunged forward in skips, plunging his hips against the heavy current at times reaching back and grasping his mother's hand and helping her with the advantage of his height.

Ella pushed against her exhaustion, knowing she had learned from her Indian friends and could endure this now because of them. Her mind drifted over memories of laughter, hardship, clumsiness, anguish, and a warm comfort she felt among these women that did not exist in her life, never had, and perhaps never would in her lifetime. These thoughts came in hot, feverish rushes as they ran for their lives, turning south now toward the great river, running often in a daze, slowing to chew jerky, trotting for a time, stopping to drink at streams, running now toward the sun into the red glow of sunrise, running through the night into dawn.

Gordon and Everett sat low in the canoe at water's edge tucked in the branches of a fallen poplar. They spoke in low, whispery voices about the raid the previous night and about what would come next in the warming spring.

"Think they'll come back for Ella? Come back to the island?" Everett asked scratching the dog's ears as she sat against his leg trying to keep her sleepy eyelids from drooping shut.

"No. Ees done. They tink she go to spirit world wit dem black demons. No come."

"I caint believe you done it, Gordon. I caint believe we ain't all dead."

"No dead yet, Evert."

They sat in silence for a time listening to swamp peepers and noting the dim cast of the rising dawn.

"What say, Gordon? Come fish and trap with me and the boy?"

Gordon lit a pipe and puffed til the bowl glowed, then handed it to Everett and spoke as he exhaled. "May-be. Ees good, dat boy. Learn fast, ey?"

"Good fisherman, too."

Gordon nodded, then sat forward a bit with the first sounds of the morning birds.

"Something comin'?" Everett asked.

"Nossir."

They rested quietly as the sun rose, and the first heat of the sun simmered over a light mist that danced slow and twirly on a damp east breeze.

"Rain come today," Gordon offered.

"Yessir, I believe you're right for once."

Gordon chuckled quietly.

The breeze picked up and creased the water with feathery wind rows of tiny waves. Everett dozed off but awoke with a start just before dropping into the deepest sleep.

Gordon sat alertly now. "They come now," he said, setting his paddle into the black water.

The dog stood and pricked her ears. Everett started.

He heard nothing but began yanking at the branches to pull them into open water. They eased the boat up to a pebbly spit just past where the stream dumped rushing water into the St. Lawrence. Everett listened hard, but heard nothing but birds chirping. Then he heard the Bluejays cry out, and the hackles stood forth on the dog's neck, and she growled low and quiet.

In a couple of minutes Gordon's braves appeared, taking long, floppy final steps across the stream mouth and leaned gasping on the gunnel, holding it for Ella and Jamie who appeared now pink-faced and bone weary, barely able to lift their legs to crawl into the giant canoe. Ella collapsed gasping in front of Everett. He draped a blanket over her shoulders and squeezed her hot hand. She squeezed back but was too winded and weary to talk.

The Indians pushed the canoe as they stepped in and took up paddles. The east breeze cooled their faces as the canoe lurched with their powerful strokes into the deep water. Jamie repositioned himself in the bow and took up a paddle. Everett turned back to Gordon and winked.

In a few minutes the spot where they set off was a distant speck, and despite the east breeze in their face, Gordon steered them into a swift channel more than offsetting the wind. They made rapid headway through deep swirling narrows, and shortly after noon glided into the vast sweep of St-Francois du Lac.

Everett set his paddle over the gunnel and nudged Ella who slept motionless in a tight bundle between his feet. She looked up and righted herself onto her knees, bracing her forearms on his knees and looking over the bow toward home. The sky was gray with clouds, the river air damp and heavy, the water glass smooth and a shimmering black as far as the eye could see. Ella watched proudly as her son sat straight-backed and stroked with strong, even motions followed in unison by the other Indians in utter silence save for the whisper of water flowing beneath them.

"They treat you okay?" Everett finally asked.

She nodded yes, and felt sadness claw at her belly as she realized the desolation Whispering Cloud must at this moment be experiencing having lost her daughter yet again.

Several hours later Everett spotted the island and pointed ahead for Ella. She nodded and held Everett's hand for a moment. In a few minutes she could recognize the shape of the trees, especially the giant willow hanging over the point with its seven trunks. The island was still barren, the leaves a couple of weeks from bursting forth. In its barren state the island looked small and vulnerable, but Ella knew that before long it would be lush and thick with green and singing with mosquitoes and crawling with more spiders than could ever be imagined.

As they approached the leeward side, red-winged black birds scratched the air with mating songs, and wind swallows carved the air already thick with moths. Ella felt a rush of warmth and fought back tears as Jamie leaned over and studied the water for signs of fish, and Everett tossed a piece of bark ahead to try to fool Jamie into thinking a fish had jumped. Everett snapped his fingers and feigned surprise, and Jamie turned back and rolled his eyes, and in his deep voice called out to Gordon, "Wandering Muskrat thinks he sees a fish."

Gordon chuckled and set his paddle, the huge canoe gliding quietly to rest at the island point.

Chapter 8

In late August, 1760, hundreds of canoes and small, armored bateaux loaded with 10,000 British troops and 700 Iroquois warriors paddled the length of Lac du St-Francois en route to Montreal. Ella and Everett anxiously watched from the point of the island as this enormous procession inched eastward in the main channel a mile to their north. Ella softly rubbed her hand over her swelling belly in hopes of calming the baby within from the feverish pace of her racing heart. She prayed that the massive fleet would continue on its murderous journey and leave them alone. It was a still day with sweltering heat, but after a time a light west breeze creased the water with tiny waves, gently urging the fleet eastward. Ella could not calm herself, however, until the last speck of the last canoe disappeared out of view past the point at Ste-Anicet.

In May, barely a month after the Wendat rescue, Ella and Everett were married by an itinerant Methodist minister who stopped by Lucy's trading post in search of clients for baptisms, marriages, belated burial services or general Christian advice and comfort. He had lost both ears to Indians but otherwise conducted himself with buoyant good cheer. The minister's arrival saved them a long trip to an English-American settlement in Ogdensburg, and on a brilliant spring day with luscious new leaves bursting yellow-green from the island trees, the minister conducted the service in "God's own church" on the island point with Jamie serving as best man. Gordon and his wife attended along with Lucy and Gilles, and after sending the minister packing with his bible and Christian trinkets in a leaky canoe, they all got smashing drunk from rum Gordon had lately distilled but not yet fully cured.

The last timed she and Everett were drunk was the night of their arrival back at the island after her rescue from the Wendat tribe. They both went swimming in the cold river and warming up later in the hut, Everett corked up his courage and blurted, "I been thinkin' I want to git married."

"And who have you been thinking ought to marry you?" she asked dryly, knowing full well he was trying his best to ask her.

"I been thinkin' you," he croaked.

"Me!" she said, pretending to be shocked.

"Yes, ma'am," Everett said, his heart pounding with fear.

She knew she didn't love Everett ferociously enough for the sort of story-book marriages young girls daydreamed about, but she knew she loved him in some elemental way that offered hope and fondness in her life. And when she allowed herself the inclination, she found him attractive, so after torturing him a few more minutes until his eyes started swimming in a daze of mournful confusion, she put her arms around him and kissed him softly on the lips and said, "Yes, Everett. I'm just teasing. Yes, I'll marry you."

A month later Lucy and Gilles married in the Catholic Church in Ste-Anicet, and this time they all celebrated at the trading post downing the finest British whiskey and French wines brought from Montreal by Henri and Renée Gaston. On the trip to the wedding, Henri and Renée downed a goodly portion of wine, and soon after they arrived, Henri proposed to Renée in a glow of lecherous spring fever. The priest was very reluctant to marry Henri and Renée out of parish and with such short notice and little preparation, but Henri offered a cash donation that changed his mind, and the Catholic priest conducted a double wedding.

Later that afternoon Henri got so drunk, he slipped off Lucy's dock and nearly drowned. For the second time in Henri's life, Everett plucked him from the river, heaved him to the dock and bounced on his chest until Henri puked up a dirty stream of muddy water and British whiskey.

"You ain't considered learnin' to swim, have you, Henri?" Everett asked as Henri coughed and sputtered.

"Mon Dieu! Mon Dieu, merci, mon ami," Henri gasped as Renée raced down the bank, her face stricken with fright, then flung herself onto Henri and kissed him with such ferocity Everett thought he might still suffocate. He straddled them both, lifted them in his arms, and carried them to dry land where they embraced in a drunken lascivious frenzy. Some weeks later Henri sent a deed of shore land sworn over to Everett with a note saying that when he got to old to fight the river, he could settle on shore and die with dry feet and a deep grave.

Jamie started work that summer as a boat builder for Gilles who set up a shop at Lucy's trading post. They built a range of useful craft, rowing bateaux, bark canoes, and the small, covered canoes that came to be known as 'The Lucy' and gradually gained a small following up and down the river.

In early September the huge fleet of British canoes neared Montreal and lost eighty men in the rapids before reorganizing and joining two other enormous British-American armies to surround French forces in Montreal. On September 8, the French gave up without a fight, ending the war and placing Canada into the hands of the British crown.

Only a few years later the Caughnawaga Mohawks were shuttled by their new British governors to a patch of land west of Montreal where their tribal customs slowly crumbled into the dreary routines of reservation life and near starvation. Many other tribes fared far worse. The Wendat village where Ella had stayed was attacked and brutally destroyed by British troops intent on making the wilderness safer for white settlers. Every man, woman, and child was slaughtered and left to rot in the hot summer sun. When Ella learned of the British raids, she insisted that Everett take her back to the Wendat village. They arrived to find scattered bones picked clean by wolves and crows amid a tangle of grape vines, saplings, emergent shrubs, weeds, wildflowers, and large patches of virulent squash with rough leaves the size of dinner plates. The cabins and long house were burned to the ground and sprouted green growth that in a year or two would devour any traces of human life. The stream flowed quietly southward, the rocks where they'd cleaned and gathered water now thick with moss and long strings of undulating algae.

Ella stood there and wept as mosquitoes hummed in growing swarms that finally drove them away.

In the ensuing years, Gordon joined Everett on the island for a few years, building a small cabin on the east point looking shoreward at the rising sun, and on the western point he built a stone mound facing the setting sun in honor of Jean-Robert. Both men fished, trapped, and hunted together, and their wives raised a thriving garden in the center two acres of the island. Gordon developed an interest in farming tobacco on a patch behind his cabin, and he and his wife purchased part of Henri's farmland holdings with a small down payment and a 5% royalty agreement for all it produced in perpetuity. It was a large tract at the river's edge on the south shore several miles east of Ste-Anicet. The fertile St. Lawrence River valley soil proved ideal for tobacco crops, and Henri and Gordon invested in scores of the long narrow government tracks at the river's edge until they owned 70,000 acres cut straight down the middle by a 40-acre sliver owned by a French pig farmer who refused to sell to an Indian. Gordon's two farms became known as far south as Virginia as among the best tobacco producers in North America. But to Gordon, his wife, and five children, the pig farm served as reminder that money and land could not earn them respect from everyone.

The men from Gordon's tribe joined forces with the British to fight the Americans during the revolution. Gordon's second son joined as a scout and was killed by American sharpshooters at Fort Ticonderoga in 1775, but this time there was no revenge. Gordon prepared to ambush the Americans with hidden canons, but the fighting never reached him. Although Montreal was taken twice, the American armies never came east of the Lachine rapids. The Americans failed to take Quebec and fell back to Lake Champlain, and thereafter most of the fighting took place far to the south. By the end of the war, Gordon was confused and dispirited, his tribe crushed, scattered, and lost. He did not know who was the enemy and returned all of his energy to farming tobacco, his warrior spirit lost to a shadowy, perpetual sadness.

Henri remained in Montreal avoiding water and boats whenever possible. He purchased several hotels, taverns, and major restaurants in the years ahead. An American general and two lieutenants visited his tavern during one of the brief occupations and complained that his food was too fancy.

"Give me steak without all the syrup," insisted the sullen American general.

"Then I feed you dog shit," Henri shouted in front of a hushed crowd of scowling patrons, aghast at the American's request.

The general stood, flipped the table onto the floor, stared at Henri, but realizing he was sorely outnumbered, stormed out with his men without further violence. The patrons clapped and whistled their approval, and Henri was thus launched toward a companion career in politics.

He and Renée Gaston, who retained her maiden name throughout their marriage, bore eleven children all of them girls except the last, a boy born with a club foot. They lost three of their girls to smallpox during a five-week stretch one winter when temperatures never rose above 25-degrees below zero. Soon after suffering her horrible losses, the once robust Renée lost thirty pounds and suffered crushing bouts of arthritis that came and went with sudden ghastly fevers leaving her each time more crippled and wracked by pain. Their daughters assumed her duties and propelled the family's restaurant and hotel holdings to ever increasing prosperity. Henri never lost his passion for his wife but after several bouts of her recurrent illness, he could barely touch her without causing yelps of agony that tortured them both with sad frustration. Despite his joy and pride in his daughters, Henri's son caused him almost perpetual sorrow. The boy become a target of derision at his school, and when Henri pulled him from formal classes and hired tutors, the boy became isolated and depressed. Henri became increasingly angered by the boy's surly, dark moods and berated him for his self-pity. At the age of twelve, the boy ran away never to return, never to be heard from again. Henri spent the rest of his life fighting off sudden throat-constricting waves of inconsolable guilt so ferocious they caused him to groan in audible misery where ever and whenever memories of his son chose to assault him. His sudden groans and rolling eyes became so familiar to friends and colleagues, that they thought him afflicted with a serious digestive disease, a fate he would have much preferred.

But Henri was too vibrant a main to be collapsed by sadness. He gained considerable power despite an influx of rich British merchants who gobbled up land and soon dominated the political and commercial landscapes of Montreal. Henri was elected to the assembly of Lower Canada and tried to pass legislation establishing French as the official language of government and commerce, but he and his majority of French 'Canadiens' were overruled by the British governor. Henri became an investor in a fierce little French-language newspaper, *Le Canadien*, and was nearly jailed when the British shut it down for its boisterous advocacy of French language and customs.

The English could not resist Henri's food, however, and the governor, himself, intervened to keep Henri out of prison so that his restaurants and taverns could remain in business. Through it all, Henri never lost sight of his enormous good fortune, and for decades after Monsieur Fourmet's death, Henri listed Le Canard Noir de Fourmet as the first item on all his menus in honor of his benefactor. Nor did he lose his fiery temper and caustic sarcasm. He often stood in the mildewed chamber of the Canadian assembly and issued forth with scathing speeches about British imperial rule and the hopeless mediocrity of British food, the primary cause, he shouted, for why British armies roamed the world.

"They search forever for a decent meal," he shouted, much to the delight of his French Canadian compatriots.

Everett and Ella remained on the island and raised two daughters and another son. Ella taught them French and proper English and gradually gathered an impressive library that they all read, save for Everett who claimed that reading hurt his eyes. The boy, Nathan, was large and big-boned like his father but harbored a bookish side and quick temper like his mother. The girls, Em and Sophie, learned to fish, hunt, row, and sail as well as any male, but in the winter of her tenth year Sophie fell through the ice and nearly drowned. She and Nathan, who was 12 at the time, had wandered too close to the channel rip while dragging a canoe along for safety as Everett required. Several inches of snow created an illusion that the ice was safe to within fifty feet or so of the dark water, and Sophie wandered out ahead of the canoe, slip-sliding and waving her arms for balance when suddenly she dropped through.

Nathan held to the gunnel of the canoe and positioned the boat near the small, dark hole where she disappeared, but she did not come back up. He shouted and waved his arms shoreward for help but a brisk north wind muffled his shouts and no one heard. Finally, he tied the rope around his chest and jumped through the hole himself, the extraordinary cold water sucking the breath from his throat. The snow cover cast a dark shadow over the water below and made it nearly impossible to see beneath the surface. Nathan had to come up several times for air and was becoming groggy and confused when he glimpsed Sophie's shimmering blond hair undulating in a patch of light near the channel where the sunlight penetrated. Nathan swam frantically toward her, but the water pulled her body closer and closer to the dark edge of deep water. Just as she was about to roll over the edge into the depths, Nathan grasped her hair and pulled her to him. He wound the rope around his arm and pulled them upward until his lungs nearly burst. Finally, he broke the surface at the canoe's edge, gasped for air and tugged his sister to the surface, but she did not breathe. He managed to muscle her over the gunnel with one arm, then pulled himself up. By now his hands were numb, his mind fuzzy and dim. He stumbled over the cross braces to the bow, and put one leg over the edge and pushed the slippery ice with his numb foot. Slowly he was able to move the canoe a full length. Figuring it was safe, he stepped out of the boat. The ice cracked, and he flopped himself over the bow just in time to keep from falling through again.

By the time he reached the island and carried Sophie into the cabin, she had not breathed for perhaps fifteen minutes. Everett pressed on her chest. He lifted her upside down and shook her until water poured from her mouth. Ella groaned in misery and prayed Sophie be spared, grasping her cold, wet lifeless hand the entire time. After another fifteen minutes of pushing and pounding her chest and despairing that she would never breathe again, Sophie coughed and sputtered and began to breathe. After a few days she was up and moving, even talking, but she was never the same. Her speech remained permanently slurred, and one eye drooped ever so slightly, and while she grew into a stunningly beautiful young woman, she remained a bit slow-witted and clingy and not quite able to cope with life's more complicated tasks. Though she remained a delight to be with, her buoyant ten-year old's personality had been frozen into her being forever by the icy river.

Nathan never quite recovered from the blame he heaped upon himself for taking his sister out on the ice that day. Perhaps if anyone had blamed him then, he might have unraveled his own culpability or benefitted from their forgiveness, but Ella insisted that he be treated as a hero and told Everett if he ever heaped an ounce of blame on Nathan, she would leave Everett forever and take his children with her. So Everett kept silent, and an odd estrangement developed between Nathan and him, not hostile so much as disconnected. Nathan became more bookish, more independent. He fished by himself and sailed alone, and while his mother would not tolerate criticism of Everett by the children, Nathan grew to consider his father doltish and dull-witted like a friendly old dog. He loved him but could not find the respect he needed. Lacking a companion in his son, Everett often took Sophie to fish with him, and Nathan would watch them row into the distance and ache with a mix of jealousy and guilt which he accepted quietly as his penance for his negligence that horrible winter day.

Em, the oldest child, was serious, ferociously independent, hard working, and stood six feet by the age of thirteen. She could shoot a gun better than Everett or her brother, and could fly fish better than any of them, a skill that later exposed her to some of the world's richest men. In her early teens, she hated herself for being so gangly and homely, but had her mother's grit and grew into her long, gaunt cheeks and became strikingly handsome and wiry strong. Em ended up as one of Lucy's great pals, and became the first woman fishing and hunting guide in the area as wealthy bankers and emerging industrialists from New York and Montreal discovered the Adirondacks and St. Lawrence River regions for their hunting vacations and summer lodges. She and Nathan contracted clients through Lucy, sometimes teaming up to guide large groups, sometimes splitting up and competing for the greatest 'kills' of duck, deer, bear, muskie, Northern pike, large mouth bass, and Atlantic salmon.

Lucy and Gilles expanded the trading post by paying the best prices for furs east of Detroit. They intercepted boats heading to Lachine, saving them a day's trip and offering free docking, better prices and better stock. They sold boats, guns, food, horses, whiskey, tobacco, seed grain, building materials, farm implements, and became an export center for fish, especially sturgeon. They raised five children, three sons and two daughters and put them to work. Two of the sons, Joe and Aurel, became river guides, and often teamed with Em and Nathan for duck hunts and fishing expeditions for wealthy clients. Their oldest son, Gilles, Jr., left the family business to join a logging operation in northern Quebec and lost his left hand in a sawmill accident when he was twenty-four. Forced into the financial side of the business, he eventually started his own timber business and brought his clients back home for hunting expeditions and learned to shoot ducks out of the air with a pistol.

Michelle, the youngest, was the most like her mother and engaged in wild teenage years and heavy bouts of drinking. She became pregnant at seventeen, and died in childbirth, leaving an infant son, Lucien, for Lucy to raise. Lucy mourned for a year after her daughter's death and took up the bottle, herself. Gilles tried to maintain the business, but it nearly collapsed until Lucy quit drinking one day when Lucien came home from school battered and bruised. His strong Indian features prompted his school mates to call him an "Injun bastard," and after the beating, he refused to return. After three days of hell drying out, Lucy took to the parish school and berated the priests with such blue language, they forbid Lucien's re-admittance and banished Lucy from the parish. Fortunately, her other daughter, Marie, had finished her studies and had been accepted for legal studies in Montreal. Lucy educated Lucien, herself, and at sixteen he joined his uncles as an assistant guide, becoming the best of them all and eventually a legend in the region.

Thanks to Gilles' and Jamie, everyone had boats and each summer, Ella, Everett, Lucy, Gilles, Gordon, and all their children could be seen from shore sailing their tiny boats across the grand sweep of Lac du St-Francois. On one afternoon during the summer of 1779, a fleet of 17 small sailboats raced in a tight formation on broad reach on their annual race around the island starting at the trading post, heading west past Everett's island, southwest a mile to Ile du Chat and returning to the trading post on a following breeze. Lucy won as always, followed closely by Em and trailed far and away last by Everett who lumbered along grumbling about the advantages of oars. Soon after that splendid afternoon, Jamie married one of Gordon's daughters and took up farming on the fertile banks of the river.

Everett remained a fisherman. One winter he had a blacksmith in Ste-Anicet forge several hundred fearsome hooks and during idle times, Everett attached each hook to a line, and each line to a long line. When the weather warmed, he trapped minnows and took his lines and minnows to ledges he knew near the channels. He baited the hooks and set them out with large anchors at either end of the long line, and the next day returned, dragged a large grappling hook to find the line, and discovered he'd caught hundreds of pounds of sturgeon attached to his night line. Smoked sturgeon and their precious eggs were in huge demand in Montreal, and Everett worked a deal with Lucy's trading post that kept them prosperous from his sturgeon lines for many years.

Ella became a competent boat woman who set off from the island at least once a week with Sophie to spend time with Gordon's wife and a scattering of other Indian women along shore. She knew that had she not been rescued that she probably would have lived and died with the Wendat tribe, and it would have been a tolerable life because the Indian women knew how to laugh and play in the face of withering hardship. Though stern with Jamie, Ella raised her children by Everett with far more tolerant hand. She did not allow them to be spanked or sharply reprimanded, and often when Everett returned from fishing, she and the children would be playing games in a torrent of chaos and howling fun. Everett never fully understood her deeper thoughts nor dared to challenge her strongest ideas, but he much enjoyed her more buoyant spirit and bouts of silliness and loved her deeply as his wife.

Each week he rowed off to pick up Jamie for an afternoon of fishing. Though it saddened him that Nathan seldom joined them, they sat often in complete silence for hours at a time calmly pulling in fish from Everett's favorite spots. When they spoke, it was usually about simple things of little consequence about which they agreed or disagreed with a series of grunts, "yessir, nossir" or with a more elaborated exclamation such as:

"I guess that's the truth, then, ain't it," Everett would say.

"Yessir, ain't nothing but," Jamie would mutter.

And then the thought would die away, and they would sit bobbing in the breeze as the great river flowed silently beneath their boat.